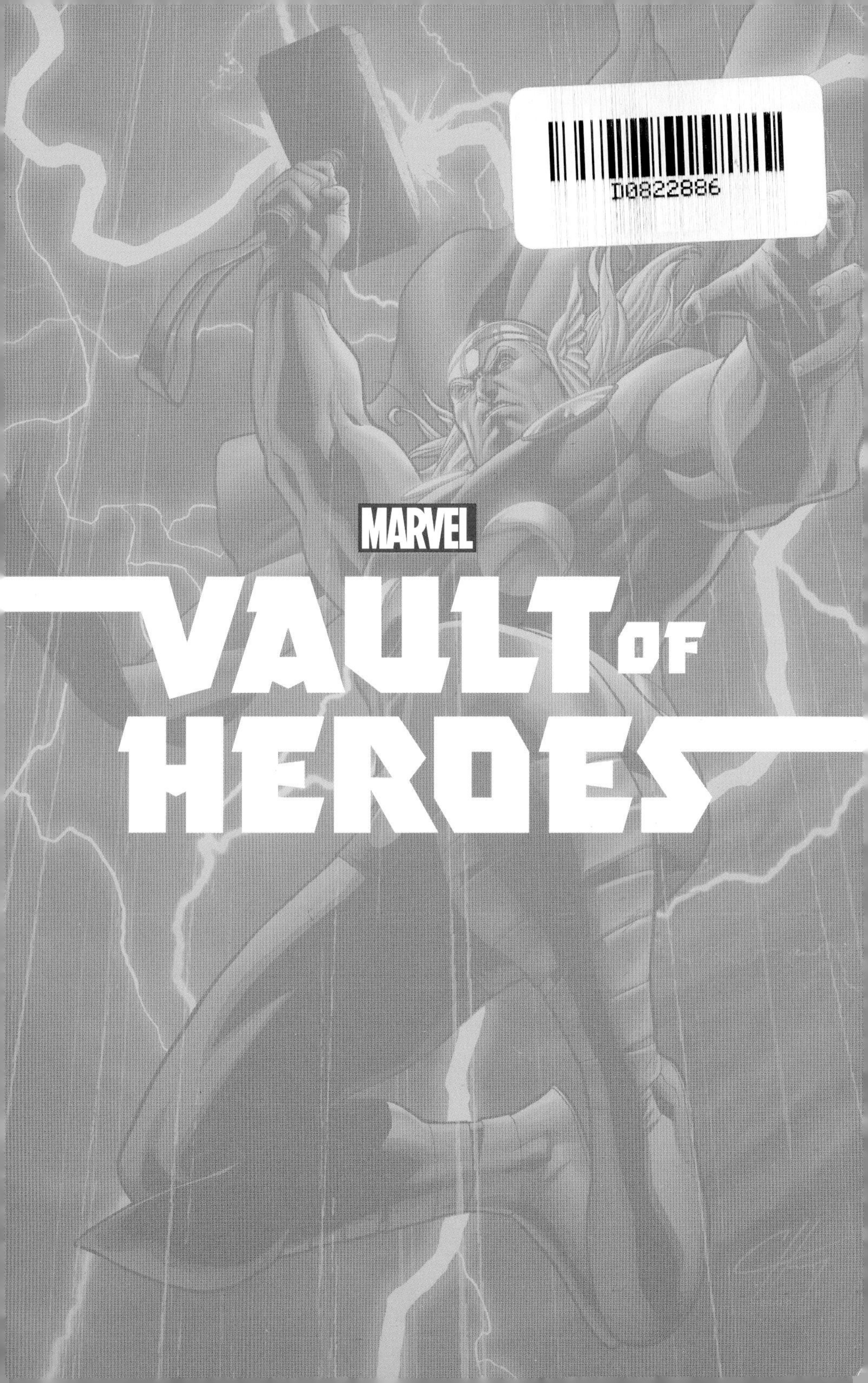
MARVEL
VAULT OF HEROES

ISBN: 978-1-68405-666-8   23 22 21 20   1 2 3 4

MARVEL VAULT OF HEROES: THOR. MARCH 2020. FIRST PRINTING. © 2020 MARVEL. The IDW logo is registered in the U.S. Patent
and Trademark Office. IDW Publishing, a division of Idea and Design Works, LLC. Editorial offices: 2765 Truxtun Road, San Diego, CA
92106. Any similarities to persons living or dead are purely coincidental. With the exception of artwork used for review purposes,
none of the contents of this publication may be reprinted without the permission of Idea and Design Works, LLC.
Printed in Korea.

IDW Publishing does not read or accept unsolicited submissions of ideas, stories, or artwork.

Originally published by MARVEL as MARVEL ADVENTURES SUPER HEROES (2008) issue #7 and 11
and MARVEL ADVENTURES SUPER HEROES (2010) issues #2, 6, 13, 14, and 19.

COVER ART BY
ESPIN, KESEL, & PANTAZIS

COLLECTION EDITS BY
JUSTIN EISINGER
AND ALONZO SIMON

COLLECTION DESIGN BY
JEFF POWELL

THOR CREATED BY
STAN LEE & JACK KIRBY

Chris Ryall, President & Publisher/CCO

Cara Morrison, Chief Financial Officer

Matthew Ruzicka, Chief Accounting Officer

David Hedgecock, Associate Publisher

John Barber, Editor-in-Chief

Justin Eisinger, Editorial Director, Graphic Novels and Collections

Jerry Bennington, VP of New Product Development

Lorelei Bunjes, VP of Technology & Information Services

Jud Meyers, Sales Director

Anna Morrow, Marketing Director

Tara McCrillis, Director of Design & Production

Mike Ford, Director of Operations

Rebekah Cahalin, General Manager

Ted Adams and Robbie Robbins, IDW Founders

Marvel Publishing:

VP Production & Special Projects: Jeff Youngquist

Assistant Editor, Special Projects: Caitlin O'Connell

Director, Licensed Publishing: Sven Larsen

SVP Print, Sales & Marketing: David Gabriel

Editor In Chief: C.B. Cebulski

Chief Creative Officer: Joe Quesada

President, Marvel Entertainment: Dan Buckley

Executive Producer: Alan Fine

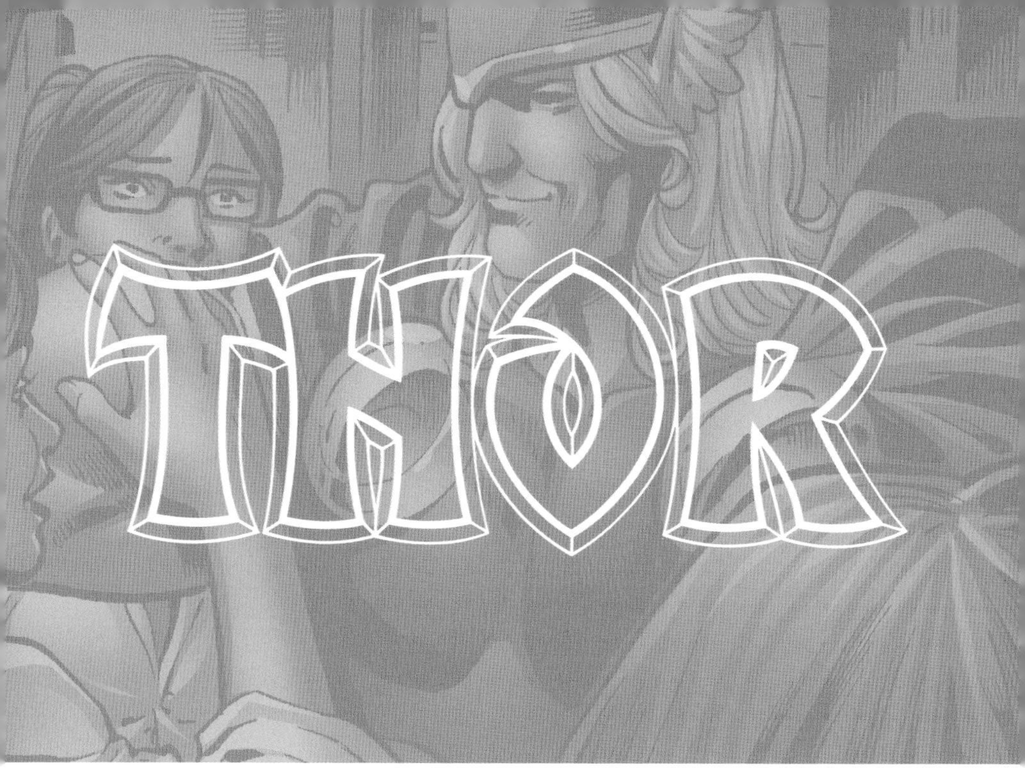
THOR

ISSUE 01

Lip Service
WRITTEN BY **LOUISE SIMONSON**
ART BY **RODNEY BUCHEMI**
COLORS BY **GURU EFX**
LETTERS BY **DAVE SHARPE**

ISSUE 02

Fire and Ice
WRITTEN BY **LOUISE SIMONSON**
PENCILS BY **JON BURAN**
INKS BY **JEREMY FREEMAN**
COLORS BY **SOTOCOLOR**
LETTERS BY **DAVE SHARPE**

ISSUE 03

Marvel Adventures Super Heroes #2
WRITTEN BY **PAUL TOBIN**
PENCILS BY **RONAN CLIQUET**
INKS BY **AMILTON SANTOS**
COLORS BY **SOTOCOLOR**
LETTERS BY **DAVE SHARPE**

ISSUE 04

Marvel Adventures Super Heroes #6
WRITTEN BY **PAUL TOBIN**
PENCILS BY **RONAN CLIQUET**
INKS BY **AMILTON SANTOS**
COLORS BY **SOTOCOLOR**
LETTERS BY **DAVE SHARPE**

ISSUE 05

Marvel Adventures Super Heroes #13
WRITTEN BY **PAUL TOBIN**
PENCILS BY **RONAN CLIQUET**
INKS BY **AMILTON SANTOS**
COLORS BY **SOTOCOLOR**
LETTERS BY **DAVE SHARPE**

ISSUE 06

Out of Time
WRITTEN BY **TODD DEZAGO**
PENCILS BY **RON LIM**
INKS BY **SCOTT KOBLISH**
COLORS BY **DIGITAL RAINBOW**
LETTERS BY **DAVE SHARPE**

ISSUE 07

If He Be Worthy
WRITTEN BY **JOE CARAMAGNA**
PENCILS BY **KEVIN SHARPE**
INKS BY **TERRY PALLOT**
COLORS BY **CHRIS SOTOMAYOR**
LETTERS BY **DAVE SHARPE**

01

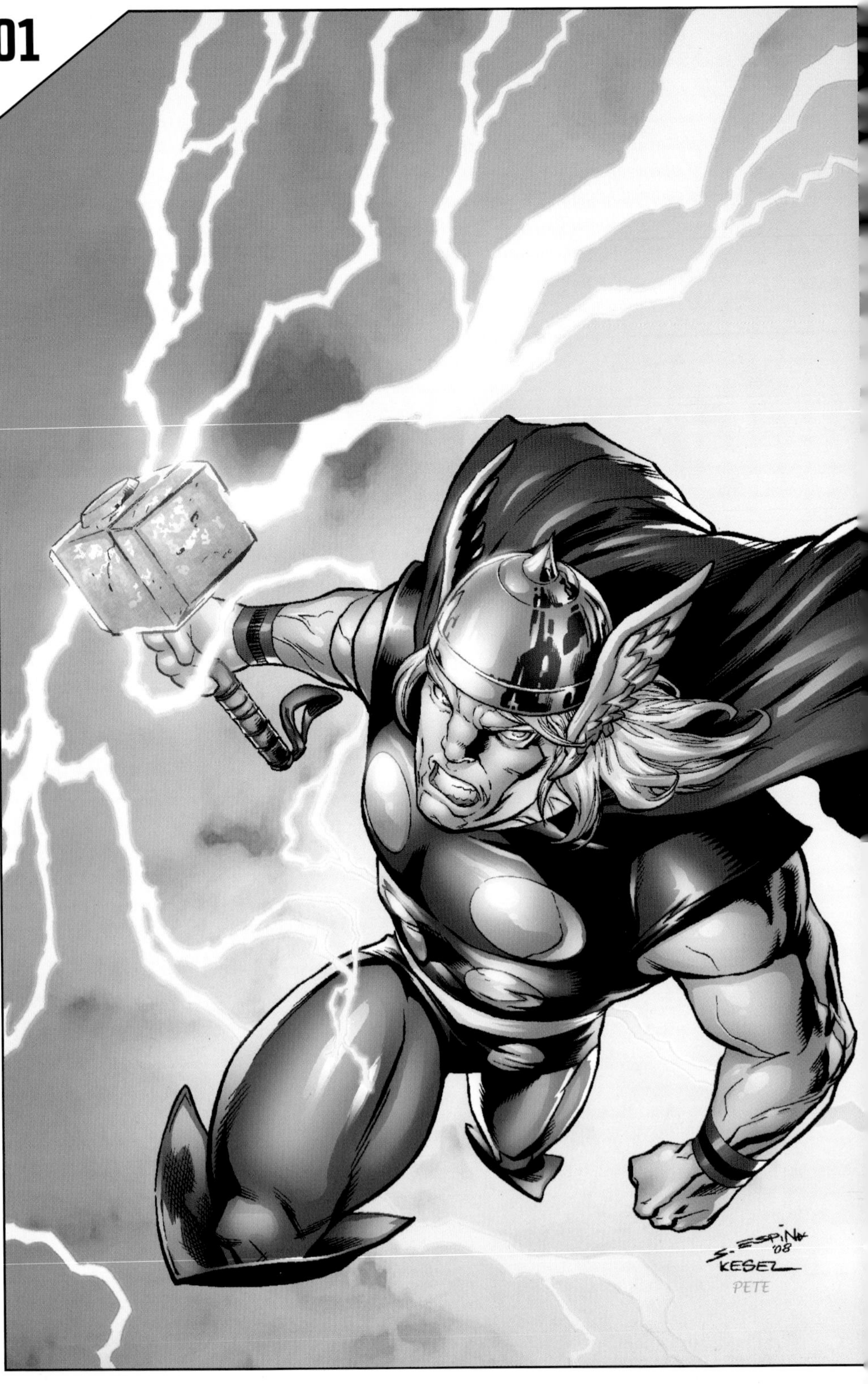
KESEL
PETE

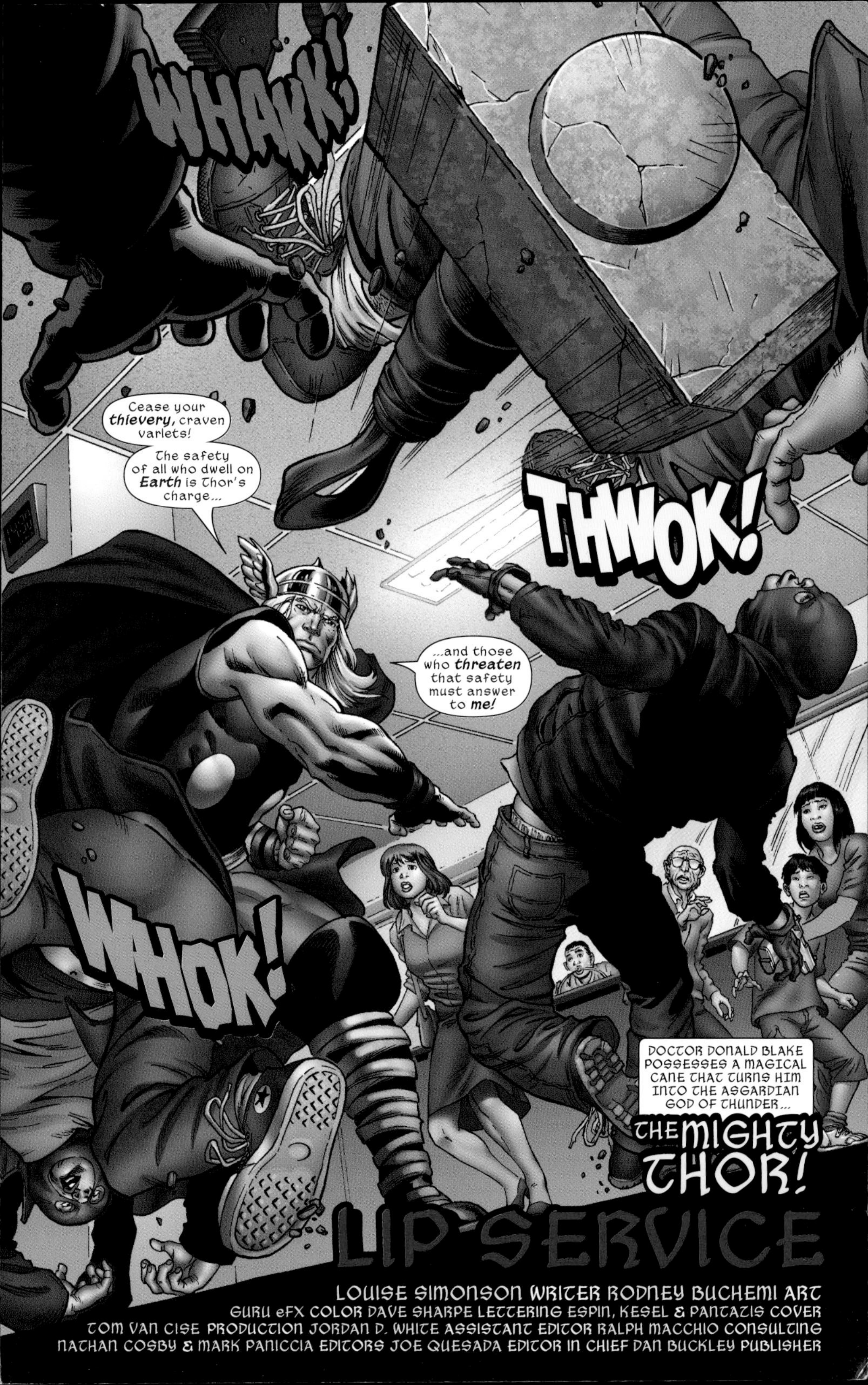

WHAKK!
Cease your thievery, craven varlets!
The safety of all who dwell on Earth is Thor's charge...
THWOK!
...and those who threaten that safety must answer to me!
WHOK!
DOCTOR DONALD BLAKE POSSESSES A MAGICAL CANE THAT TURNS HIM INTO THE ASGARDIAN GOD OF THUNDER...
THE MIGHTY THOR!
LIP SERVICE
LOUISE SIMONSON WRITER RODNEY BUCHEMI ART
GURU eFX COLOR DAVE SHARPE LETTERING ESPIN, KESEL & PANTAZIS COVER
TOM VAN CISE PRODUCTION JORDAN D. WHITE ASSISTANT EDITOR RALPH MACCHIO CONSULTING
NATHAN COSBY & MARK PANICCIA EDITORS JOE QUESADA EDITOR IN CHIEF DAN BUCKLEY PUBLISHER

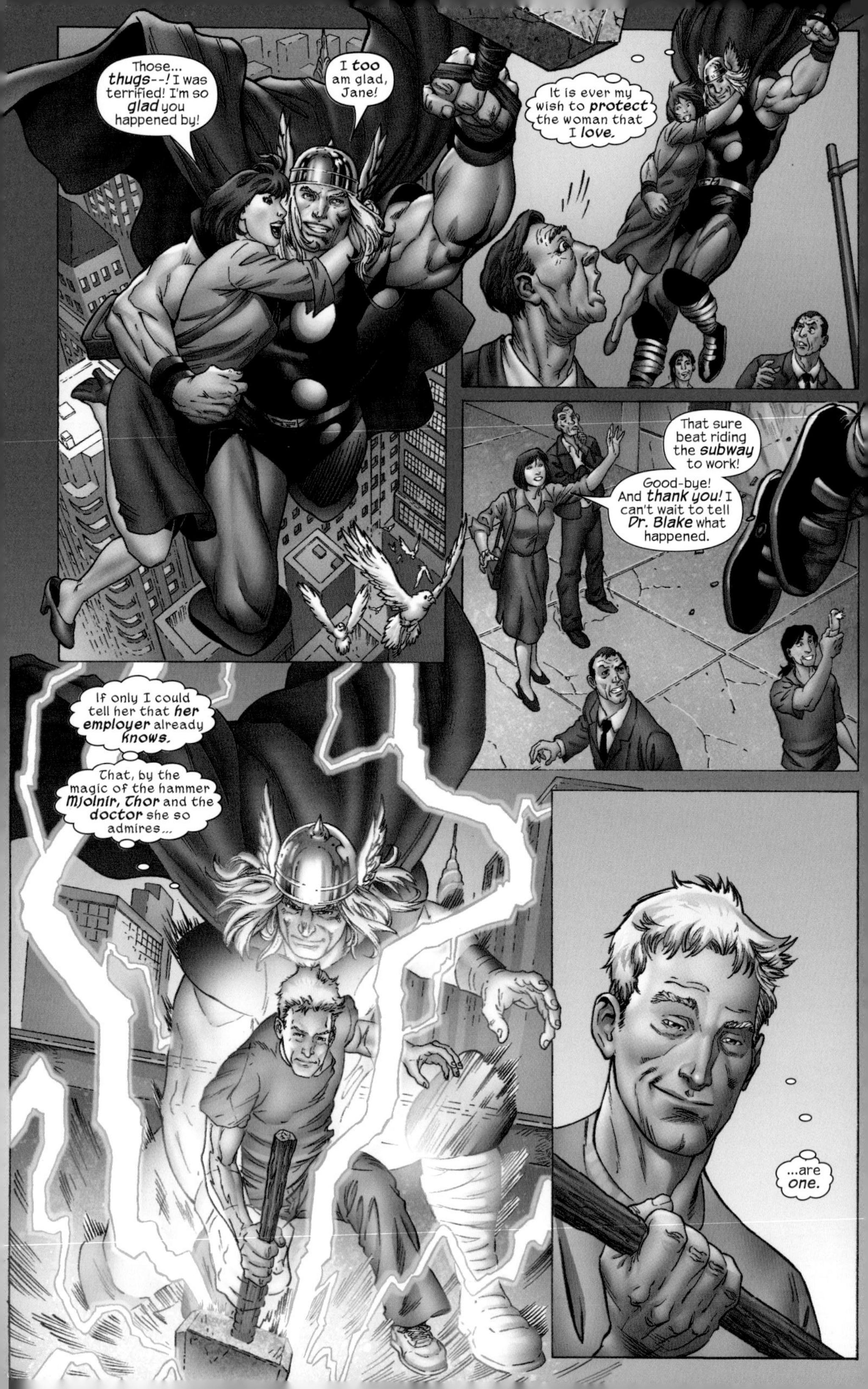
Those... thugs--! I was terrified! I'm so glad you happened by!
I too am glad, Jane!
It is ever my wish to protect the woman that I love.
That sure beat riding the subway to work!
Good-bye! And thank you! I can't wait to tell Dr. Blake what happened.
If only I could tell her that her employer already knows.
That, by the magic of the hammer Mjolnir, Thor and the doctor she so admires...
...are one.

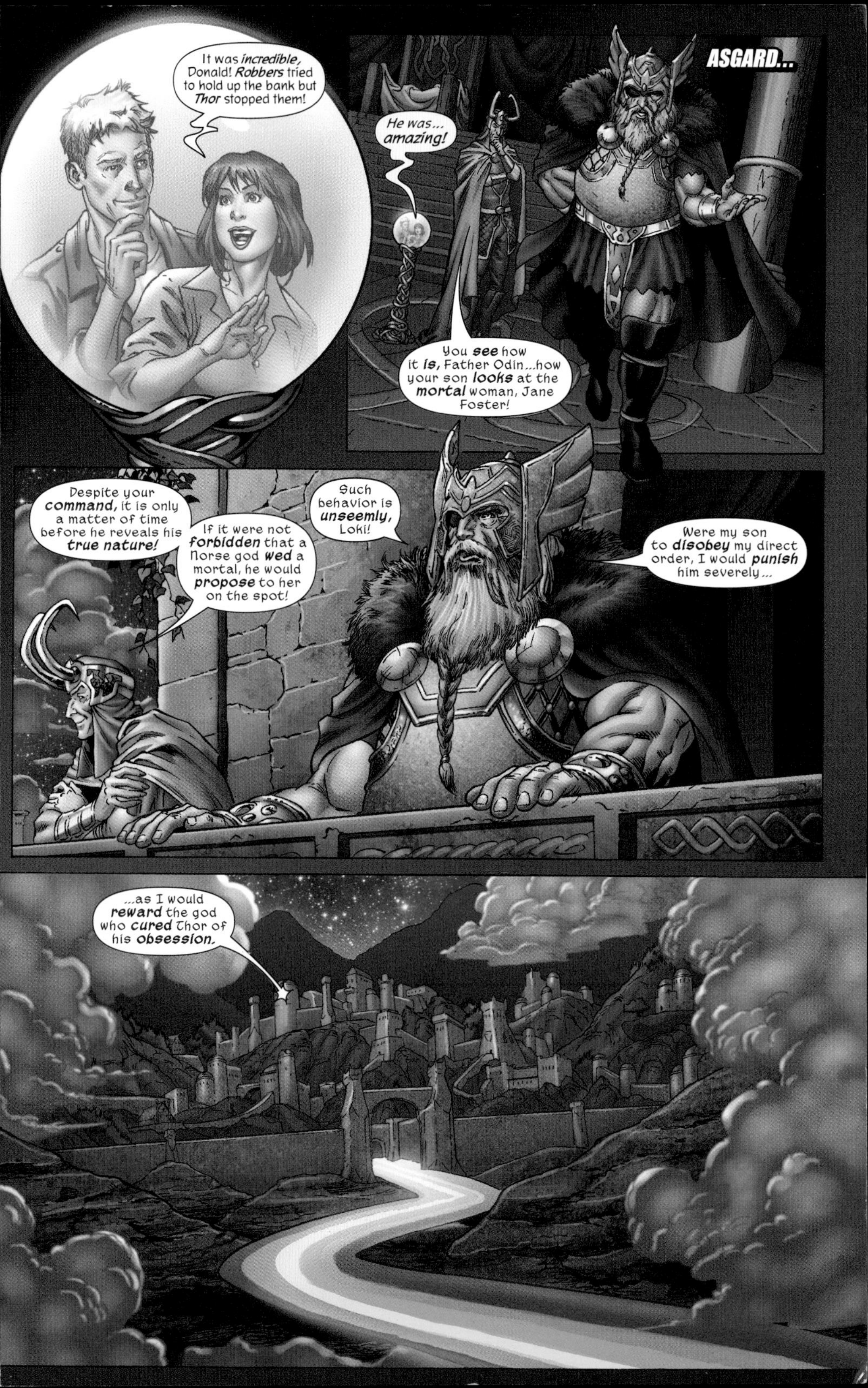
ASGARD...
It was incredible, Donald! Robbers tried to hold up the bank but Thor stopped them!
He was... amazing!
You see how it is, Father Odin...how your son looks at the mortal woman, Jane Foster!
Despite your command, it is only a matter of time before he reveals his true nature!
If it were not forbidden that a Norse god wed a mortal, he would propose to her on the spot!
Such behavior is unseemly, Loki!
Were my son to disobey my direct order, I would punish him severely...
...as I would reward the god who cured Thor of his obsession.

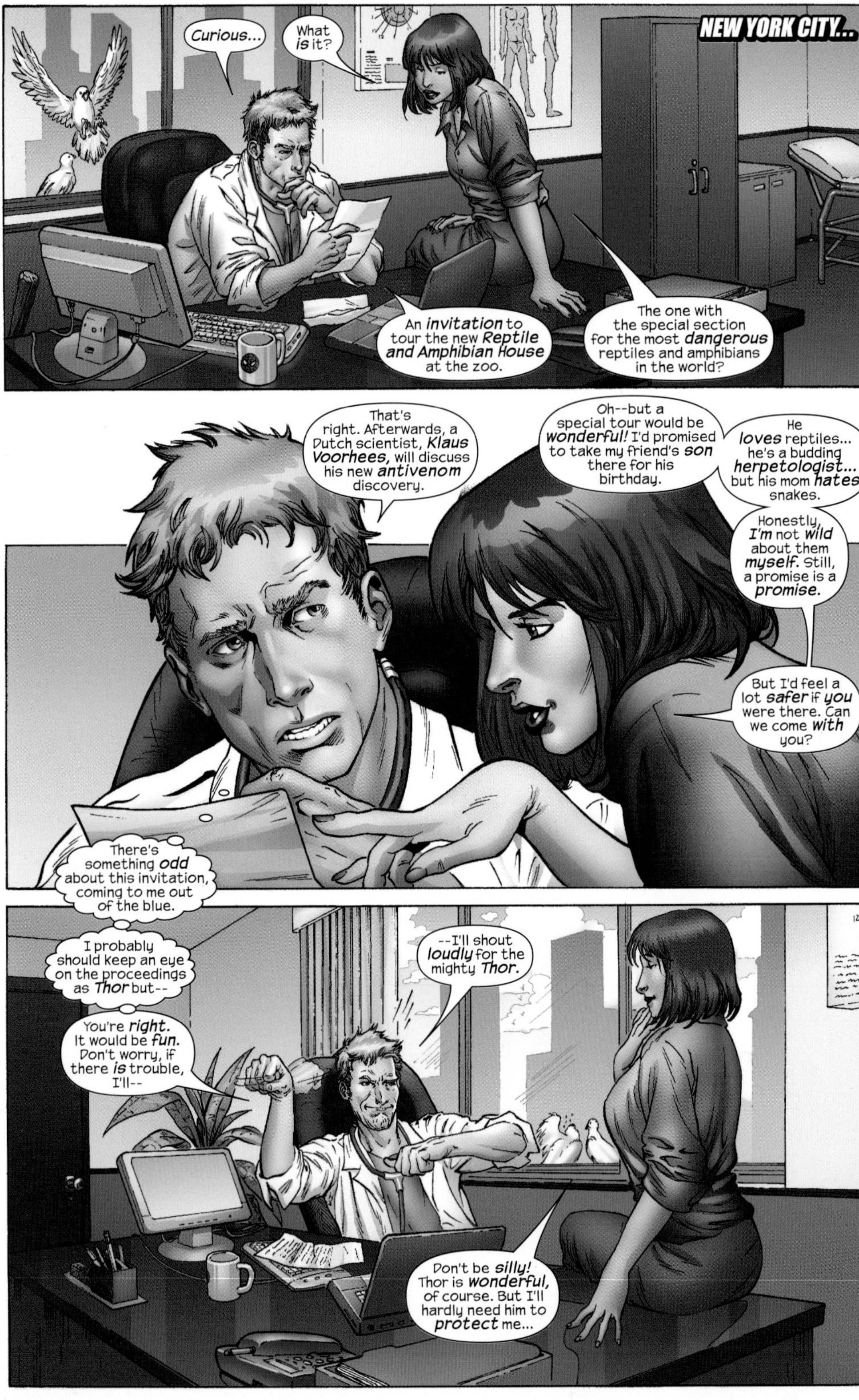

NEW YORK CITY...
Curious...
What *is* it?
An *invitation* to tour the new *Reptile and Amphibian House* at the zoo.
The one with the special section for the most *dangerous* reptiles and amphibians in the world?
That's right. Afterwards, a Dutch scientist, *Klaus Voorhees,* will discuss his new *antivenom* discovery.
Oh--but a special tour would be *wonderful!* I'd promised to take my friend's *son* there for his birthday.
He *loves* reptiles... he's a budding *herpetologist...* but his mom *hates* snakes.
Honestly, *I'm* not *wild* about them *myself.* Still, a promise is a *promise.*
But I'd feel a lot *safer* if *you* were there. Can we come *with* you?
There's something *odd* about this invitation, coming to me out of the blue.
I probably should keep an eye on the proceedings as *Thor* but--
You're *right.* It would be *fun.* Don't worry, if there *is* trouble, I'll--
--I'll shout *loudly* for the mighty *Thor.*
Don't be *silly!* Thor is *wonderful,* of course. But I'll hardly need him to *protect* me...

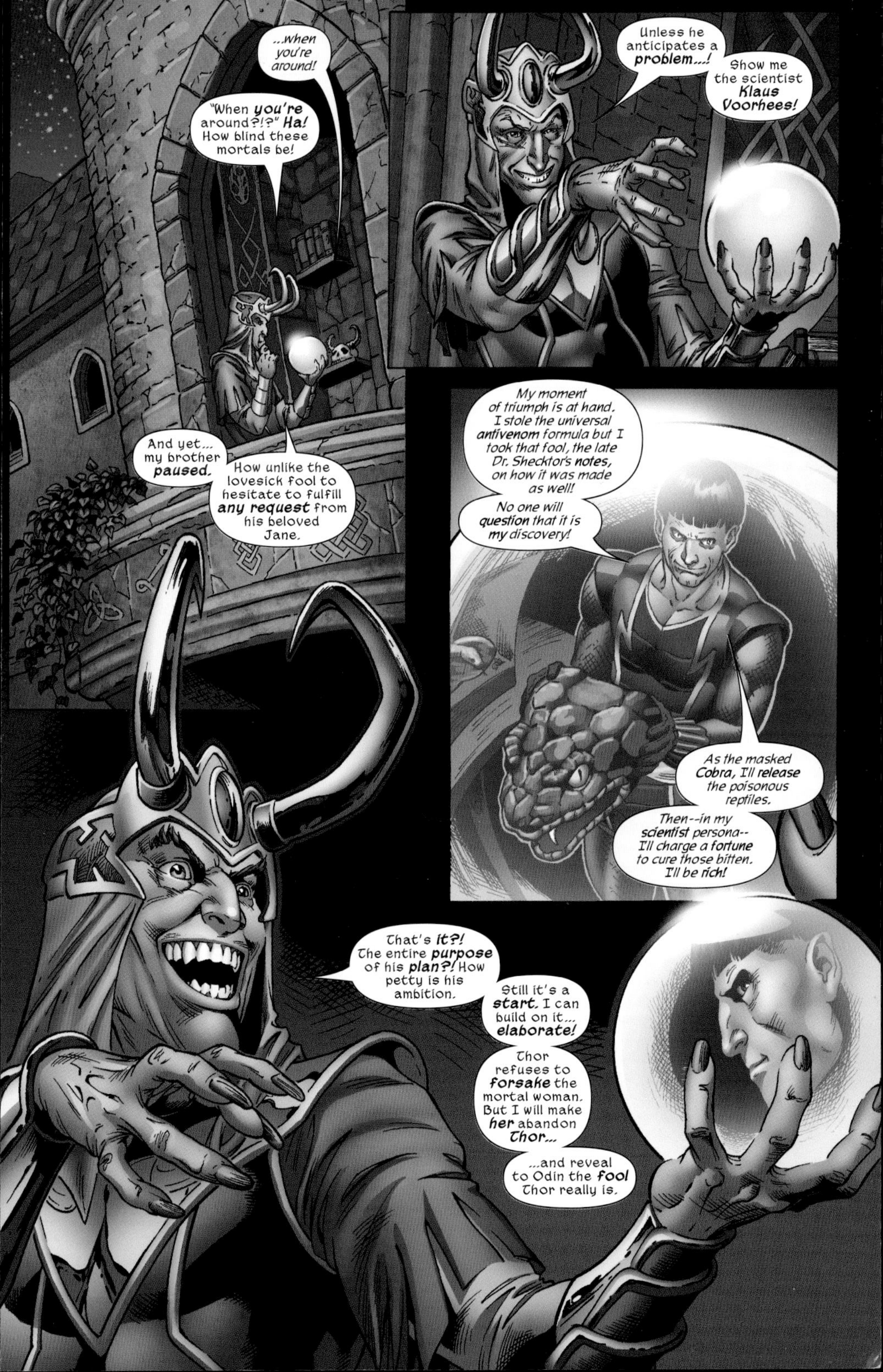
...when you're around!
"When you're around?!?" Ha! How blind these mortals be!
Unless he anticipates a problem...!
Show me the scientist Klaus Voorhees!
And yet... my brother paused.
How unlike the lovesick fool to hesitate to fulfill any request from his beloved Jane.
My moment of triumph is at hand. I stole the universal antivenom formula but I took that fool, the late Dr. Shecktor's notes, on how it was made as well!
No one will question that it is my discovery!
As the masked Cobra, I'll release the poisonous reptiles.
Then--in my scientist persona--I'll charge a fortune to cure those bitten. I'll be rich!
That's it?! The entire purpose of his plan?! How petty is his ambition.
Still it's a start. I can build on it... elaborate!
Thor refuses to forsake the mortal woman. But I will make her abandon Thor...
...and reveal to Odin the fool Thor really is.

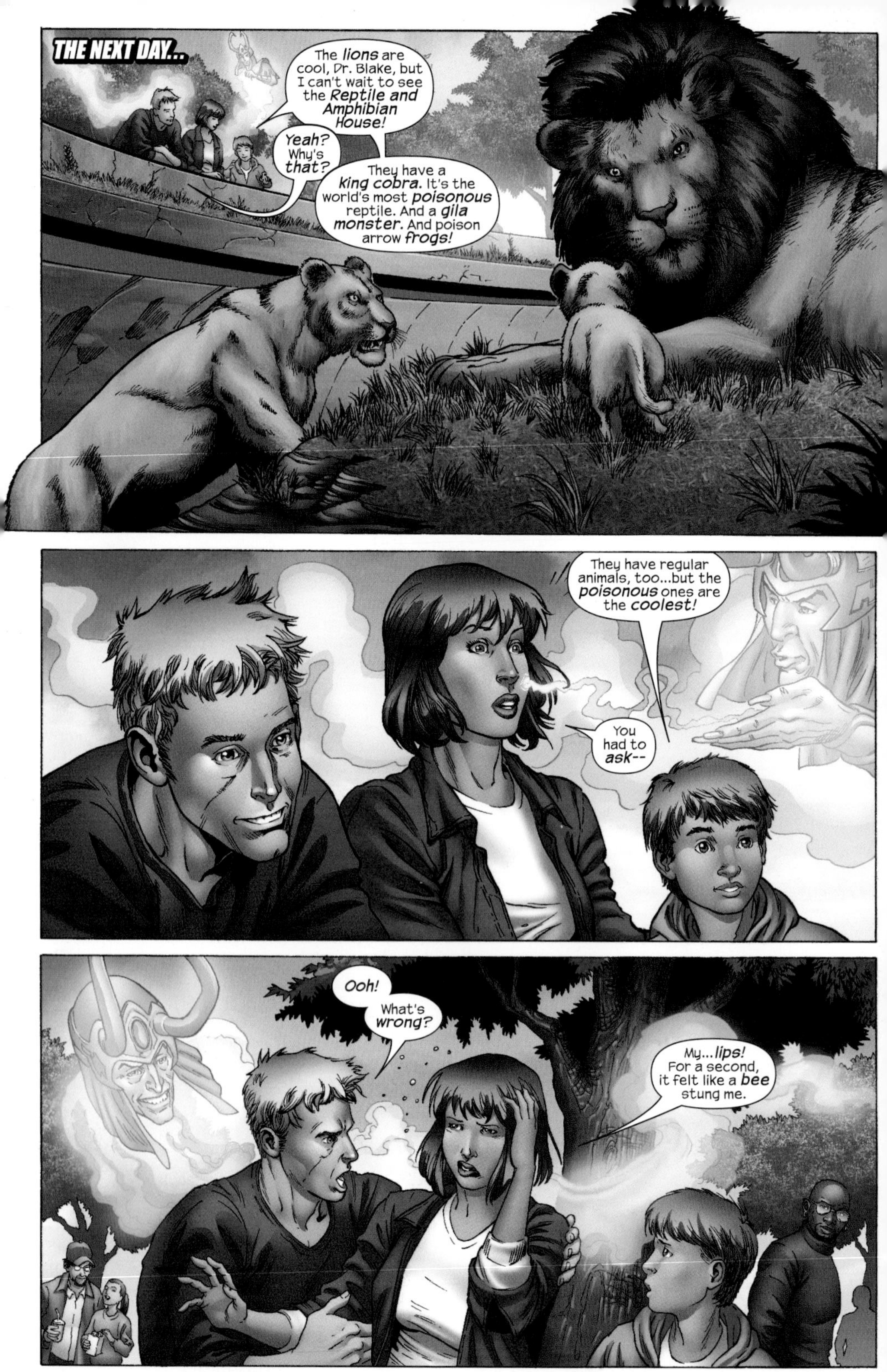
THE NEXT DAY...
The lions are cool, Dr. Blake, but I can't wait to see the Reptile and Amphibian House!
Yeah? Why's that?
They have a king cobra. It's the world's most poisonous reptile. And a gila monster. And poison arrow frogs!
They have regular animals, too...but the poisonous ones are the coolest!
You had to ask--
Ooh!
What's wrong?
My...lips! For a second, it felt like a bee stung me.

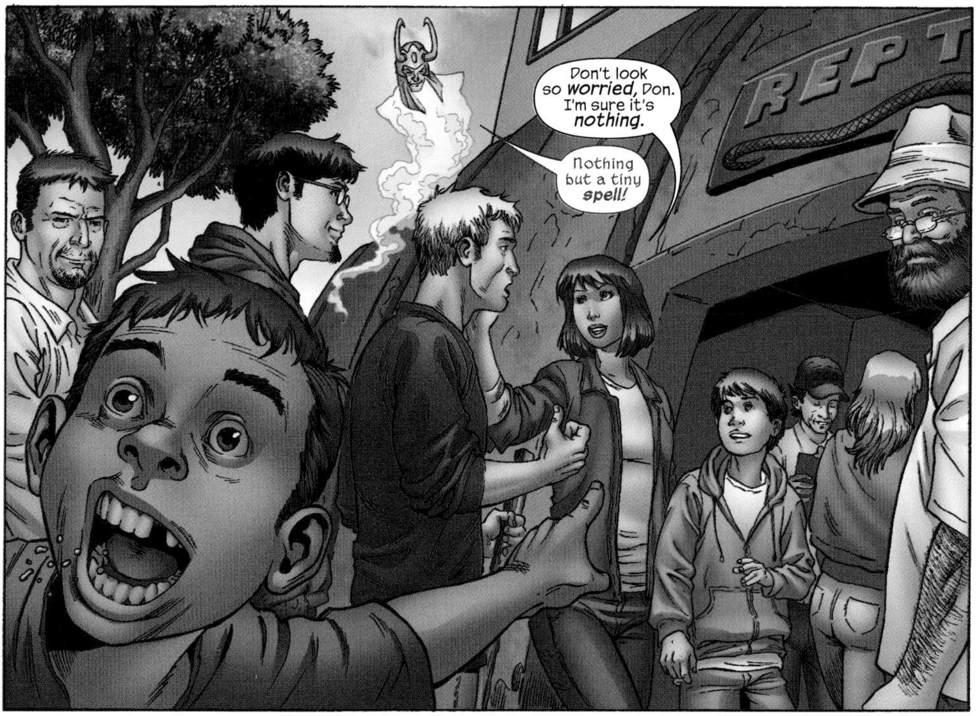
REPT
Don't look so worried, Don. I'm sure it's nothing.
Nothing but a tiny spell!

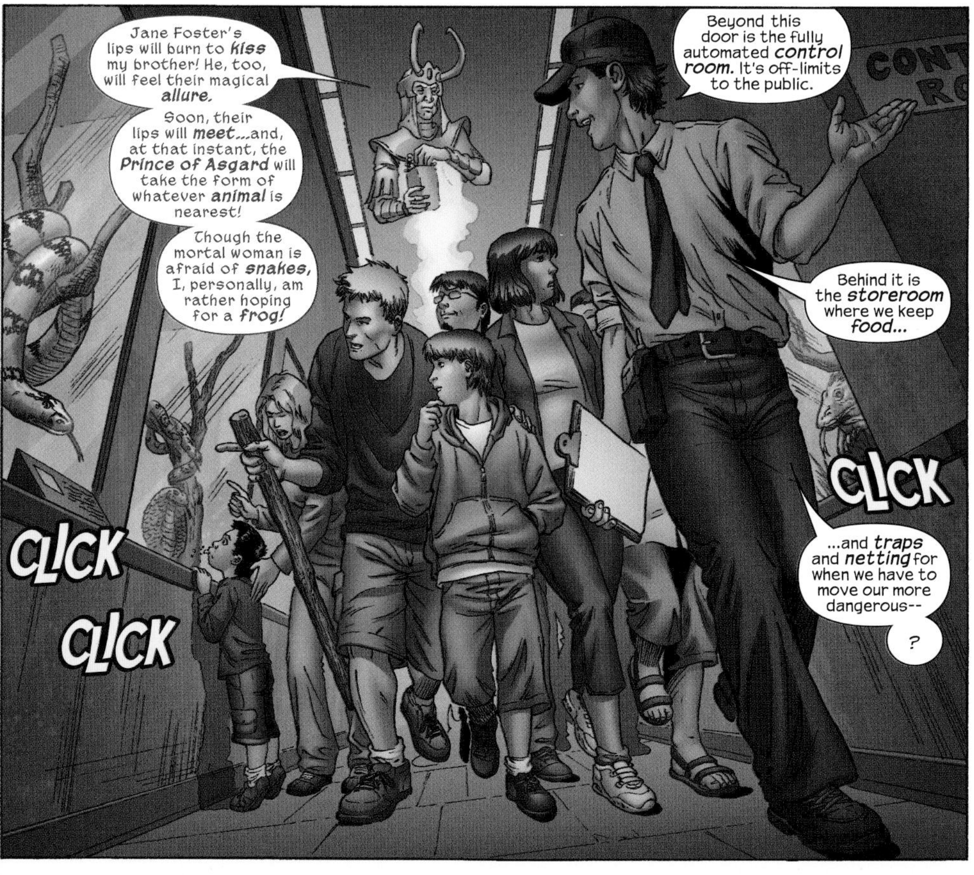
Jane Foster's lips will burn to kiss my brother! He, too, will feel their magical allure.
Soon, their lips will meet...and, at that instant, the Prince of Asgard will take the form of whatever animal is nearest!
Though the mortal woman is afraid of snakes, I, personally, am rather hoping for a frog!
Beyond this door is the fully automated control room. It's off-limits to the public.
CONT
RO
Behind it is the storeroom where we keep food...
CLICK
CLICK
CLICK
...and traps and netting for when we have to move our more dangerous--
?

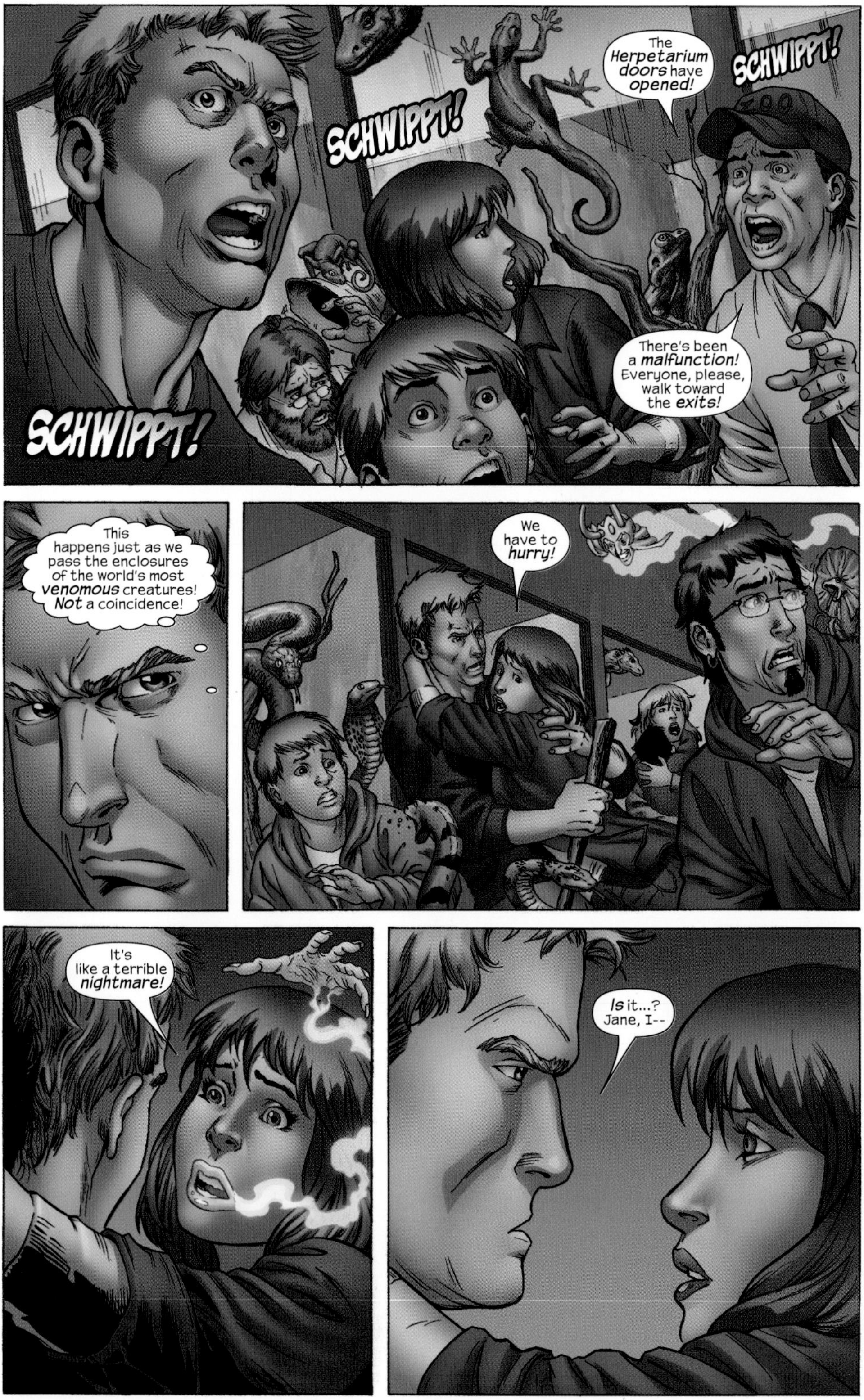
The Herpetarium doors have opened!
SCHWIPPT!
SCHWIPPT!
There's been a malfunction! Everyone, please, walk toward the exits!
SCHWIPPT!
This happens just as we pass the enclosures of the world's most venomous creatures! Not a coincidence!
We have to hurry!
It's like a terrible nightmare!
Is it...? Jane, I--

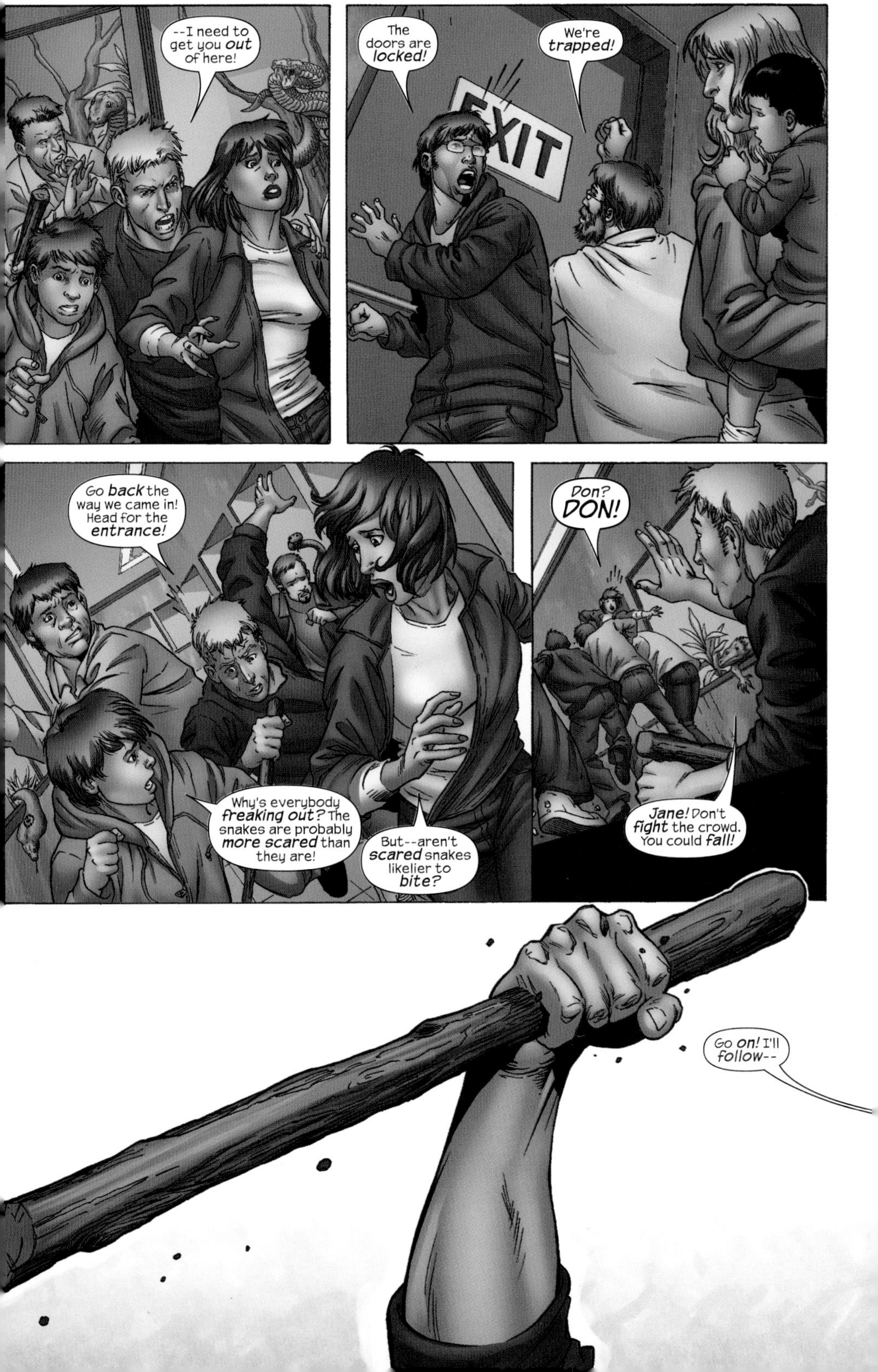
--I need to get you out of here!
The doors are locked!
EXIT
We're trapped!
Go back the way we came in! Head for the entrance!
Why's everybody freaking out? The snakes are probably more scared than they are!
But--aren't scared snakes likelier to bite?
Don? DON!
Jane! Don't fight the crowd. You could fall!
Go on! I'll follow--

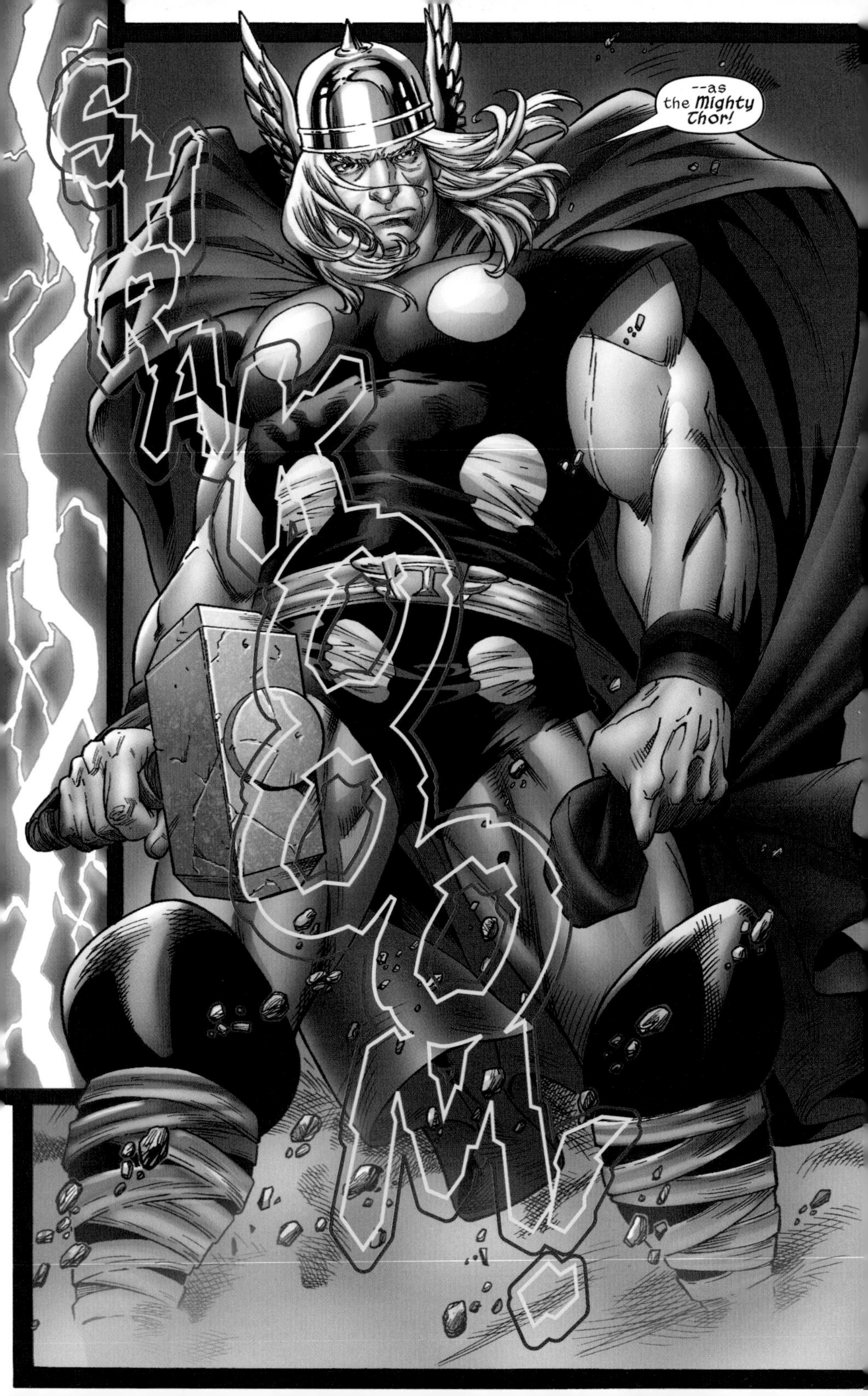
--as the *Mighty Thor!*

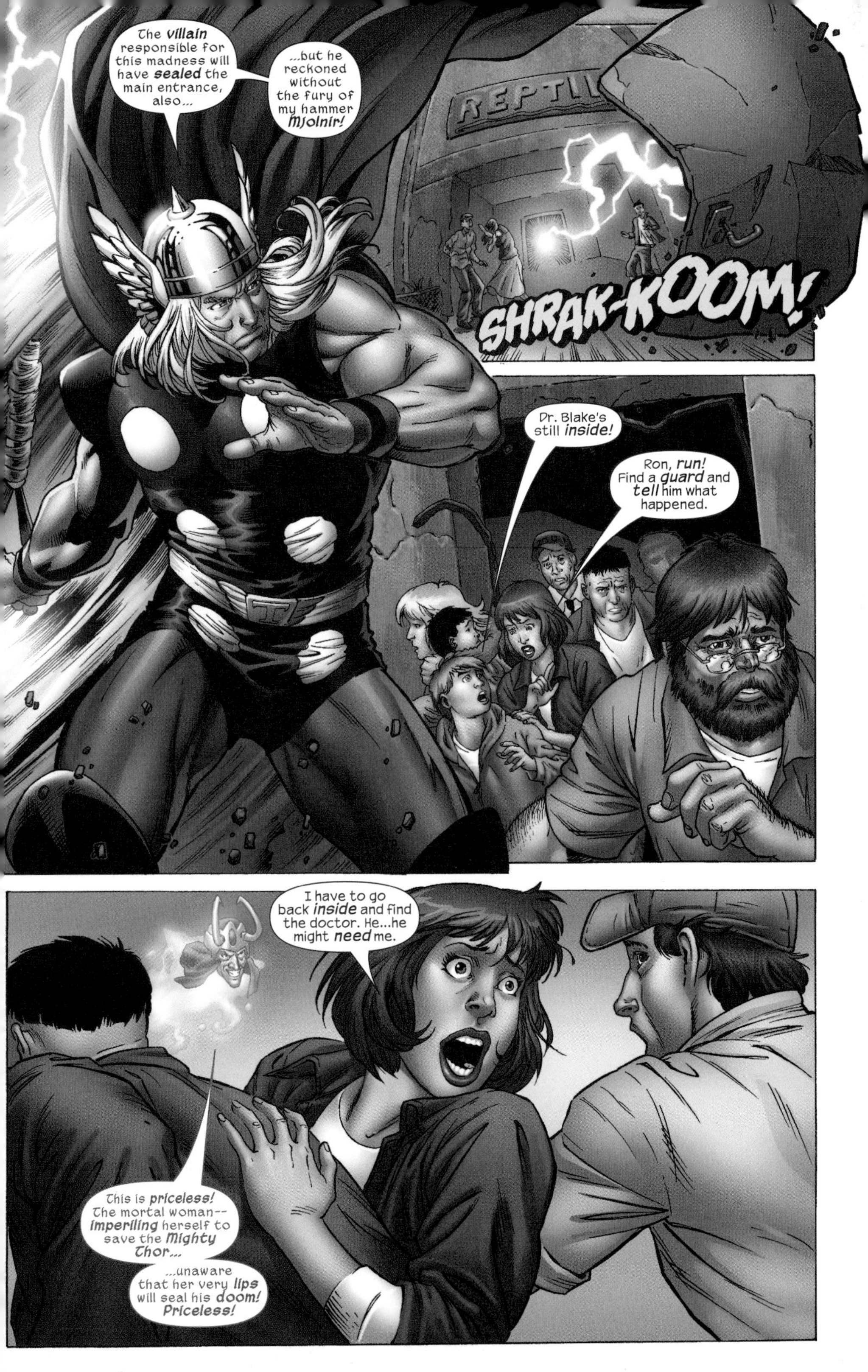
The villain responsible for this madness will have sealed the main entrance, also...
...but he reckoned without the fury of my hammer Mjolnir!
REPTIL
SHRAK-KOOM!
Dr. Blake's still inside!
Ron, run! Find a guard and tell him what happened.
I have to go back inside and find the doctor. He...he might need me.
This is priceless! The mortal woman-- imperiling herself to save the Mighty Thor...
...unaware that her very lips will seal his doom! Priceless!

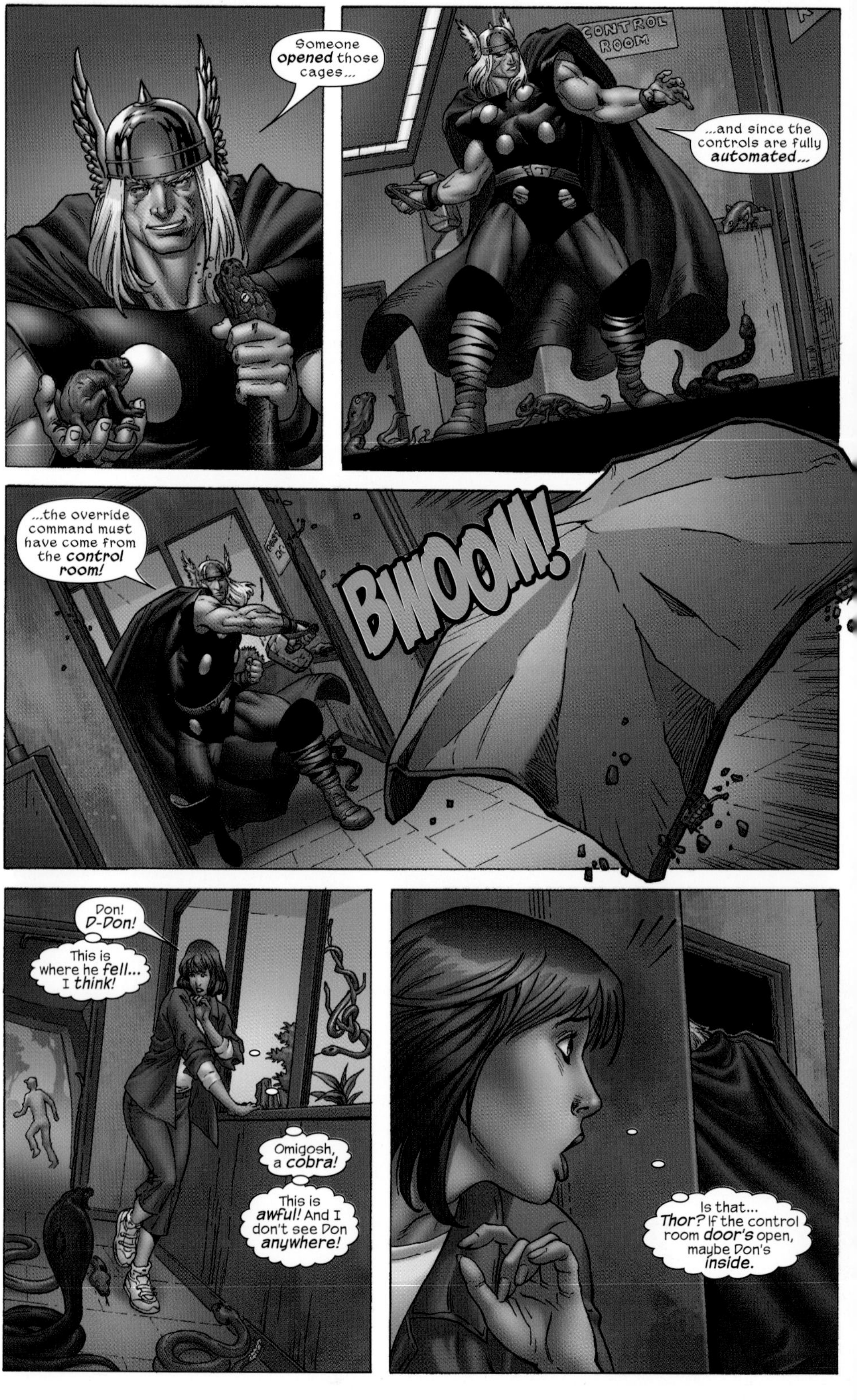
Someone opened those cages...
...and since the controls are fully automated...
CONTROL ROOM
...the override command must have come from the control room!
BWOOM!
Don! D-Don!
This is where he fell... I think!
Omigosh, a cobra!
This is awful! And I don't see Don anywhere!
Is that... Thor? If the control room door's open, maybe Don's inside.

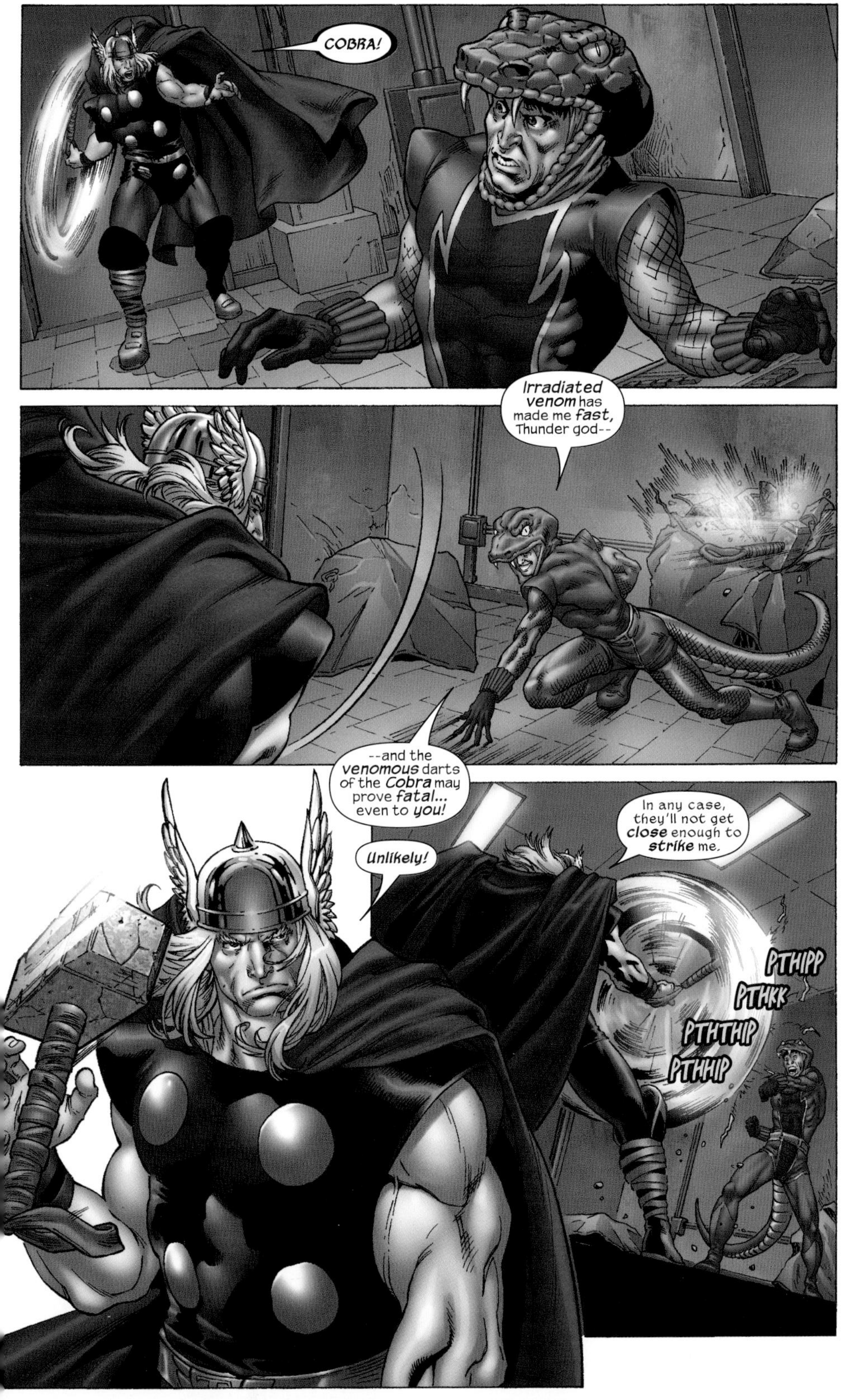
COBRA!
Irradiated venom has made me fast, Thunder god--
--and the venomous darts of the Cobra may prove fatal... even to you!
Unlikely!
In any case, they'll not get close enough to strike me.
PTHIPP
PTHKK
PTHTHIP
PTHHIP

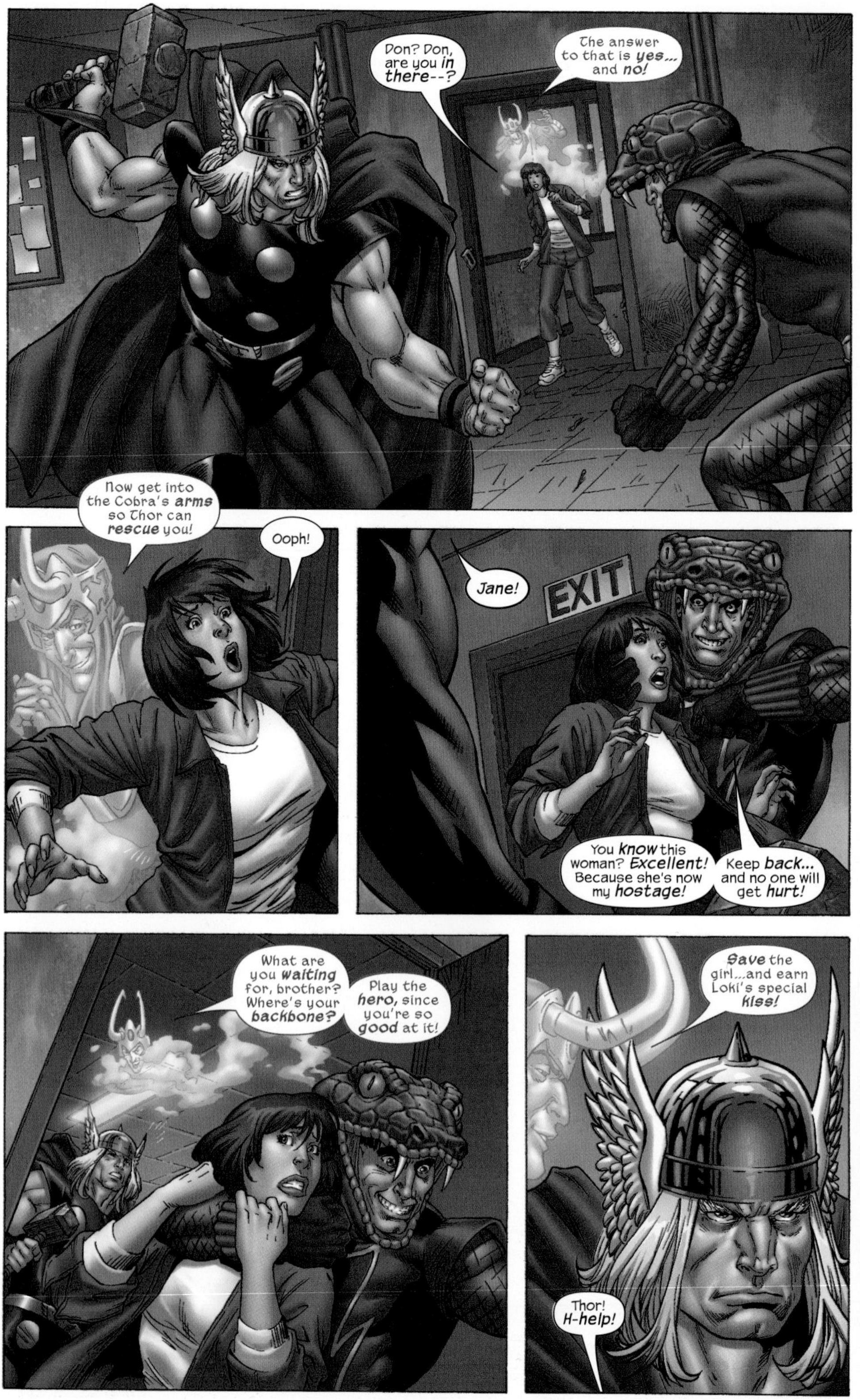
Don? Don, are you in there--?
The answer to that is yes... and no!
Now get into the Cobra's arms so Thor can rescue you!
Ooph!
Jane!
You know this woman? Excellent! Because she's now my hostage!
Keep back... and no one will get hurt!
What are you waiting for, brother? Where's your backbone?
Play the hero, since you're so good at it!
Save the girl...and earn Loki's special kiss!
Thor! H-help!

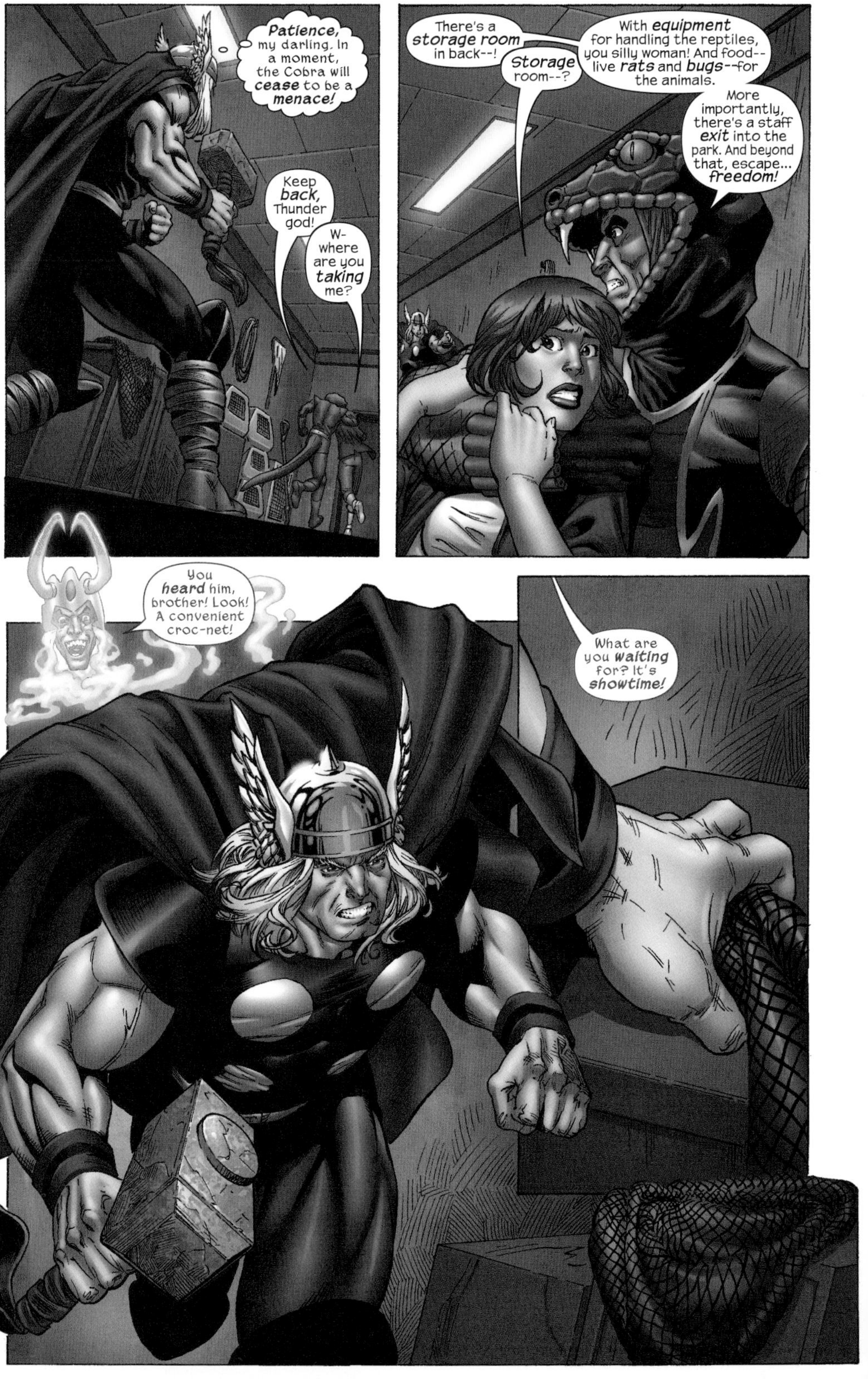
Patience, my darling. In a moment, the Cobra will cease to be a menace!
Keep back, Thunder god!
W-where are you taking me?
There's a storage room in back--!
Storage room--?
With equipment for handling the reptiles, you silly woman! And food--live rats and bugs--for the animals.
More importantly, there's a staff exit into the park. And beyond that, escape... freedom!
You heard him, brother! Look! A convenient croc-net!
What are you waiting for? It's showtime!

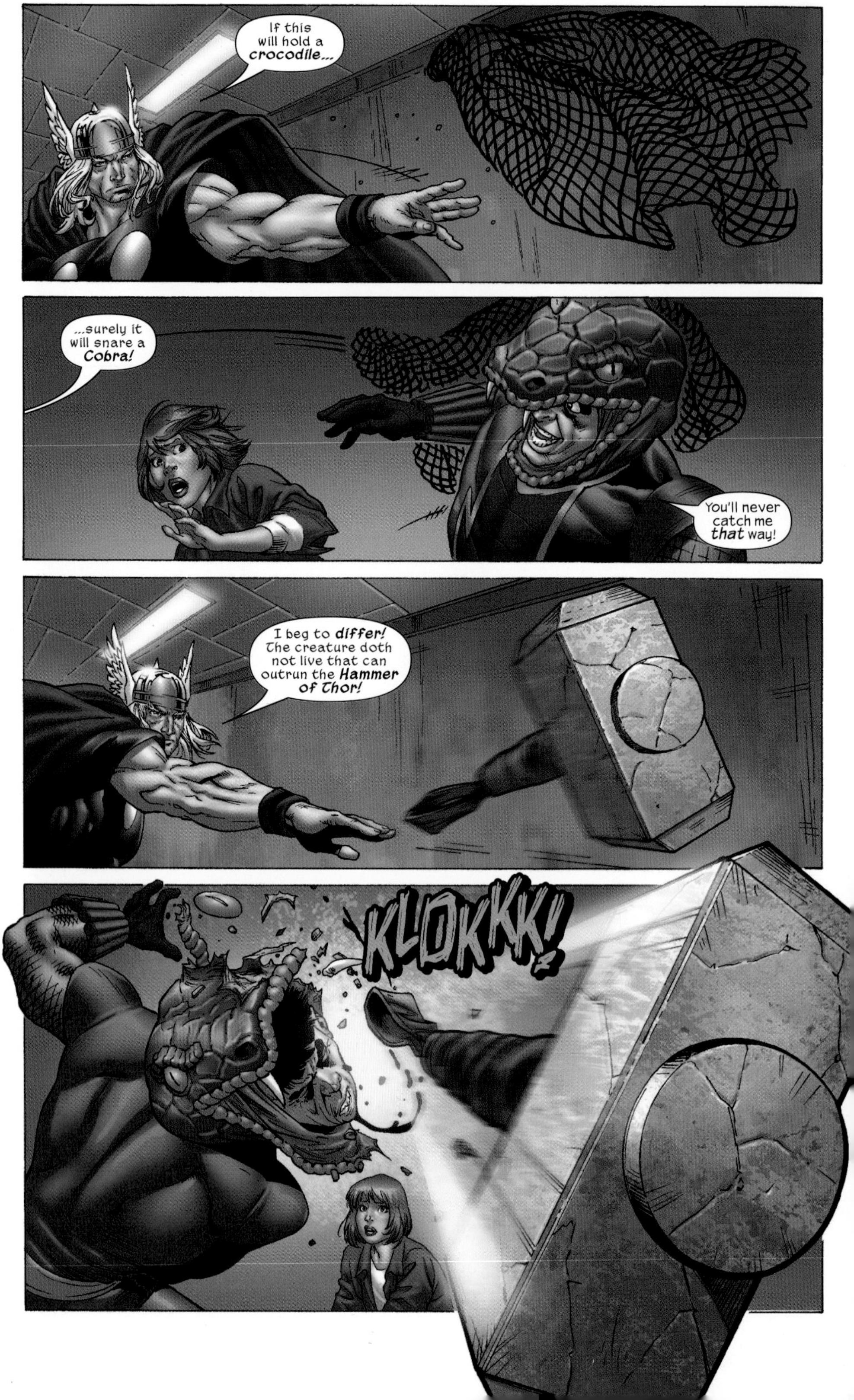
If this will hold a crocodile...
...surely it will snare a Cobra!
You'll never catch me that way!
I beg to differ! The creature doth not live that can outrun the Hammer of Thor!
KLOKKK!

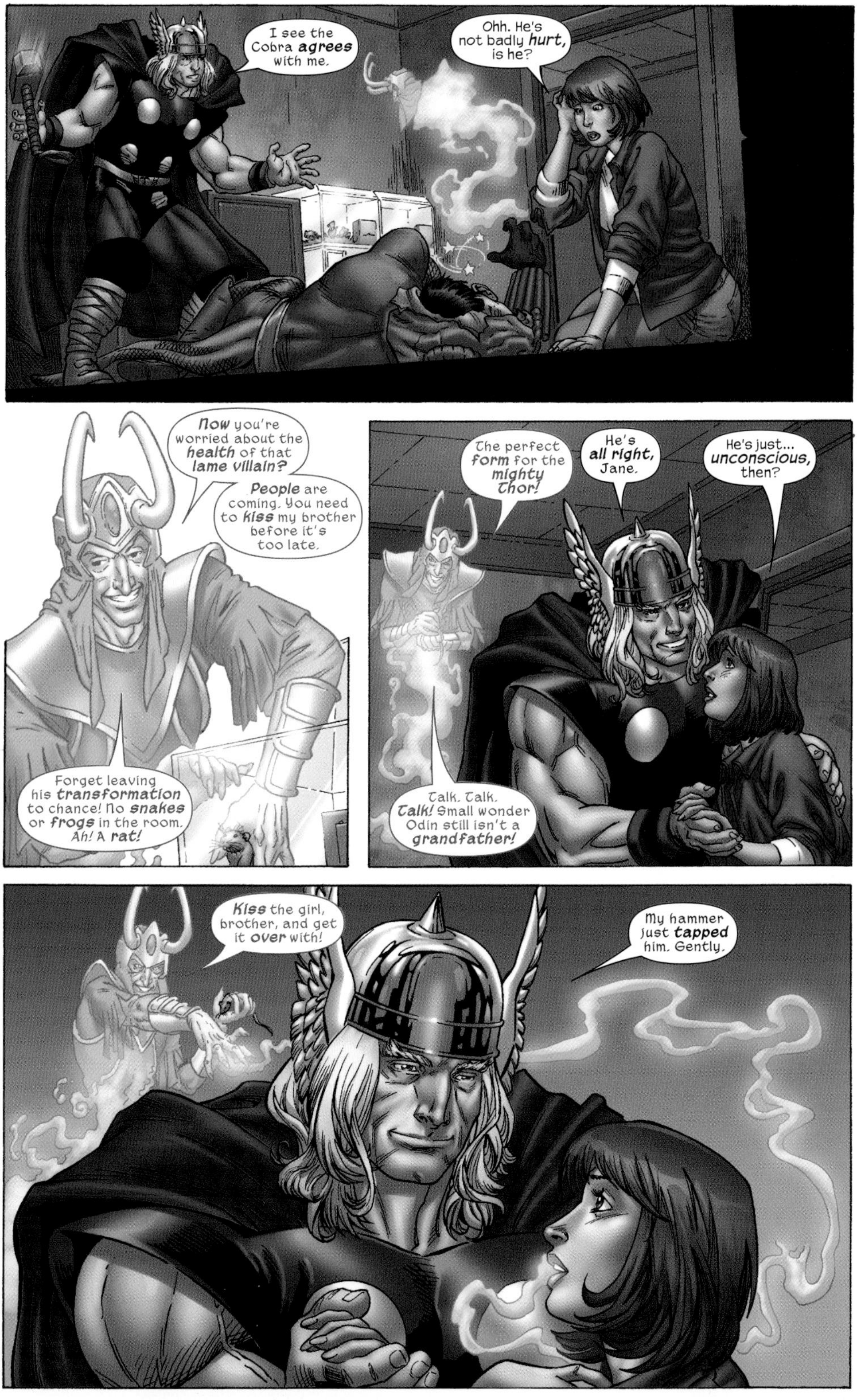
I see the Cobra agrees with me.
Ohh. He's not badly hurt, is he?
Now you're worried about the health of that lame villain?
People are coming. You need to kiss my brother before it's too late.
Forget leaving his transformation to chance! No snakes or frogs in the room. Ah! A rat!
The perfect form for the mighty Thor!
He's all right, Jane.
He's just... unconscious, then?
Talk. Talk. Talk! Small wonder Odin still isn't a grandfather!
Kiss the girl, brother, and get it over with!
My hammer just tapped him. Gently.

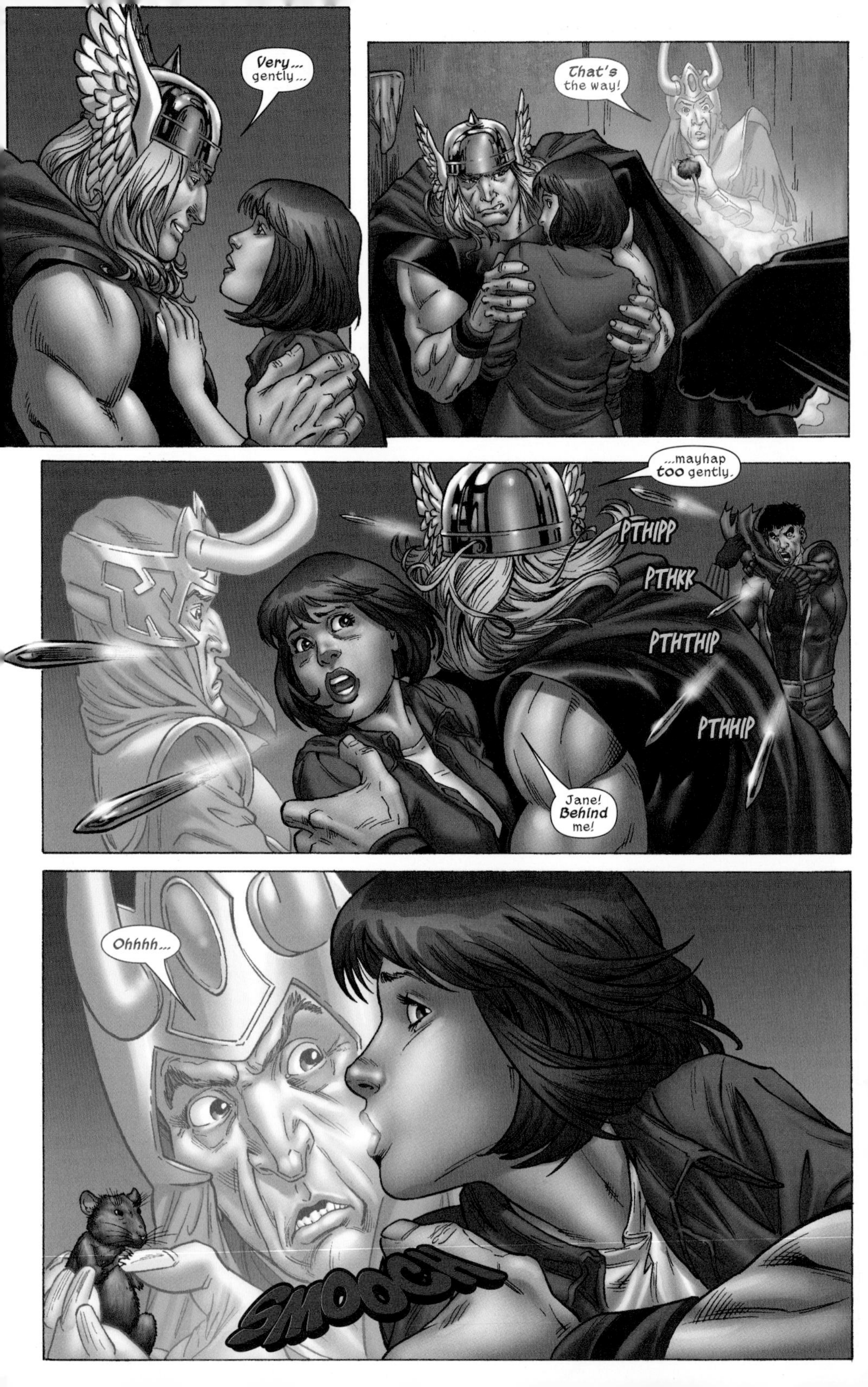

Very... gently...
That's the way!
...mayhap too gently.
PTHIPP
PTHKK
PTHTHIP
PTHHIP
Jane! Behind me!
Ohhhh...
SMOOCH

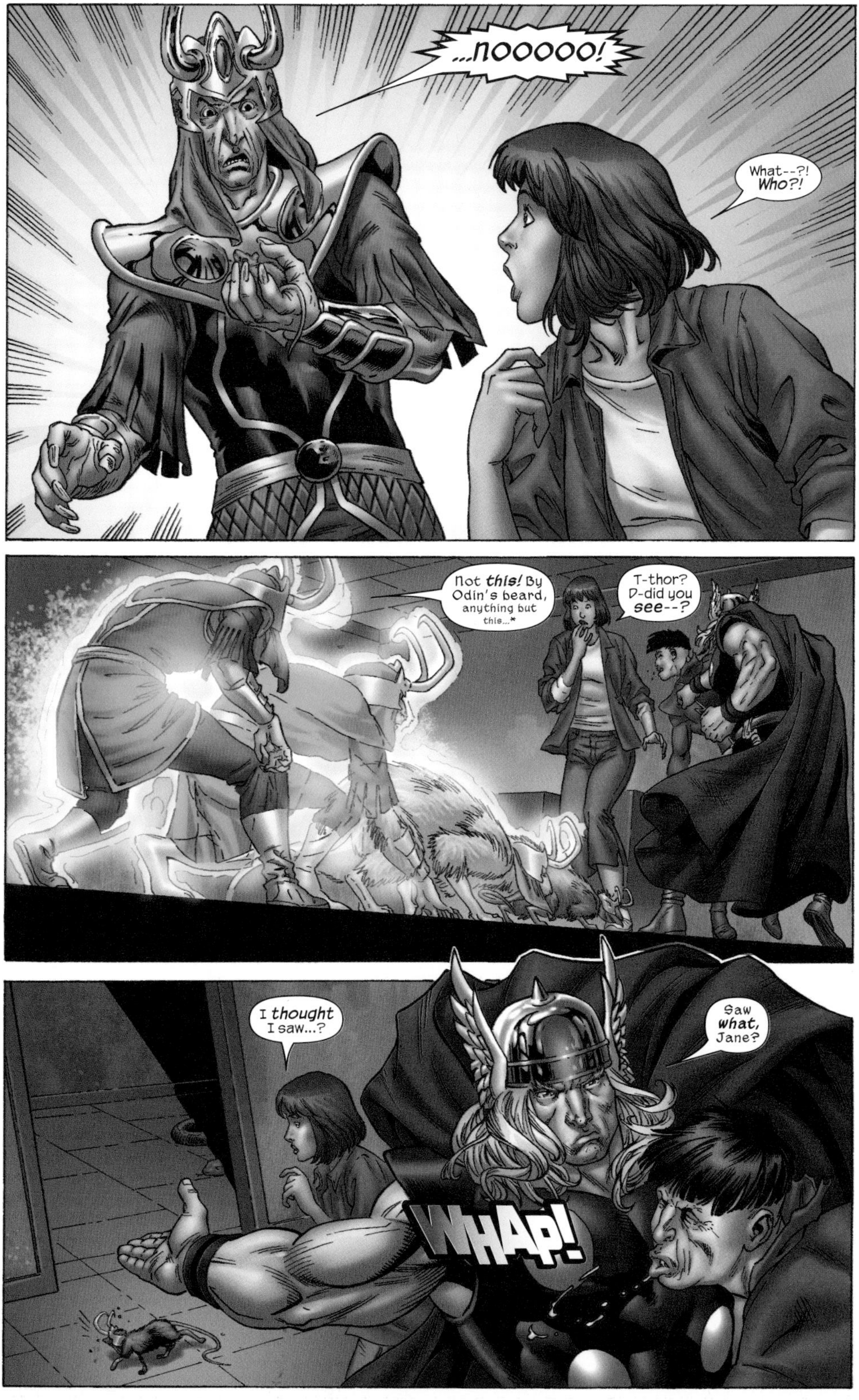
...NOOOOO!
What--?! Who?!
Not this! By Odin's beard, anything but this...*
T-thor? D-did you see--?
I thought I saw...?
Saw what, Jane?
WHAP!

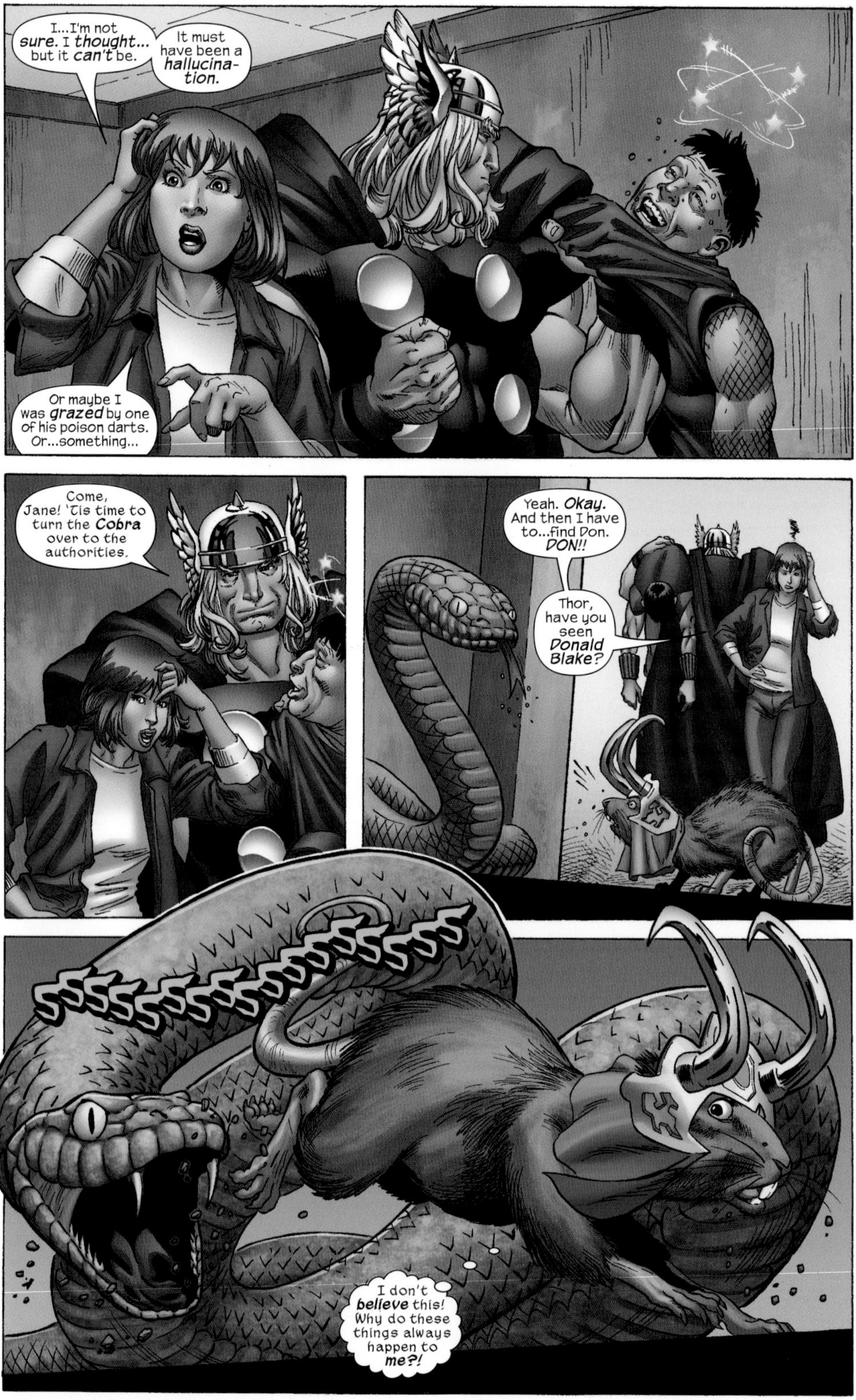
I...I'm not sure. I thought... but it can't be.
It must have been a hallucination.
Or maybe I was grazed by one of his poison darts. Or...something...
Come, Jane! 'Tis time to turn the Cobra over to the authorities.
Yeah. Okay. And then I have to...find Don. DON!!
Thor, have you seen Donald Blake?
SSSSSSSSSSSSSSSSSSSS
I don't believe this! Why do these things always happen to me?!

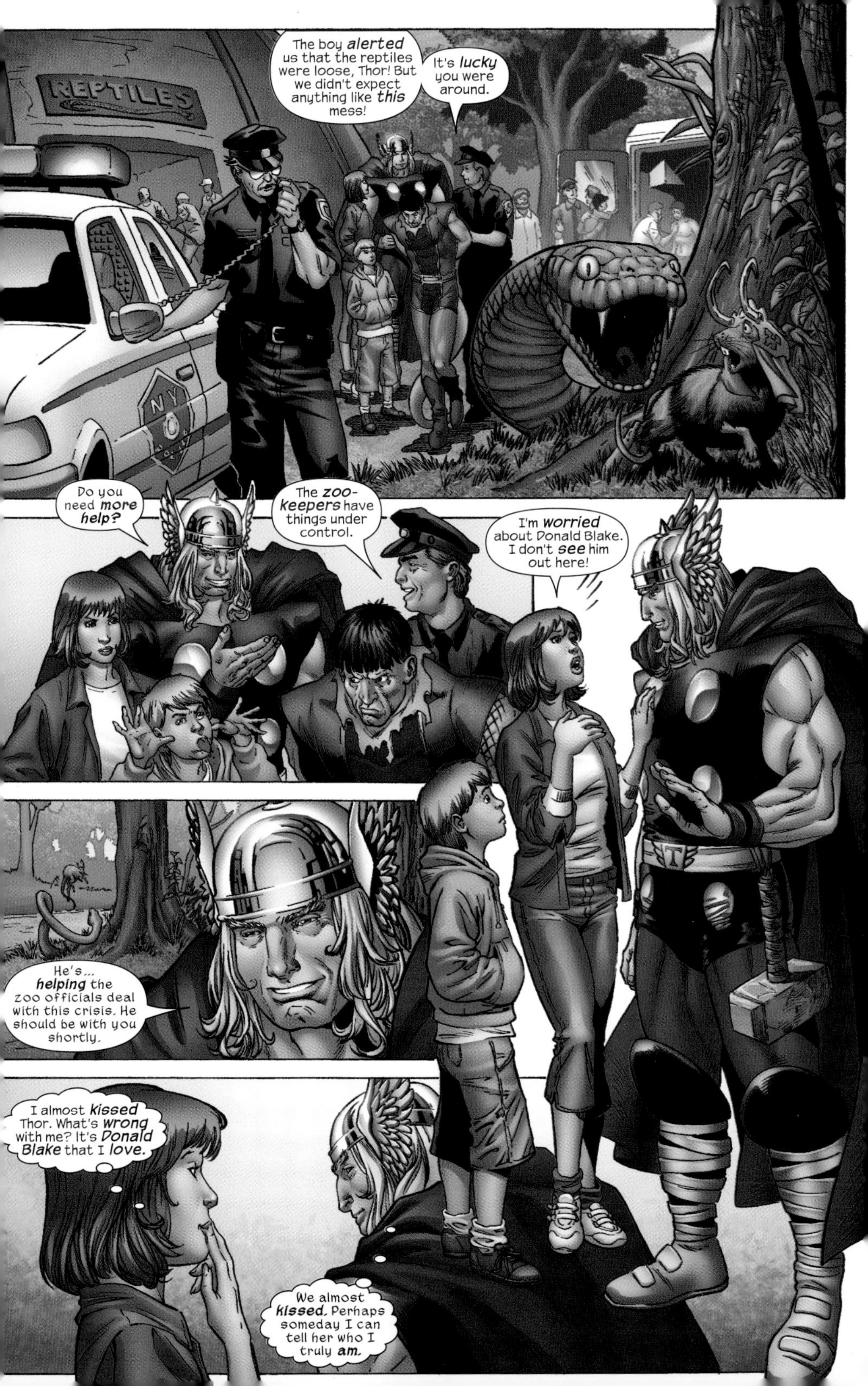

REPTILES
The boy alerted us that the reptiles were loose, Thor! But we didn't expect anything like this mess!
It's lucky you were around.
NY
Do you need more help?
The zoo-keepers have things under control.
I'm worried about Donald Blake. I don't see him out here!
He's... helping the zoo officials deal with this crisis. He should be with you shortly.
I almost kissed Thor. What's wrong with me? It's Donald Blake that I love.
We almost kissed. Perhaps someday I can tell her who I truly am.

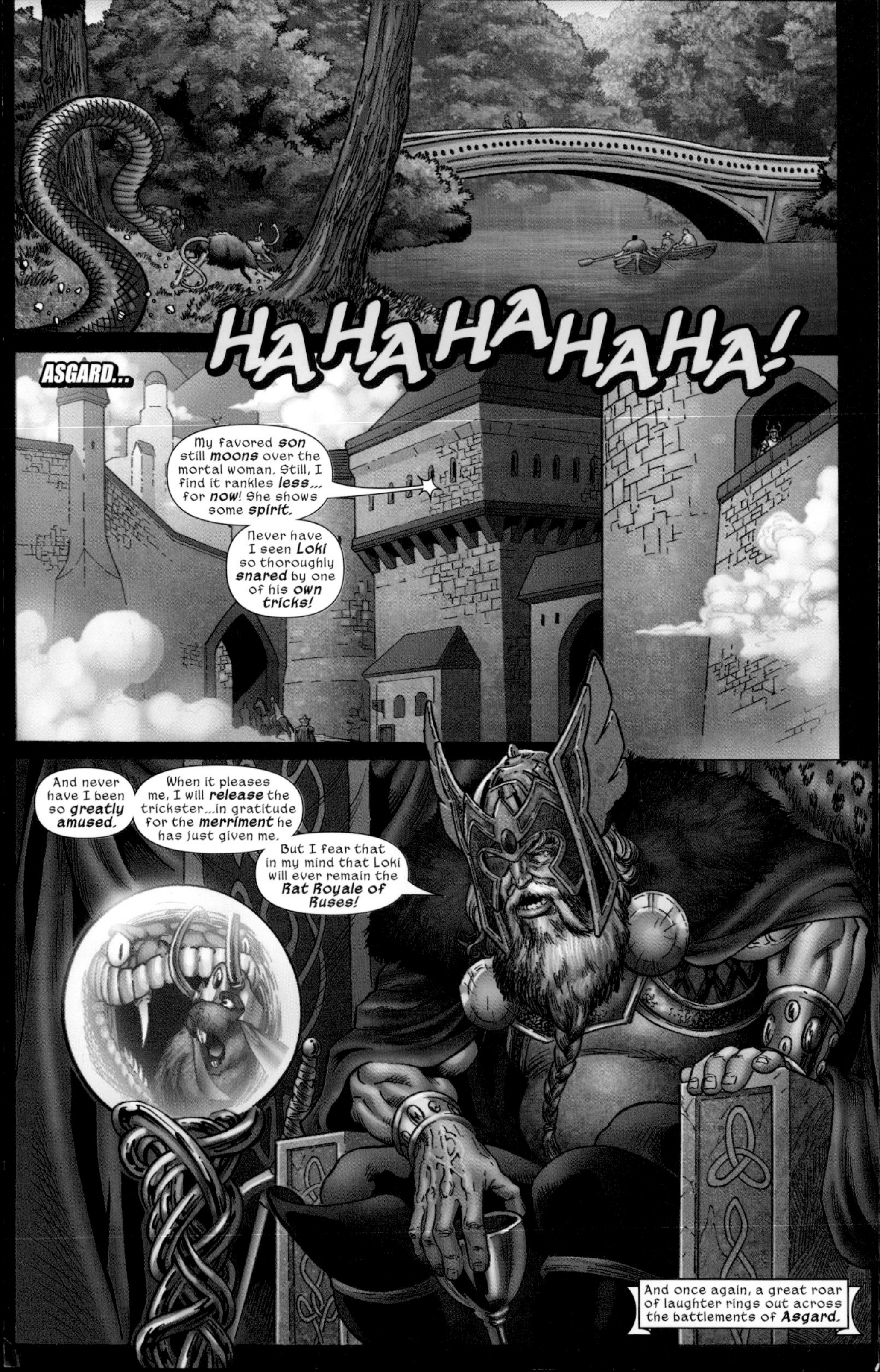
HAHAHAHAHAHA!
ASGARD...
My favored son still moons over the mortal woman. Still, I find it rankles less... for now! She shows some spirit.
Never have I seen Loki so thoroughly snared by one of his own tricks!
And never have I been so greatly amused.
When it pleases me, I will release the trickster...in gratitude for the merriment he has just given me.
But I fear that in my mind that Loki will ever remain the Rat Royale of Ruses!
And once again, a great roar of laughter rings out across the battlements of Asgard.

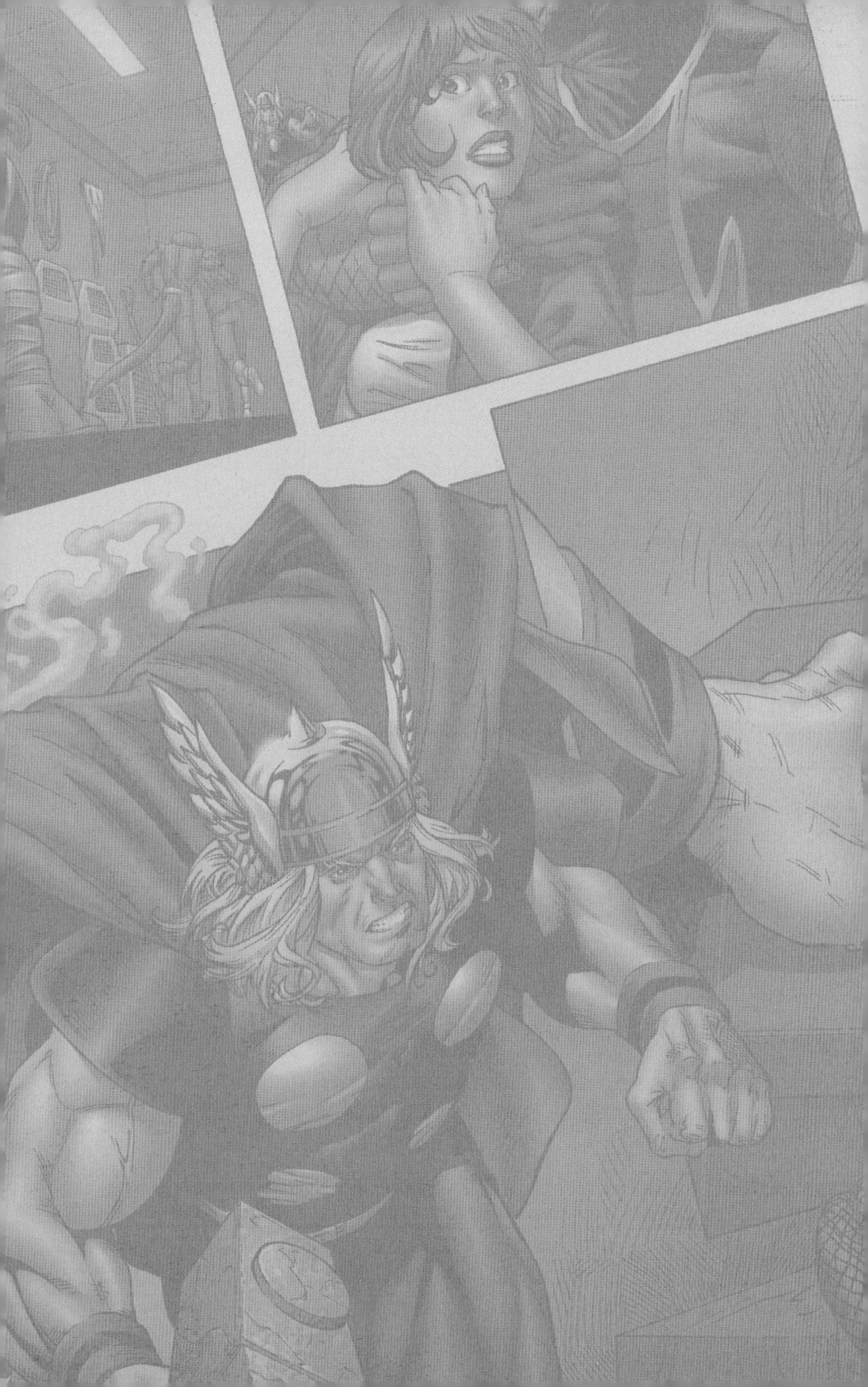

02

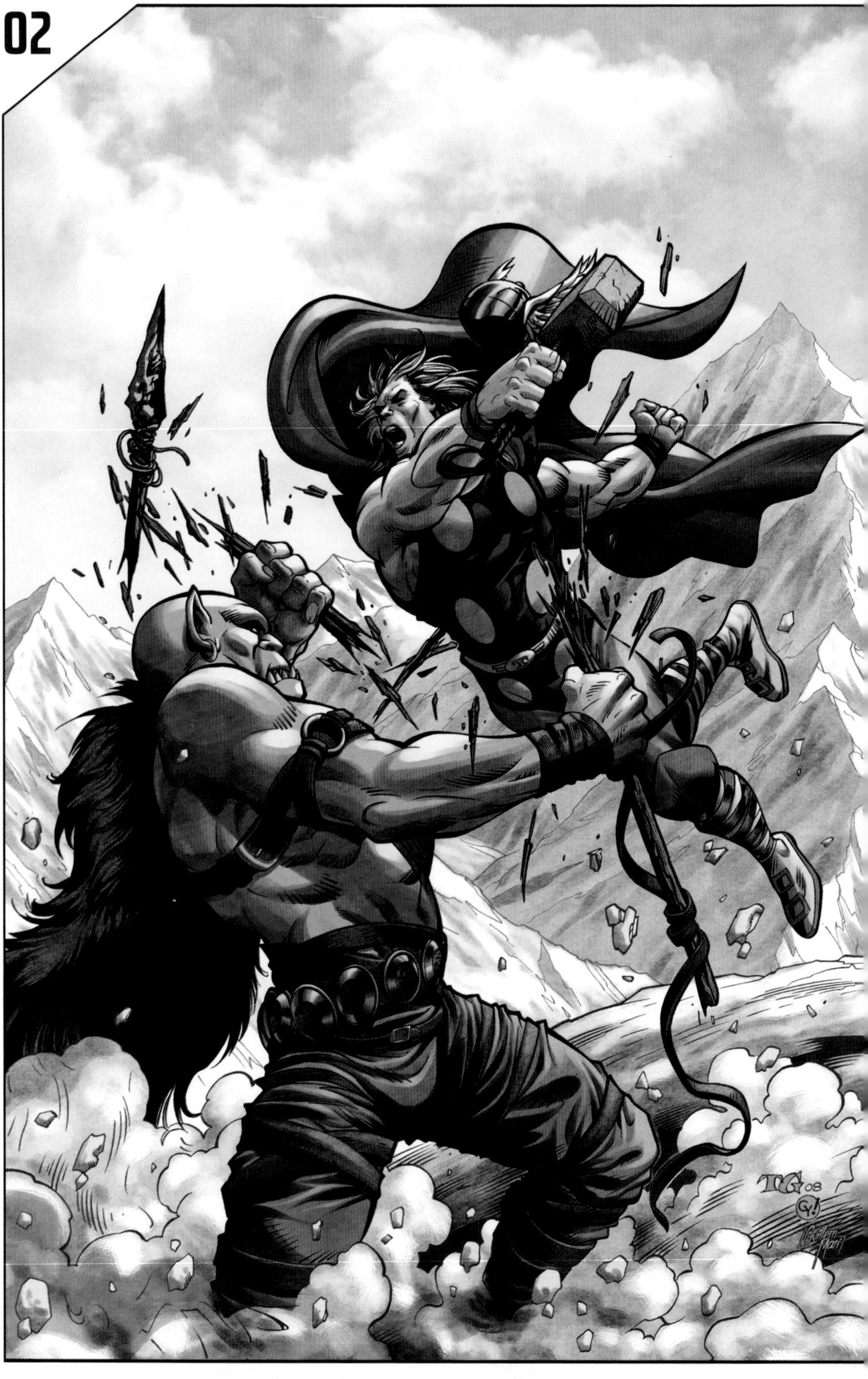

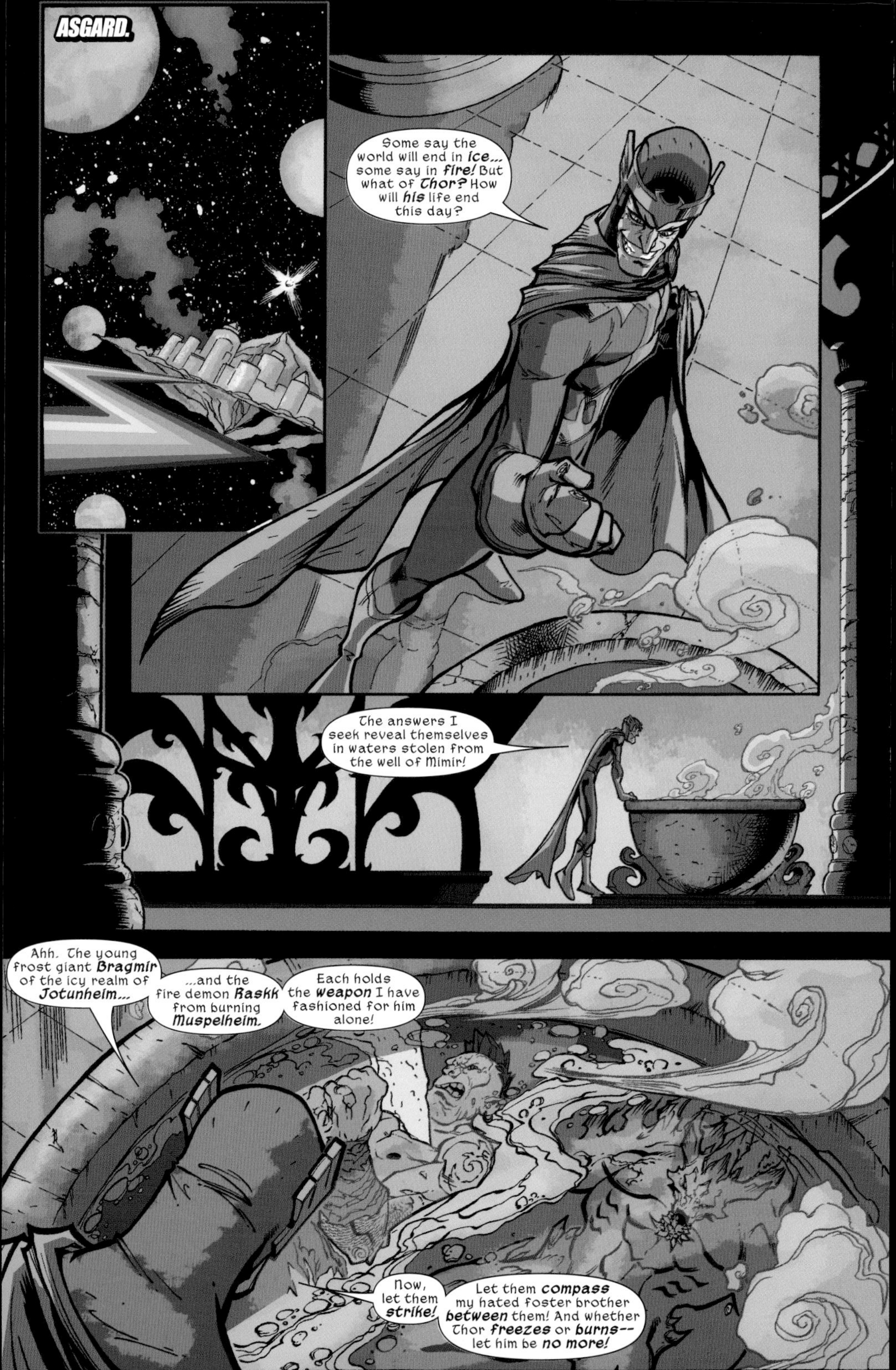

ASGARD.
Some say the world will end in ice... some say in fire! But what of Thor? How will his life end this day?
The answers I seek reveal themselves in waters stolen from the well of Mimir!
Ahh. The young frost giant Bragmir of the icy realm of Jotunheim...
...and the fire demon Raskk from burning Muspelheim.
Each holds the weapon I have fashioned for him alone!
Now, let them strike!
Let them compass my hated foster brother between them! And whether Thor freezes or burns-- let him be no more!

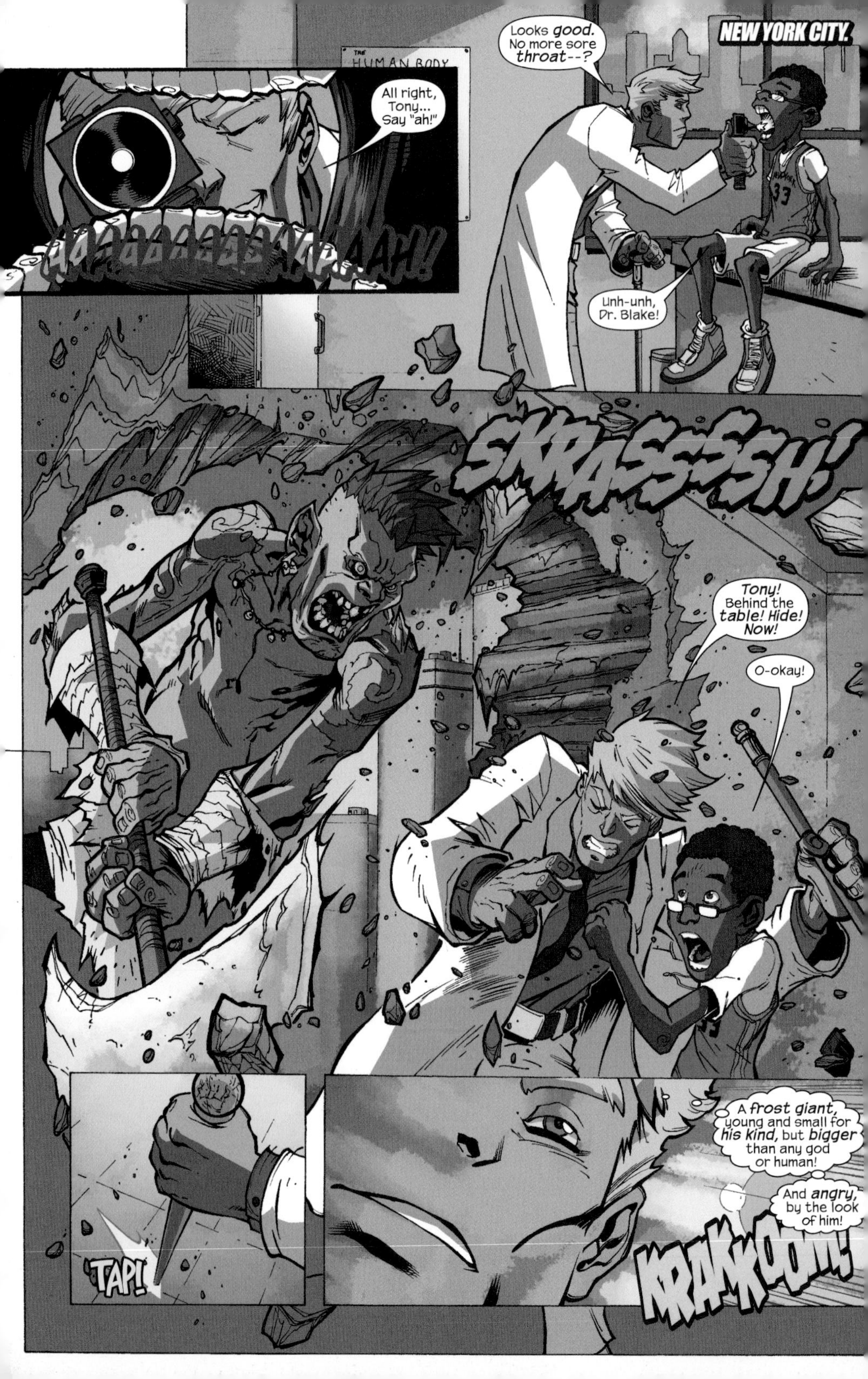
NEW YORK CITY.
All right, Tony... Say "ah!"
AAAAAAAAAAAAAAAAH!
Looks good. No more sore throat--?
Unh-unh, Dr. Blake!
SKRASSSSH!
Tony! Behind the table! Hide! Now!
O-okay!
TAP!
A frost giant, young and small for his kind, but bigger than any god or human!
And angry, by the look of him!
KRAKKOOM!

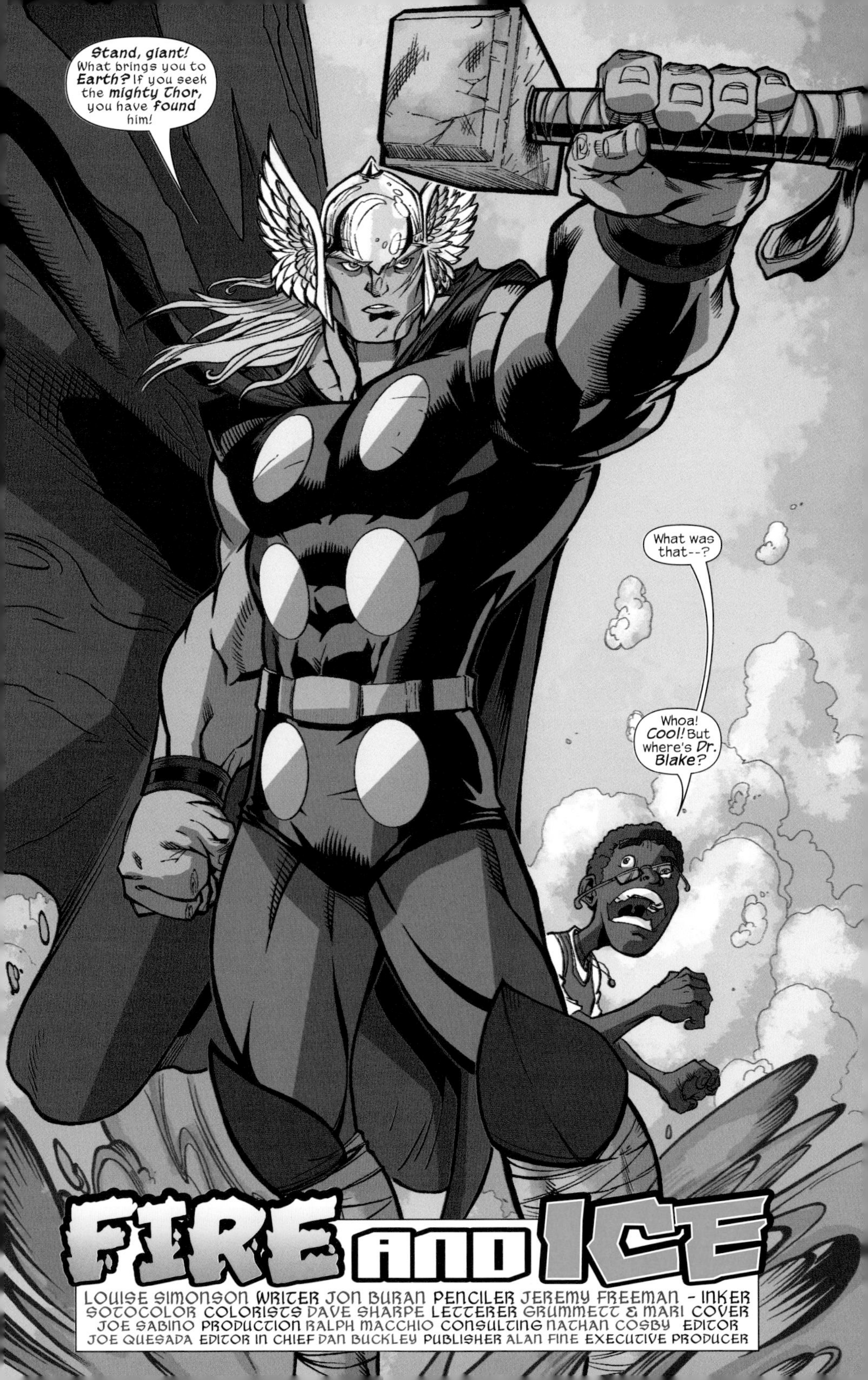

Stand, giant! What brings you to Earth? If you seek the mighty Thor, you have found him!
What was that--?
Whoa! Cool! But where's Dr. Blake?
FIRE AND ICE
LOUISE SIMONSON WRITER JON BURAN PENCILER JEREMY FREEMAN - INKER
SOTOCOLOR COLORISTS DAVE SHARPE LETTERER GRUMMETT & MARI COVER
JOE SABINO PRODUCTION RALPH MACCHIO CONSULTING NATHAN COSBY EDITOR
JOE QUESADA EDITOR IN CHIEF DAN BUCKLEY PUBLISHER ALAN FINE EXECUTIVE PRODUCER

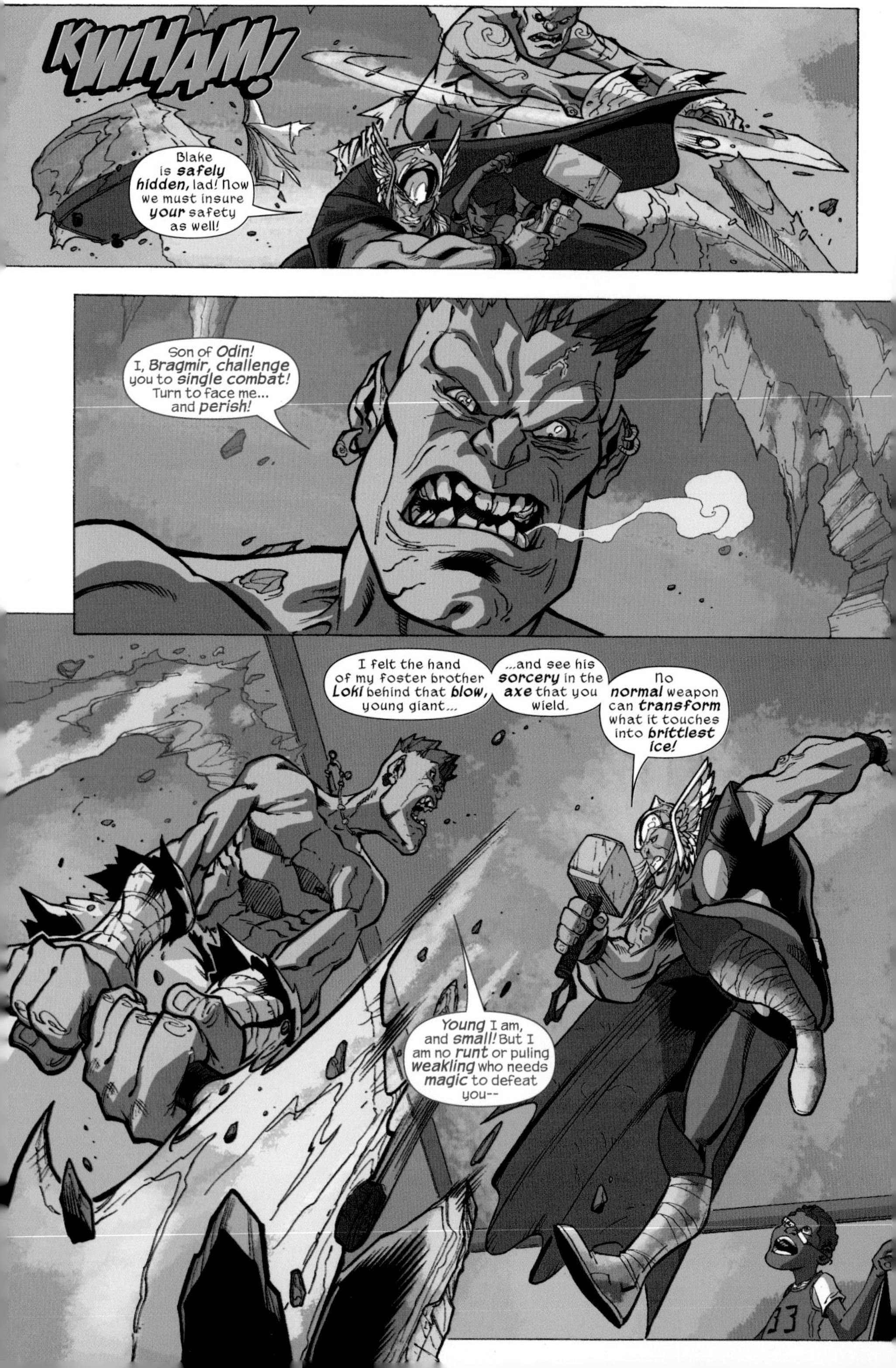
KWHAM!
Blake is safely hidden, lad! Now we must insure your safety as well!
Son of Odin! I, Bragmir, challenge you to single combat! Turn to face me... and perish!
I felt the hand of my foster brother Loki behind that blow, young giant...
...and see his sorcery in the axe that you wield.
No normal weapon can transform what it touches into brittlest ice!
Young I am, and small! But I am no runt or puling weakling who needs magic to defeat you--

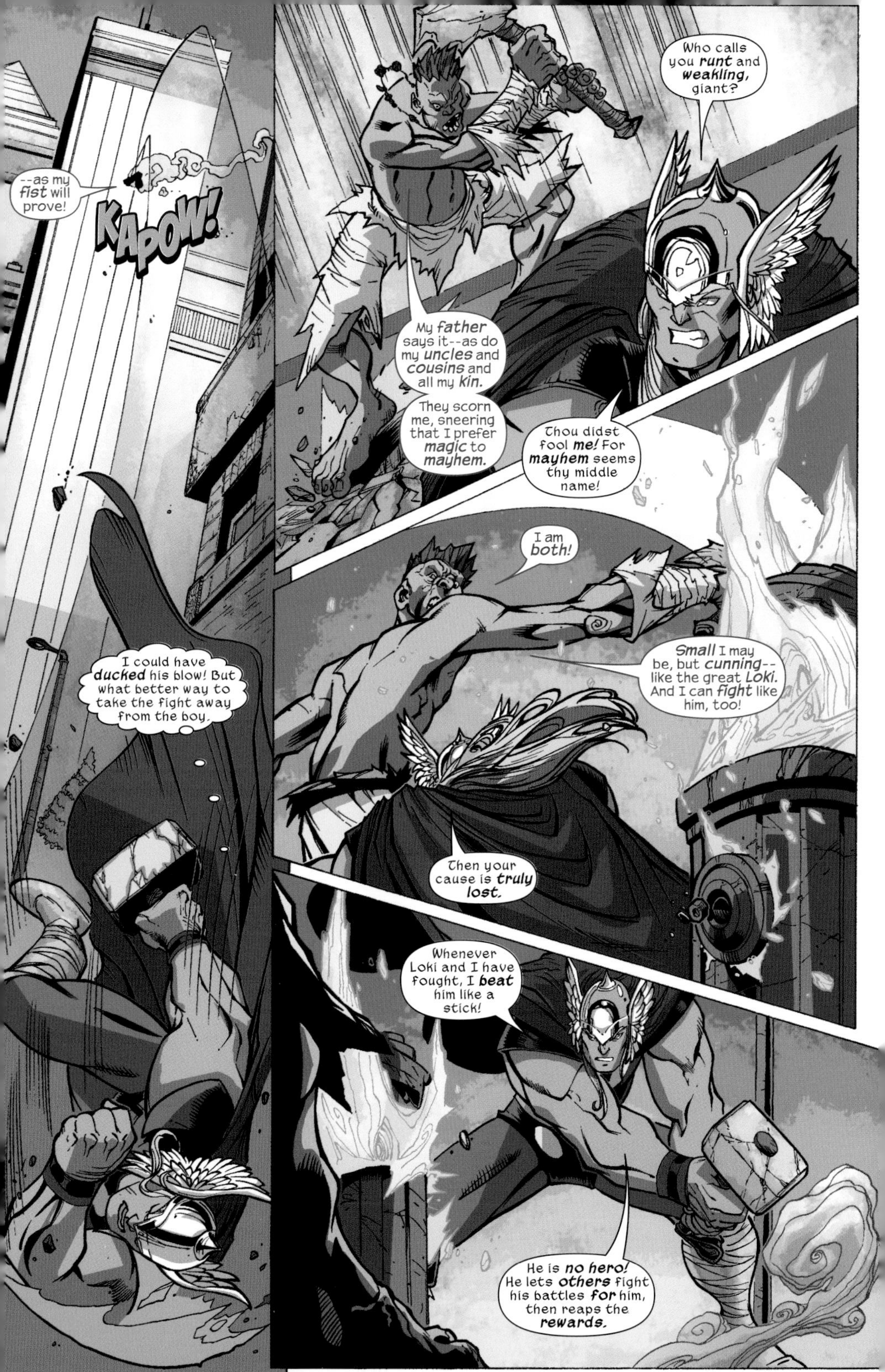
--as my fist will prove!
KAPOW!
I could have ducked his blow! But what better way to take the fight away from the boy.
Who calls you runt and weakling, giant?
My father says it--as do my uncles and cousins and all my kin.
They scorn me, sneering that I prefer magic to mayhem.
Thou didst fool me! For mayhem seems thy middle name!
I am both!
Small I may be, but cunning--like the great Loki. And I can fight like him, too!
Then your cause is truly lost.
Whenever Loki and I have fought, I beat him like a stick!
He is no hero! He lets others fight his battles for him, then reaps the rewards.

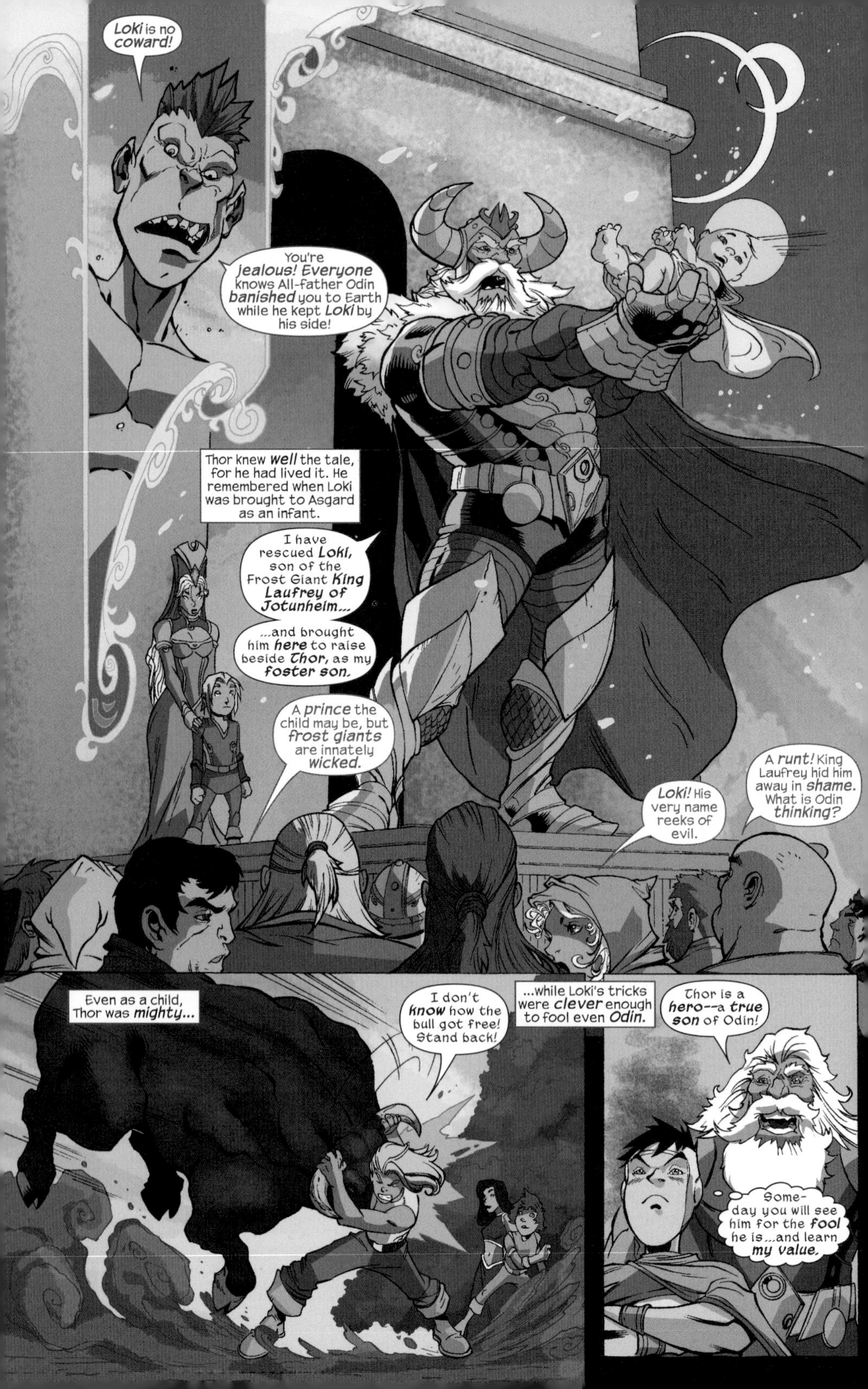

Loki is no coward!
You're jealous! Everyone knows All-father Odin banished you to Earth while he kept Loki by his side!
Thor knew well the tale, for he had lived it. He remembered when Loki was brought to Asgard as an infant.
I have rescued Loki, son of the Frost Giant King Laufrey of Jotunheim...
...and brought him here to raise beside Thor, as my foster son.
A prince the child may be, but frost giants are innately wicked.
Loki! His very name reeks of evil.
A runt! King Laufrey hid him away in shame. What is Odin thinking?
Even as a child, Thor was mighty...
I don't know how the bull got free! Stand back!
...while Loki's tricks were clever enough to fool even Odin.
Thor is a hero--a true son of Odin!
Some-day you will see him for the fool he is...and learn my value.

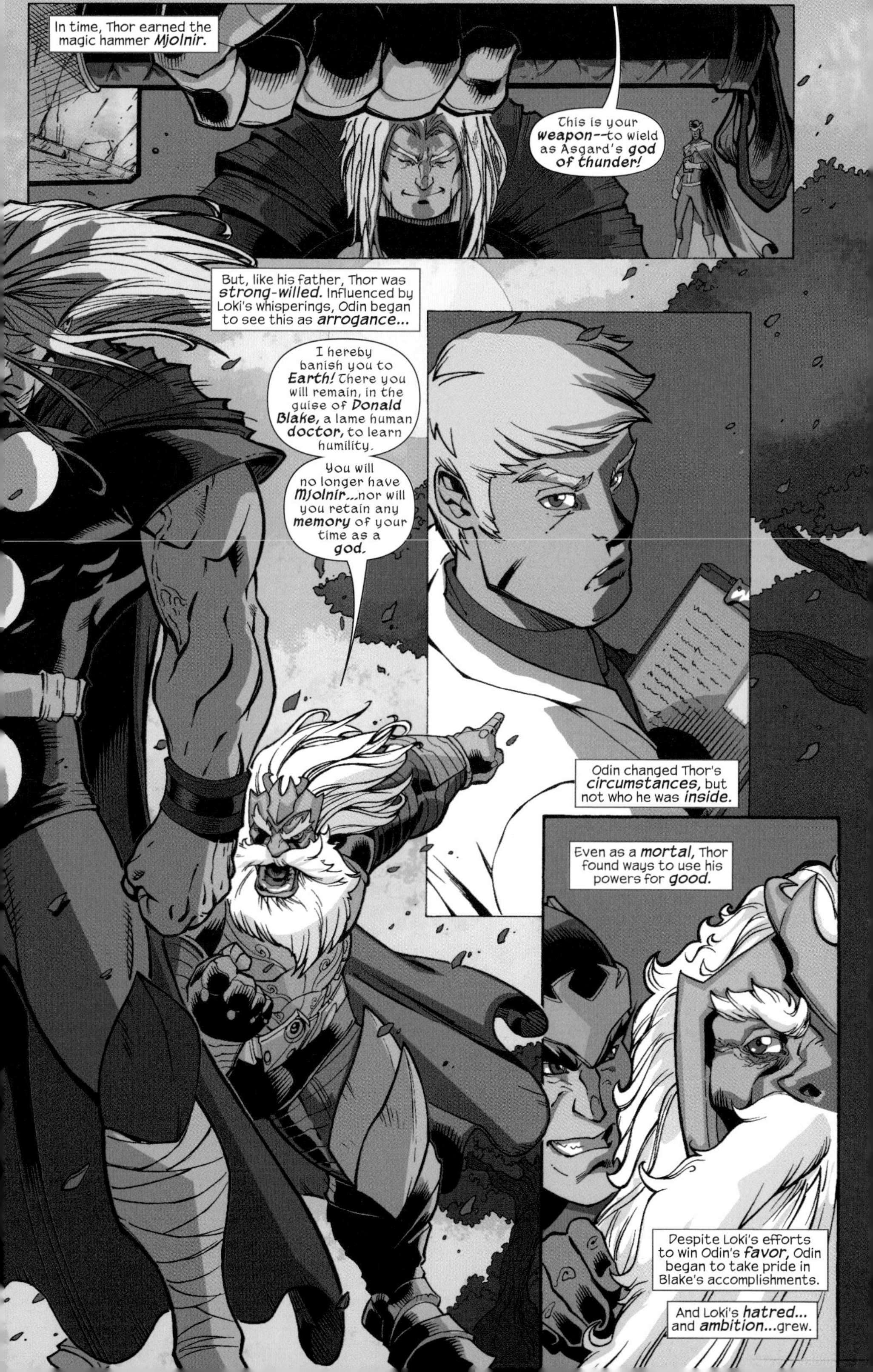
In time, Thor earned the magic hammer Mjolnir.
This is your weapon--to wield as Asgard's god of thunder!
But, like his father, Thor was strong-willed. Influenced by Loki's whisperings, Odin began to see this as arrogance...
I hereby banish you to Earth! There you will remain, in the guise of Donald Blake, a lame human doctor, to learn humility.
You will no longer have Mjolnir...nor will you retain any memory of your time as a god.
Odin changed Thor's circumstances, but not who he was inside.
Even as a mortal, Thor found ways to use his powers for good.
Despite Loki's efforts to win Odin's favor, Odin began to take pride in Blake's accomplishments.
And Loki's hatred... and ambition...grew.

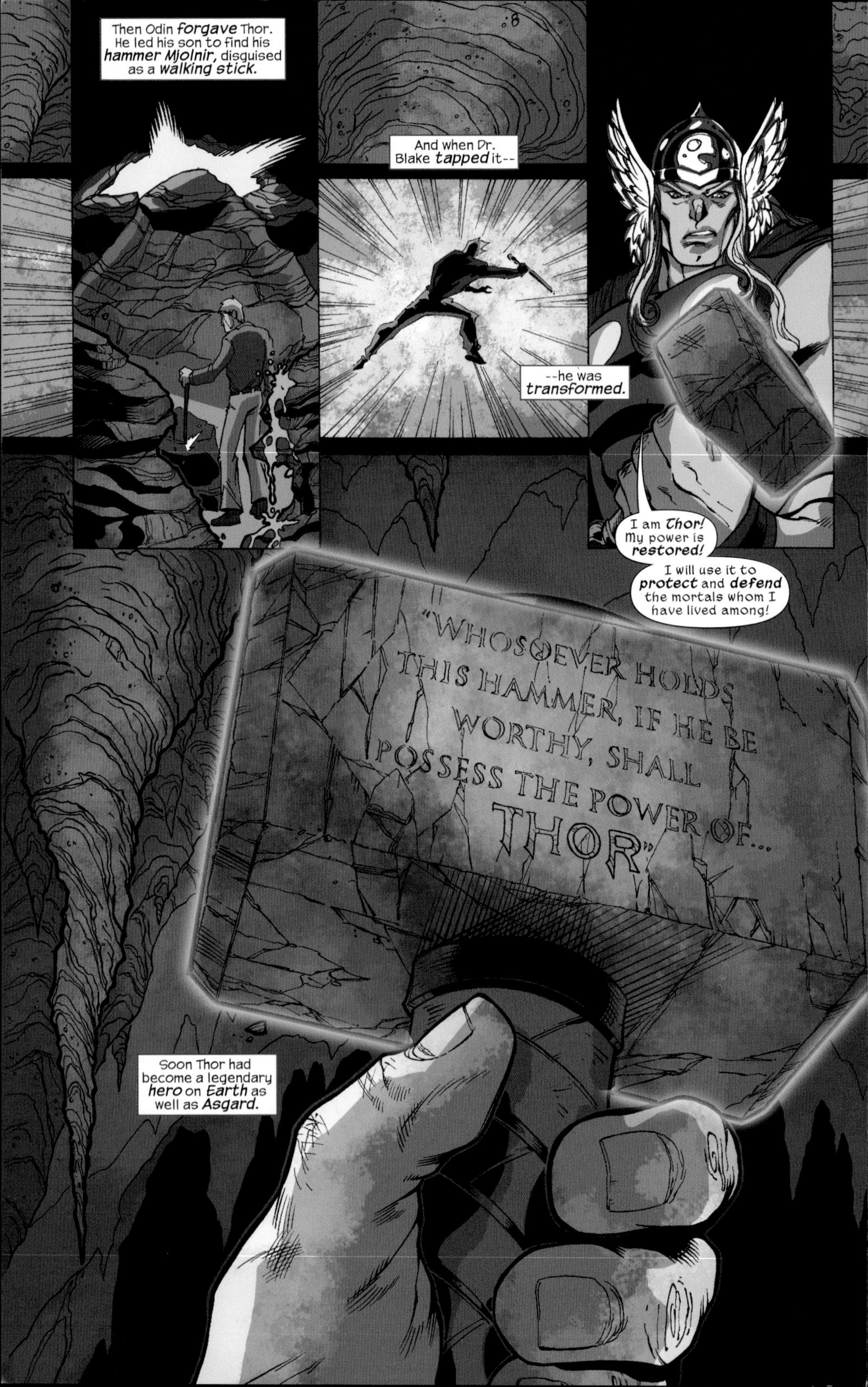
Then Odin forgave Thor. He led his son to find his hammer Mjolnir, disguised as a walking stick.
And when Dr. Blake tapped it--
--he was transformed.
I am Thor! My power is restored!
I will use it to protect and defend the mortals whom I have lived among!
"WHOSOEVER HOLDS THIS HAMMER, IF HE BE WORTHY, SHALL POSSESS THE POWER OF... THOR"
Soon Thor had become a legendary hero on Earth as well as Asgard.

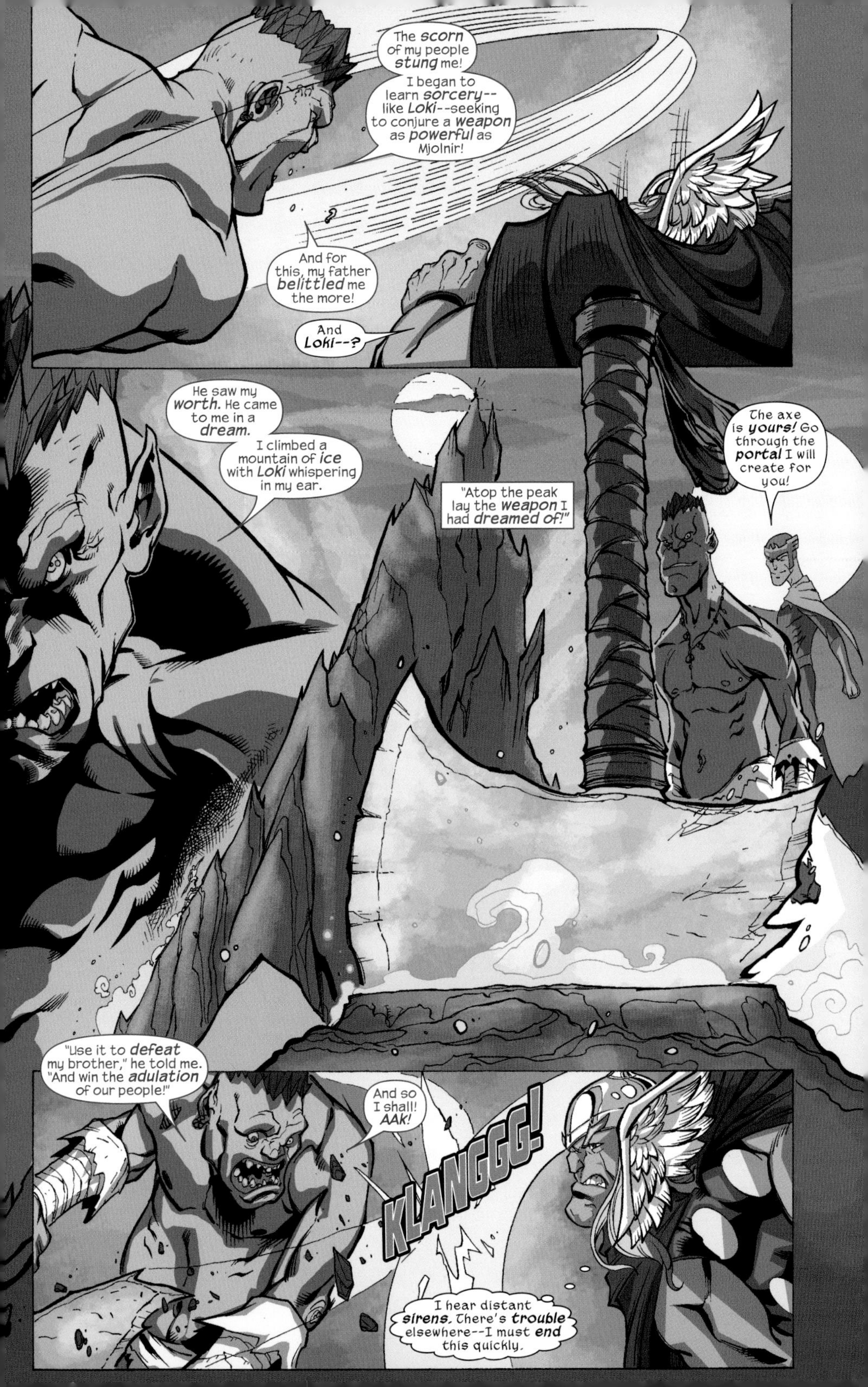

The scorn of my people stung me!
I began to learn sorcery--like Loki--seeking to conjure a weapon as powerful as Mjolnir!
And for this, my father belittled me the more!
And Loki--?
He saw my worth. He came to me in a dream.
I climbed a mountain of ice with Loki whispering in my ear.
"Atop the peak lay the weapon I had dreamed of!"
The axe is yours! Go through the portal I will create for you!
"Use it to defeat my brother," he told me. "And win the adulation of our people!"
And so I shall! AAK!
KLANGGG!
I hear distant sirens. There's trouble elsewhere--I must end this quickly.

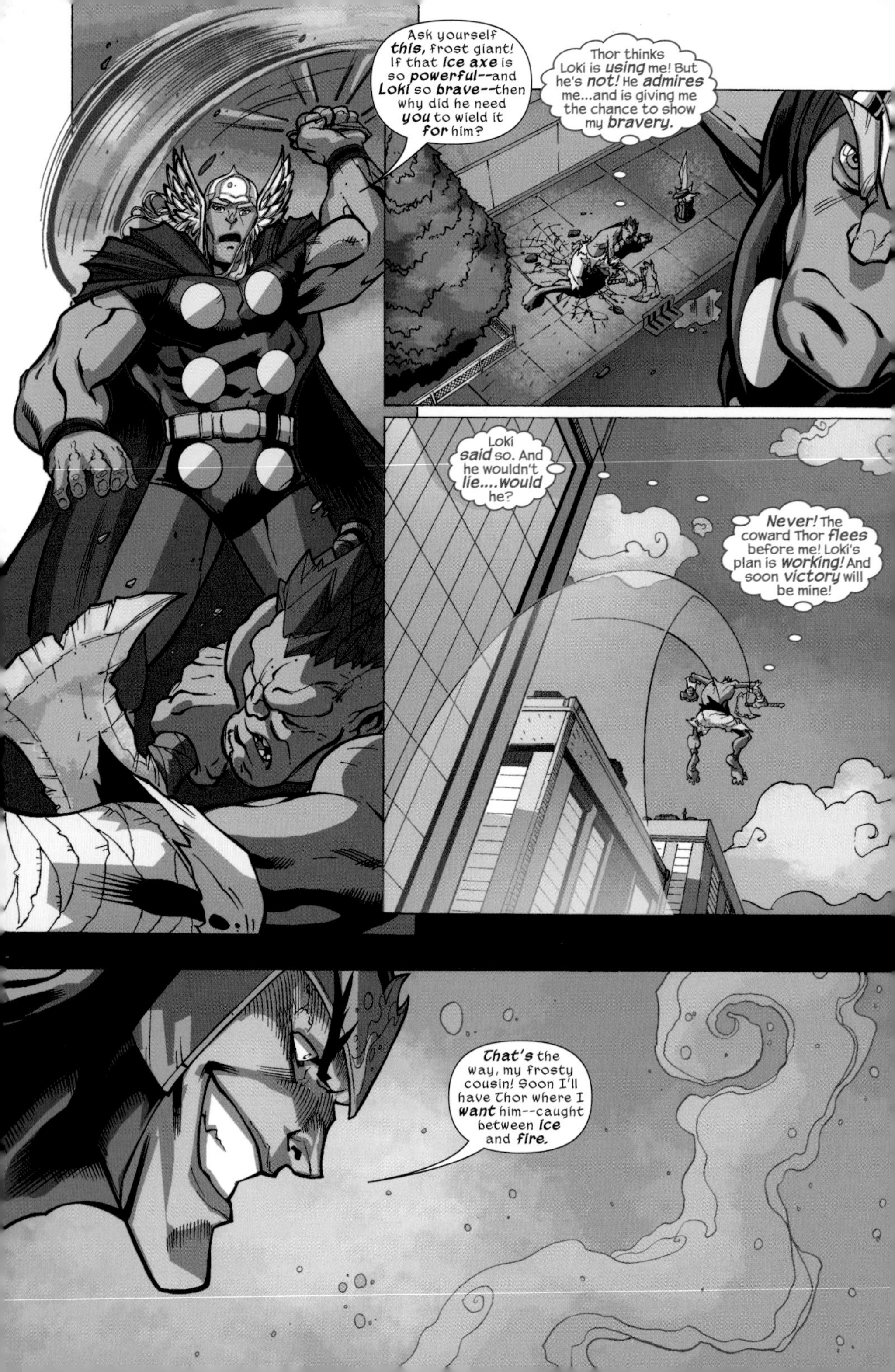

Ask yourself this, frost giant! If that ice axe is so powerful--and Loki so brave--then why did he need you to wield it for him?
Thor thinks Loki is using me! But he's not! He admires me...and is giving me the chance to show my bravery.
Loki said so. And he wouldn't lie....would he?
Never! The coward Thor flees before me! Loki's plan is working! And soon victory will be mine!
That's the way, my frosty cousin! Soon I'll have Thor where I want him--caught between ice and fire.

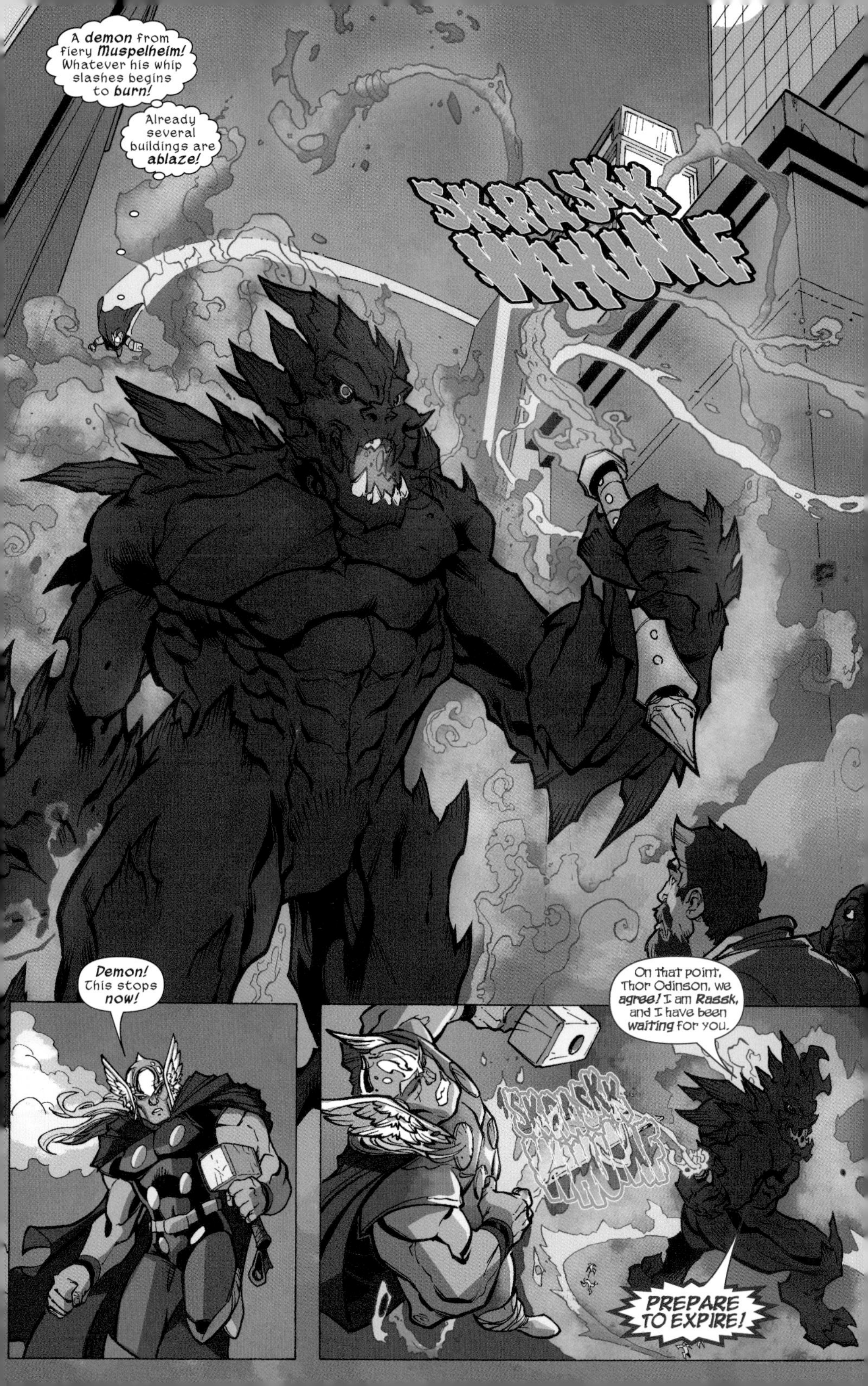
A demon from fiery Muspelheim! Whatever his whip slashes begins to burn!
Already several buildings are ablaze!
SKRASKK
WHUMF
Demon! This stops now!
On that point, Thor Odinson, we agree! I am Rassk, and I have been waiting for you.
SKRASKK
WHUMF
PREPARE TO EXPIRE!

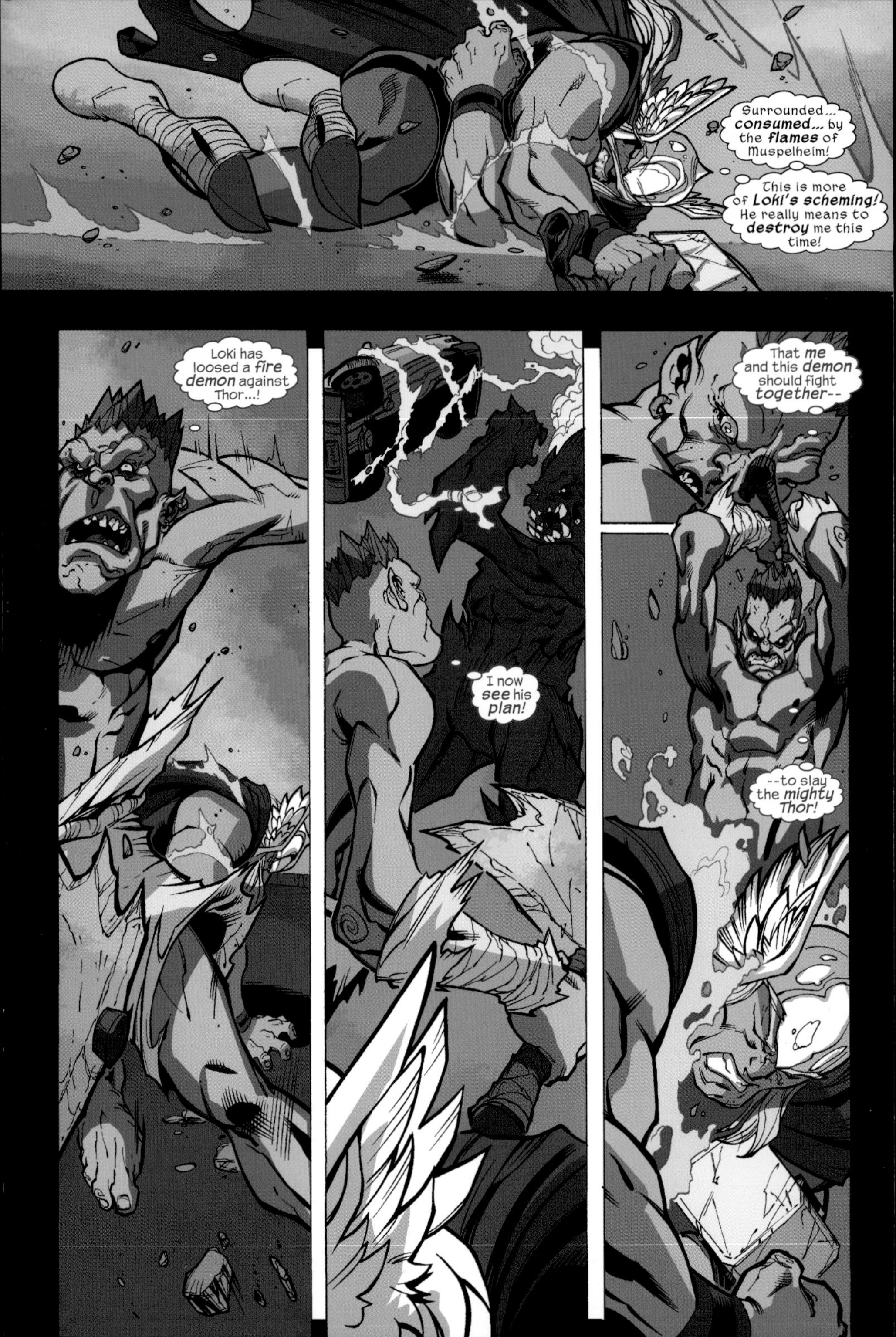

Surrounded... consumed... by the flames of Muspelheim!
This is more of Loki's scheming! He really means to destroy me this time!
Loki has loosed a fire demon against Thor...!
I now see his plan!
That me and this demon should fight together--
--to slay the mighty Thor!

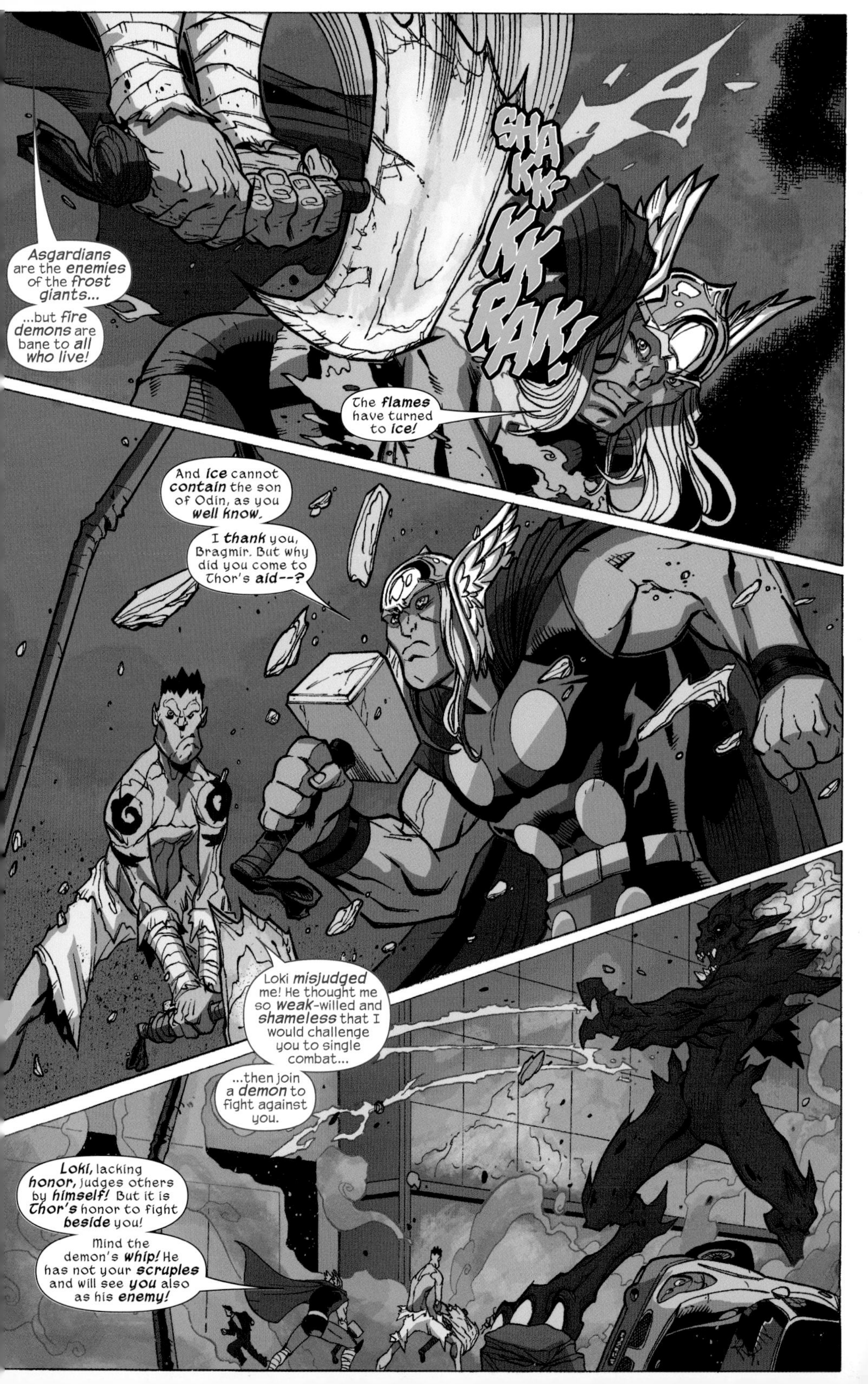
SHAKKK-KKRAK!
Asgardians are the enemies of the frost giants...
...but fire demons are bane to all who live!
The flames have turned to ice!
And ice cannot contain the son of Odin, as you well know.
I thank you, Bragmir. But why did you come to Thor's aid--?
Loki misjudged me! He thought me so weak-willed and shameless that I would challenge you to single combat...
...then join a demon to fight against you.
Loki, lacking honor, judges others by himself! But it is Thor's honor to fight beside you!
Mind the demon's whip! He has not your scruples and will see you also as his enemy!

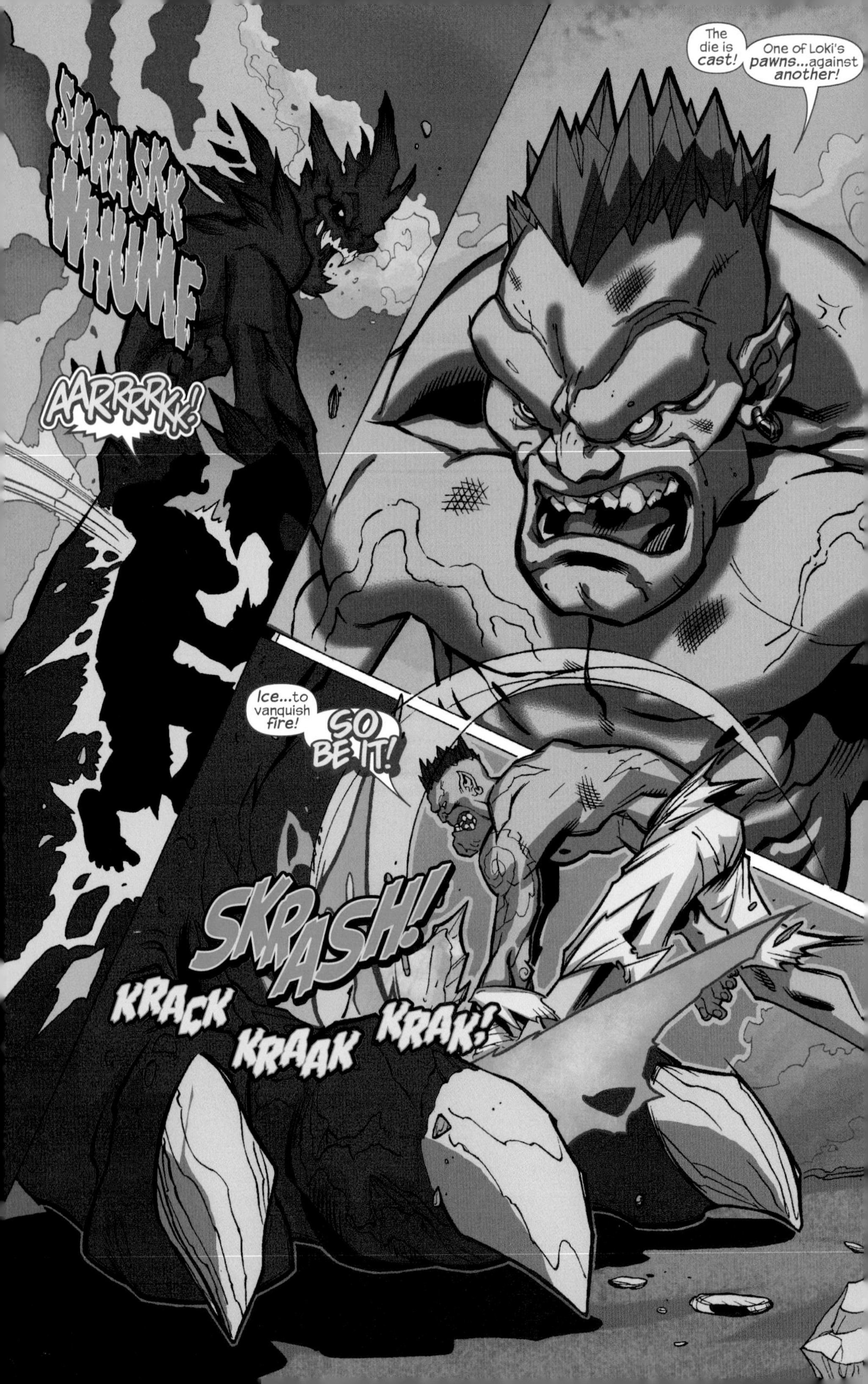
SKRASKK WHUMF
AARRRRKK!
The die is cast!
One of Loki's pawns...against another!
Ice...to vanquish fire!
SO BE IT!
SKRASH!
KRACK
KRAAK
KRAK!

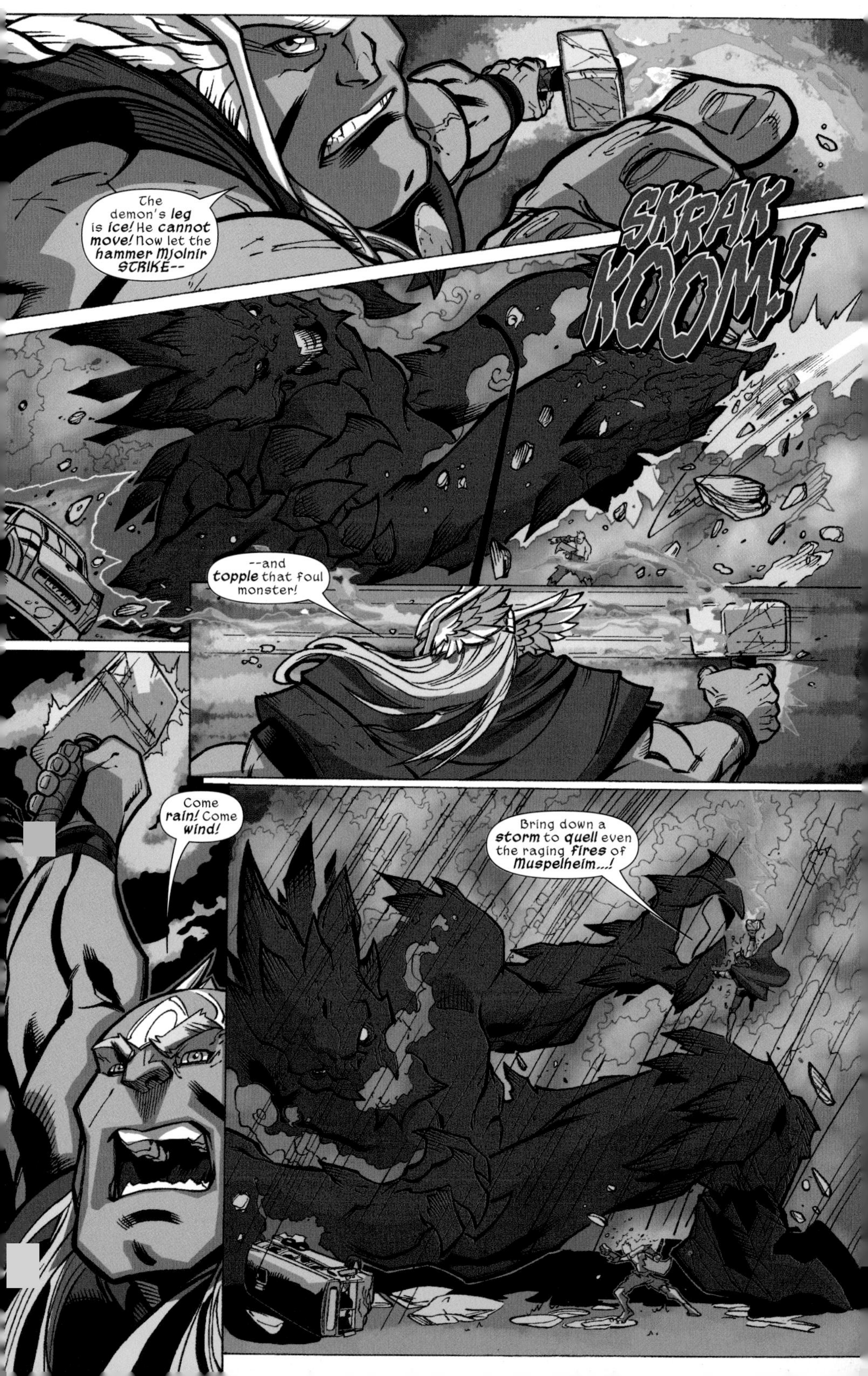

The demon's leg is ice! He cannot move! Now let the hammer Mjolnir STRIKE--
SKRAK KOOM!
--and topple that foul monster!
Come rain! Come wind!
Bring down a storm to quell even the raging fires of Muspelheim...!

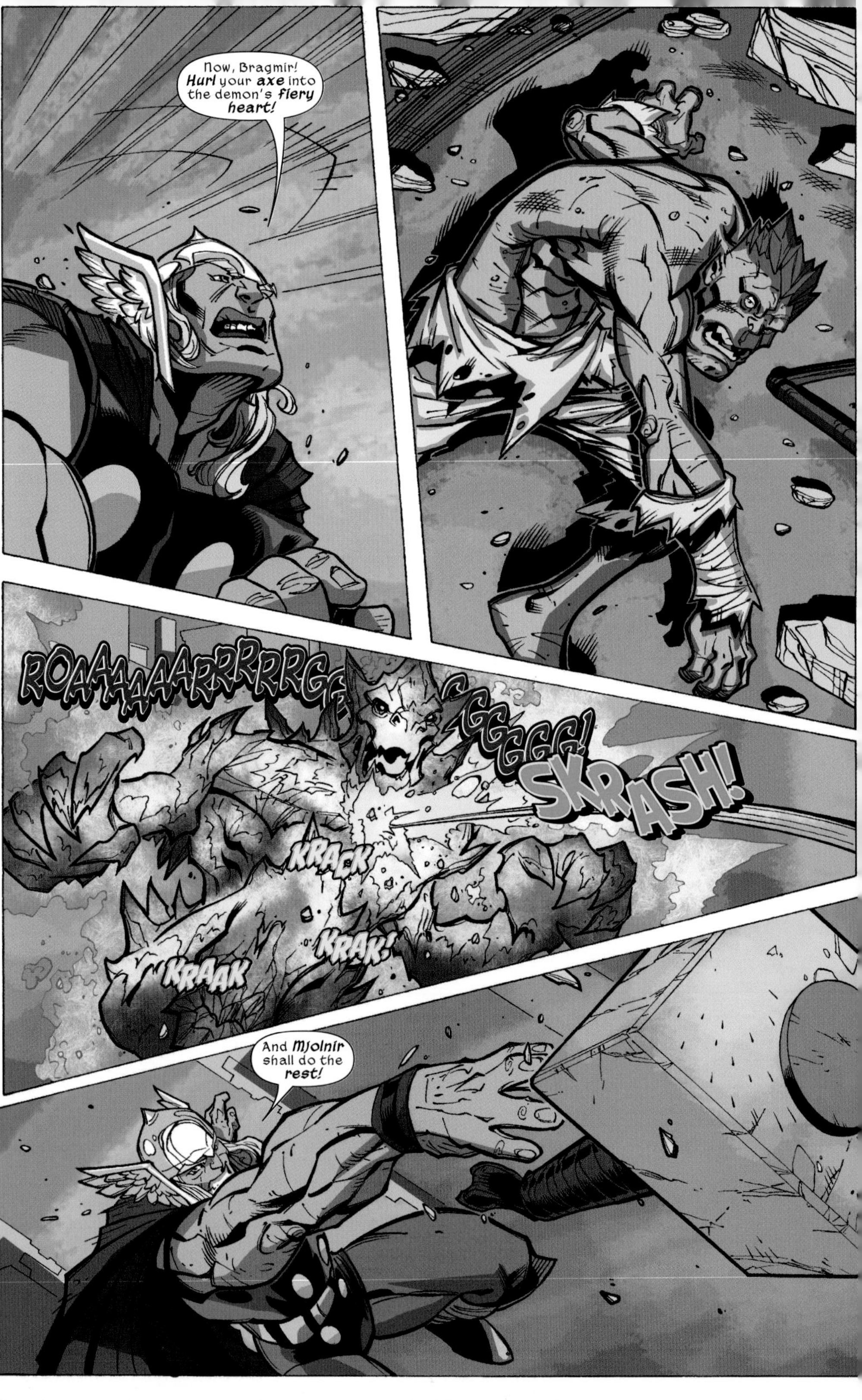
Now, Bragmir! Hurl your axe into the demon's fiery heart!
ROAAAAAARRRRRGGGGGG!
SKRASH!
KRACK
KRAK!
KRAAK
And Mjolnir shall do the rest!

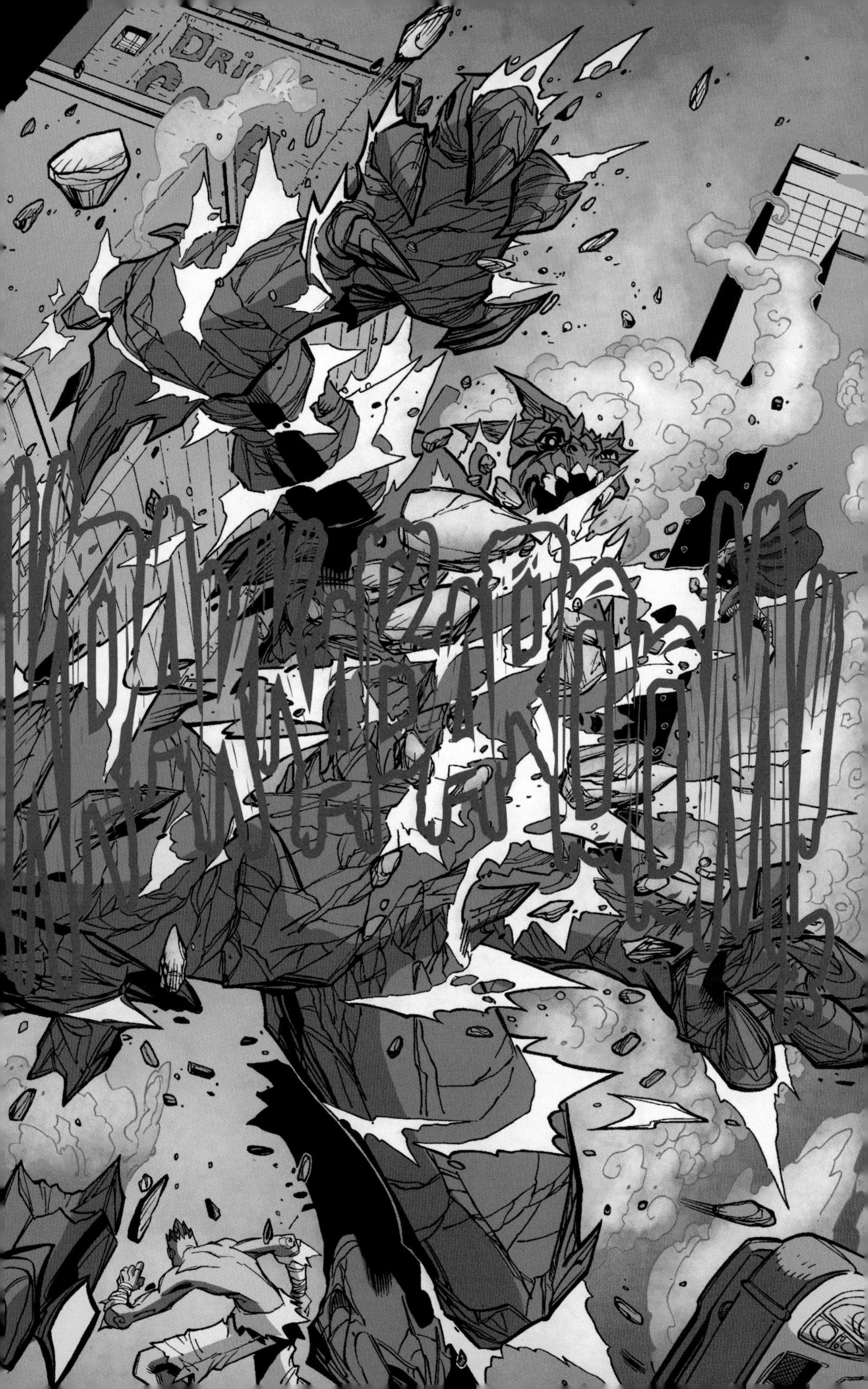

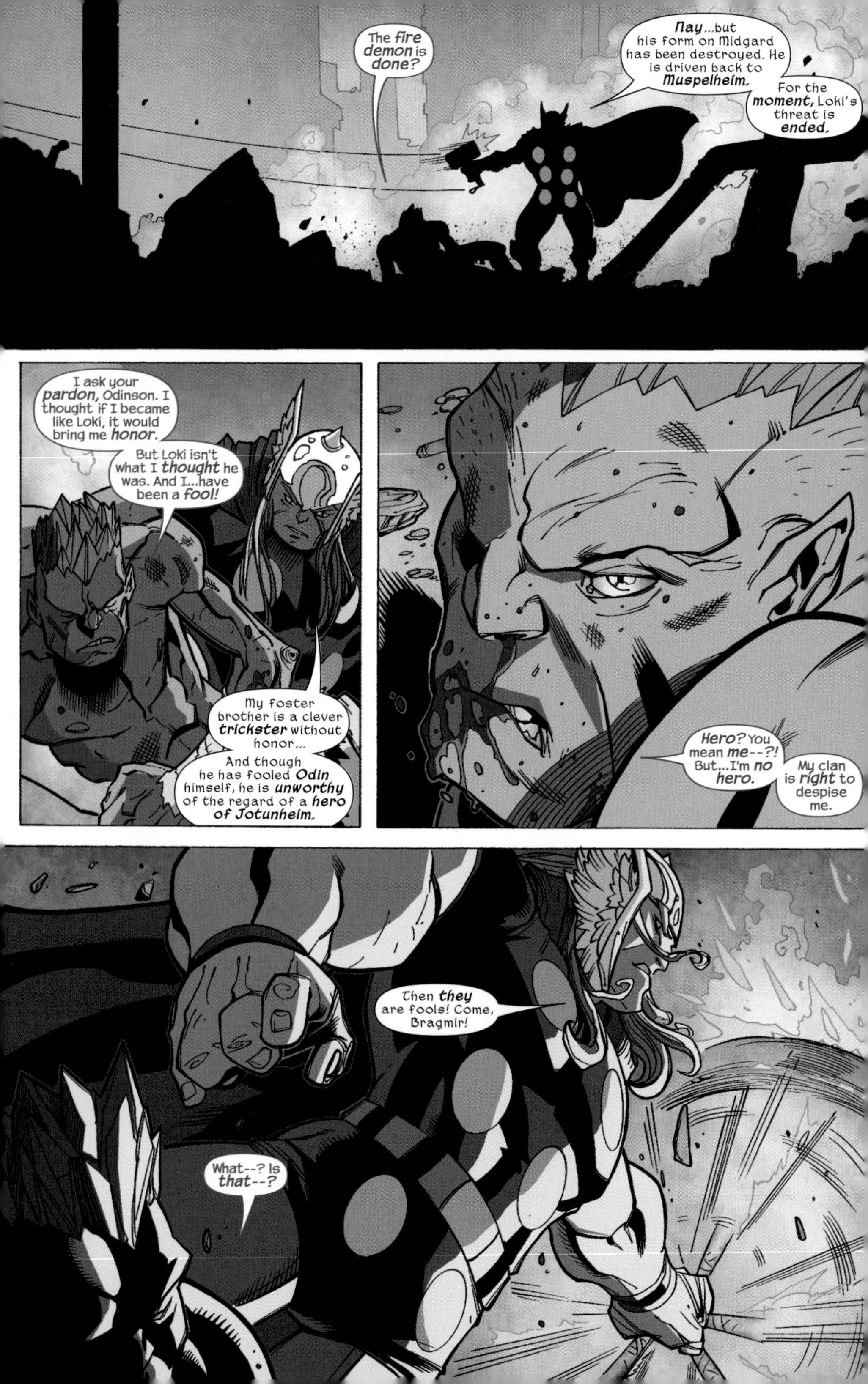
The fire demon is done?
Nay...but his form on Midgard has been destroyed. He is driven back to Muspelheim.
For the moment, Loki's threat is ended.
I ask your pardon, Odinson. I thought if I became like Loki, it would bring me honor.
But Loki isn't what I thought he was. And I...have been a fool!
My foster brother is a clever trickster without honor...
And though he has fooled Odin himself, he is unworthy of the regard of a hero of Jotunheim.
Hero? You mean me--?! But...I'm no hero.
My clan is right to despise me.
Then they are fools! Come, Bragmir!
What--? Is that--?

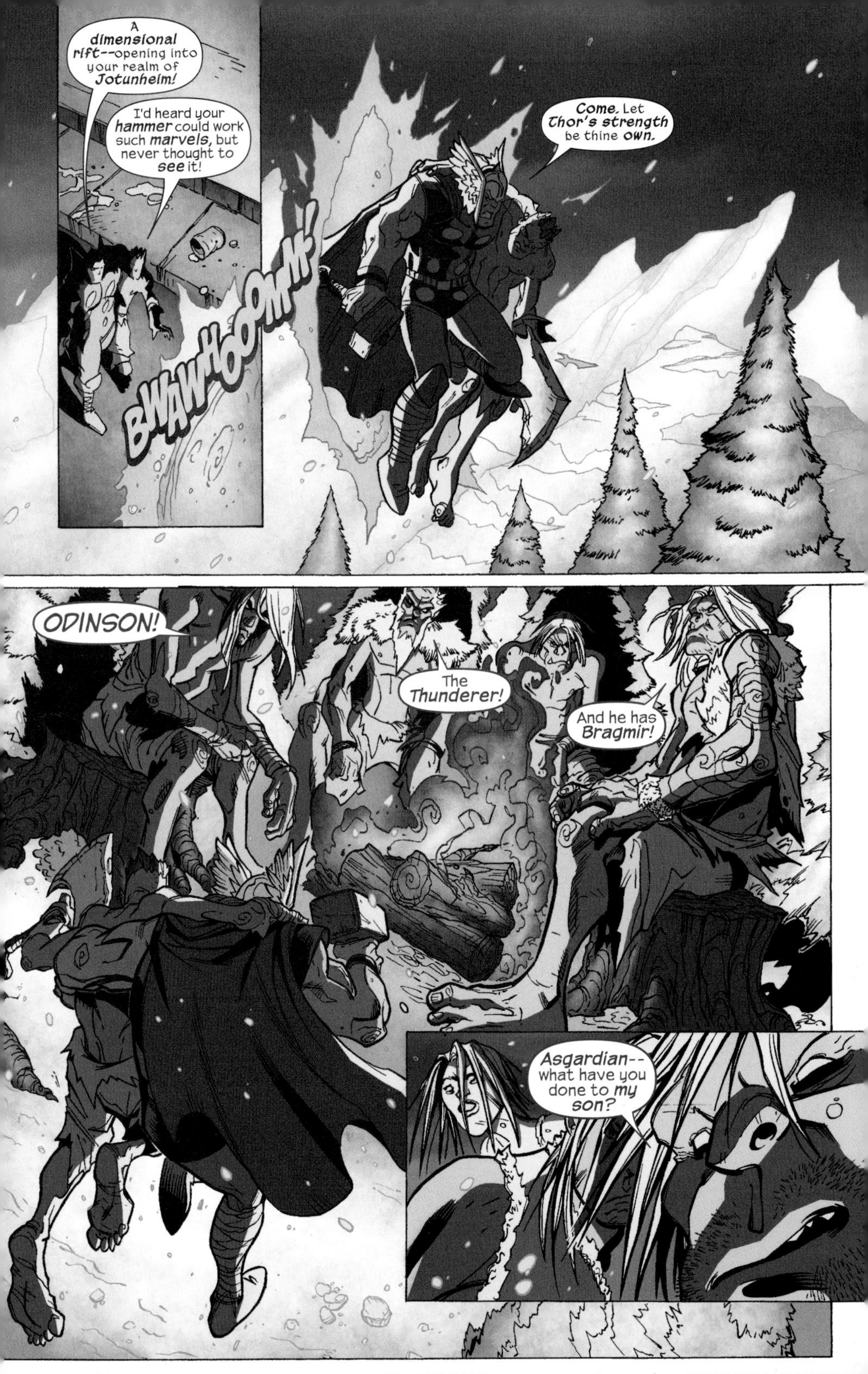
A dimensional rift--opening into your realm of Jotunheim!
I'd heard your hammer could work such marvels, but never thought to see it!
BWAWHOOOMM!
Come. Let Thor's strength be thine own.
ODINSON!
The Thunderer!
And he has Bragmir!
Asgardian--what have you done to my son?

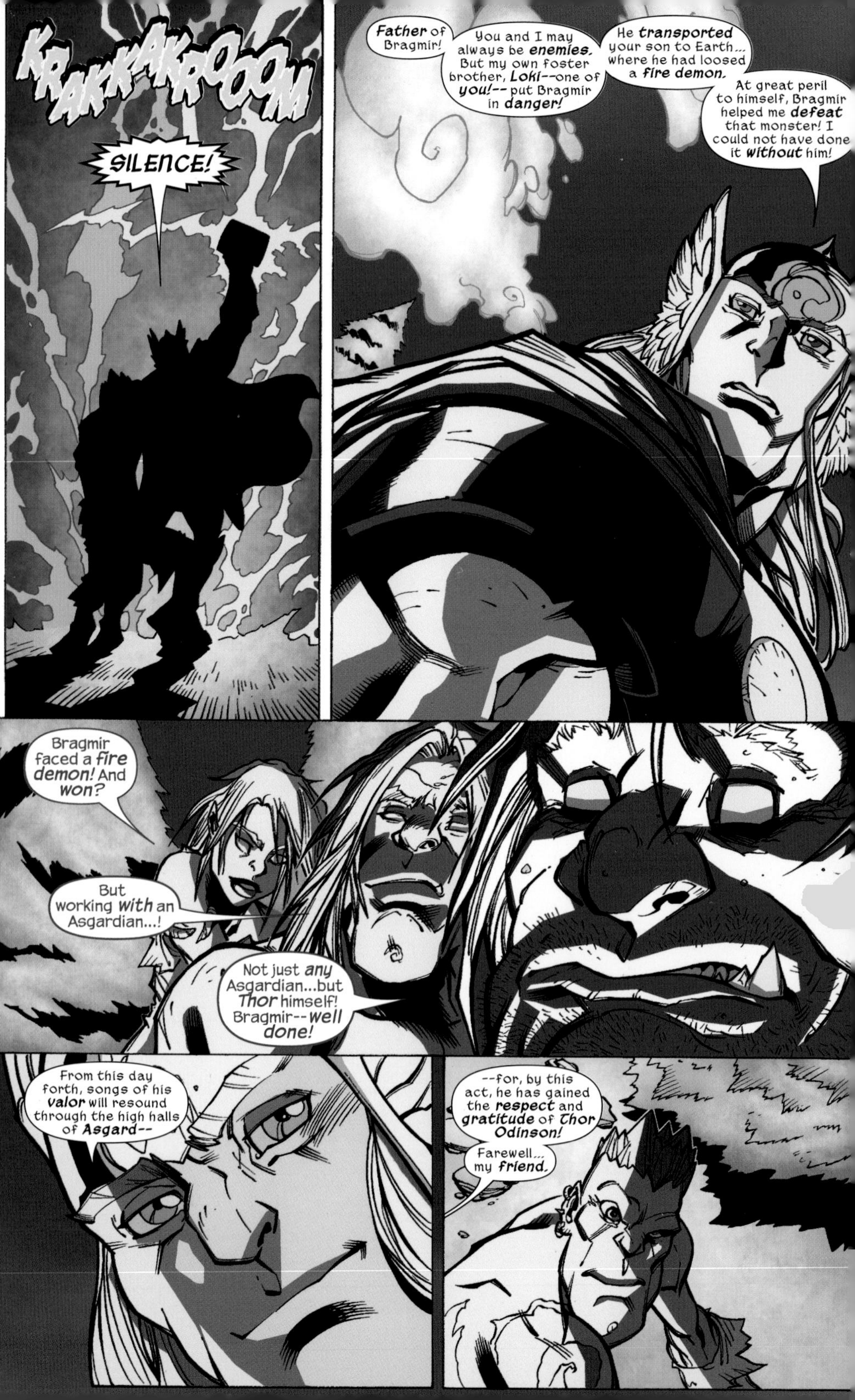
KRAKKAKROOOOM
SILENCE!
Father of Bragmir!
You and I may always be enemies. But my own foster brother, Loki--one of you!--put Bragmir in danger!
He transported your son to Earth... where he had loosed a fire demon.
At great peril to himself, Bragmir helped me defeat that monster! I could not have done it without him!
Bragmir faced a fire demon! And won?
But working with an Asgardian...!
Not just any Asgardian...but Thor himself! Bragmir--well done!
From this day forth, songs of his valor will resound through the high halls of Asgard--
--for, by this act, he has gained the respect and gratitude of Thor Odinson!
Farewell... my friend.

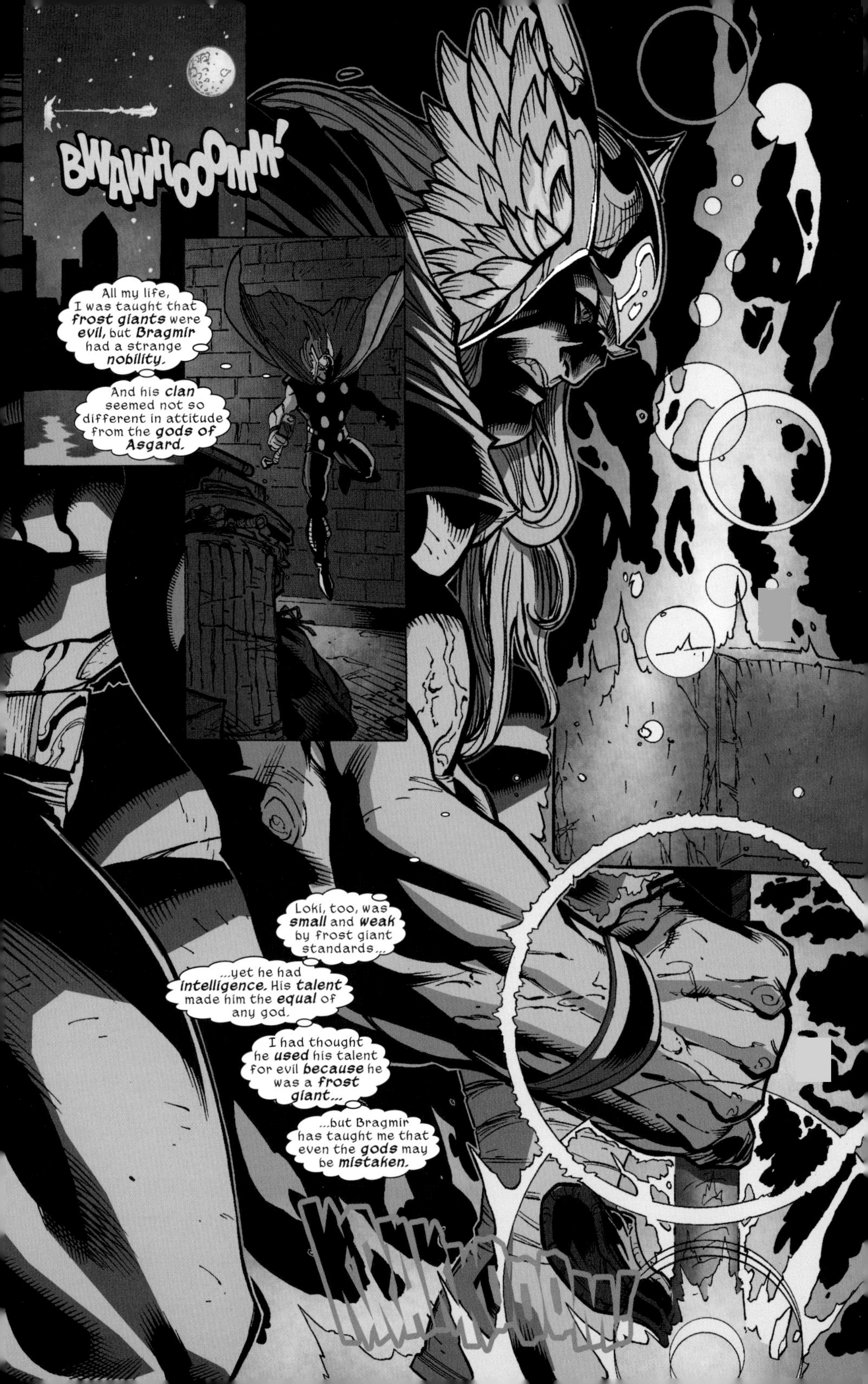
BWAWHOOOMM!
All my life, I was taught that frost giants were evil, but Bragmir had a strange nobility.
And his clan seemed not so different in attitude from the gods of Asgard.
Loki, too, was small and weak by frost giant standards...
...yet he had intelligence. His talent made him the equal of any god.
I had thought he used his talent for evil because he was a frost giant...
...but Bragmir has taught me that even the gods may be mistaken.

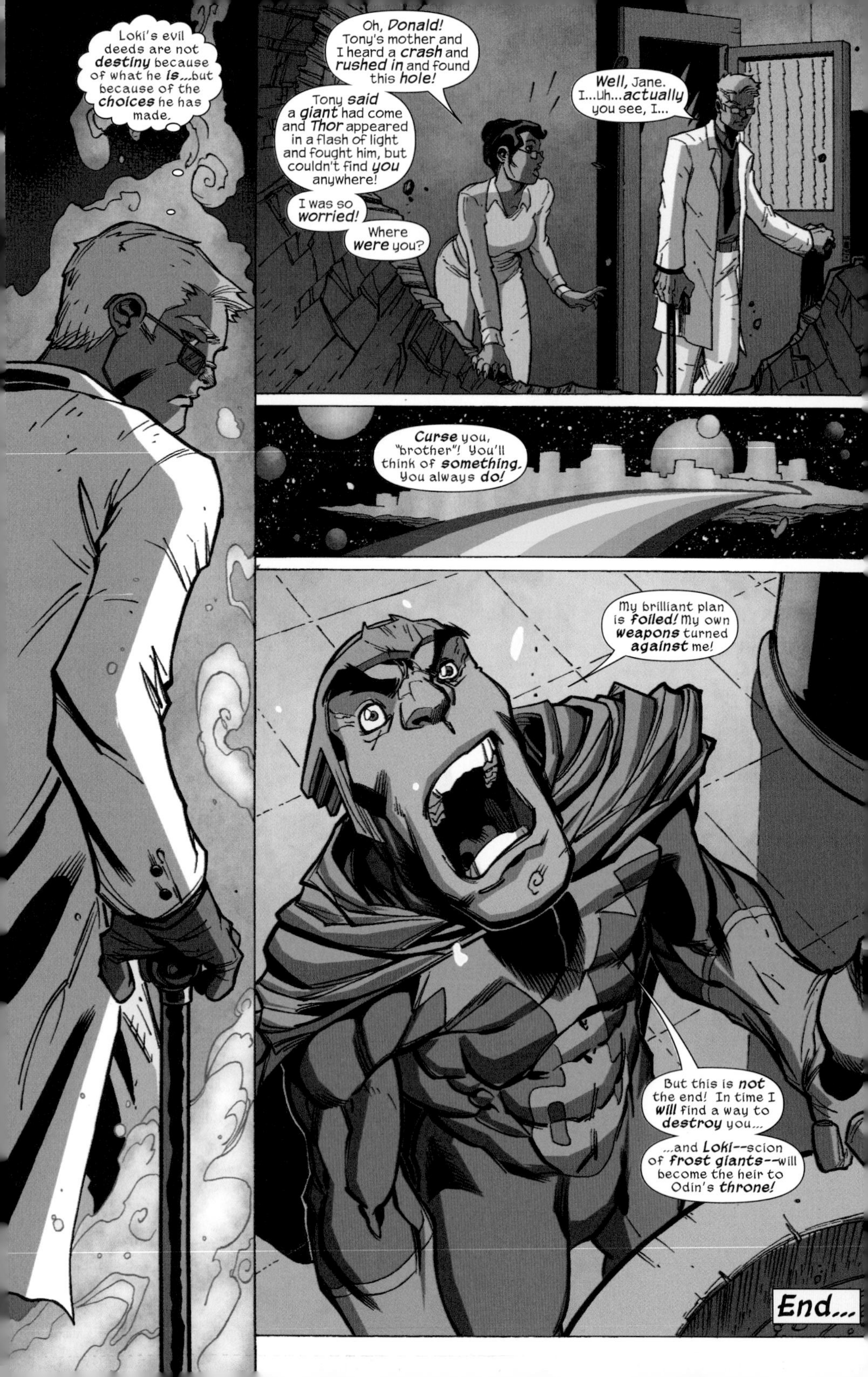
Loki's evil deeds are not destiny because of what he is...but because of the choices he has made.
Oh, Donald! Tony's mother and I heard a crash and rushed in and found this hole!
Tony said a giant had come and Thor appeared in a flash of light and fought him, but couldn't find you anywhere!
I was so worried!
Where were you?
Well, Jane. I...uh...actually you see, I...
Curse you, "brother"! You'll think of something. You always do!
My brilliant plan is foiled! My own weapons turned against me!
But this is not the end! In time I will find a way to destroy you...
...and Loki--scion of frost giants--will become the heir to Odin's throne!
End...

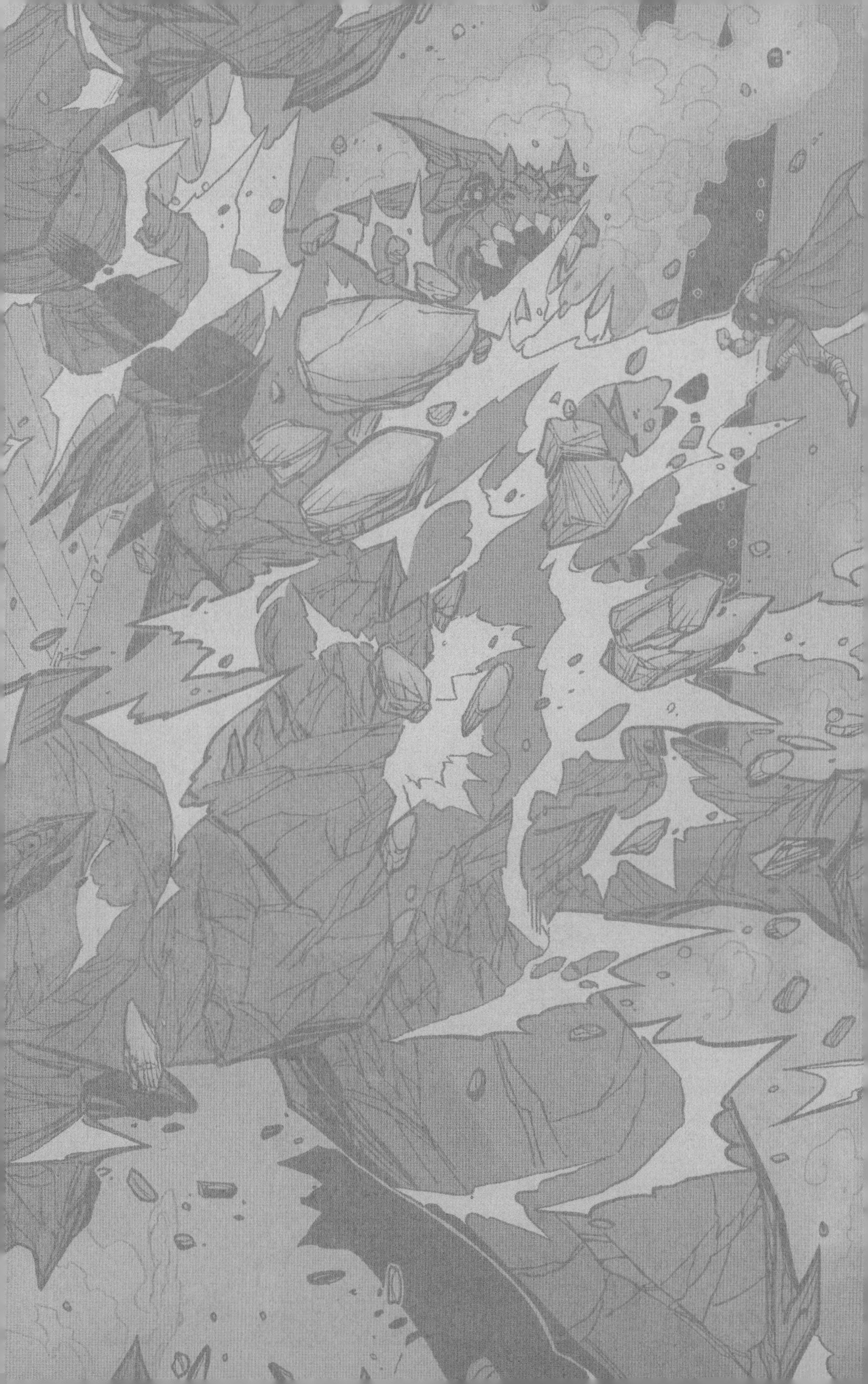

03

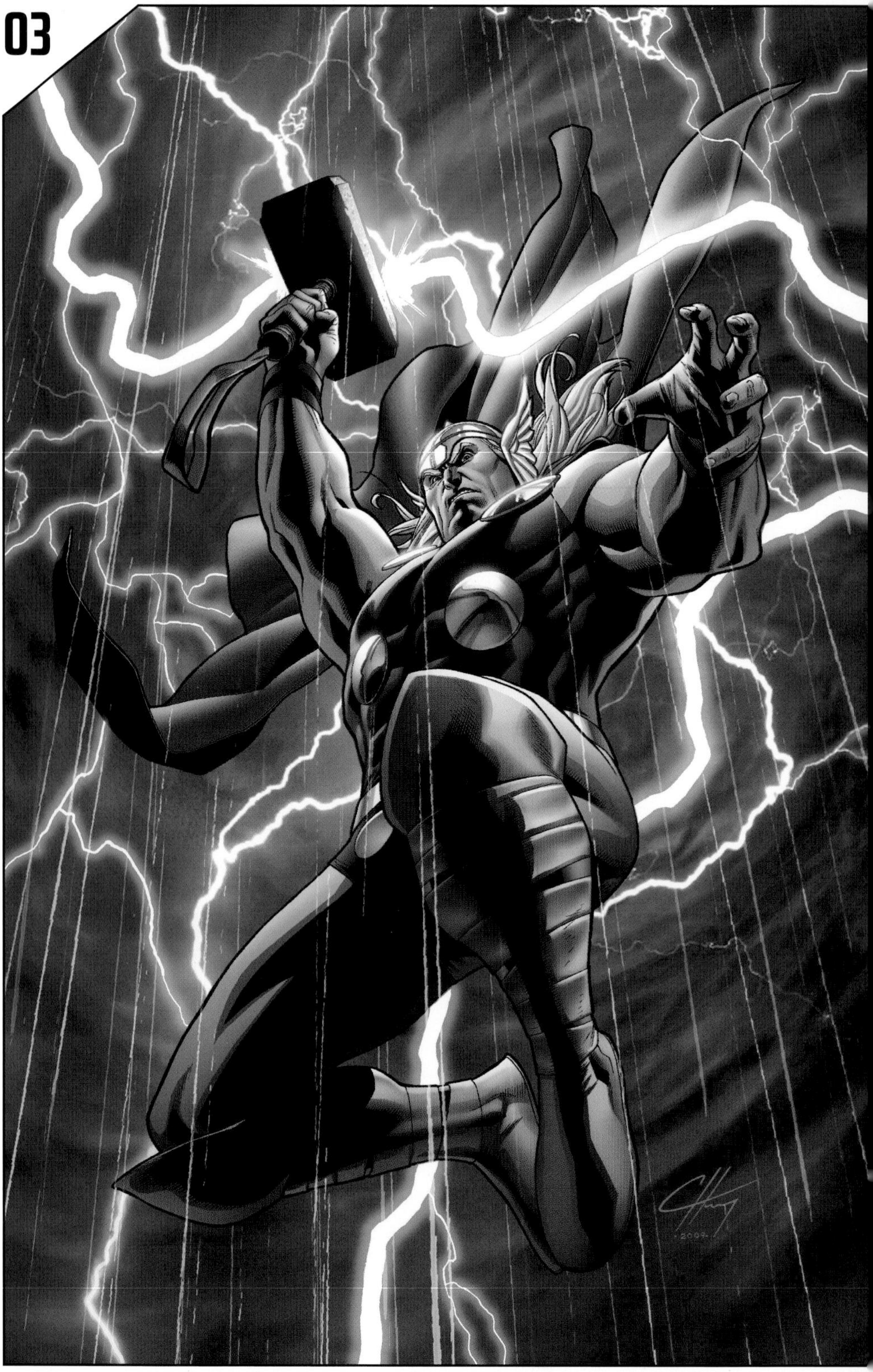

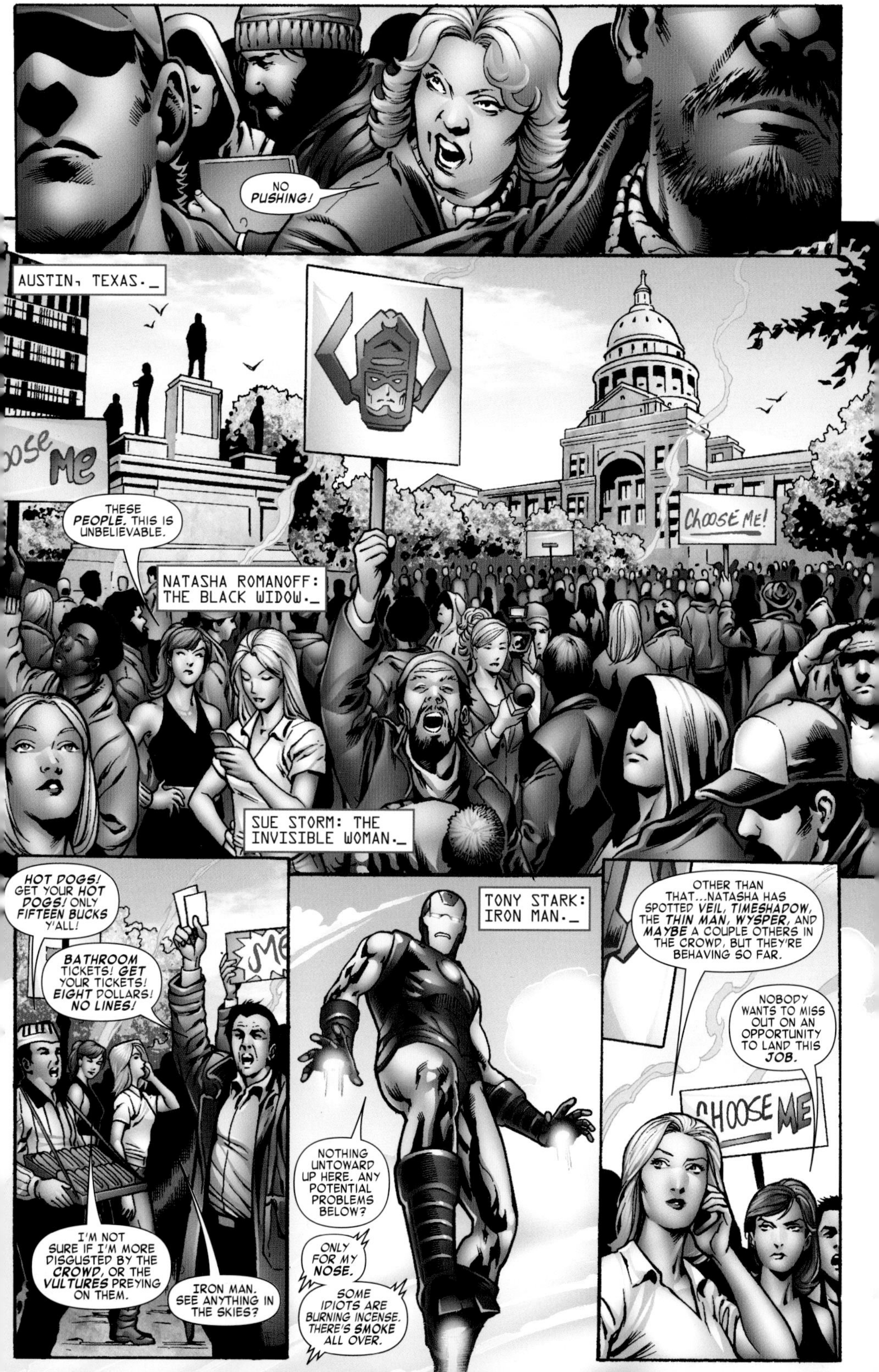

NO PUSHING!
AUSTIN, TEXAS._
CHOOSE ME
THESE PEOPLE. THIS IS UNBELIEVABLE.
NATASHA ROMANOFF: THE BLACK WIDOW._
CHOOSE ME!
SUE STORM: THE INVISIBLE WOMAN._
HOT DOGS! GET YOUR HOT DOGS! ONLY FIFTEEN BUCKS Y'ALL!
BATHROOM TICKETS! GET YOUR TICKETS! EIGHT DOLLARS! NO LINES!
I'M NOT SURE IF I'M MORE DISGUSTED BY THE CROWD, OR THE VULTURES PREYING ON THEM.
IRON MAN. SEE ANYTHING IN THE SKIES?
TONY STARK: IRON MAN._
NOTHING UNTOWARD UP HERE. ANY POTENTIAL PROBLEMS BELOW?
ONLY FOR MY NOSE.
SOME IDIOTS ARE BURNING INCENSE. THERE'S SMOKE ALL OVER.
OTHER THAN THAT...NATASHA HAS SPOTTED VEIL, TIMESHADOW, THE THIN MAN, WYSPER, AND MAYBE A COUPLE OTHERS IN THE CROWD, BUT THEY'RE BEHAVING SO FAR.
NOBODY WANTS TO MISS OUT ON AN OPPORTUNITY TO LAND THIS JOB.
CHOOSE ME

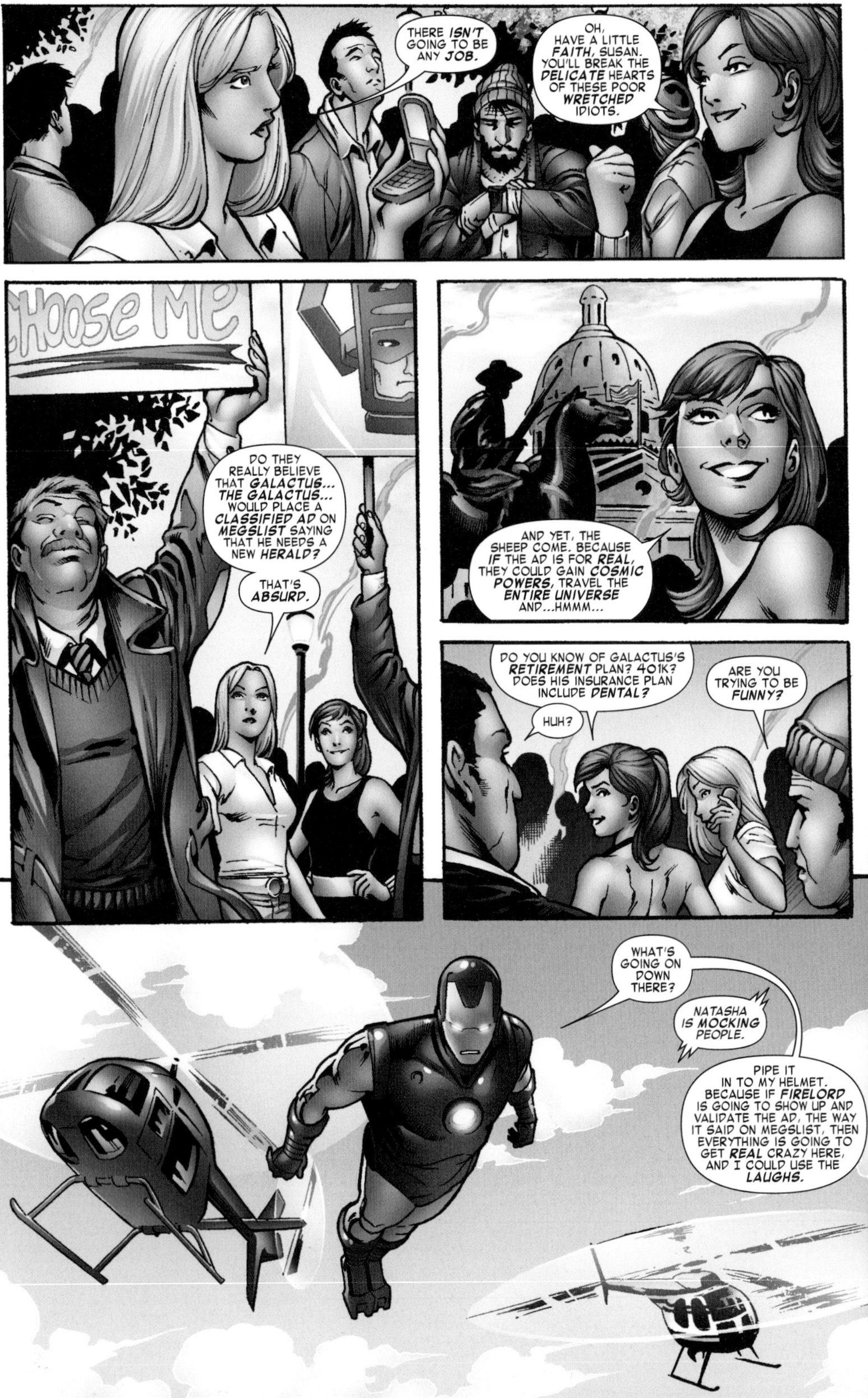
THERE ISN'T GOING TO BE ANY JOB.
OH, HAVE A LITTLE FAITH, SUSAN. YOU'LL BREAK THE DELICATE HEARTS OF THESE POOR WRETCHED IDIOTS.
CHOOSE ME
DO THEY REALLY BELIEVE THAT GALACTUS... THE GALACTUS... WOULD PLACE A CLASSIFIED AD ON MEGSLIST SAYING THAT HE NEEDS A NEW HERALD?
THAT'S ABSURD.
AND YET, THE SHEEP COME. BECAUSE IF THE AD IS FOR REAL, THEY COULD GAIN COSMIC POWERS, TRAVEL THE ENTIRE UNIVERSE AND...HMMM...
DO YOU KNOW OF GALACTUS'S RETIREMENT PLAN? 401K? DOES HIS INSURANCE PLAN INCLUDE DENTAL?
HUH?
ARE YOU TRYING TO BE FUNNY?
WHAT'S GOING ON DOWN THERE?
NATASHA IS MOCKING PEOPLE.
PIPE IT IN TO MY HELMET. BECAUSE IF FIRELORD IS GOING TO SHOW UP AND VALIDATE THE AD, THE WAY IT SAID ON MEGSLIST, THEN EVERYTHING IS GOING TO GET REAL CRAZY HERE, AND I COULD USE THE LAUGHS.

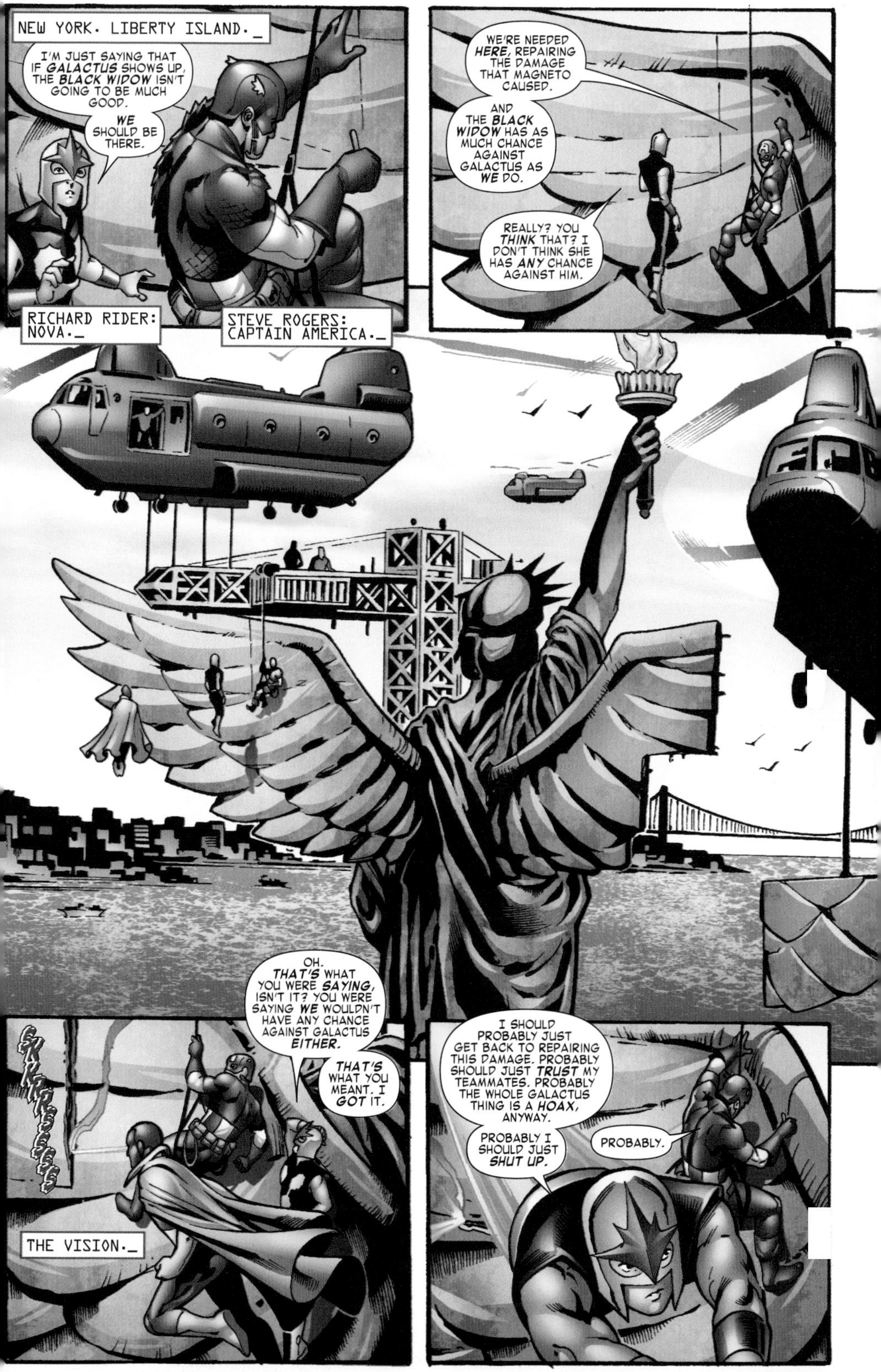

NEW YORK. LIBERTY ISLAND._
I'M JUST SAYING THAT IF GALACTUS SHOWS UP, THE BLACK WIDOW ISN'T GOING TO BE MUCH GOOD.
WE SHOULD BE THERE.
RICHARD RIDER: NOVA._
STEVE ROGERS: CAPTAIN AMERICA._
WE'RE NEEDED HERE, REPAIRING THE DAMAGE THAT MAGNETO CAUSED.
AND THE BLACK WIDOW HAS AS MUCH CHANCE AGAINST GALACTUS AS WE DO.
REALLY? YOU THINK THAT? I DON'T THINK SHE HAS ANY CHANCE AGAINST HIM.
OH. THAT'S WHAT YOU WERE SAYING, ISN'T IT? YOU WERE SAYING WE WOULDN'T HAVE ANY CHANCE AGAINST GALACTUS EITHER.
THAT'S WHAT YOU MEANT. I GOT IT.
SKRRSSSSS
THE VISION._
I SHOULD PROBABLY JUST GET BACK TO REPAIRING THIS DAMAGE. PROBABLY SHOULD JUST TRUST MY TEAMMATES. PROBABLY THE WHOLE GALACTUS THING IS A HOAX, ANYWAY.
PROBABLY I SHOULD JUST SHUT UP.
PROBABLY.

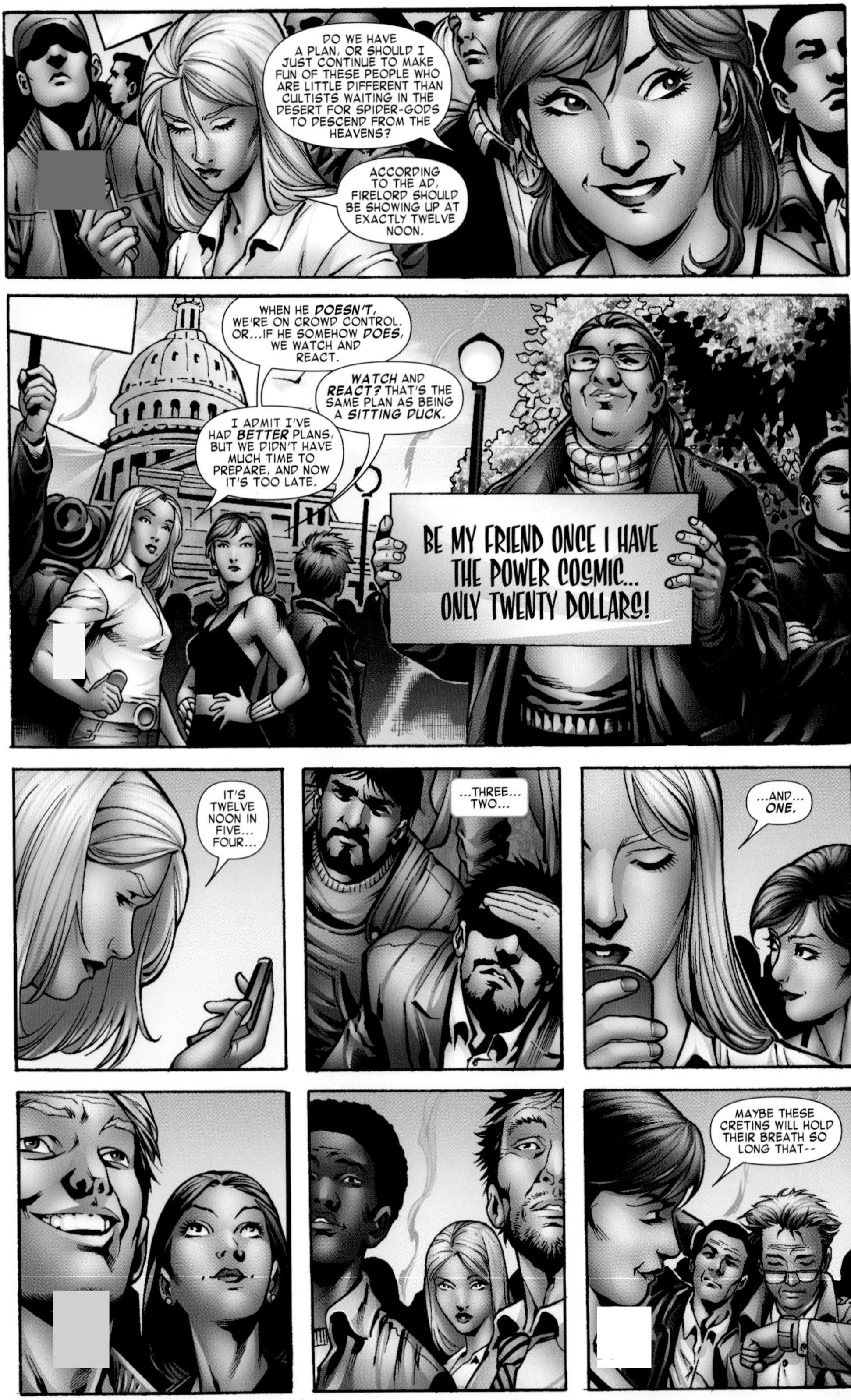
DO WE HAVE A PLAN, OR SHOULD I JUST CONTINUE TO MAKE FUN OF THESE PEOPLE WHO ARE LITTLE DIFFERENT THAN CULTISTS WAITING IN THE DESERT FOR SPIDER-GODS TO DESCEND FROM THE HEAVENS?
ACCORDING TO THE AD, FIRELORD SHOULD BE SHOWING UP AT EXACTLY TWELVE NOON.
WHEN HE DOESN'T, WE'RE ON CROWD CONTROL. OR...IF HE SOMEHOW DOES, WE WATCH AND REACT.
WATCH AND REACT? THAT'S THE SAME PLAN AS BEING A SITTING DUCK.
I ADMIT I'VE HAD BETTER PLANS, BUT WE DIDN'T HAVE MUCH TIME TO PREPARE, AND NOW IT'S TOO LATE.
BE MY FRIEND ONCE I HAVE THE POWER COSMIC... ONLY TWENTY DOLLARS!
IT'S TWELVE NOON IN FIVE... FOUR...
...THREE... TWO...
...AND... ONE.
MAYBE THESE CRETINS WILL HOLD THEIR BREATH SO LONG THAT--

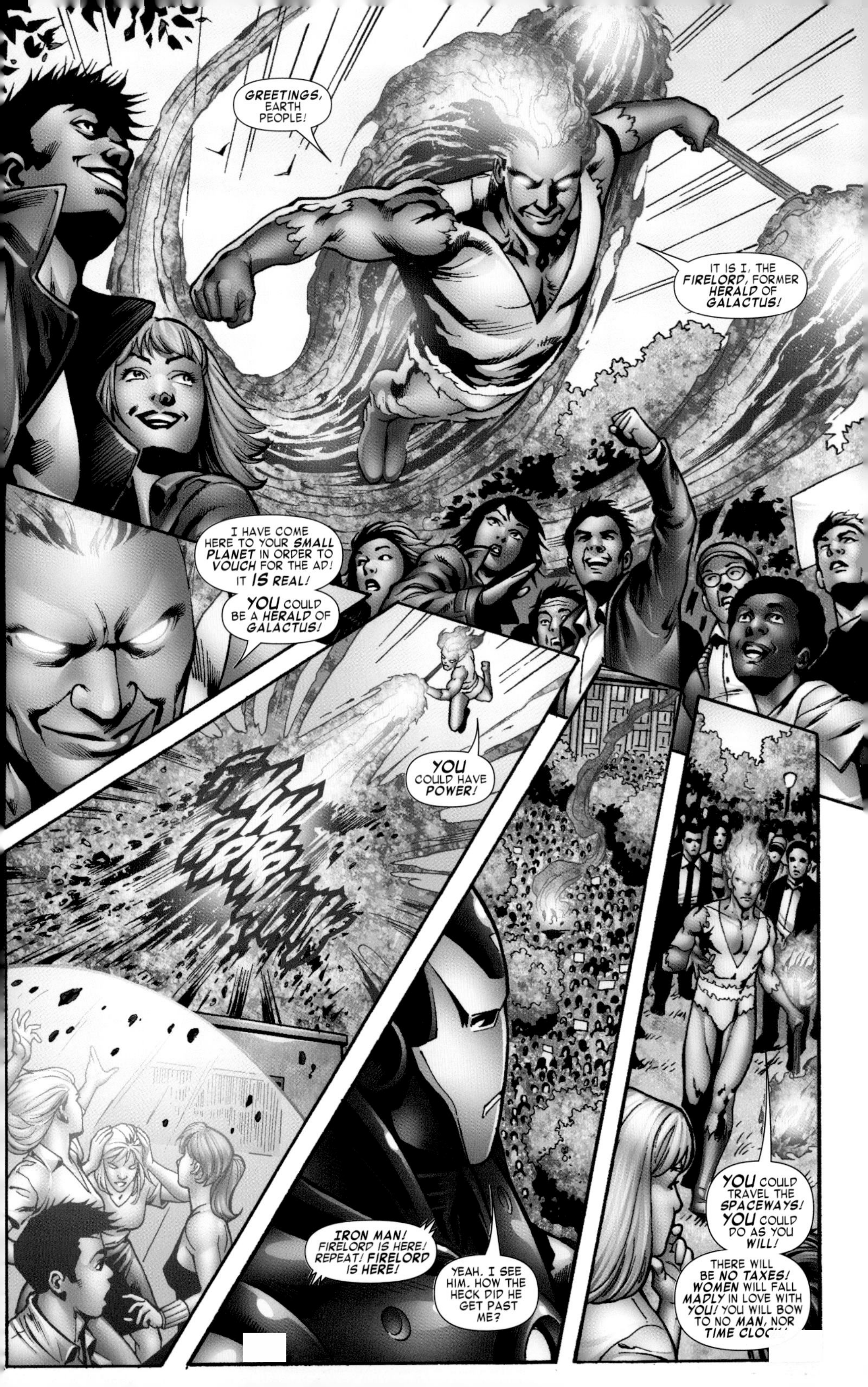
GREETINGS, EARTH PEOPLE!
IT IS I, THE FIRELORD, FORMER HERALD OF GALACTUS!
I HAVE COME HERE TO YOUR SMALL PLANET IN ORDER TO VOUCH FOR THE AD! IT IS REAL!
YOU COULD BE A HERALD OF GALACTUS!
YOU COULD HAVE POWER!
IRON MAN! FIRELORD IS HERE! REPEAT! FIRELORD IS HERE!
YEAH. I SEE HIM. HOW THE HECK DID HE GET PAST ME?
YOU COULD TRAVEL THE SPACEWAYS! YOU COULD DO AS YOU WILL!
THERE WILL BE NO TAXES! WOMEN WILL FALL MADLY IN LOVE WITH YOU! YOU WILL BOW TO NO MAN, NOR TIME CLOC

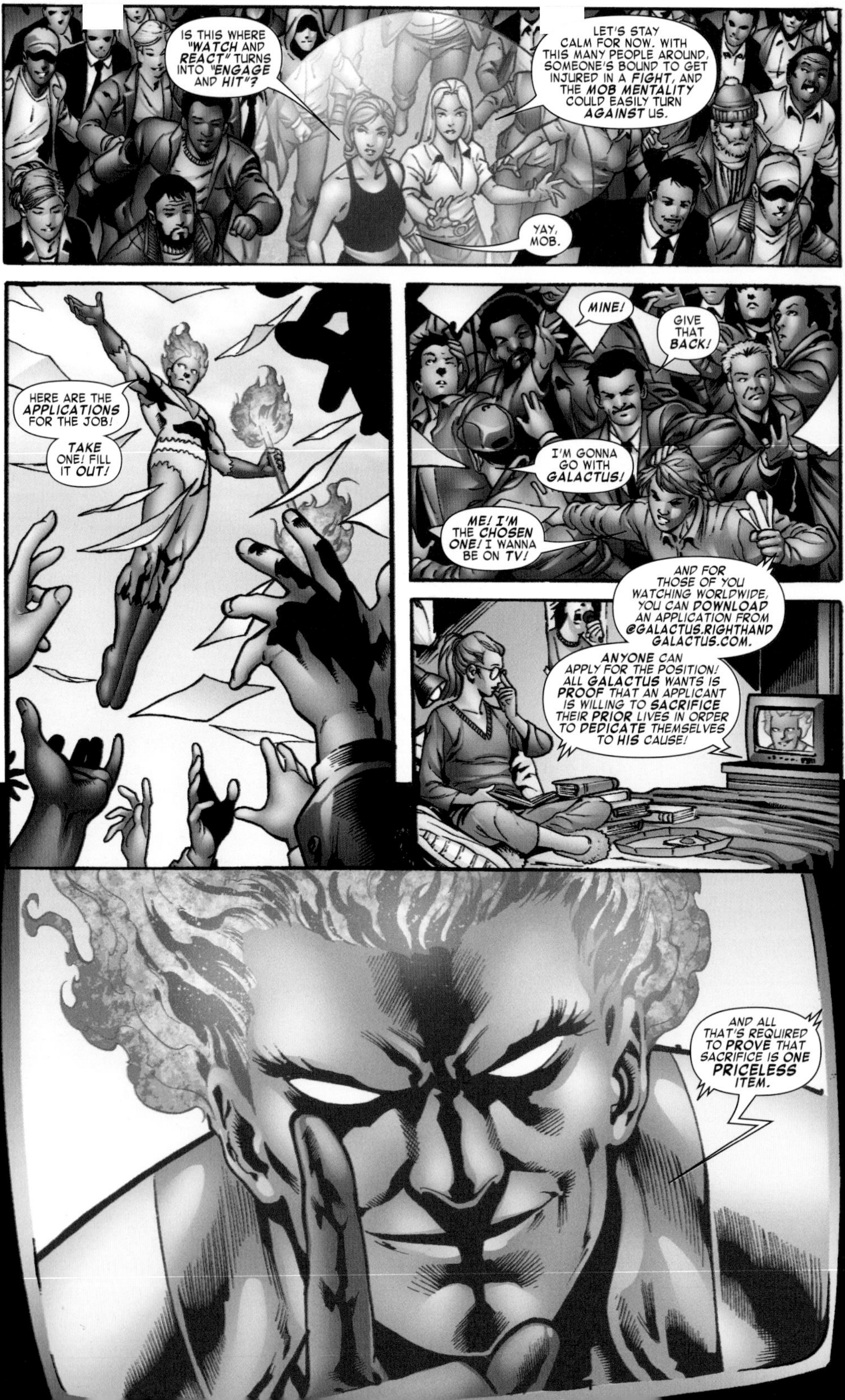
IS THIS WHERE "WATCH AND REACT" TURNS INTO "ENGAGE AND HIT"?
LET'S STAY CALM FOR NOW. WITH THIS MANY PEOPLE AROUND, SOMEONE'S BOUND TO GET INJURED IN A FIGHT, AND THE MOB MENTALITY COULD EASILY TURN AGAINST US.
YAY, MOB.
HERE ARE THE APPLICATIONS FOR THE JOB!
TAKE ONE! FILL IT OUT!
MINE!
GIVE THAT BACK!
I'M GONNA GO WITH GALACTUS!
ME! I'M THE CHOSEN ONE! I WANNA BE ON TV!
AND FOR THOSE OF YOU WATCHING WORLDWIDE, YOU CAN DOWNLOAD AN APPLICATION FROM @GALACTUS.RIGHTHAND GALACTUS.COM.
ANYONE CAN APPLY FOR THE POSITION! ALL GALACTUS WANTS IS PROOF THAT AN APPLICANT IS WILLING TO SACRIFICE THEIR PRIOR LIVES IN ORDER TO DEDICATE THEMSELVES TO HIS CAUSE!
AND ALL THAT'S REQUIRED TO PROVE THAT SACRIFICE IS ONE PRICELESS ITEM.

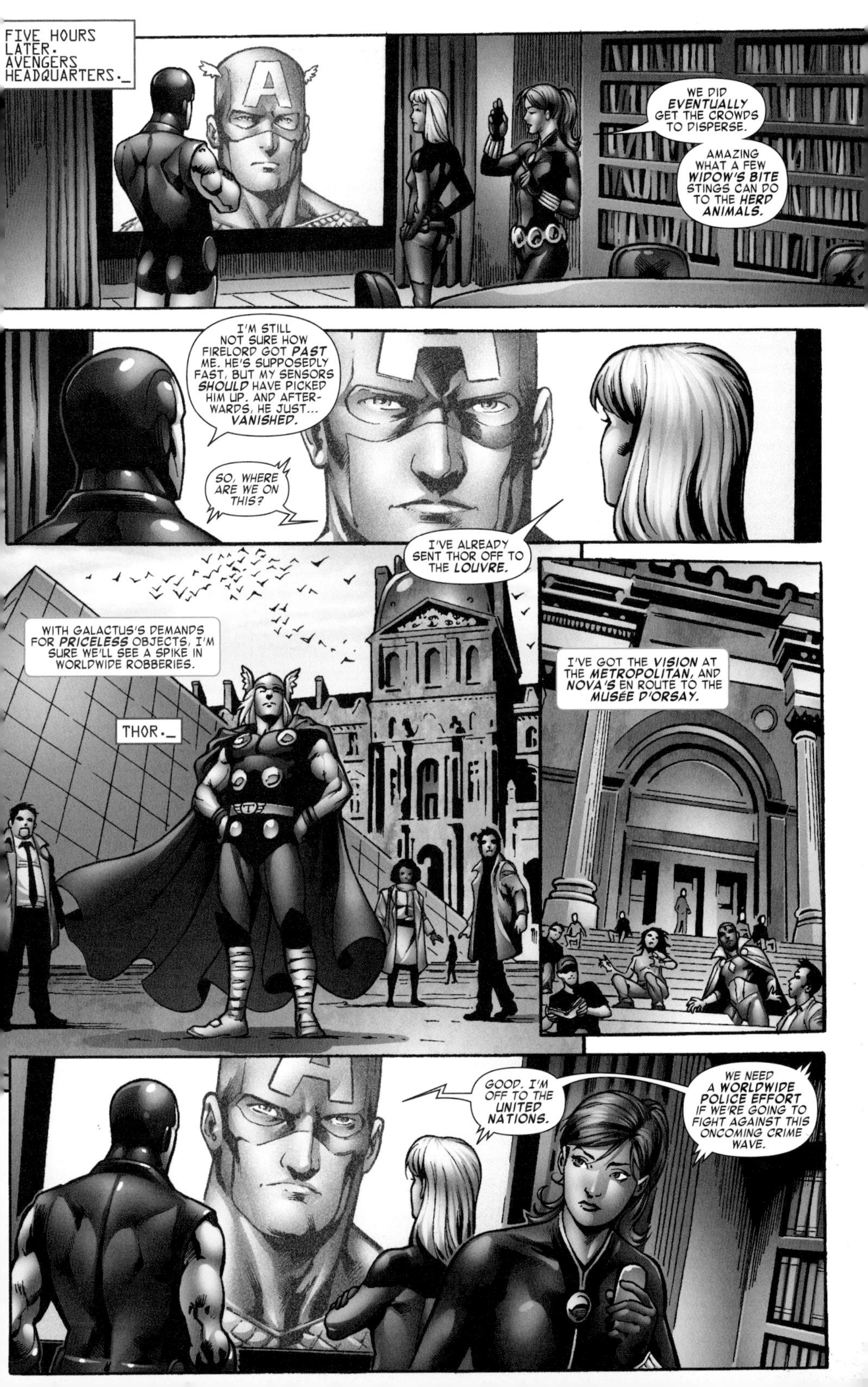

FIVE HOURS LATER. AVENGERS HEADQUARTERS._
WE DID EVENTUALLY GET THE CROWDS TO DISPERSE.
AMAZING WHAT A FEW WIDOW'S BITE STINGS CAN DO TO THE HERD ANIMALS.
I'M STILL NOT SURE HOW FIRELORD GOT PAST ME. HE'S SUPPOSEDLY FAST, BUT MY SENSORS SHOULD HAVE PICKED HIM UP. AND AFTERWARDS, HE JUST... VANISHED.
SO, WHERE ARE WE ON THIS?
I'VE ALREADY SENT THOR OFF TO THE LOUVRE.
WITH GALACTUS'S DEMANDS FOR PRICELESS OBJECTS, I'M SURE WE'LL SEE A SPIKE IN WORLDWIDE ROBBERIES.
THOR._
I'VE GOT THE VISION AT THE METROPOLITAN, AND NOVA'S EN ROUTE TO THE MUSÉE D'ORSAY.
GOOD. I'M OFF TO THE UNITED NATIONS.
WE NEED A WORLDWIDE POLICE EFFORT IF WE'RE GOING TO FIGHT AGAINST THIS ONCOMING CRIME WAVE.

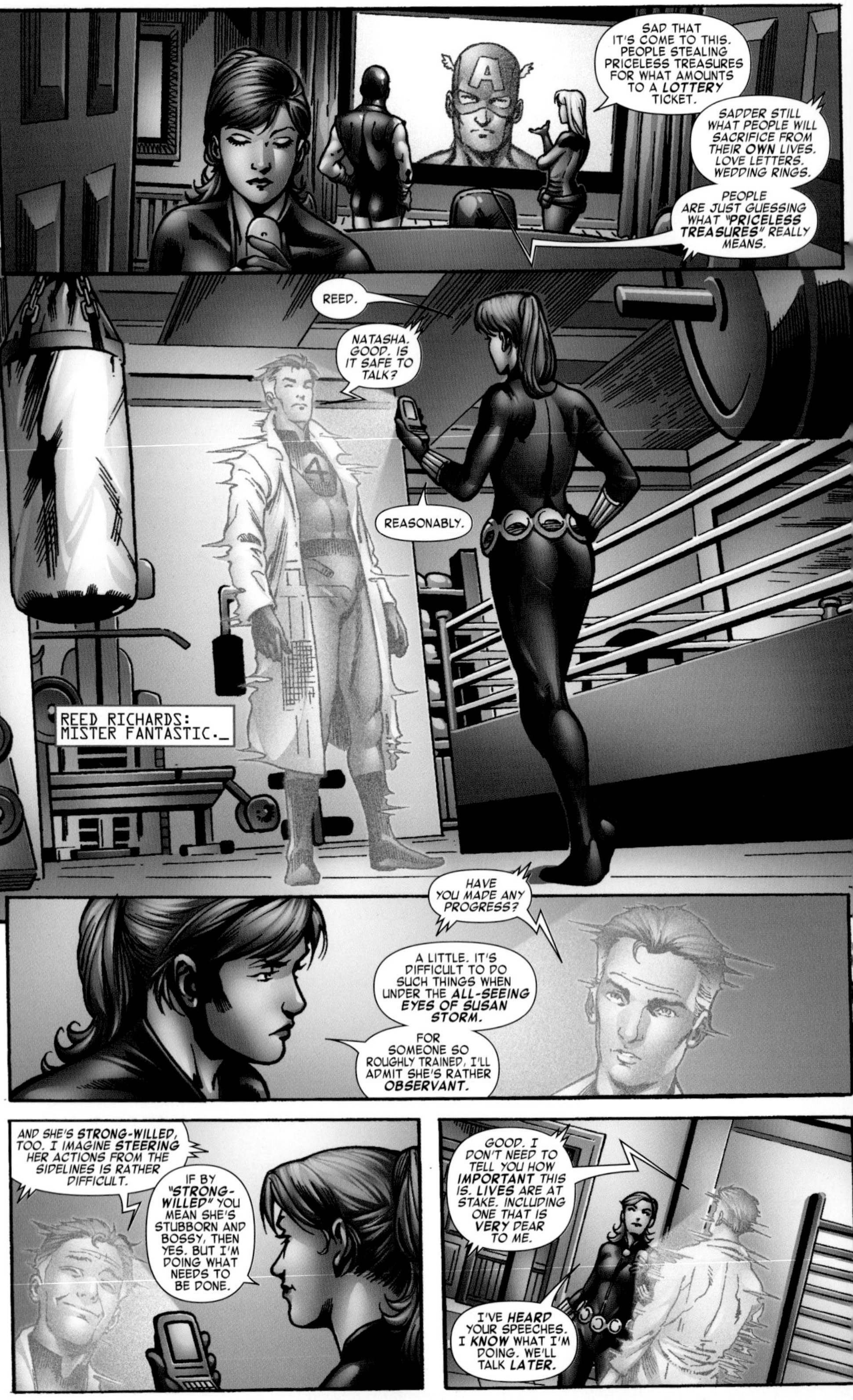
SAD THAT IT'S COME TO THIS. PEOPLE STEALING PRICELESS TREASURES FOR WHAT AMOUNTS TO A LOTTERY TICKET.
SADDER STILL WHAT PEOPLE WILL SACRIFICE FROM THEIR OWN LIVES. LOVE LETTERS. WEDDING RINGS.
PEOPLE ARE JUST GUESSING WHAT "PRICELESS TREASURES" REALLY MEANS.
REED.
NATASHA. GOOD. IS IT SAFE TO TALK?
REASONABLY.
REED RICHARDS: MISTER FANTASTIC._
HAVE YOU MADE ANY PROGRESS?
A LITTLE. IT'S DIFFICULT TO DO SUCH THINGS WHEN UNDER THE ALL-SEEING EYES OF SUSAN STORM.
FOR SOMEONE SO ROUGHLY TRAINED, I'LL ADMIT SHE'S RATHER OBSERVANT.
AND SHE'S STRONG-WILLED, TOO. I IMAGINE STEERING HER ACTIONS FROM THE SIDELINES IS RATHER DIFFICULT.
IF BY "STRONG-WILLED" YOU MEAN SHE'S STUBBORN AND BOSSY, THEN YES. BUT I'M DOING WHAT NEEDS TO BE DONE.
GOOD. I DON'T NEED TO TELL YOU HOW IMPORTANT THIS IS. LIVES ARE AT STAKE. INCLUDING ONE THAT IS VERY DEAR TO ME.
I'VE HEARD YOUR SPEECHES. I KNOW WHAT I'M DOING. WE'LL TALK LATER.

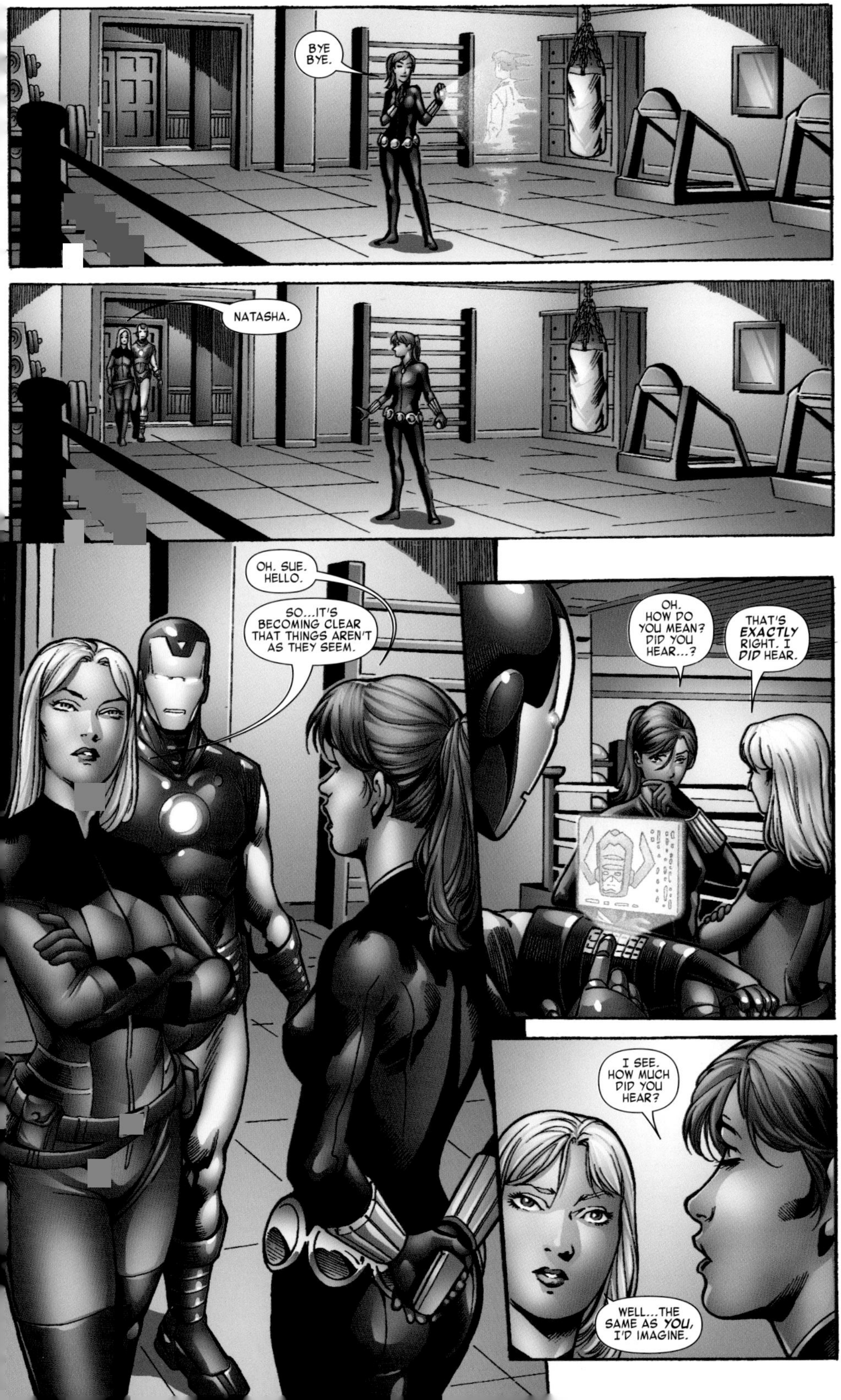
BYE BYE.
NATASHA.
OH. SUE. HELLO.
SO...IT'S BECOMING CLEAR THAT THINGS AREN'T AS THEY SEEM.
OH. HOW DO YOU MEAN? DID YOU HEAR...?
THAT'S *EXACTLY* RIGHT. I *DID* HEAR.
I SEE. HOW MUCH DID YOU HEAR?
WELL...THE SAME AS *YOU*, I'D IMAGINE.

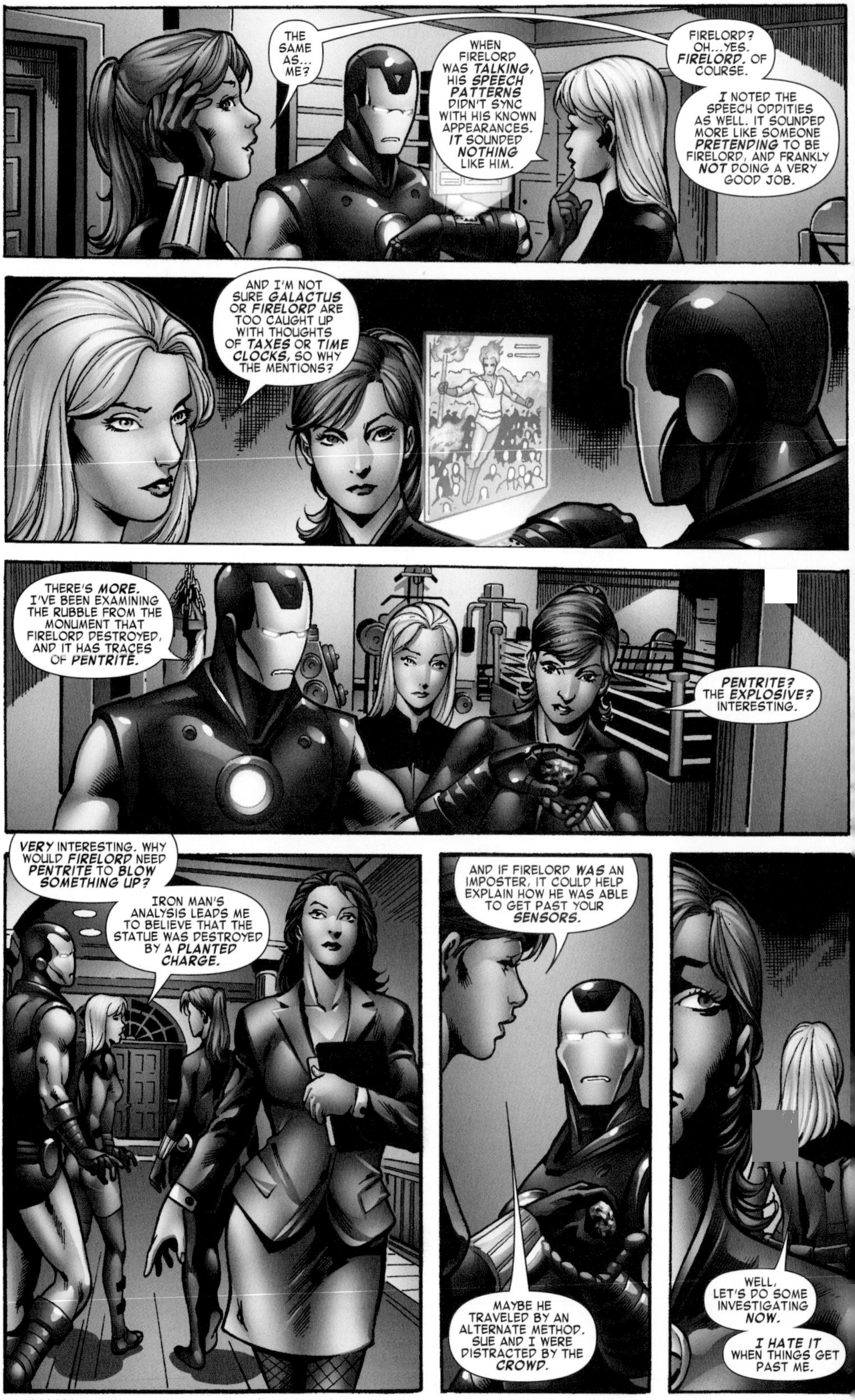
THE SAME AS... ME?
WHEN FIRELORD WAS TALKING, HIS SPEECH PATTERNS DIDN'T SYNC WITH HIS KNOWN APPEARANCES. IT SOUNDED NOTHING LIKE HIM.
FIRELORD? OH...YES. FIRELORD. OF COURSE.
I NOTED THE SPEECH ODDITIES AS WELL. IT SOUNDED MORE LIKE SOMEONE PRETENDING TO BE FIRELORD, AND FRANKLY NOT DOING A VERY GOOD JOB.
AND I'M NOT SURE GALACTUS OR FIRELORD ARE TOO CAUGHT UP WITH THOUGHTS OF TAXES OR TIME CLOCKS, SO WHY THE MENTIONS?
THERE'S MORE. I'VE BEEN EXAMINING THE RUBBLE FROM THE MONUMENT THAT FIRELORD DESTROYED, AND IT HAS TRACES OF PENTRITE.
PENTRITE? THE EXPLOSIVE? INTERESTING.
VERY INTERESTING. WHY WOULD FIRELORD NEED PENTRITE TO BLOW SOMETHING UP?
IRON MAN'S ANALYSIS LEADS ME TO BELIEVE THAT THE STATUE WAS DESTROYED BY A PLANTED CHARGE.
AND IF FIRELORD WAS AN IMPOSTER, IT COULD HELP EXPLAIN HOW HE WAS ABLE TO GET PAST YOUR SENSORS.
MAYBE HE TRAVELED BY AN ALTERNATE METHOD. SUE AND I WERE DISTRACTED BY THE CROWD.
WELL, LET'S DO SOME INVESTIGATING NOW.
I HATE IT WHEN THINGS GET PAST ME.

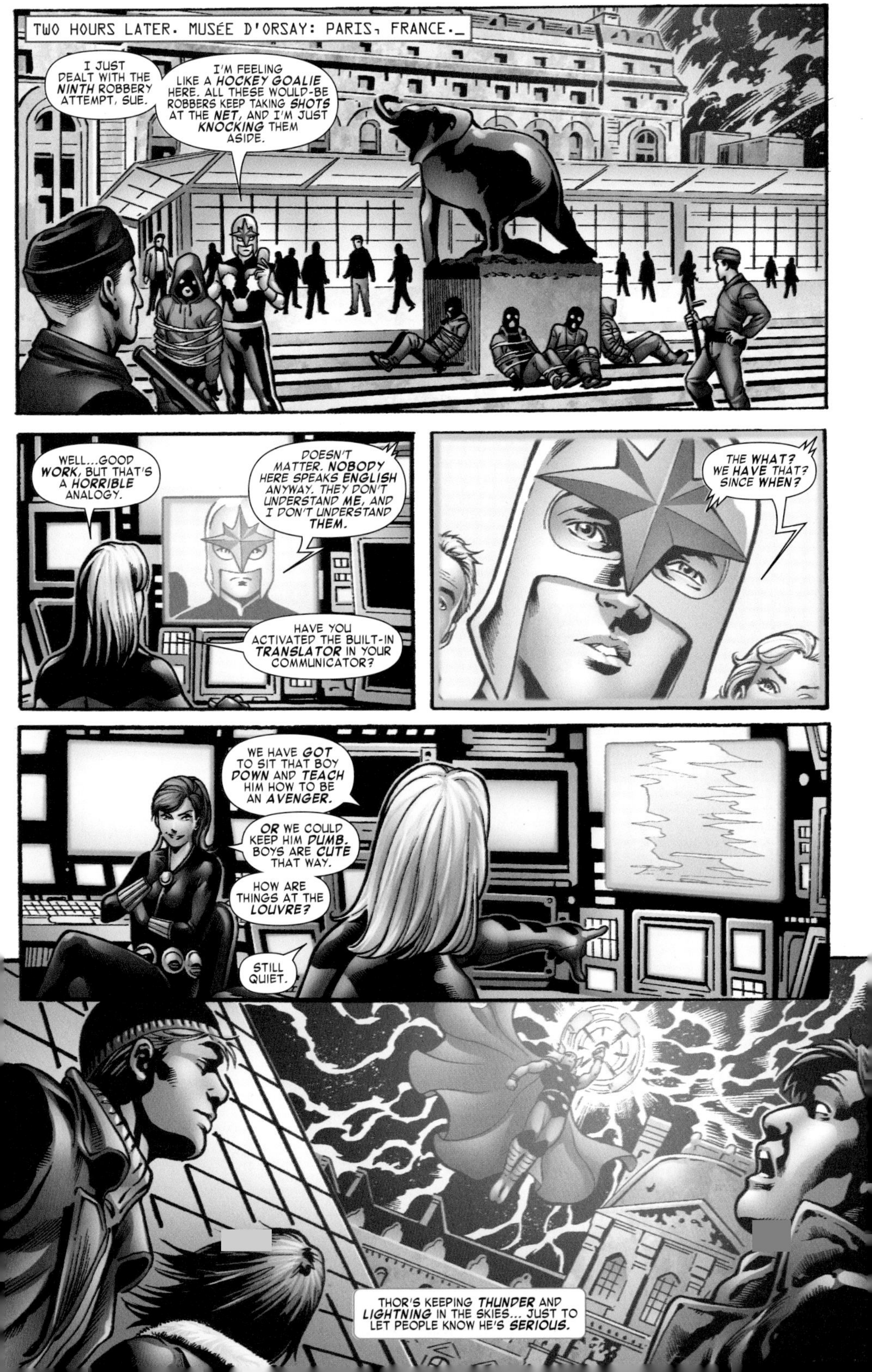

TWO HOURS LATER. MUSÉE D'ORSAY: PARIS, FRANCE._
I JUST DEALT WITH THE NINTH ROBBERY ATTEMPT, SUE.
I'M FEELING LIKE A HOCKEY GOALIE HERE. ALL THESE WOULD-BE ROBBERS KEEP TAKING SHOTS AT THE NET, AND I'M JUST KNOCKING THEM ASIDE.
WELL...GOOD WORK, BUT THAT'S A HORRIBLE ANALOGY.
DOESN'T MATTER. NOBODY HERE SPEAKS ENGLISH ANYWAY. THEY DON'T UNDERSTAND ME, AND I DON'T UNDERSTAND THEM.
HAVE YOU ACTIVATED THE BUILT-IN TRANSLATOR IN YOUR COMMUNICATOR?
THE WHAT? WE HAVE THAT? SINCE WHEN?
WE HAVE GOT TO SIT THAT BOY DOWN AND TEACH HIM HOW TO BE AN AVENGER.
OR WE COULD KEEP HIM DUMB. BOYS ARE CUTE THAT WAY.
HOW ARE THINGS AT THE LOUVRE?
STILL QUIET.
THOR'S KEEPING THUNDER AND LIGHTNING IN THE SKIES... JUST TO LET PEOPLE KNOW HE'S SERIOUS.

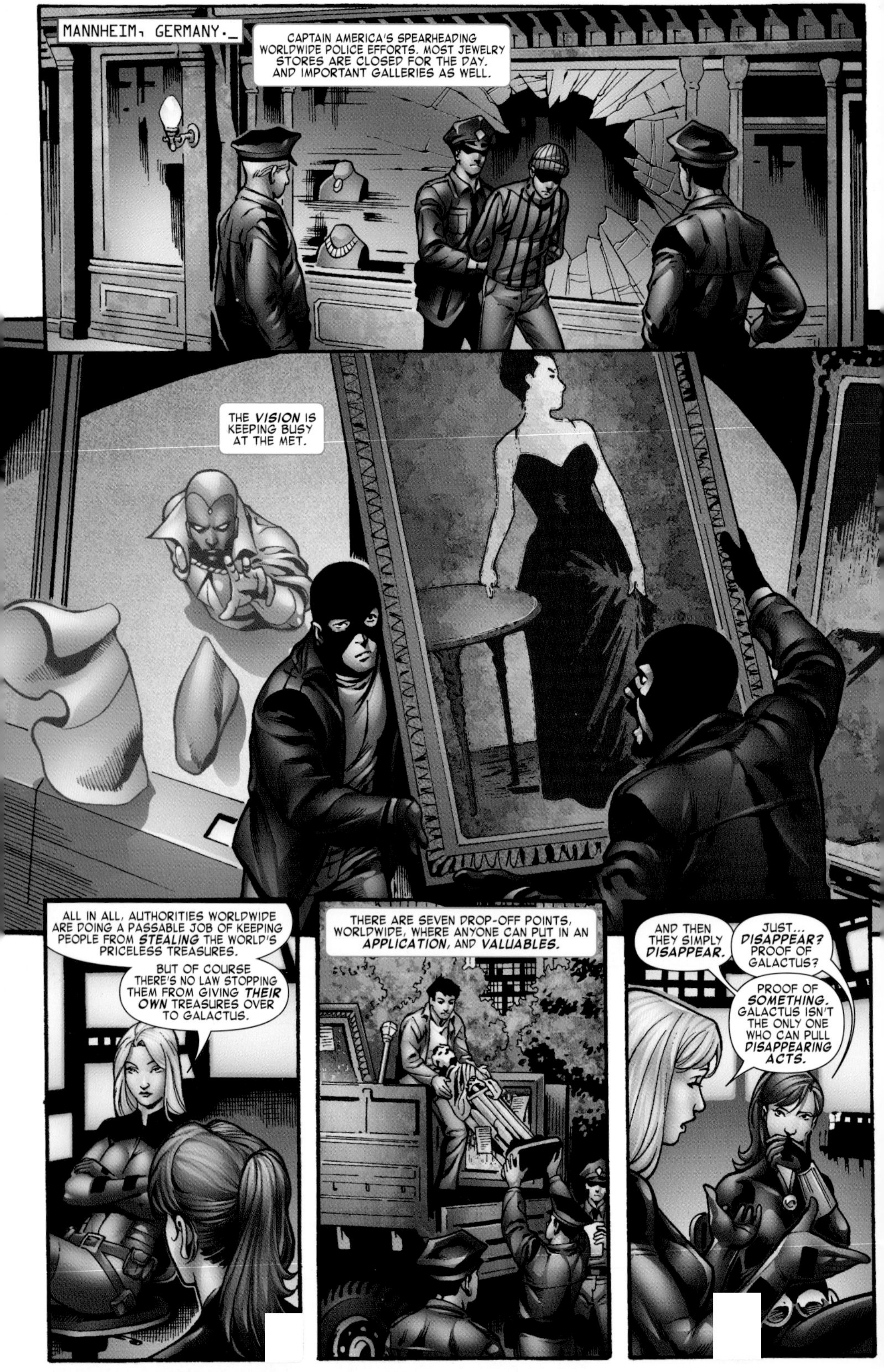
MANNHEIM, GERMANY._
CAPTAIN AMERICA'S SPEARHEADING WORLDWIDE POLICE EFFORTS. MOST JEWELRY STORES ARE CLOSED FOR THE DAY. AND IMPORTANT GALLERIES AS WELL.
THE VISION IS KEEPING BUSY AT THE MET.
ALL IN ALL, AUTHORITIES WORLDWIDE ARE DOING A PASSABLE JOB OF KEEPING PEOPLE FROM STEALING THE WORLD'S PRICELESS TREASURES.
BUT OF COURSE THERE'S NO LAW STOPPING THEM FROM GIVING THEIR OWN TREASURES OVER TO GALACTUS.
THERE ARE SEVEN DROP-OFF POINTS, WORLDWIDE, WHERE ANYONE CAN PUT IN AN APPLICATION, AND VALUABLES.
AND THEN THEY SIMPLY DISAPPEAR.
JUST... DISAPPEAR? PROOF OF GALACTUS?
PROOF OF SOMETHING. GALACTUS ISN'T THE ONLY ONE WHO CAN PULL DISAPPEARING ACTS.

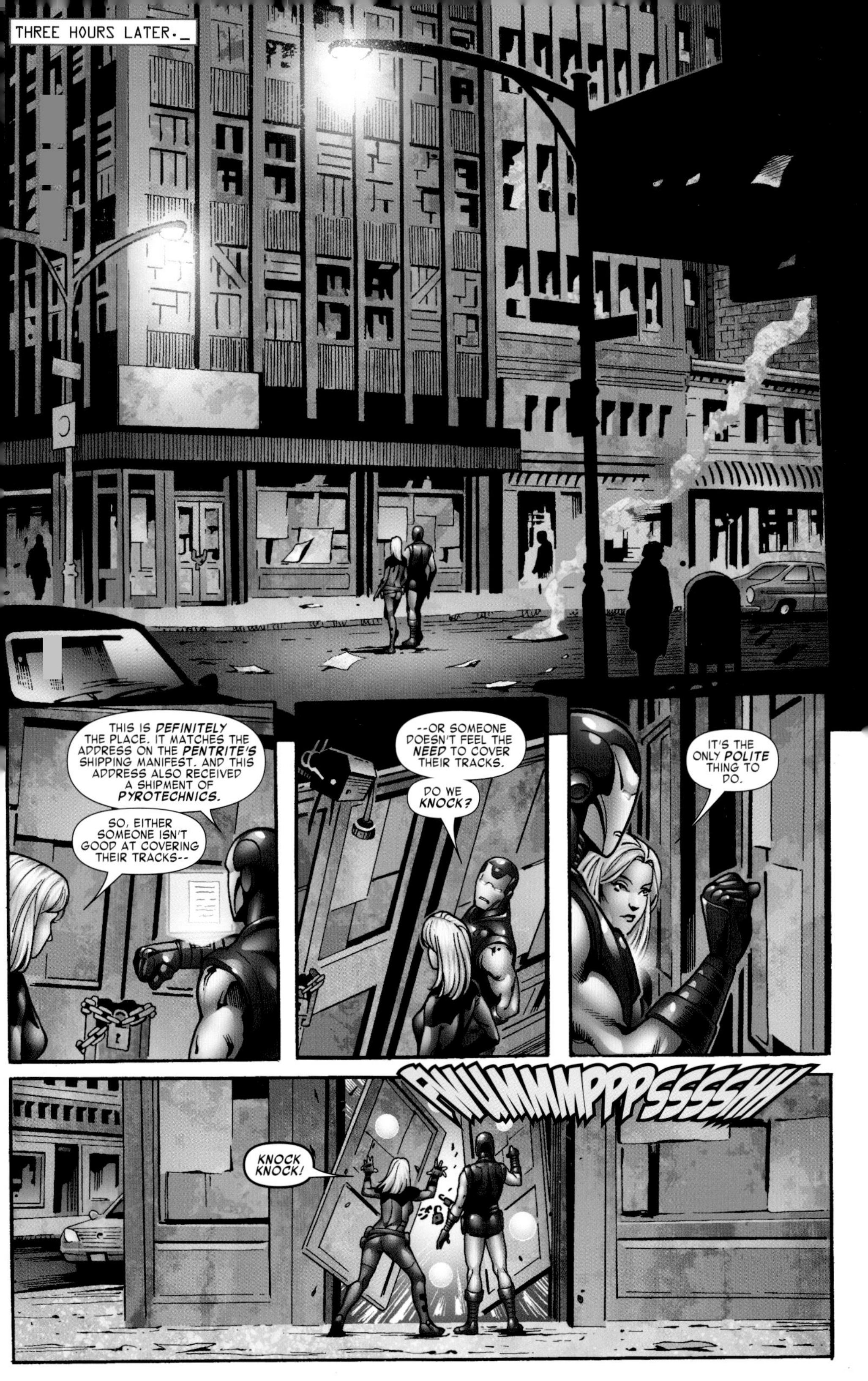
THREE HOURS LATER._
THIS IS DEFINITELY THE PLACE. IT MATCHES THE ADDRESS ON THE PENTRITE'S SHIPPING MANIFEST. AND THIS ADDRESS ALSO RECEIVED A SHIPMENT OF PYROTECHNICS.
SO, EITHER SOMEONE ISN'T GOOD AT COVERING THEIR TRACKS--
--OR SOMEONE DOESN'T FEEL THE NEED TO COVER THEIR TRACKS.
DO WE KNOCK?
IT'S THE ONLY POLITE THING TO DO.
BNUMMMPPPSSSSSH
KNOCK KNOCK!

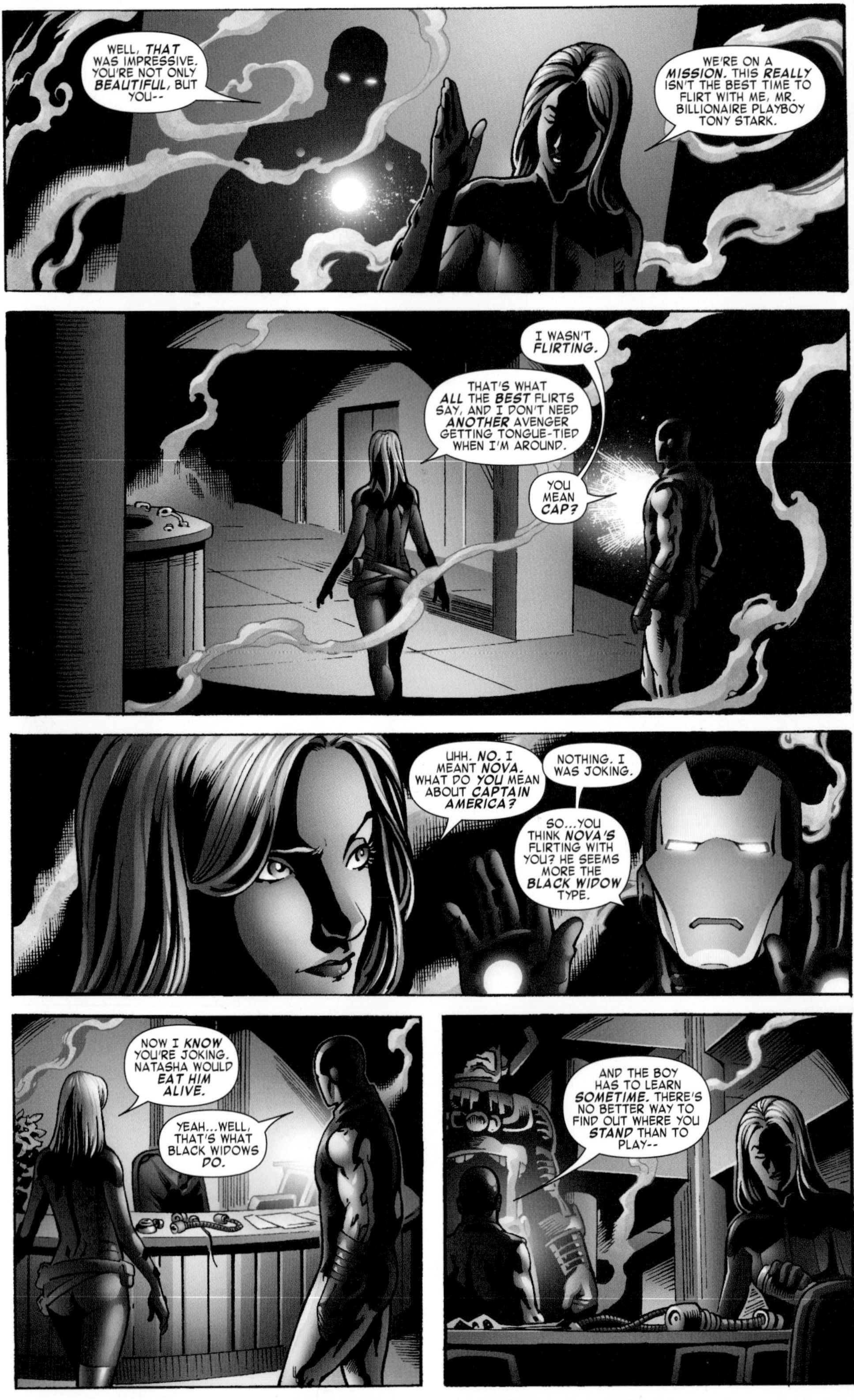
WELL, THAT WAS IMPRESSIVE. YOU'RE NOT ONLY BEAUTIFUL, BUT YOU--
WE'RE ON A MISSION. THIS REALLY ISN'T THE BEST TIME TO FLIRT WITH ME, MR. BILLIONAIRE PLAYBOY TONY STARK.
I WASN'T FLIRTING.
THAT'S WHAT ALL THE BEST FLIRTS SAY, AND I DON'T NEED ANOTHER AVENGER GETTING TONGUE-TIED WHEN I'M AROUND.
YOU MEAN CAP?
UHH. NO. I MEANT NOVA. WHAT DO YOU MEAN ABOUT CAPTAIN AMERICA?
NOTHING. I WAS JOKING.
SO...YOU THINK NOVA'S FLIRTING WITH YOU? HE SEEMS MORE THE BLACK WIDOW TYPE.
NOW I KNOW YOU'RE JOKING. NATASHA WOULD EAT HIM ALIVE.
YEAH...WELL, THAT'S WHAT BLACK WIDOWS DO.
AND THE BOY HAS TO LEARN SOMETIME. THERE'S NO BETTER WAY TO FIND OUT WHERE YOU STAND THAN TO PLAY--

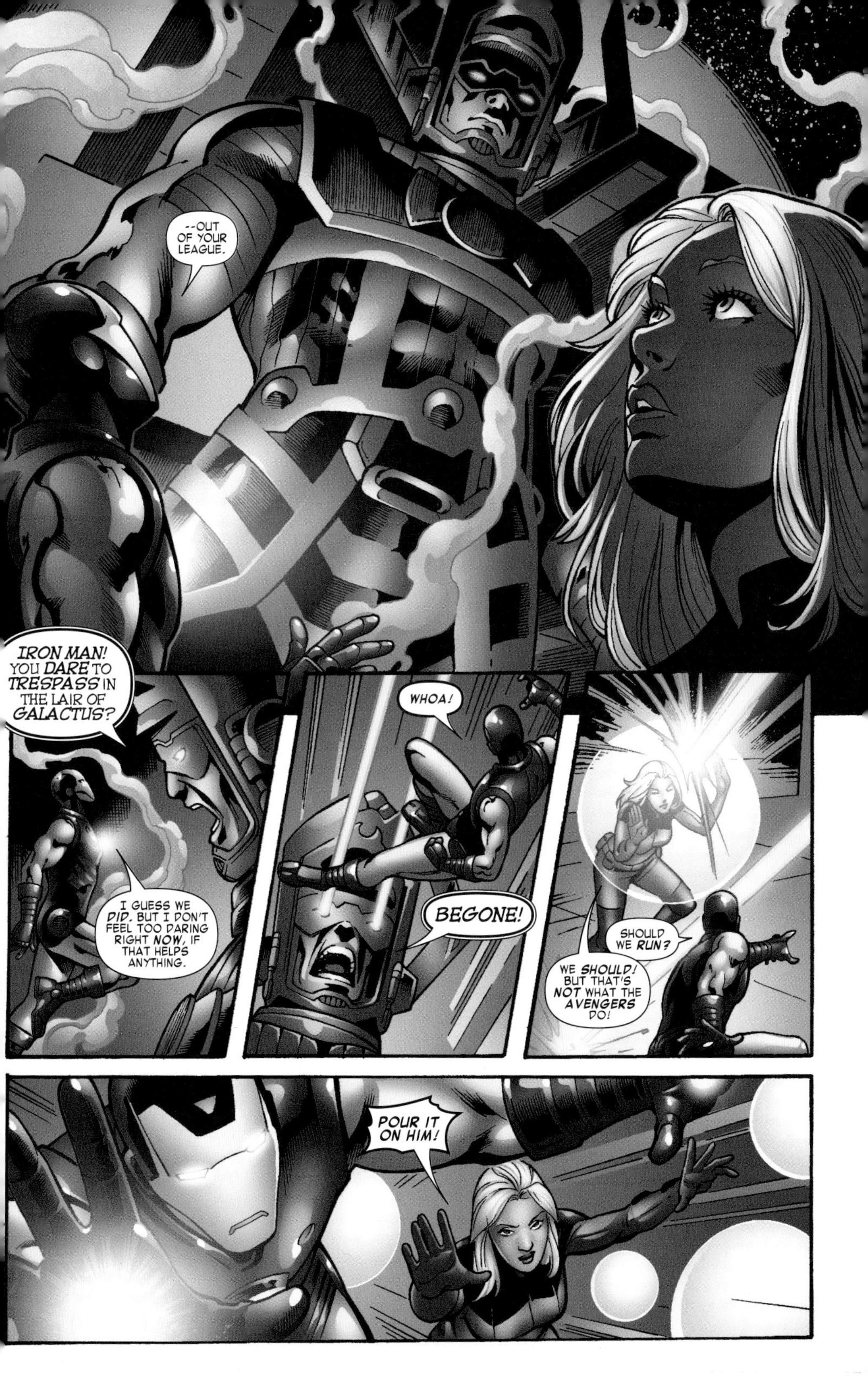
--OUT OF YOUR LEAGUE.
IRON MAN! YOU DARE TO TRESPASS IN THE LAIR OF GALACTUS?
I GUESS WE DID. BUT I DON'T FEEL TOO DARING RIGHT NOW, IF THAT HELPS ANYTHING.
WHOA!
BEGONE!
SHOULD WE RUN?
WE SHOULD! BUT THAT'S NOT WHAT THE AVENGERS DO!
POUR IT ON HIM!

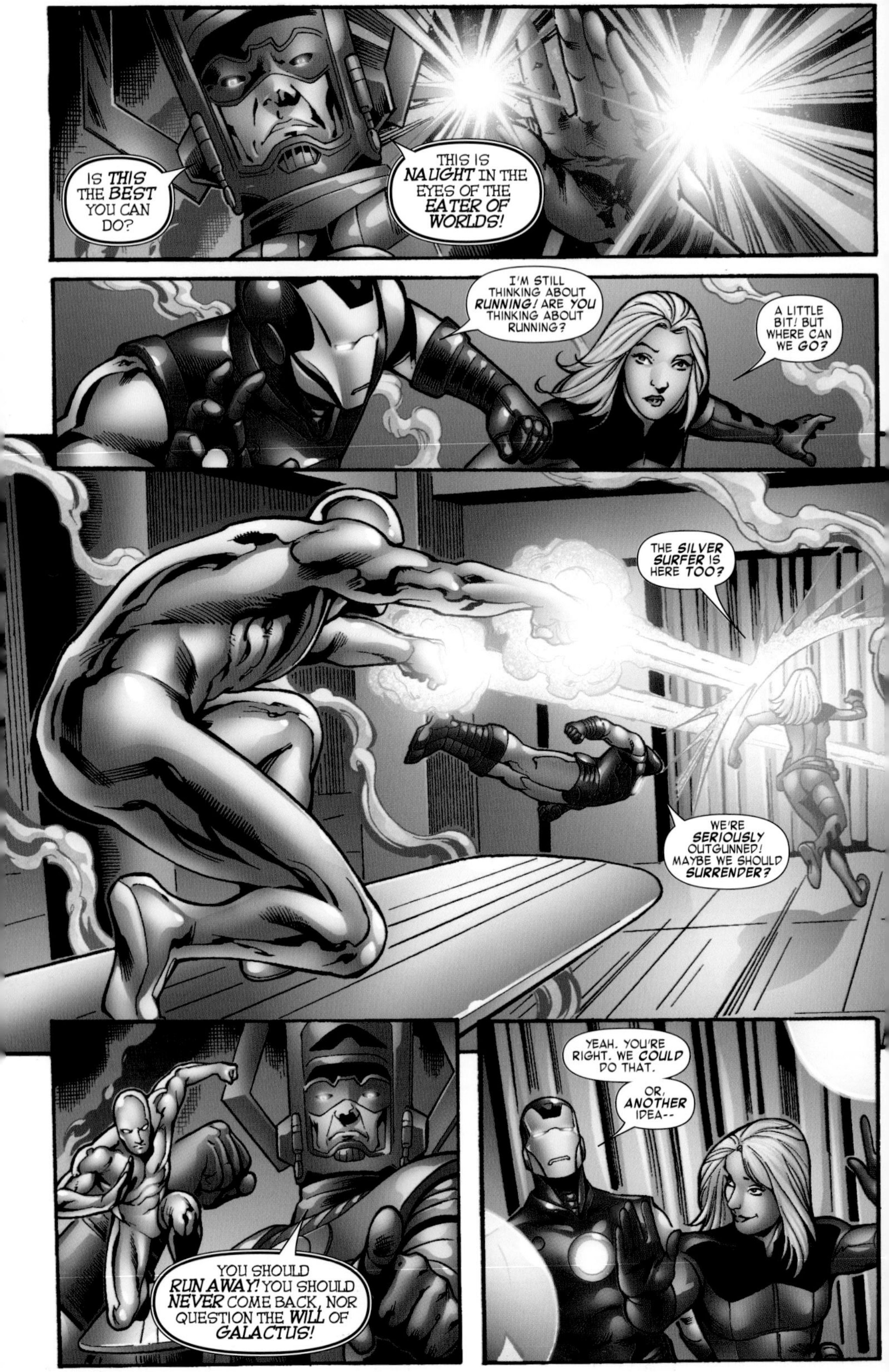
IS THIS THE BEST YOU CAN DO?
THIS IS NAUGHT IN THE EYES OF THE EATER OF WORLDS!
I'M STILL THINKING ABOUT RUNNING! ARE YOU THINKING ABOUT RUNNING?
A LITTLE BIT! BUT WHERE CAN WE GO?
THE SILVER SURFER IS HERE TOO?
WE'RE SERIOUSLY OUTGUNNED! MAYBE WE SHOULD SURRENDER?
YOU SHOULD RUN AWAY! YOU SHOULD NEVER COME BACK, NOR QUESTION THE WILL OF GALACTUS!
YEAH. YOU'RE RIGHT. WE COULD DO THAT.
OR, ANOTHER IDEA--

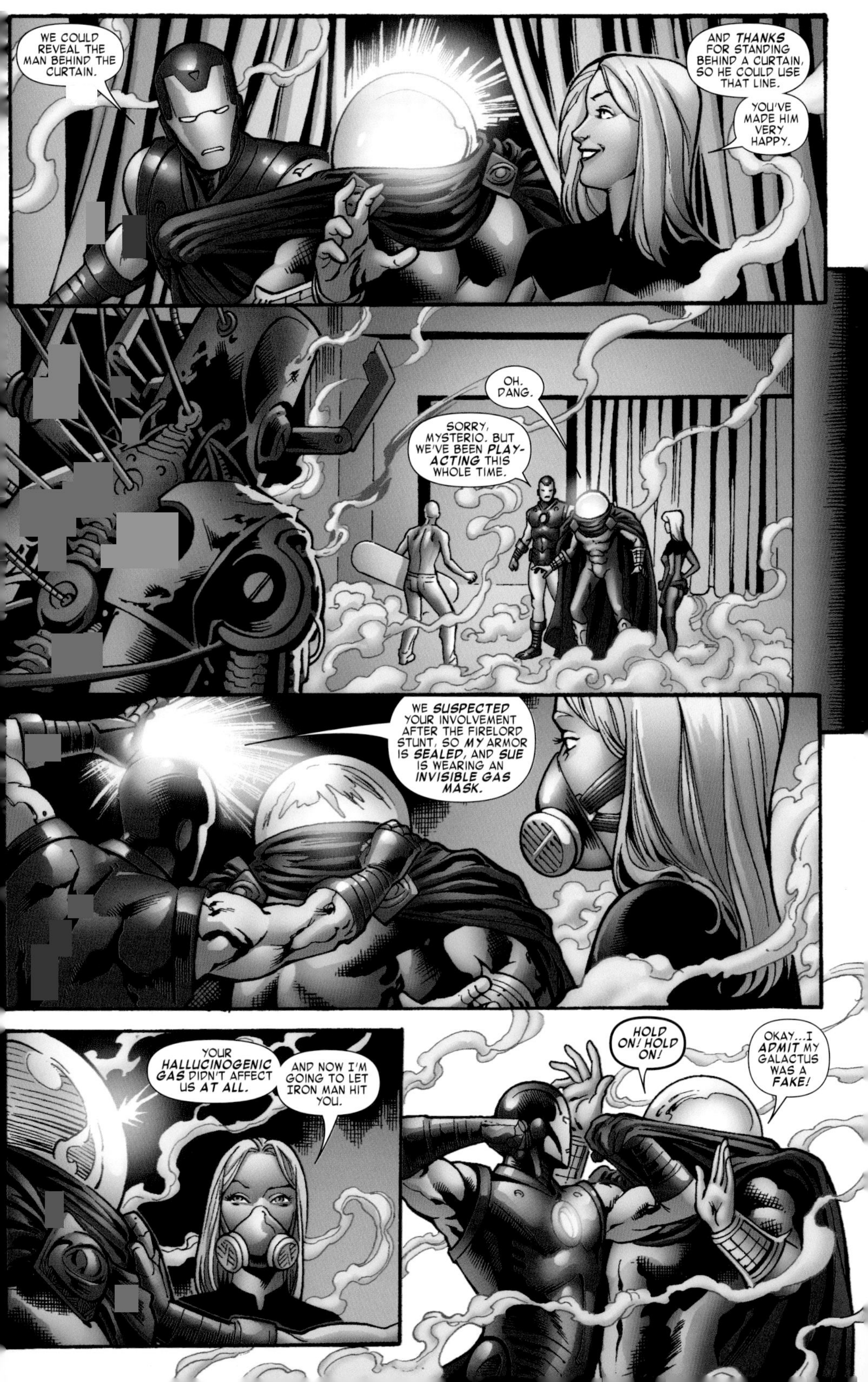
WE COULD REVEAL THE MAN BEHIND THE CURTAIN.
AND THANKS FOR STANDING BEHIND A CURTAIN, SO HE COULD USE THAT LINE.
YOU'VE MADE HIM VERY HAPPY.
OH. DANG.
SORRY, MYSTERIO. BUT WE'VE BEEN PLAY-ACTING THIS WHOLE TIME.
WE SUSPECTED YOUR INVOLVEMENT AFTER THE FIRELORD STUNT, SO MY ARMOR IS SEALED, AND SUE IS WEARING AN INVISIBLE GAS MASK.
YOUR HALLUCINOGENIC GAS DIDN'T AFFECT US AT ALL.
AND NOW I'M GOING TO LET IRON MAN HIT YOU.
HOLD ON! HOLD ON!
OKAY...I ADMIT MY GALACTUS WAS A FAKE!

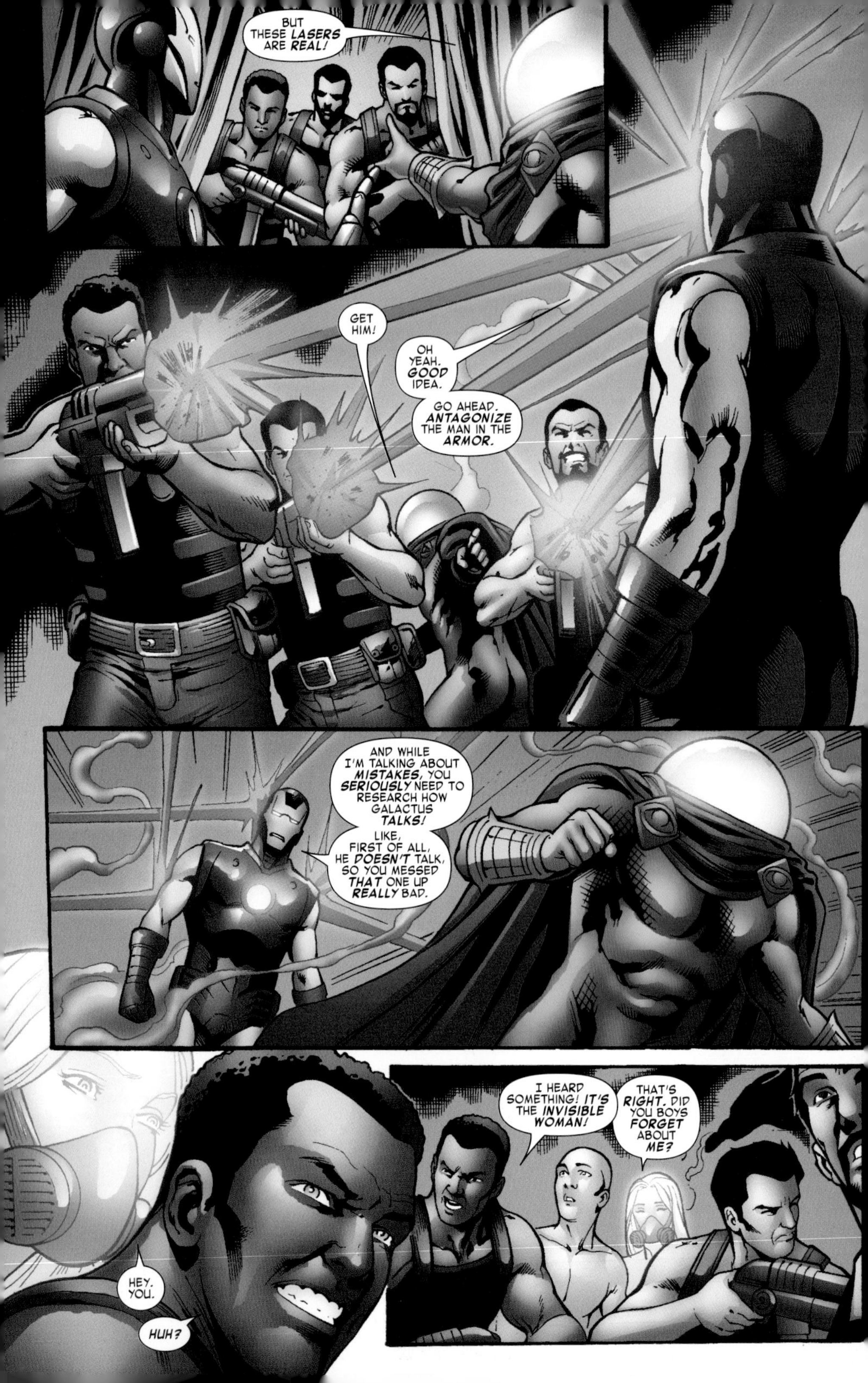

BUT THESE LASERS ARE REAL!
GET HIM!
OH YEAH. GOOD IDEA.
GO AHEAD. ANTAGONIZE THE MAN IN THE ARMOR.
AND WHILE I'M TALKING ABOUT MISTAKES, YOU SERIOUSLY NEED TO RESEARCH HOW GALACTUS TALKS!
LIKE, FIRST OF ALL, HE DOESN'T TALK, SO YOU MESSED THAT ONE UP REALLY BAD.
I HEARD SOMETHING! IT'S THE INVISIBLE WOMAN!
THAT'S RIGHT. DID YOU BOYS FORGET ABOUT ME?
HEY. YOU.
HUH?

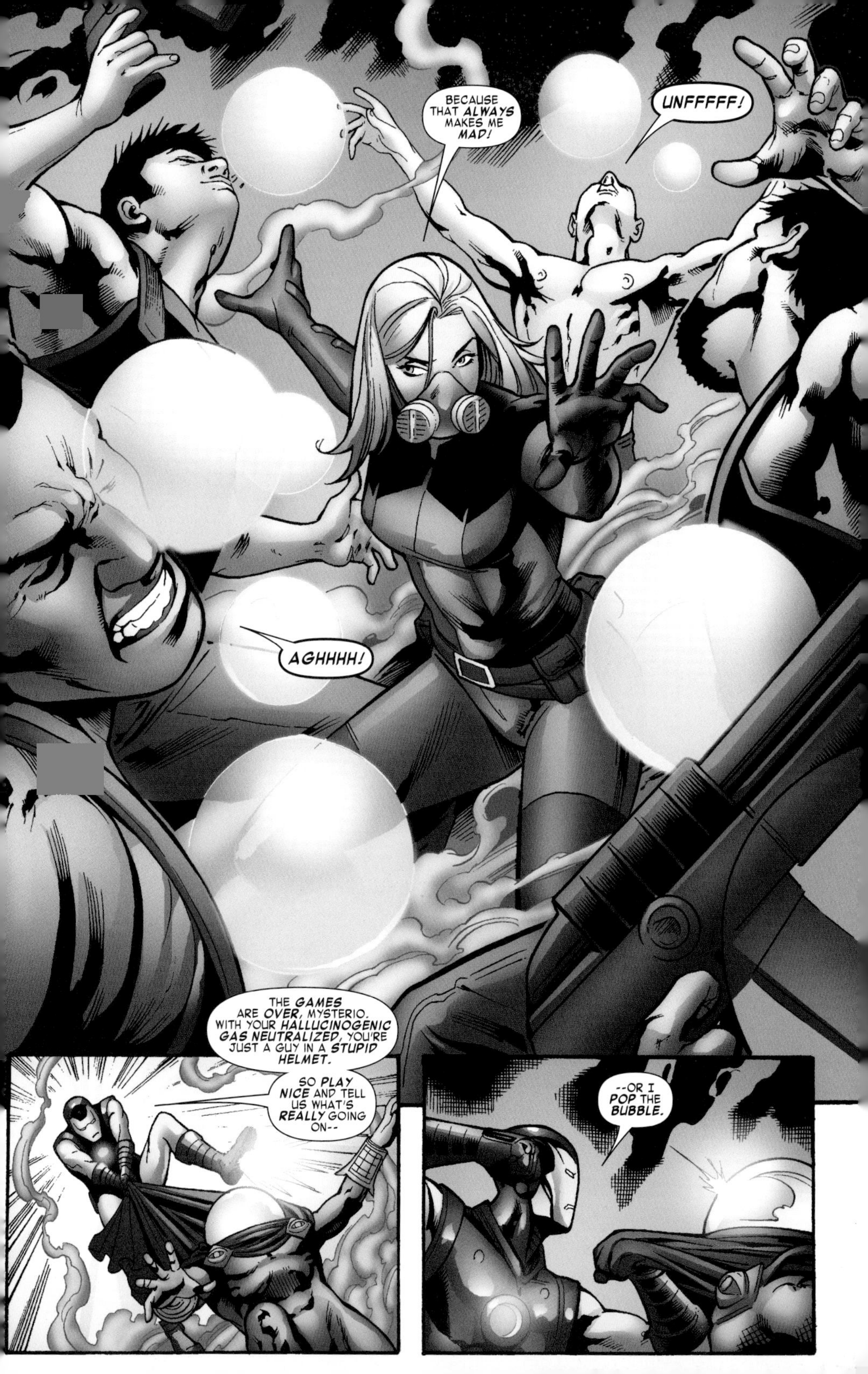
BECAUSE THAT ALWAYS MAKES ME MAD!
UNFFFFF!
AGHHHH!
THE GAMES ARE OVER, MYSTERIO. WITH YOUR HALLUCINOGENIC GAS NEUTRALIZED, YOU'RE JUST A GUY IN A STUPID HELMET.
SO PLAY NICE AND TELL US WHAT'S REALLY GOING ON--
--OR I POP THE BUBBLE.

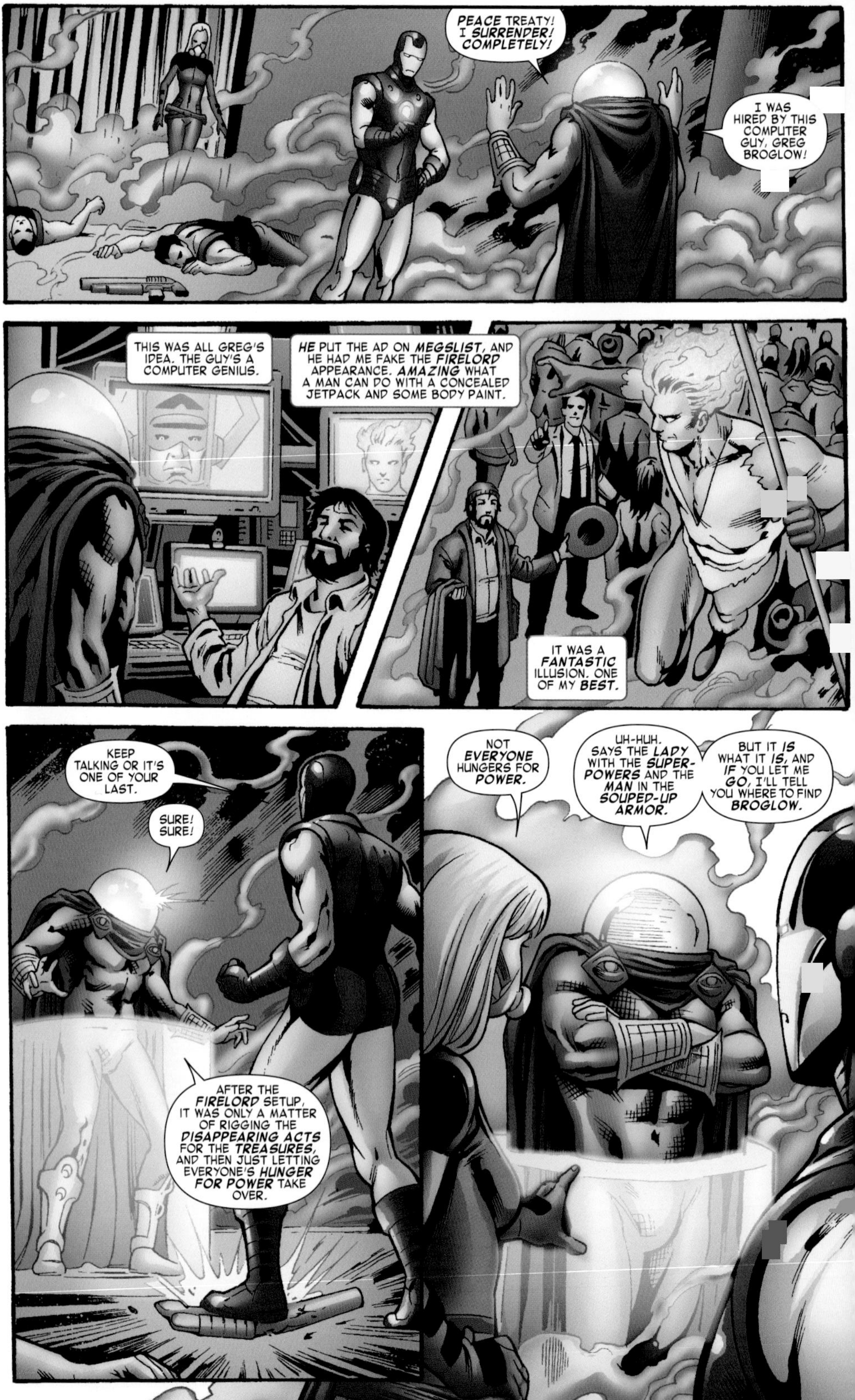
PEACE TREATY! I SURRENDER! COMPLETELY!
I WAS HIRED BY THIS COMPUTER GUY, GREG BROGLOW!
THIS WAS ALL GREG'S IDEA. THE GUY'S A COMPUTER GENIUS.
HE PUT THE AD ON MEGSLIST, AND HE HAD ME FAKE THE FIRELORD APPEARANCE. AMAZING WHAT A MAN CAN DO WITH A CONCEALED JETPACK AND SOME BODY PAINT.
IT WAS A FANTASTIC ILLUSION. ONE OF MY BEST.
KEEP TALKING OR IT'S ONE OF YOUR LAST.
SURE! SURE!
AFTER THE FIRELORD SETUP, IT WAS ONLY A MATTER OF RIGGING THE DISAPPEARING ACTS FOR THE TREASURES, AND THEN JUST LETTING EVERYONE'S HUNGER FOR POWER TAKE OVER.
NOT EVERYONE HUNGERS FOR POWER.
UH-HUH. SAYS THE LADY WITH THE SUPER-POWERS AND THE MAN IN THE SOUPED-UP ARMOR.
BUT IT IS WHAT IT IS, AND IF YOU LET ME GO, I'LL TELL YOU WHERE TO FIND BROGLOW.

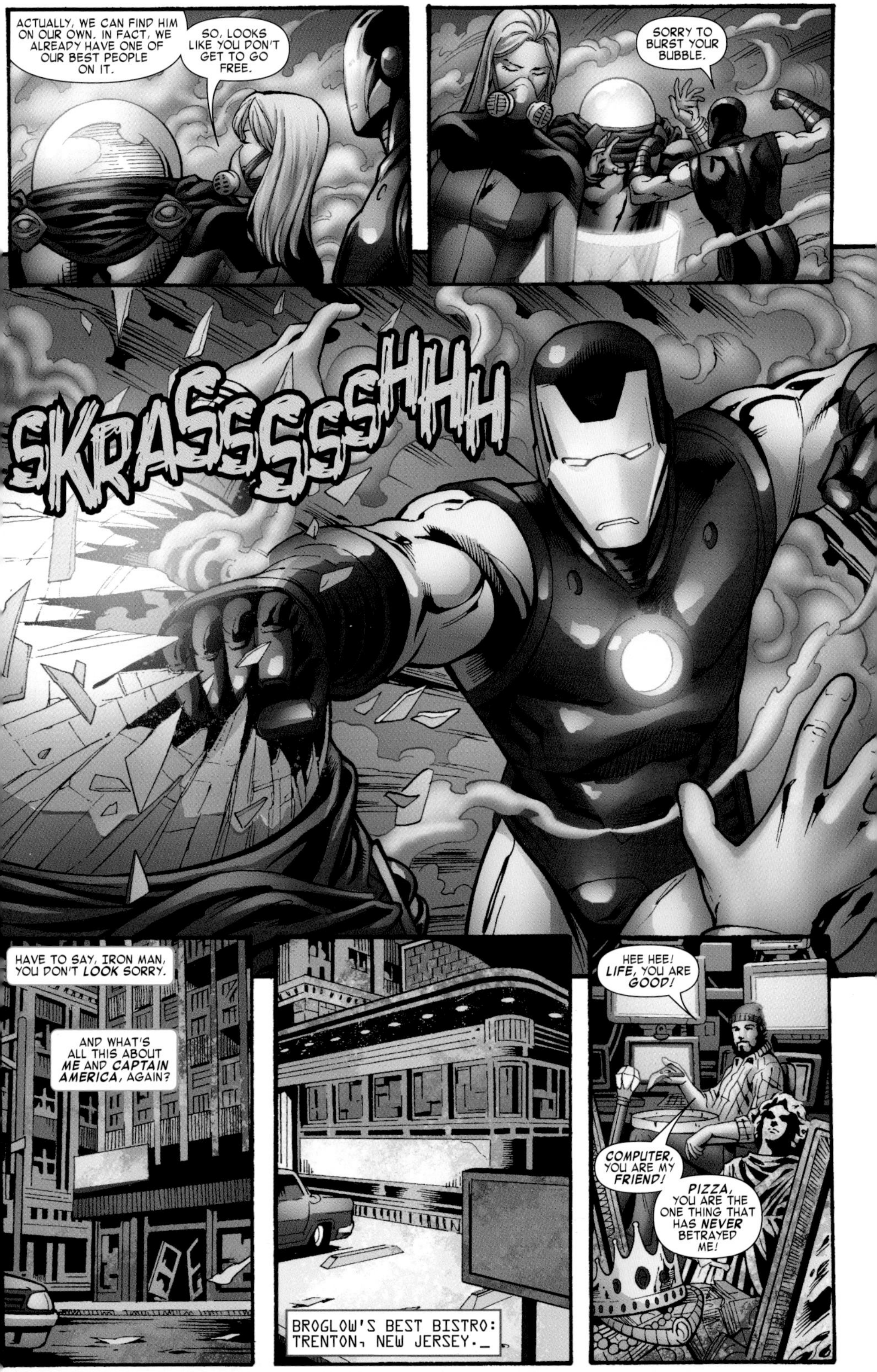
ACTUALLY, WE CAN FIND HIM ON OUR OWN. IN FACT, WE ALREADY HAVE ONE OF OUR BEST PEOPLE ON IT.
SO, LOOKS LIKE YOU DON'T GET TO GO FREE.
SORRY TO BURST YOUR BUBBLE.
SKRASSSSSSHHH
HAVE TO SAY, IRON MAN, YOU DON'T LOOK SORRY.
AND WHAT'S ALL THIS ABOUT ME AND CAPTAIN AMERICA, AGAIN?
BROGLOW'S BEST BISTRO: TRENTON, NEW JERSEY.
HEE HEE! LIFE, YOU ARE GOOD!
COMPUTER, YOU ARE MY FRIEND!
PIZZA, YOU ARE THE ONE THING THAT HAS NEVER BETRAYED ME!

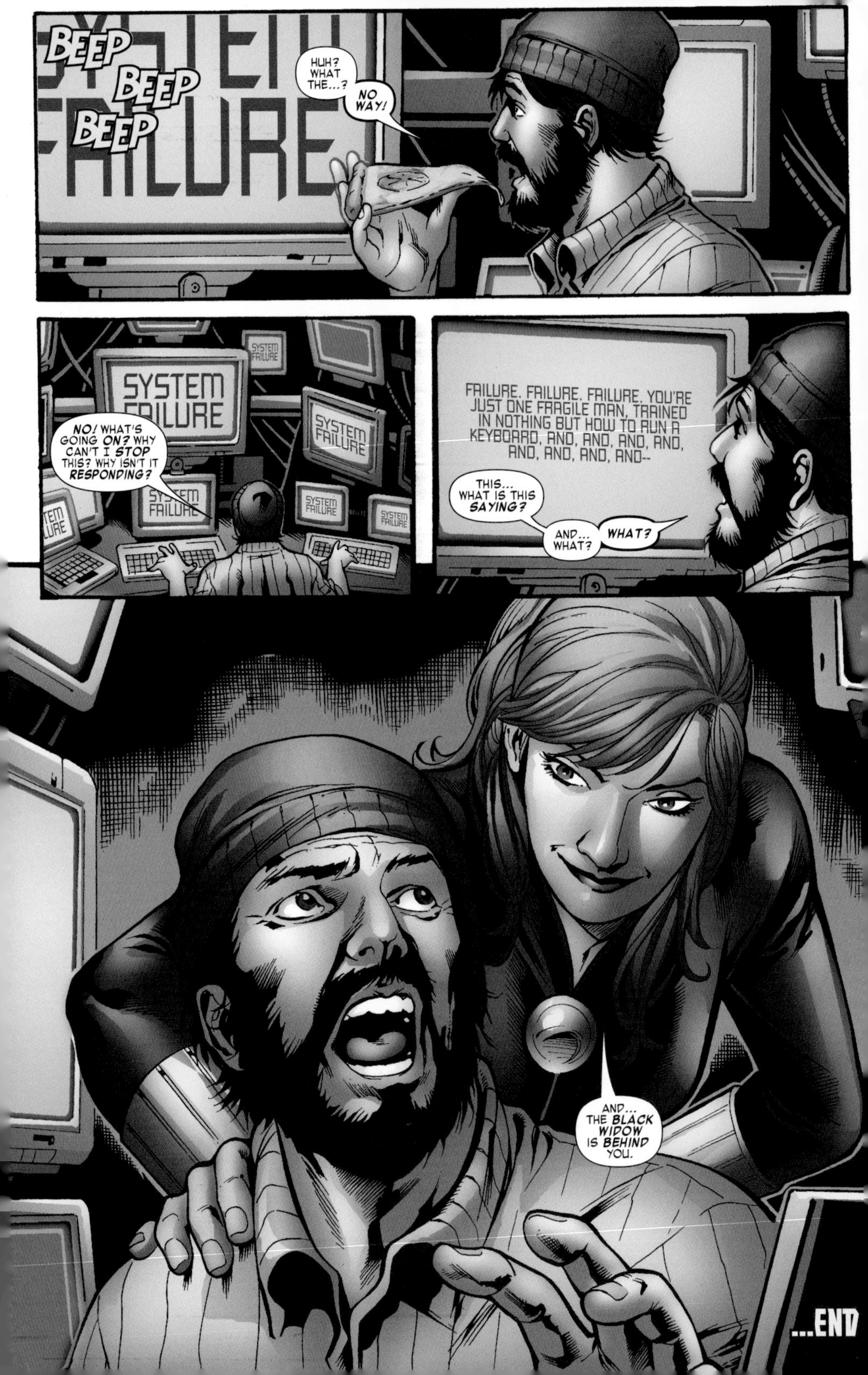

BEEP BEEP BEEP
SYSTEM FAILURE
HUH? WHAT THE...?
NO WAY!
SYSTEM FAILURE
NO! WHAT'S GOING ON? WHY CAN'T I STOP THIS? WHY ISN'T IT RESPONDING?
FAILURE. FAILURE. FAILURE. YOU'RE JUST ONE FRAGILE MAN, TRAINED IN NOTHING BUT HOW TO RUN A KEYBOARD, AND, AND, AND, AND, AND, AND, AND, AND--
THIS... WHAT IS THIS SAYING?
AND... WHAT?
WHAT?
AND... THE BLACK WIDOW IS BEHIND YOU.
...END

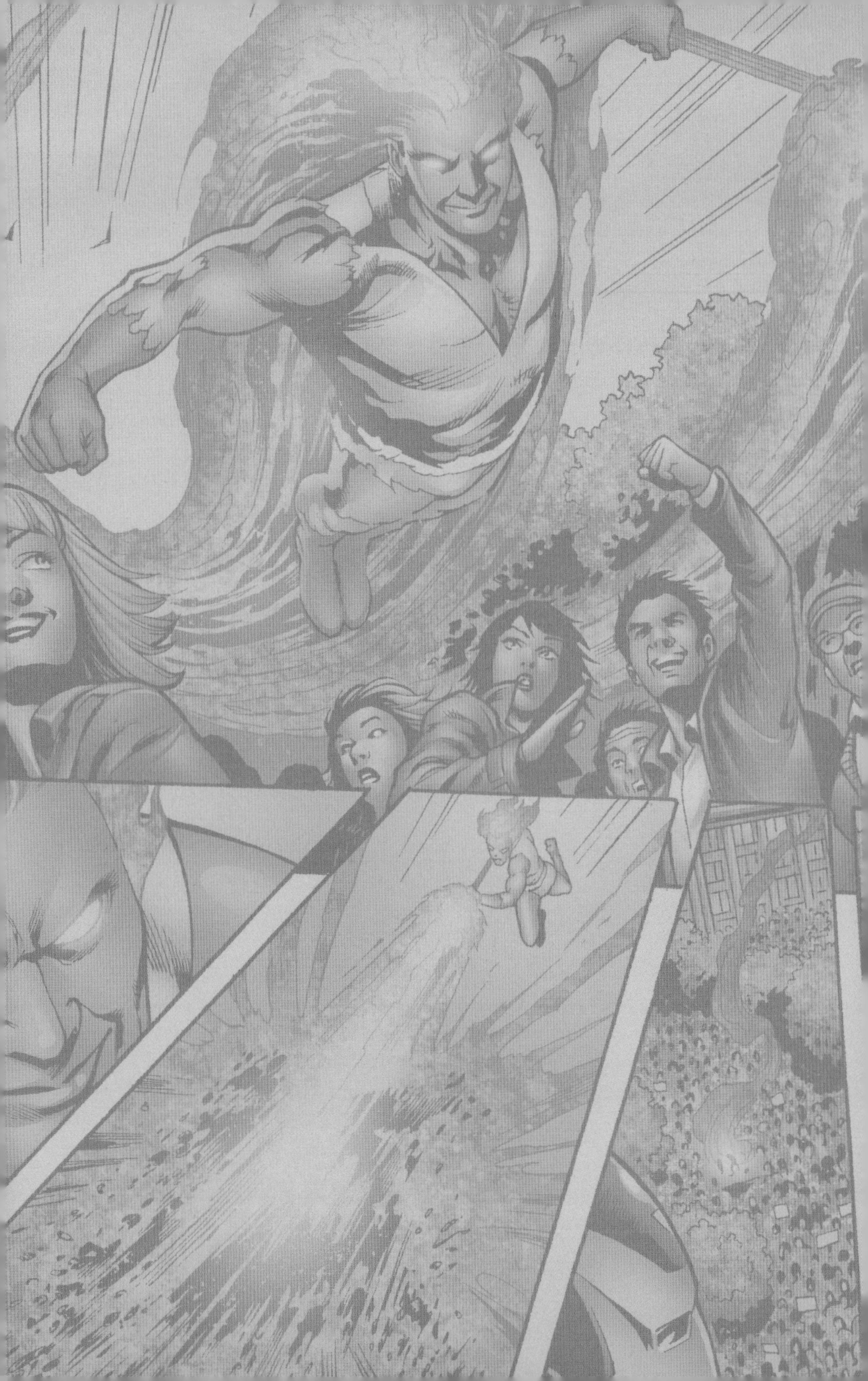

04

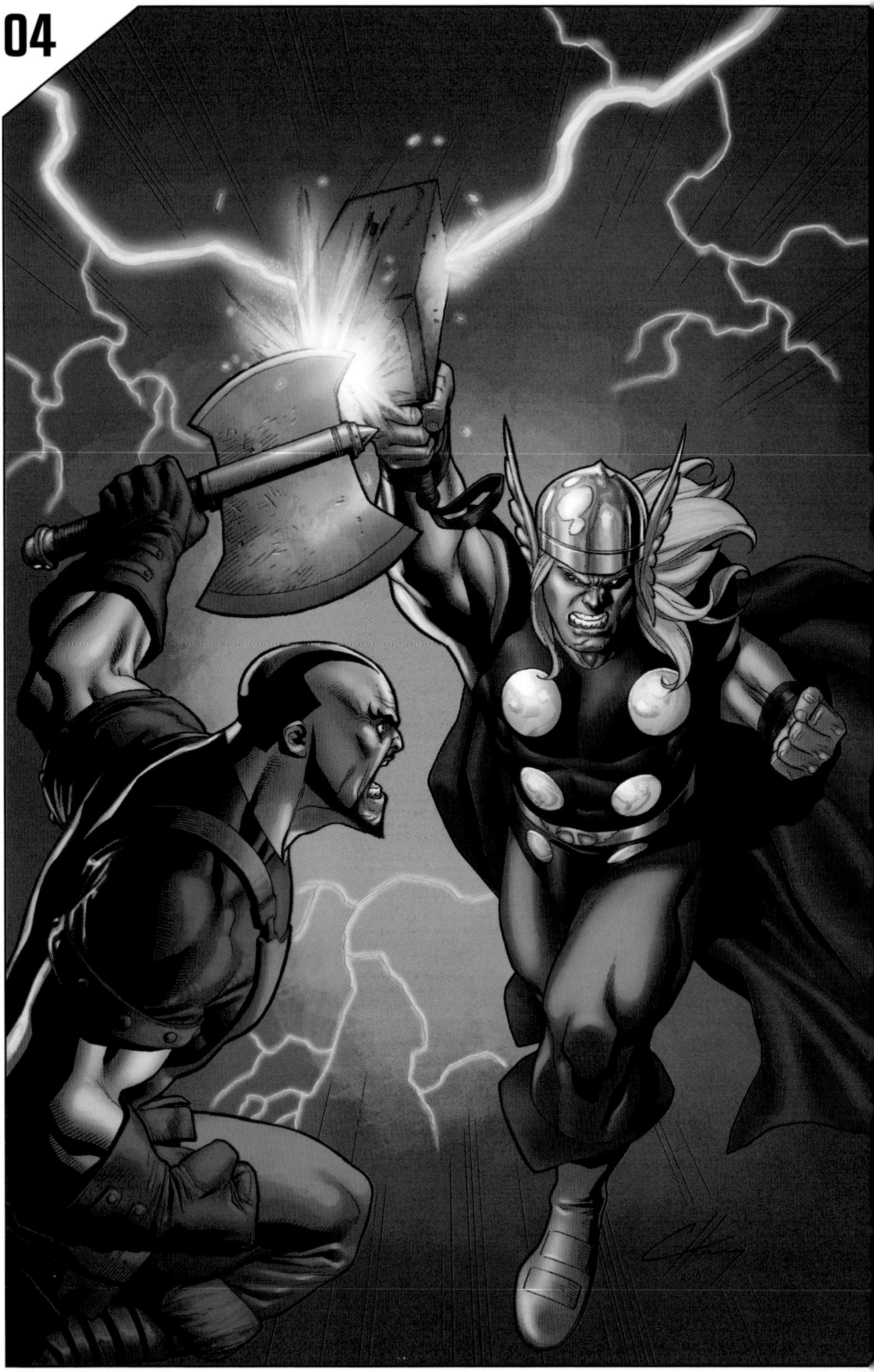

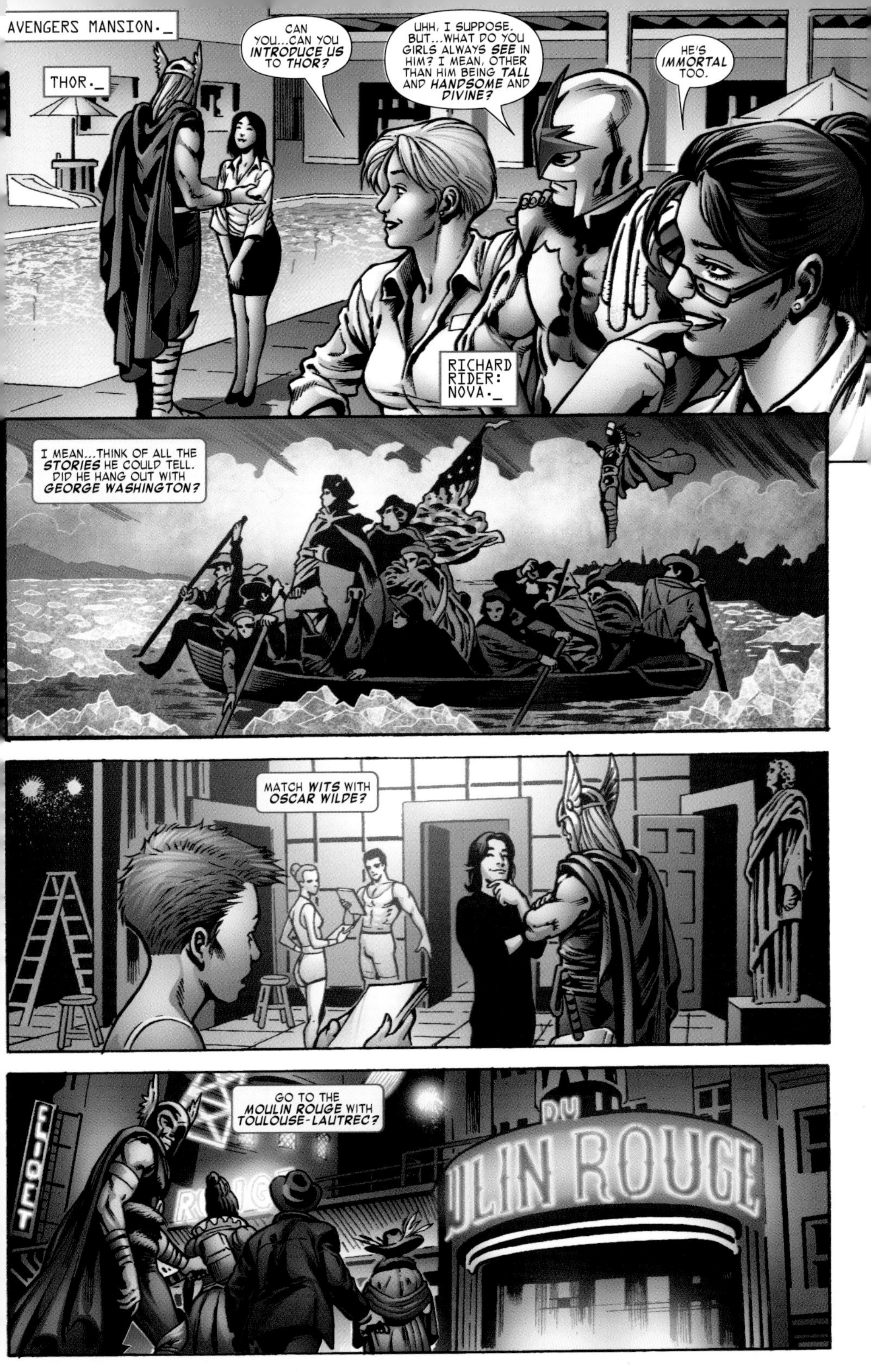
AVENGERS MANSION._
THOR._
CAN YOU...CAN YOU INTRODUCE US TO THOR?
UHH, I SUPPOSE. BUT...WHAT DO YOU GIRLS ALWAYS SEE IN HIM? I MEAN, OTHER THAN HIM BEING TALL AND HANDSOME AND DIVINE?
HE'S IMMORTAL TOO.
RICHARD RIDER: NOVA._
I MEAN...THINK OF ALL THE STORIES HE COULD TELL. DID HE HANG OUT WITH GEORGE WASHINGTON?
MATCH WITS WITH OSCAR WILDE?
GO TO THE MOULIN ROUGE WITH TOULOUSE-LAUTREC?
DU
ULIN ROUGE

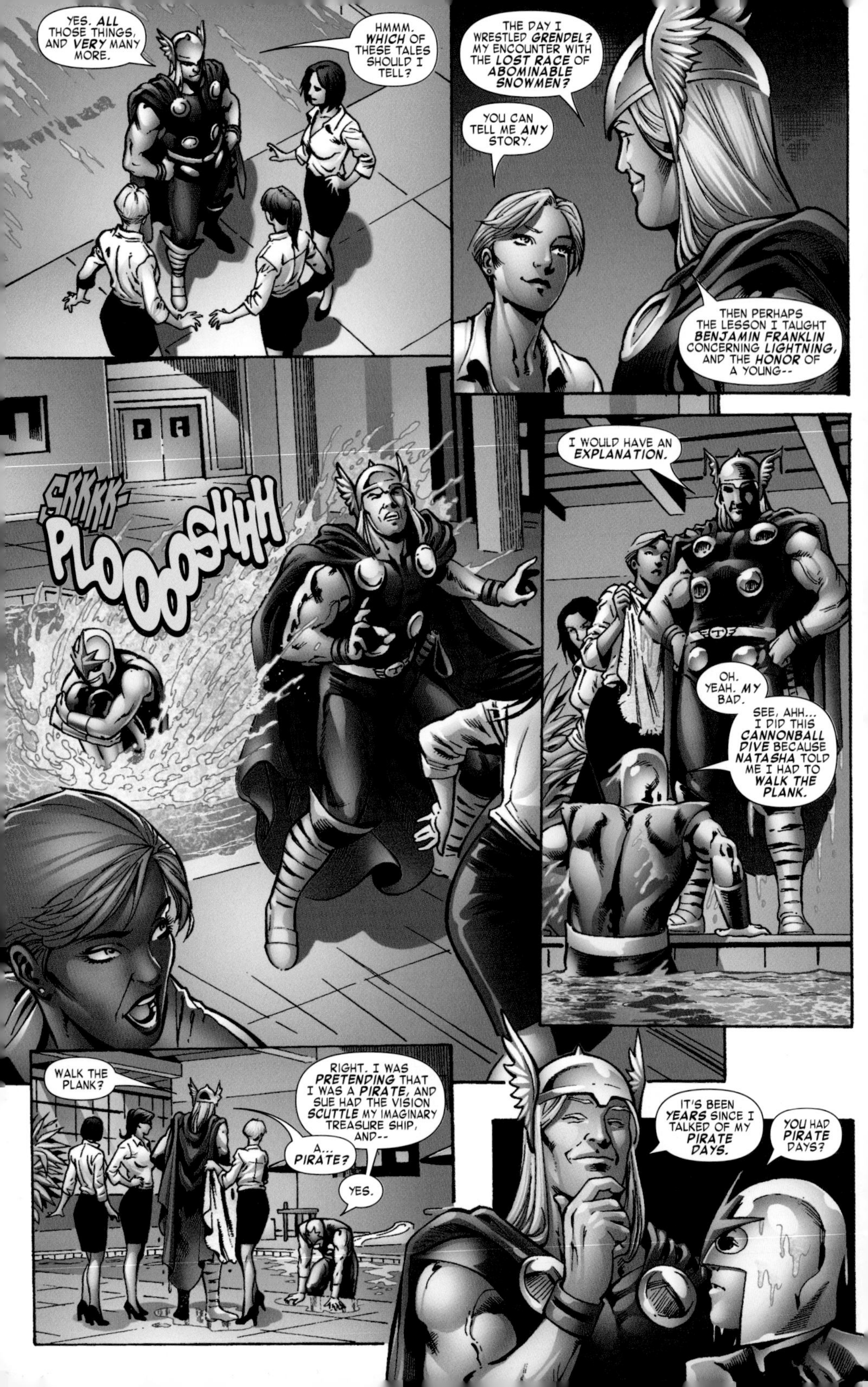
YES. ALL THOSE THINGS, AND VERY MANY MORE.
HMMM. WHICH OF THESE TALES SHOULD I TELL?
THE DAY I WRESTLED GRENDEL? MY ENCOUNTER WITH THE LOST RACE OF ABOMINABLE SNOWMEN?
YOU CAN TELL ME ANY STORY.
THEN PERHAPS THE LESSON I TAUGHT BENJAMIN FRANKLIN CONCERNING LIGHTNING, AND THE HONOR OF A YOUNG--
SKKKK-PLOOOOSHHH
I WOULD HAVE AN EXPLANATION.
OH. YEAH. MY BAD.
SEE, AHH... I DID THIS CANNONBALL DIVE BECAUSE NATASHA TOLD ME I HAD TO WALK THE PLANK.
WALK THE PLANK?
RIGHT. I WAS PRETENDING THAT I WAS A PIRATE, AND SUE HAD THE VISION SCUTTLE MY IMAGINARY TREASURE SHIP, AND--
A... PIRATE?
YES.
IT'S BEEN YEARS SINCE I TALKED OF MY PIRATE DAYS.
YOU HAD PIRATE DAYS?

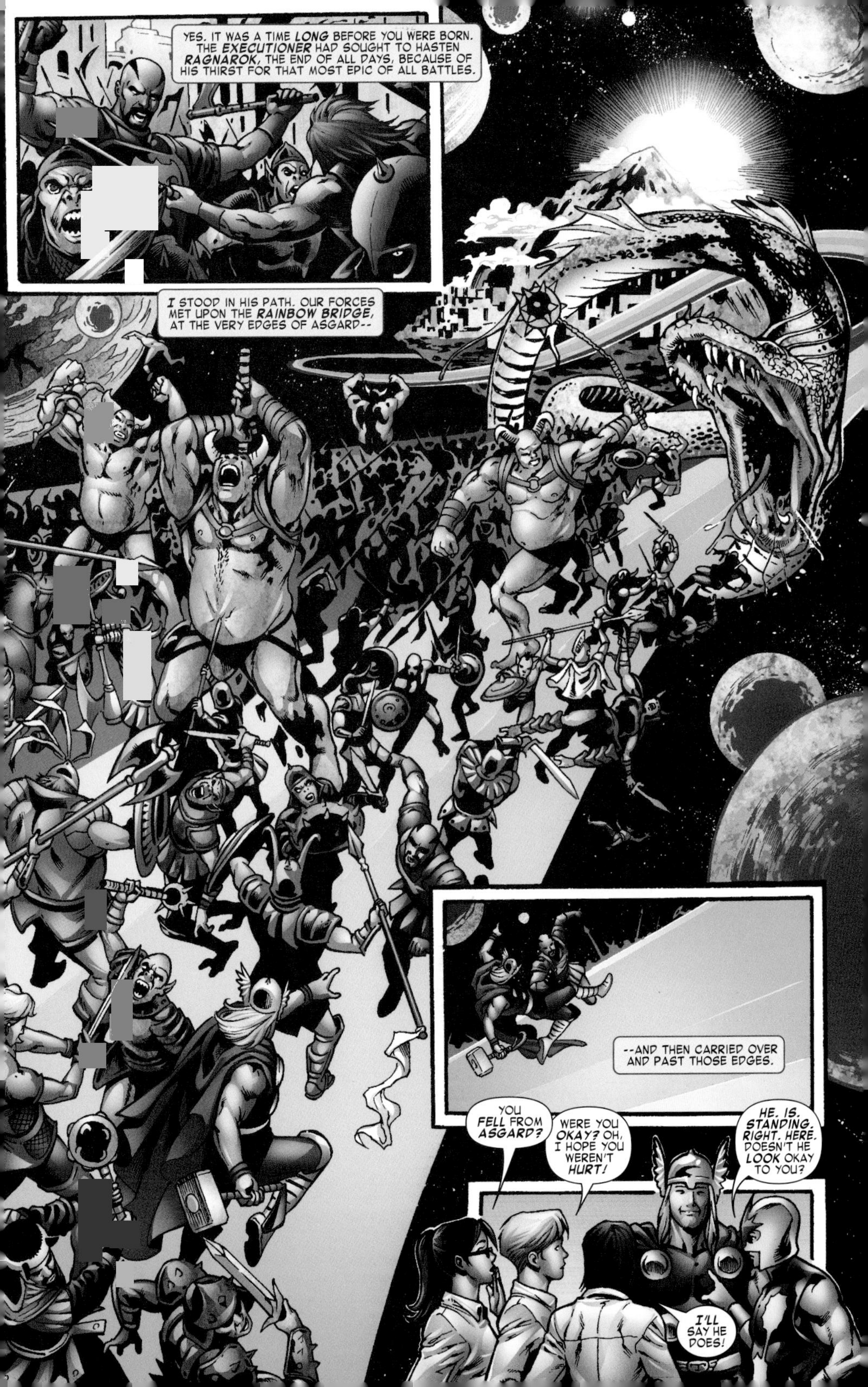
YES. IT WAS A TIME LONG BEFORE YOU WERE BORN. THE EXECUTIONER HAD SOUGHT TO HASTEN RAGNAROK, THE END OF ALL DAYS, BECAUSE OF HIS THIRST FOR THAT MOST EPIC OF ALL BATTLES.
I STOOD IN HIS PATH. OUR FORCES MET UPON THE RAINBOW BRIDGE, AT THE VERY EDGES OF ASGARD--
--AND THEN CARRIED OVER AND PAST THOSE EDGES.
YOU FELL FROM ASGARD?
WERE YOU OKAY? OH, I HOPE YOU WEREN'T HURT!
HE. IS. STANDING. RIGHT. HERE. DOESN'T HE LOOK OKAY TO YOU?
I'LL SAY HE DOES!

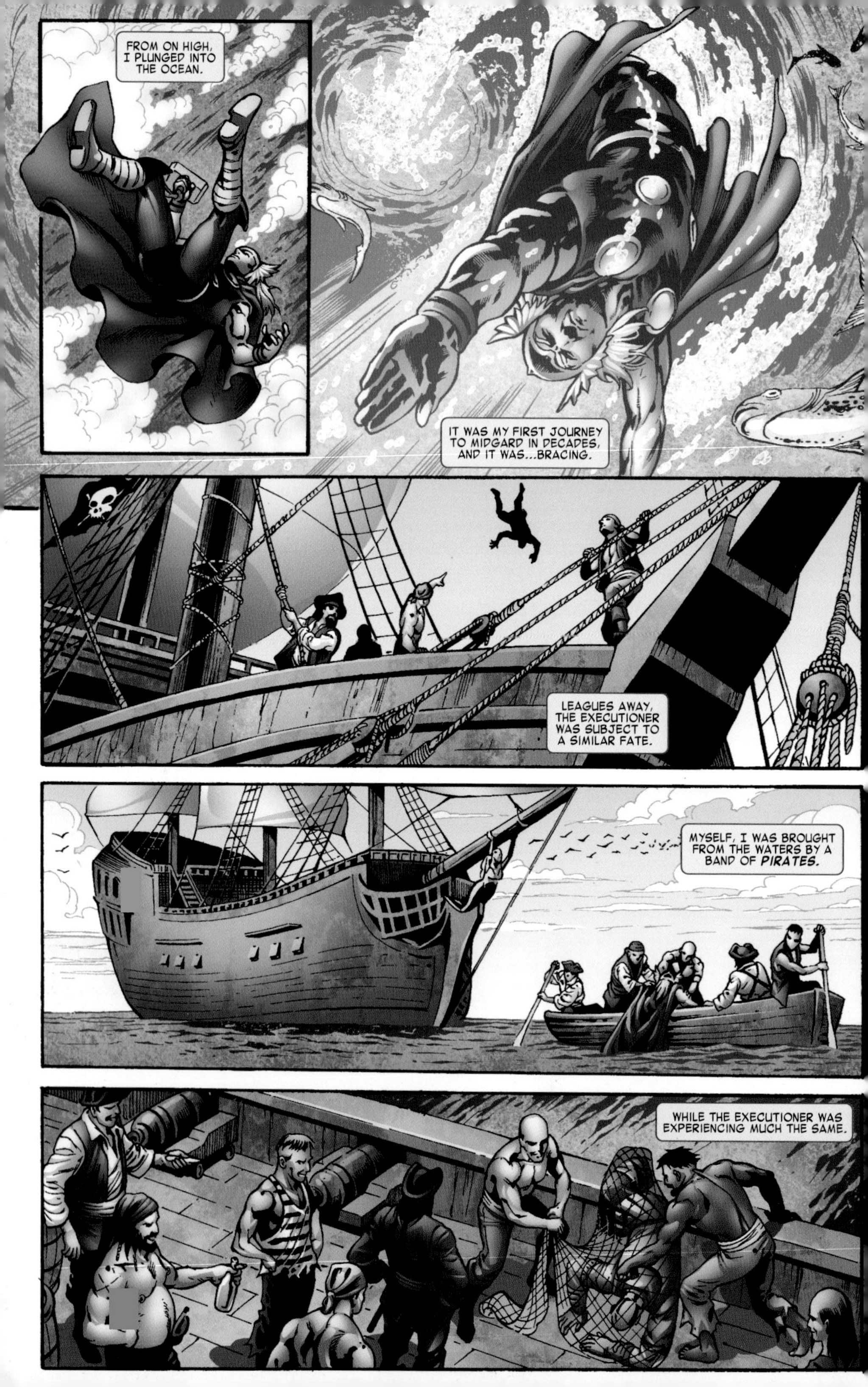
FROM ON HIGH, I PLUNGED INTO THE OCEAN.
IT WAS MY FIRST JOURNEY TO MIDGARD IN DECADES, AND IT WAS...BRACING.
LEAGUES AWAY, THE EXECUTIONER WAS SUBJECT TO A SIMILAR FATE.
MYSELF, I WAS BROUGHT FROM THE WATERS BY A BAND OF *PIRATES.*
WHILE THE EXECUTIONER WAS EXPERIENCING MUCH THE SAME.

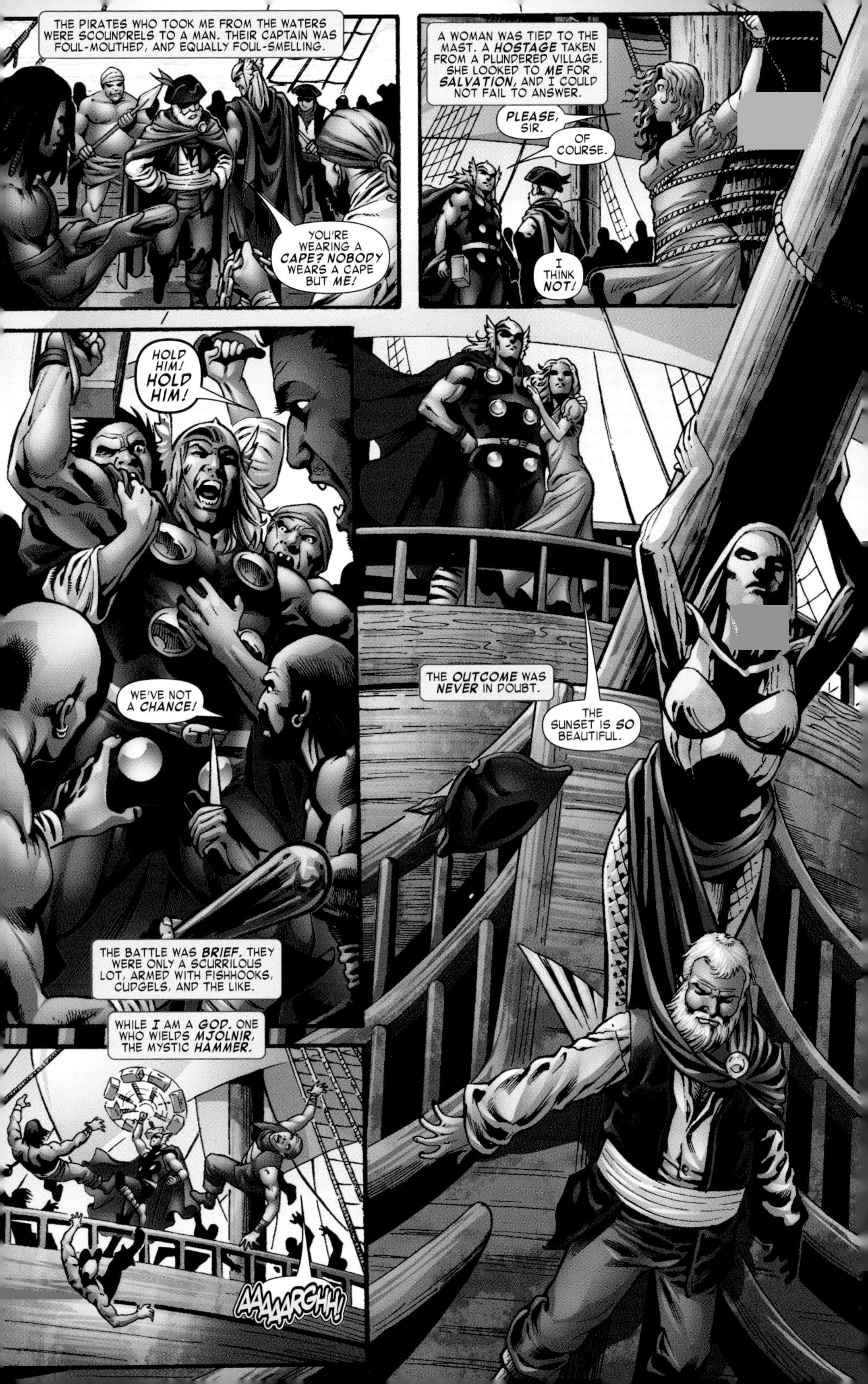
THE PIRATES WHO TOOK ME FROM THE WATERS WERE SCOUNDRELS TO A MAN. THEIR CAPTAIN WAS FOUL-MOUTHED, AND EQUALLY FOUL-SMELLING.
YOU'RE WEARING A CAPE? NOBODY WEARS A CAPE BUT ME!
A WOMAN WAS TIED TO THE MAST. A HOSTAGE TAKEN FROM A PLUNDERED VILLAGE. SHE LOOKED TO ME FOR SALVATION, AND I COULD NOT FAIL TO ANSWER.
PLEASE, SIR.
OF COURSE.
I THINK NOT!
HOLD HIM! HOLD HIM!
WE'VE NOT A CHANCE!
THE BATTLE WAS BRIEF. THEY WERE ONLY A SCURRILOUS LOT, ARMED WITH FISHHOOKS, CUDGELS, AND THE LIKE.
WHILE I AM A GOD. ONE WHO WIELDS MJOLNIR, THE MYSTIC HAMMER.
AAAAARGHH!
THE OUTCOME WAS NEVER IN DOUBT.
THE SUNSET IS SO BEAUTIFUL.

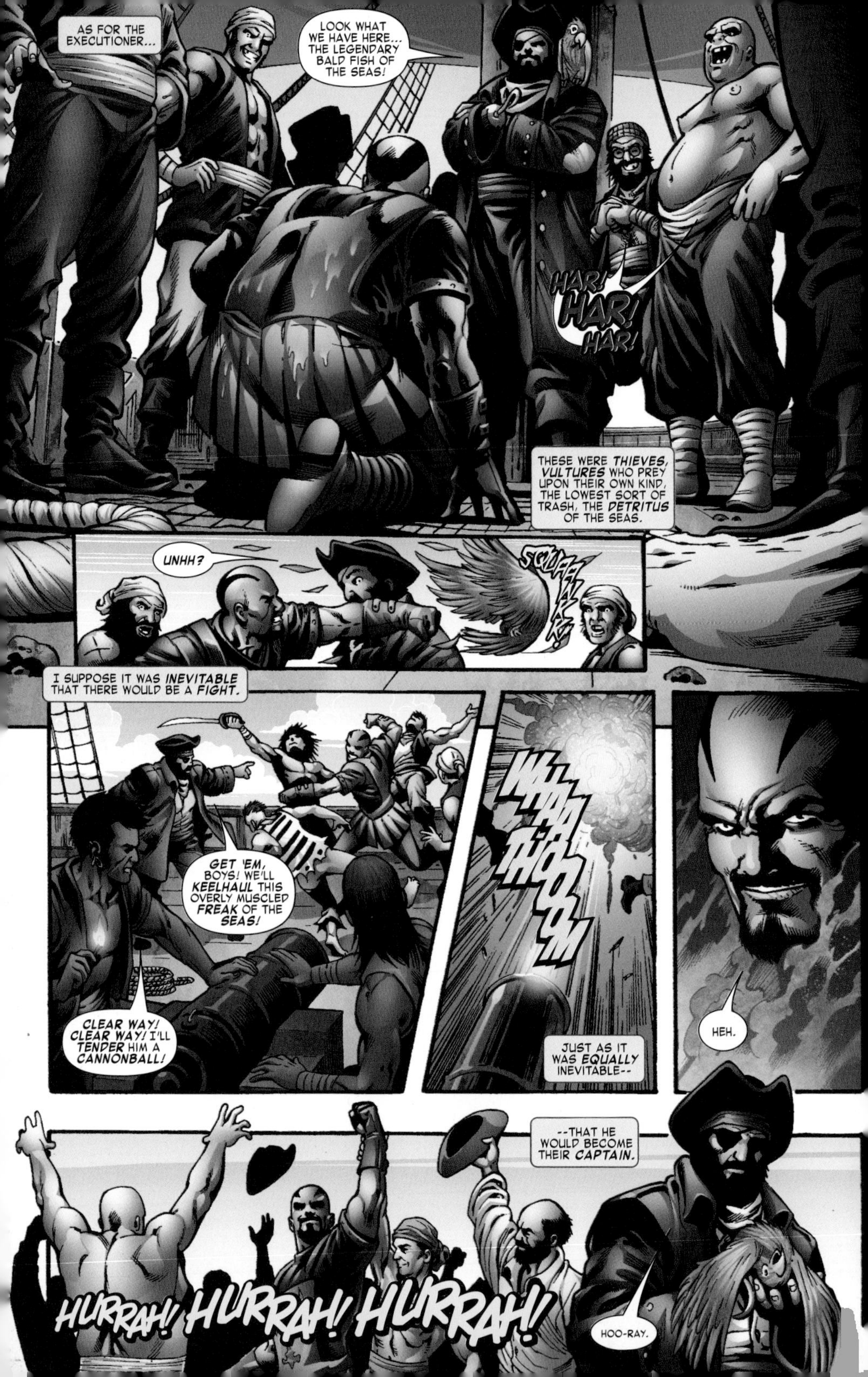

AS FOR THE EXECUTIONER...
LOOK WHAT WE HAVE HERE... THE LEGENDARY BALD FISH OF THE SEAS!
HAR! HAR! HAR!
THESE WERE THIEVES, VULTURES WHO PREY UPON THEIR OWN KIND, THE LOWEST SORT OF TRASH, THE DETRITUS OF THE SEAS.
UNHH?
I SUPPOSE IT WAS INEVITABLE THAT THERE WOULD BE A FIGHT.
GET 'EM, BOYS! WE'LL KEELHAUL THIS OVERLY MUSCLED FREAK OF THE SEAS!
CLEAR WAY! CLEAR WAY! I'LL TENDER HIM A CANNONBALL!
JUST AS IT WAS EQUALLY INEVITABLE--
HEH.
--THAT HE WOULD BECOME THEIR CAPTAIN.
HURRAH! HURRAH! HURRAH!
HOO-RAY.

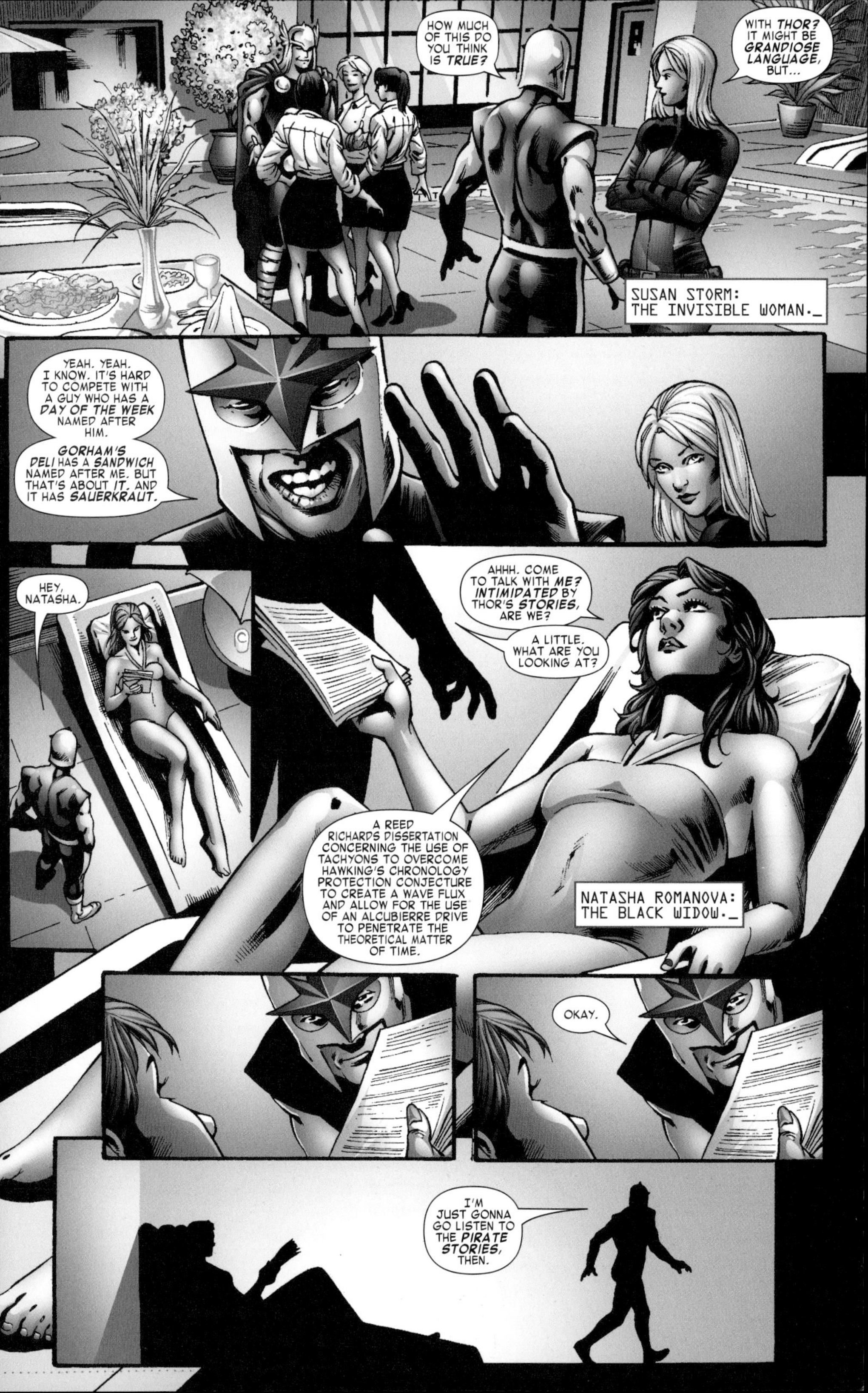

HOW MUCH OF THIS DO YOU THINK IS *TRUE?*
WITH *THOR?* IT MIGHT BE *GRANDIOSE LANGUAGE,* BUT...
SUSAN STORM: THE INVISIBLE WOMAN._
YEAH. YEAH. I KNOW. IT'S HARD TO COMPETE WITH A GUY WHO HAS A *DAY OF THE WEEK* NAMED AFTER HIM.
GORHAM'S DELI HAS A *SANDWICH* NAMED AFTER ME. BUT THAT'S ABOUT *IT.* AND IT HAS *SAUERKRAUT.*
HEY, NATASHA.
AHHH. COME TO TALK WITH *ME? INTIMIDATED* BY THOR'S *STORIES,* ARE WE?
A LITTLE. WHAT ARE YOU LOOKING AT?
A REED RICHARDS DISSERTATION CONCERNING THE USE OF TACHYONS TO OVERCOME HAWKING'S CHRONOLOGY PROTECTION CONJECTURE TO CREATE A WAVE FLUX AND ALLOW FOR THE USE OF AN ALCUBIERRE DRIVE TO PENETRATE THE THEORETICAL MATTER OF TIME.
NATASHA ROMANOVA: THE BLACK WIDOW._
OKAY.
I'M JUST GONNA GO LISTEN TO THE *PIRATE STORIES,* THEN.

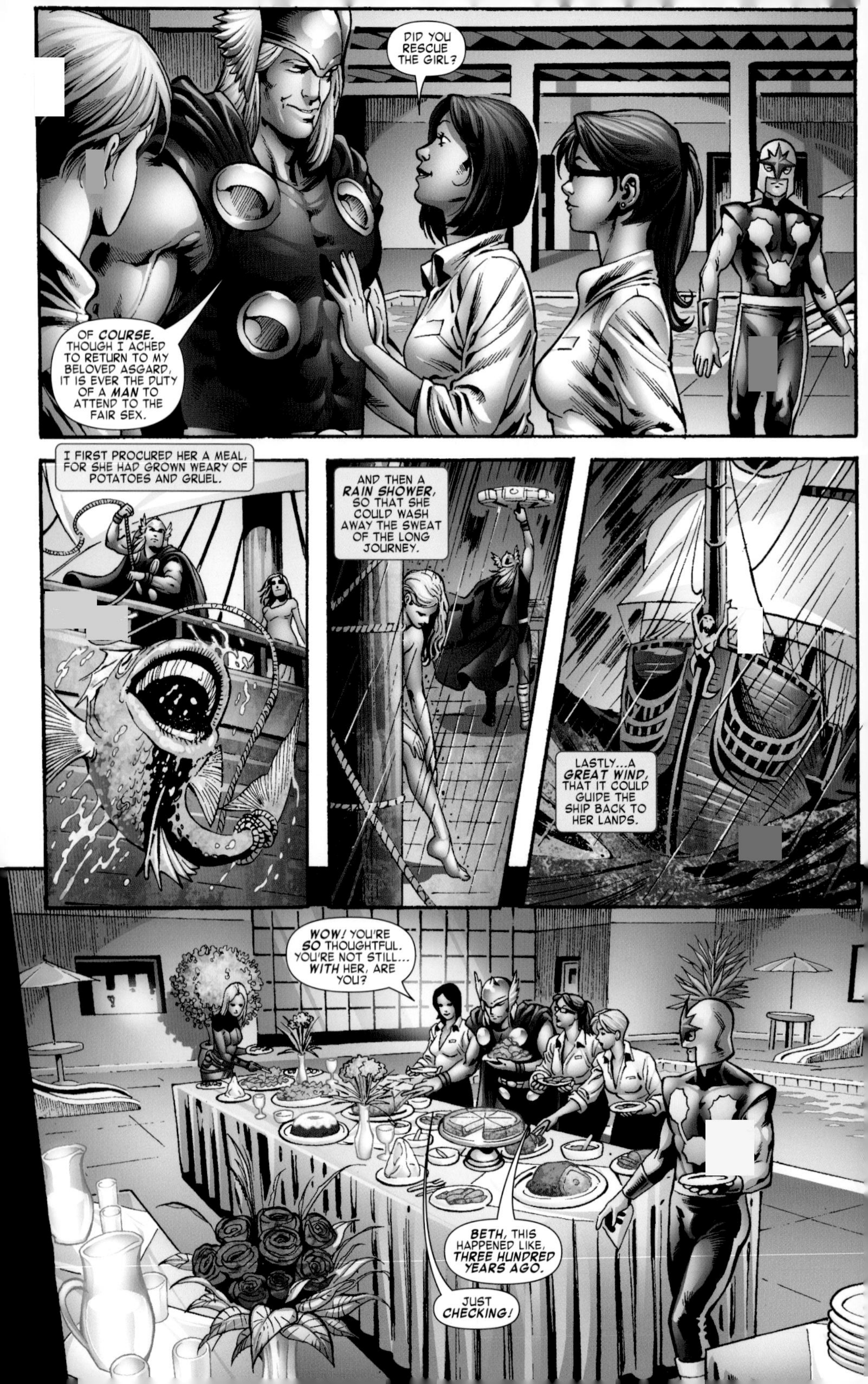
DID YOU RESCUE THE GIRL?
OF COURSE. THOUGH I ACHED TO RETURN TO MY BELOVED ASGARD, IT IS EVER THE DUTY OF A MAN TO ATTEND TO THE FAIR SEX.
I FIRST PROCURED HER A MEAL, FOR SHE HAD GROWN WEARY OF POTATOES AND GRUEL.
AND THEN A RAIN SHOWER, SO THAT SHE COULD WASH AWAY THE SWEAT OF THE LONG JOURNEY.
LASTLY...A GREAT WIND, THAT IT COULD GUIDE THE SHIP BACK TO HER LANDS.
WOW! YOU'RE SO THOUGHTFUL. YOU'RE NOT STILL... WITH HER, ARE YOU?
BETH, THIS HAPPENED LIKE, THREE HUNDRED YEARS AGO.
JUST CHECKING!

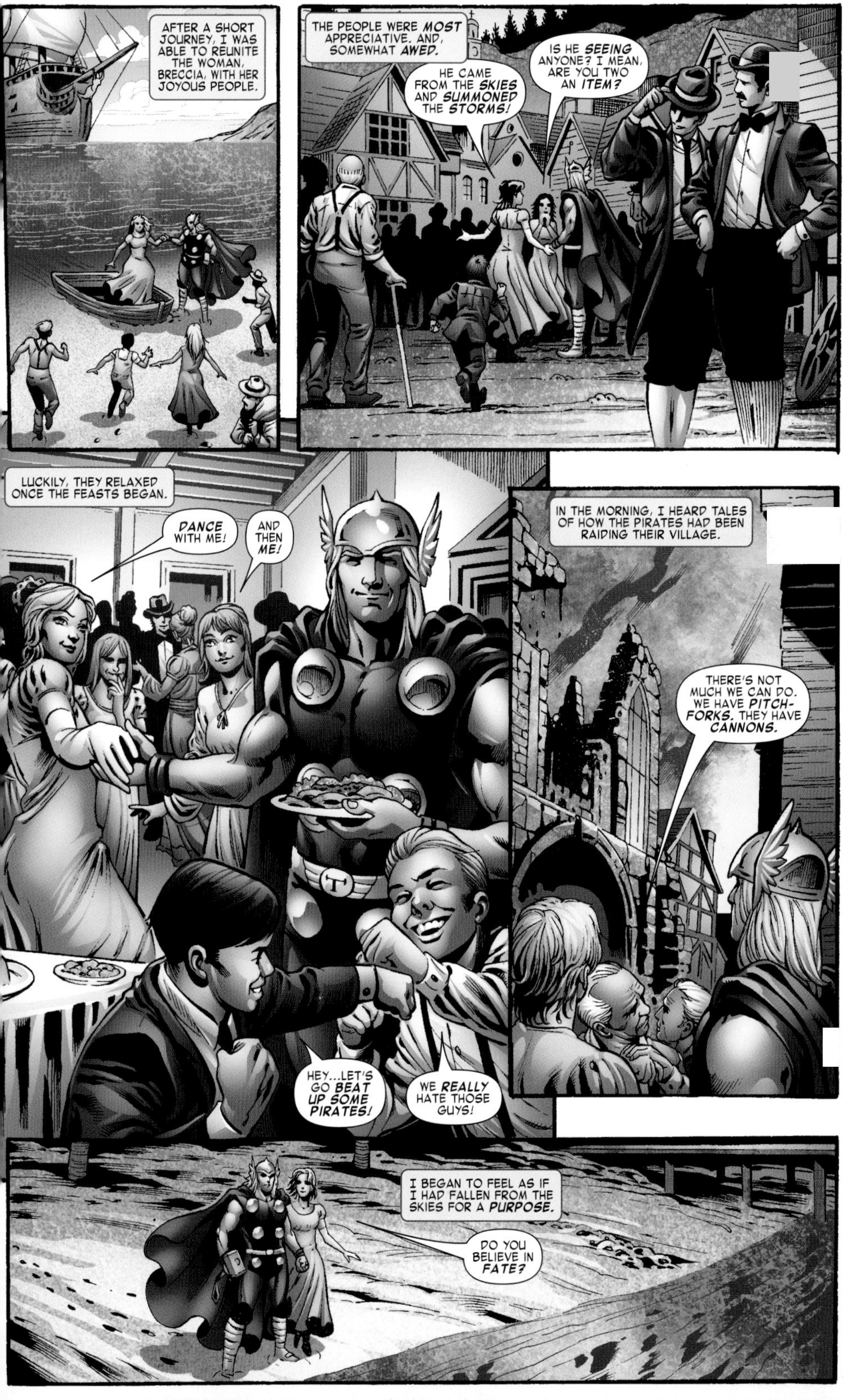
AFTER A SHORT JOURNEY, I WAS ABLE TO REUNITE THE WOMAN, BRECCIA, WITH HER JOYOUS PEOPLE.
THE PEOPLE WERE *MOST* APPRECIATIVE. AND, SOMEWHAT *AWED*.
HE CAME FROM THE *SKIES* AND *SUMMONED* THE *STORMS*!
IS HE *SEEING* ANYONE? I MEAN, ARE YOU TWO AN *ITEM?*
LUCKILY, THEY RELAXED ONCE THE FEASTS BEGAN.
DANCE WITH ME!
AND THEN *ME!*
HEY...LET'S GO *BEAT UP SOME PIRATES!*
WE *REALLY* HATE THOSE GUYS!
IN THE MORNING, I HEARD TALES OF HOW THE PIRATES HAD BEEN RAIDING THEIR VILLAGE.
THERE'S NOT MUCH WE CAN DO. WE HAVE *PITCH-FORKS.* THEY HAVE *CANNONS.*
I BEGAN TO FEEL AS IF I HAD FALLEN FROM THE SKIES FOR A *PURPOSE.*
DO YOU BELIEVE IN *FATE?*

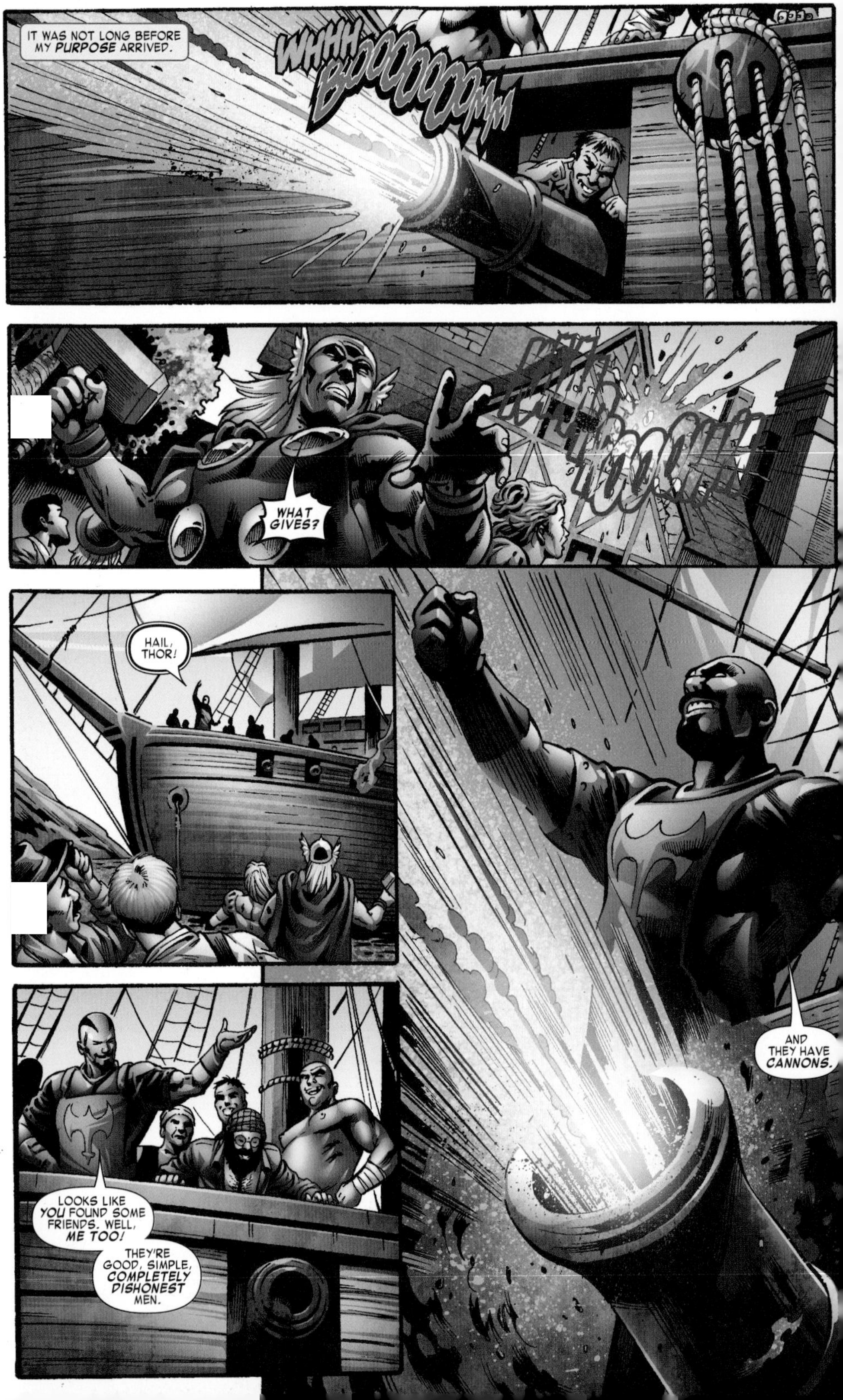
IT WAS NOT LONG BEFORE MY PURPOSE ARRIVED.
WHAT GIVES?
HAIL, THOR!
LOOKS LIKE YOU FOUND SOME FRIENDS. WELL, ME TOO!
THEY'RE GOOD, SIMPLE, COMPLETELY DISHONEST MEN.
AND THEY HAVE CANNONS.

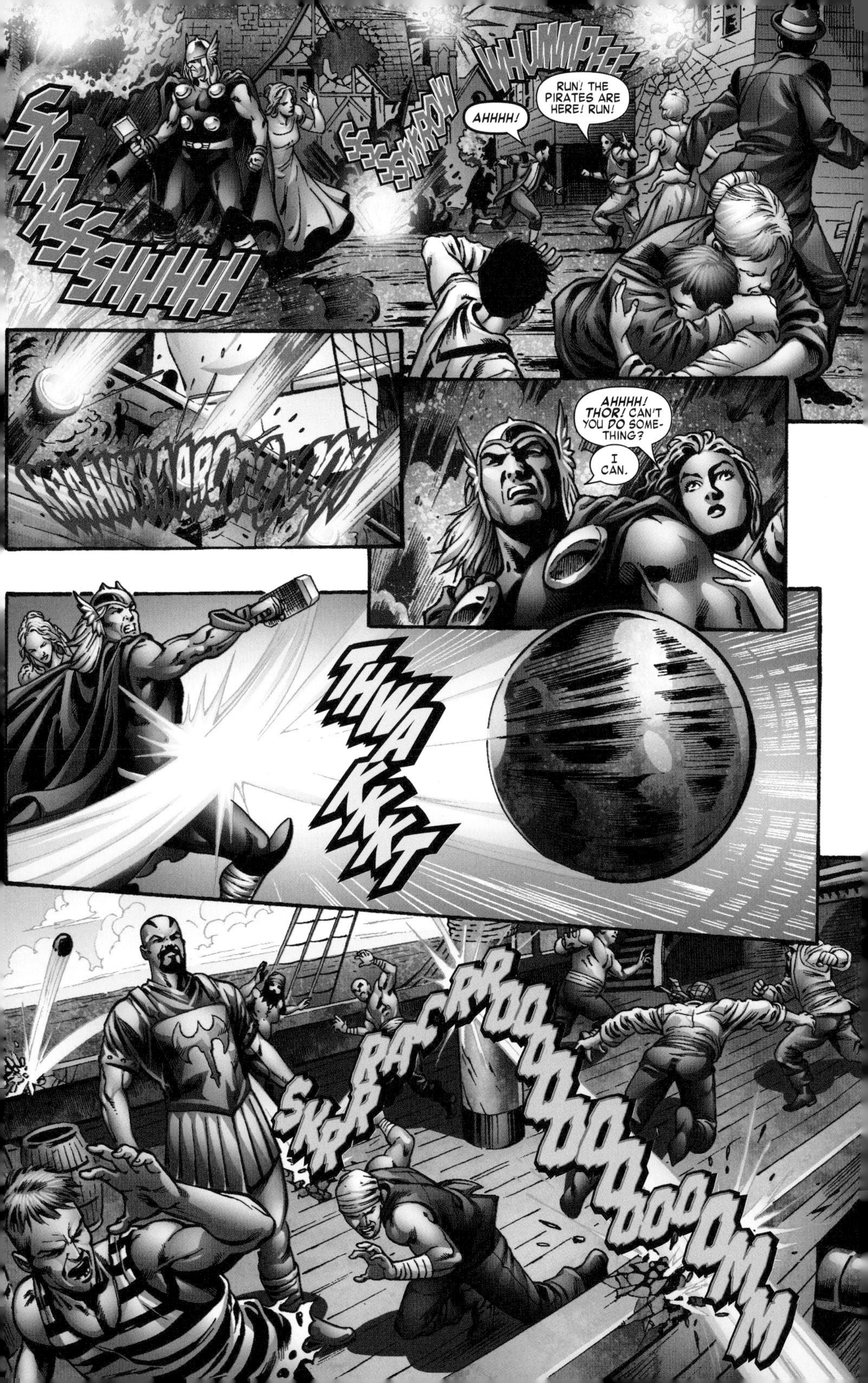
SKRAASSHHHHH
SSSSSKKROW
WHUMMPFFF
AHHHH!
RUN! THE PIRATES ARE HERE! RUN!
AHHHH! THOR! CAN'T YOU DO SOMETHING?
I CAN.
THWAKKKKT
SKRRRACRROOOOOOOOOOOOOOOMM

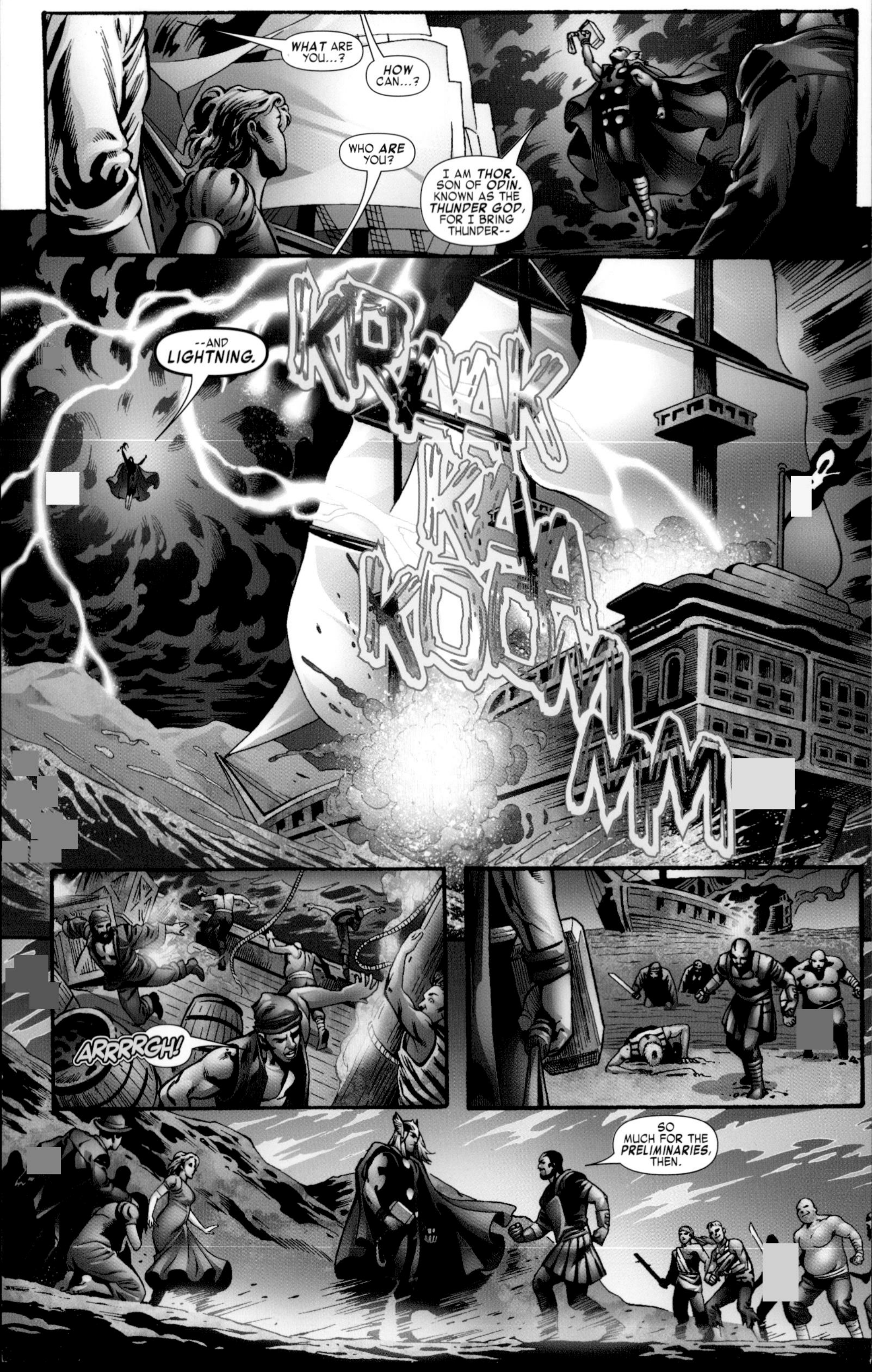
WHAT ARE YOU...?
HOW CAN...?
WHO ARE YOU?
I AM THOR. SON OF ODIN. KNOWN AS THE THUNDER GOD, FOR I BRING THUNDER--
--AND LIGHTNING.
ARRRRGH!
SO MUCH FOR THE PRELIMINARIES, THEN.

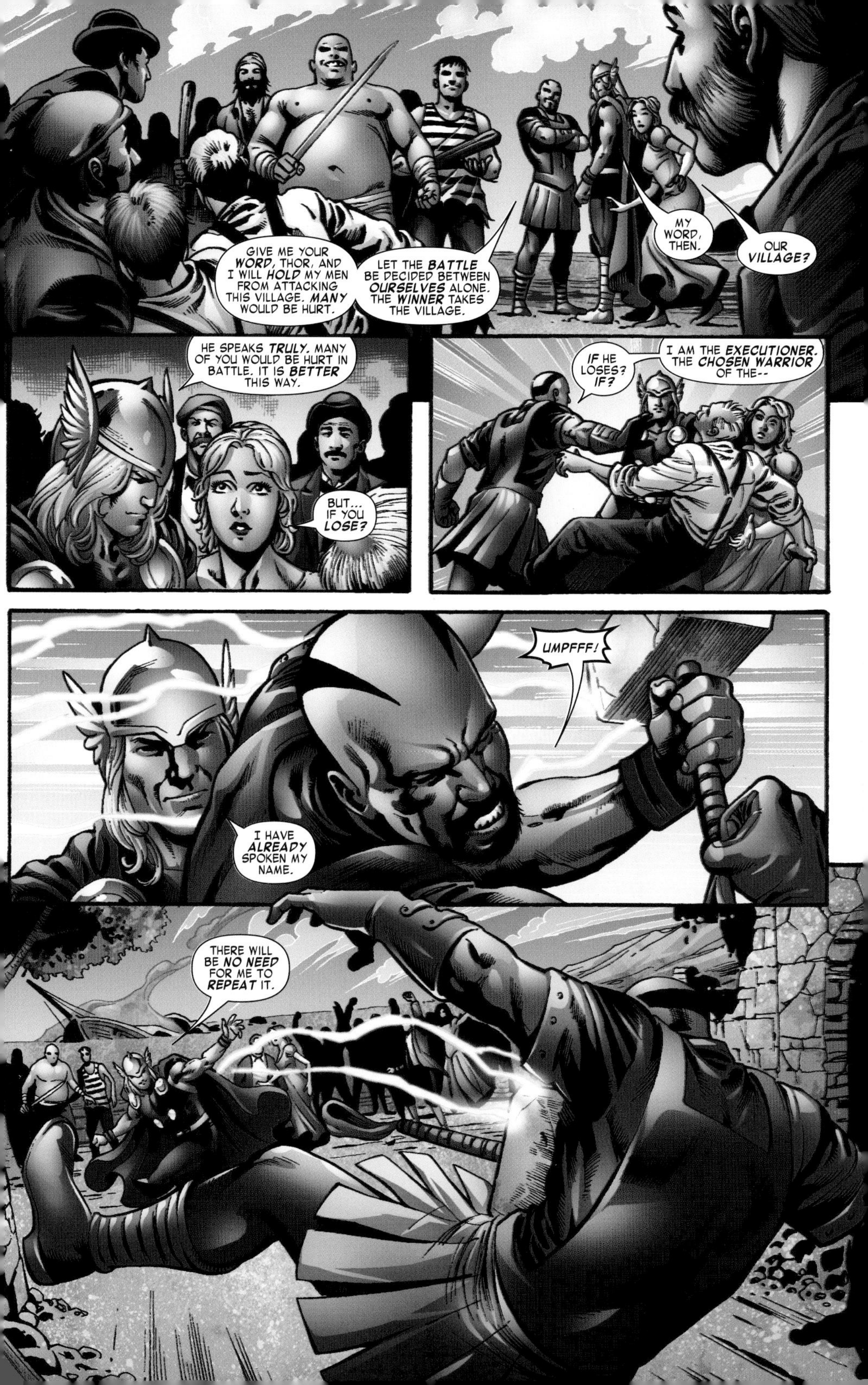

GIVE ME YOUR WORD, THOR, AND I WILL HOLD MY MEN FROM ATTACKING THIS VILLAGE. MANY WOULD BE HURT.
LET THE BATTLE BE DECIDED BETWEEN OURSELVES ALONE. THE WINNER TAKES THE VILLAGE.
MY WORD, THEN.
OUR VILLAGE?
HE SPEAKS TRULY. MANY OF YOU WOULD BE HURT IN BATTLE. IT IS BETTER THIS WAY.
BUT... IF YOU LOSE?
IF HE LOSES? IF?
I AM THE EXECUTIONER. THE CHOSEN WARRIOR OF THE--
UMPFFF!
I HAVE ALREADY SPOKEN MY NAME.
THERE WILL BE NO NEED FOR ME TO REPEAT IT.

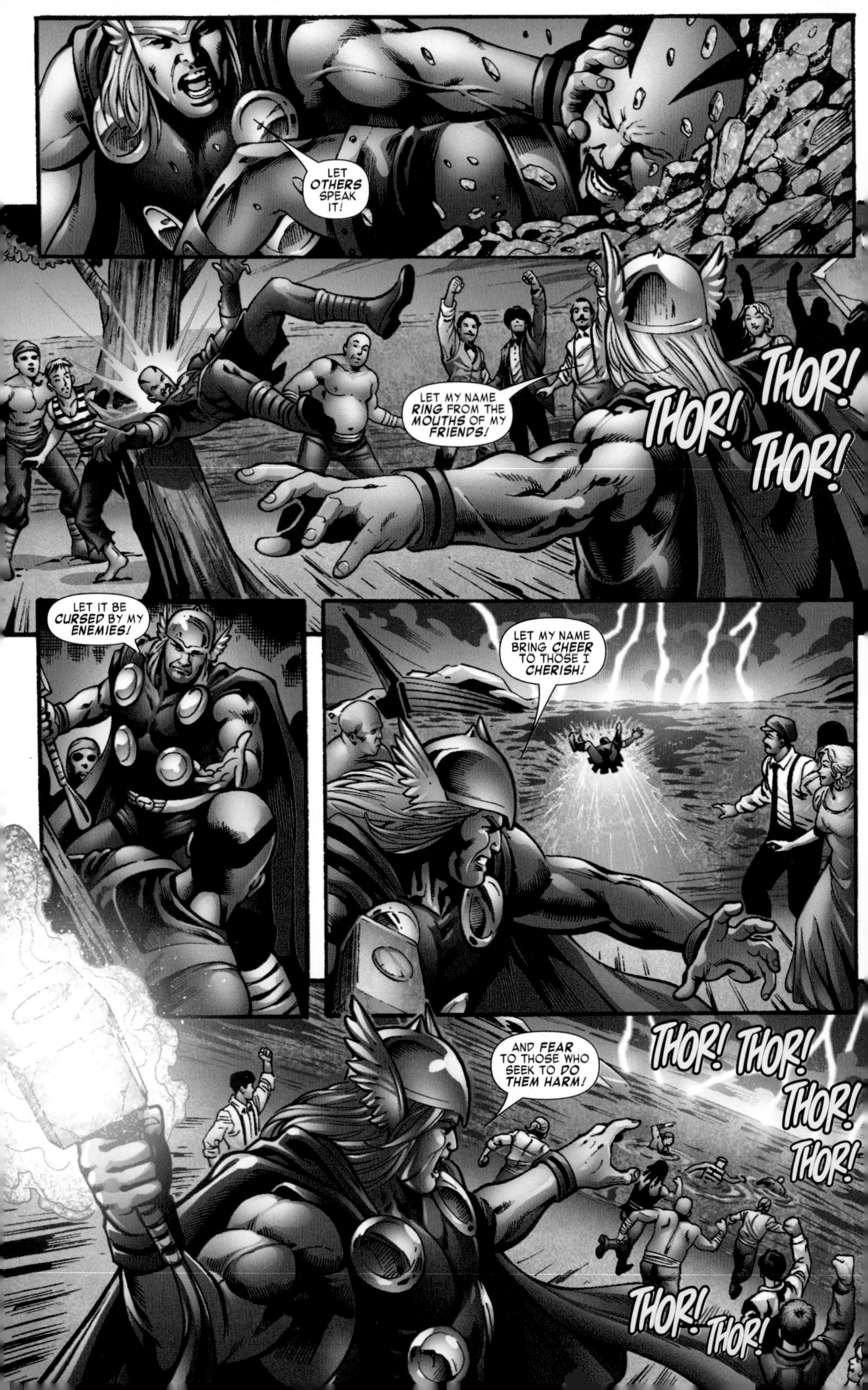
LET OTHERS SPEAK IT!
LET MY NAME RING FROM THE MOUTHS OF MY FRIENDS!
THOR! THOR! THOR!
LET IT BE CURSED BY MY ENEMIES!
LET MY NAME BRING CHEER TO THOSE I CHERISH!
AND FEAR TO THOSE WHO SEEK TO DO THEM HARM!
THOR! THOR! THOR! THOR!
THOR! THOR!

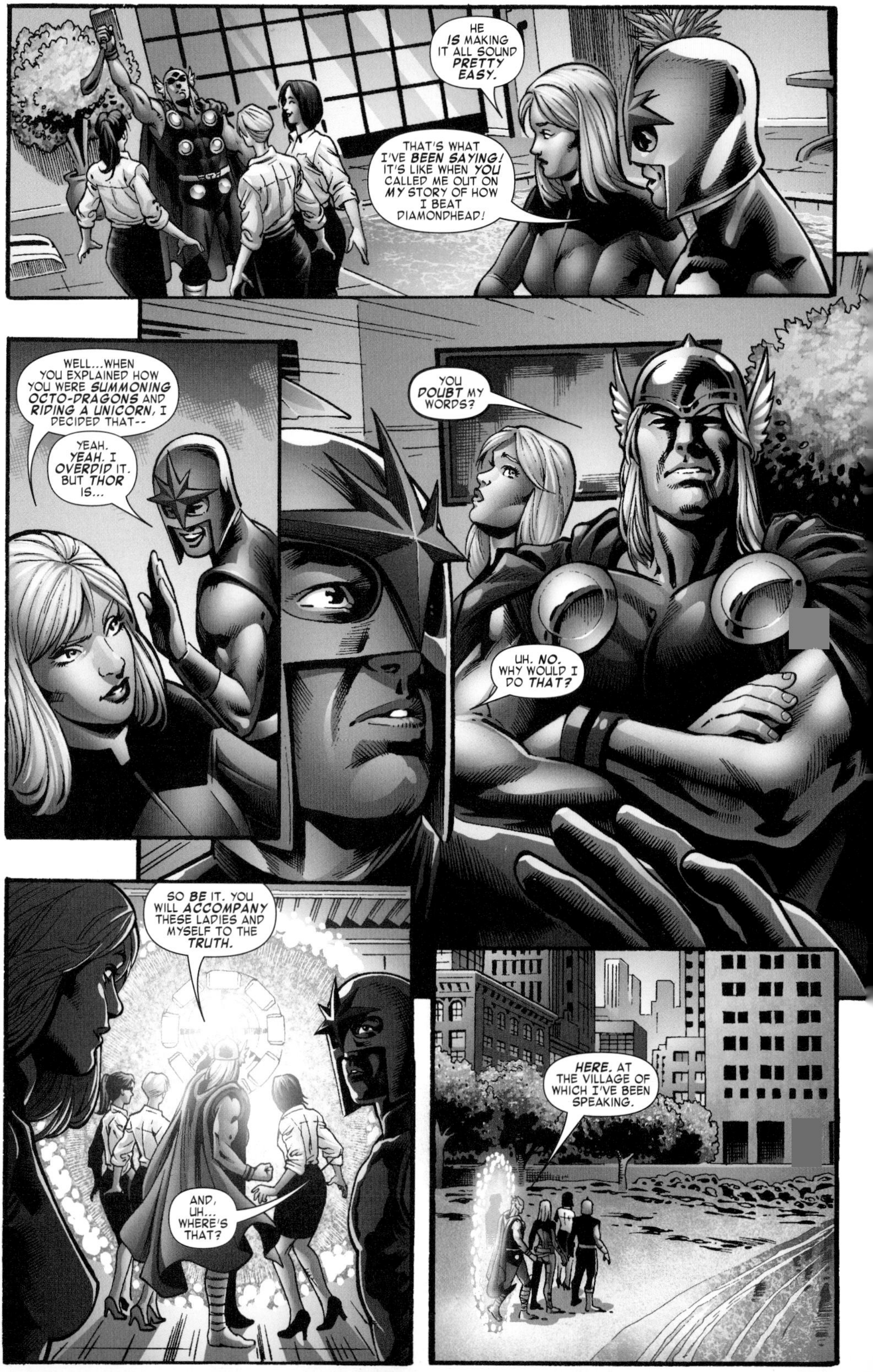
HE IS MAKING IT ALL SOUND PRETTY EASY.
THAT'S WHAT I'VE BEEN SAYING! IT'S LIKE WHEN YOU CALLED ME OUT ON MY STORY OF HOW I BEAT DIAMONDHEAD!
WELL...WHEN YOU EXPLAINED HOW YOU WERE SUMMONING OCTO-DRAGONS AND RIDING A UNICORN, I DECIDED THAT--
YEAH. YEAH. I OVERDID IT. BUT THOR IS...
YOU DOUBT MY WORDS?
UH. NO. WHY WOULD I DO THAT?
SO BE IT. YOU WILL ACCOMPANY THESE LADIES AND MYSELF TO THE TRUTH.
AND, UH... WHERE'S THAT?
HERE. AT THE VILLAGE OF WHICH I'VE BEEN SPEAKING.

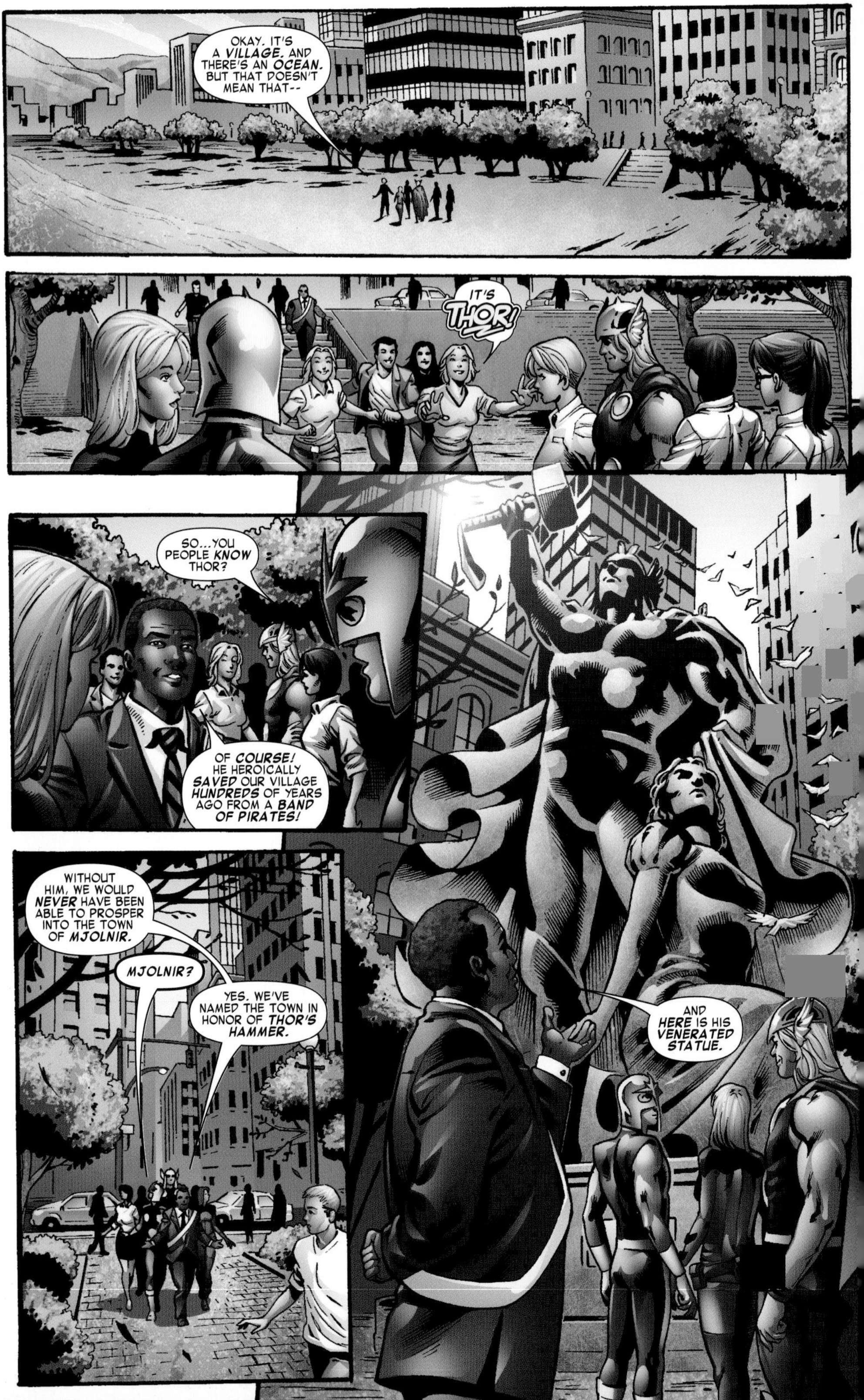

OKAY. IT'S A VILLAGE. AND THERE'S AN OCEAN. BUT THAT DOESN'T MEAN THAT--
IT'S THOR!
SO...YOU PEOPLE KNOW THOR?
OF COURSE! HE HEROICALLY SAVED OUR VILLAGE HUNDREDS OF YEARS AGO FROM A BAND OF PIRATES!
WITHOUT HIM, WE WOULD NEVER HAVE BEEN ABLE TO PROSPER INTO THE TOWN OF MJOLNIR.
MJOLNIR?
YES. WE'VE NAMED THE TOWN IN HONOR OF THOR'S HAMMER.
AND HERE IS HIS VENERATED STATUE.

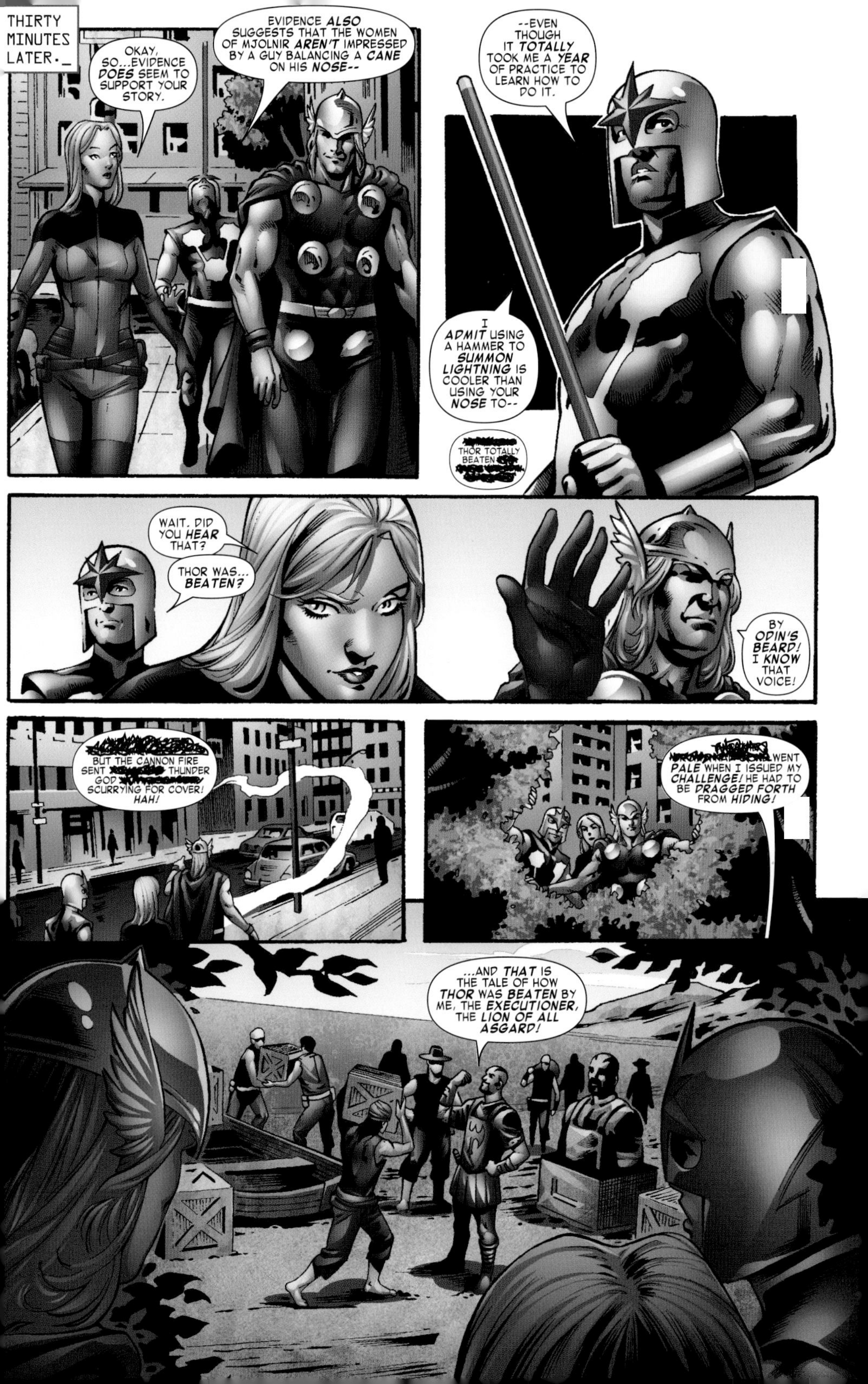

THIRTY MINUTES LATER._
OKAY, SO...EVIDENCE DOES SEEM TO SUPPORT YOUR STORY.
EVIDENCE ALSO SUGGESTS THAT THE WOMEN OF MJOLNIR AREN'T IMPRESSED BY A GUY BALANCING A CANE ON HIS NOSE--
--EVEN THOUGH IT TOTALLY TOOK ME A YEAR OF PRACTICE TO LEARN HOW TO DO IT.
I ADMIT USING A HAMMER TO SUMMON LIGHTNING IS COOLER THAN USING YOUR NOSE TO--
[redacted] THOR TOTALLY BEATEN [redacted]
WAIT. DID YOU HEAR THAT?
THOR WAS... BEATEN?
BY ODIN'S BEARD! I KNOW THAT VOICE!
[redacted] BUT THE CANNON FIRE SENT [redacted] THUNDER GOD [redacted] SCURRYING FOR COVER! HAH!
[redacted] WENT PALE WHEN I ISSUED MY CHALLENGE! HE HAD TO BE DRAGGED FORTH FROM HIDING!
...AND THAT IS THE TALE OF HOW THOR WAS BEATEN BY ME, THE EXECUTIONER, THE LION OF ALL ASGARD!

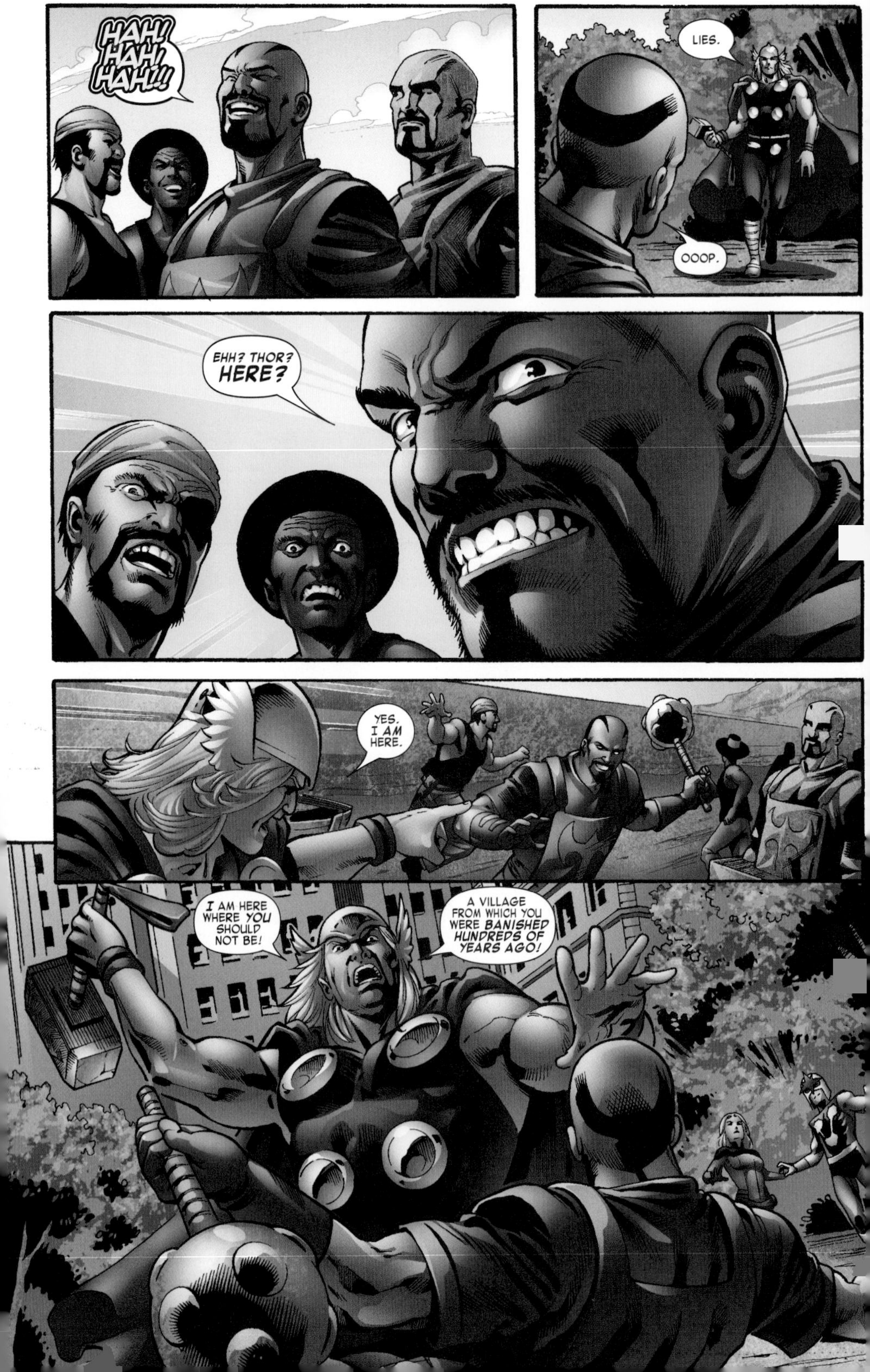
HAH! HAH! HAH!!!
LIES.
OOOP.
EHH? THOR? HERE?
YES. I AM HERE.
I AM HERE WHERE YOU SHOULD NOT BE!
A VILLAGE FROM WHICH YOU WERE BANISHED HUNDREDS OF YEARS AGO!

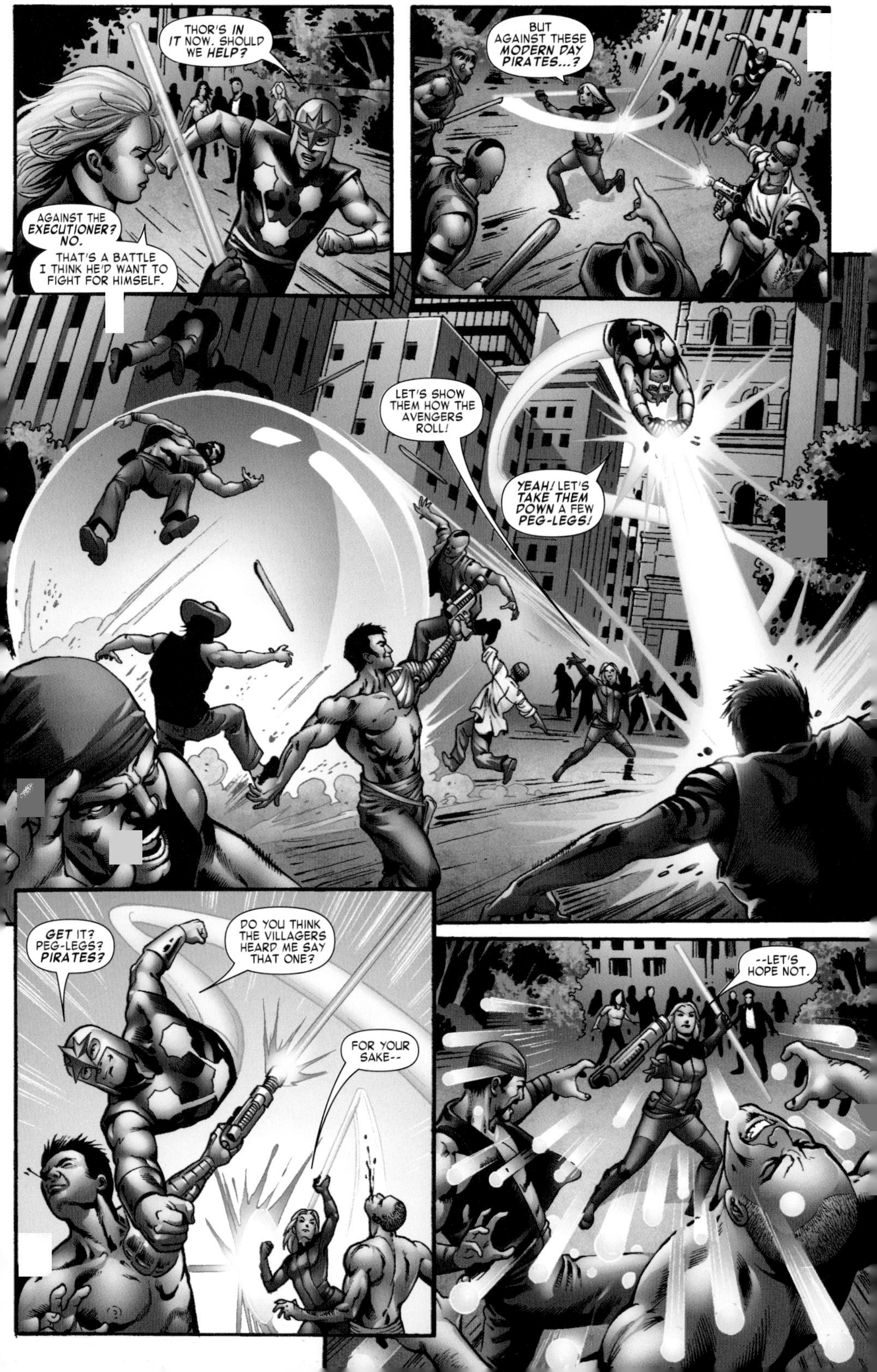
THOR'S IN IT NOW. SHOULD WE HELP?
AGAINST THE EXECUTIONER? NO.
THAT'S A BATTLE I THINK HE'D WANT TO FIGHT FOR HIMSELF.
BUT AGAINST THESE MODERN DAY PIRATES...?
LET'S SHOW THEM HOW THE AVENGERS ROLL!
YEAH! LET'S TAKE THEM DOWN A FEW PEG-LEGS!
GET IT? PEG-LEGS? PIRATES?
DO YOU THINK THE VILLAGERS HEARD ME SAY THAT ONE?
FOR YOUR SAKE--
--LET'S HOPE NOT.

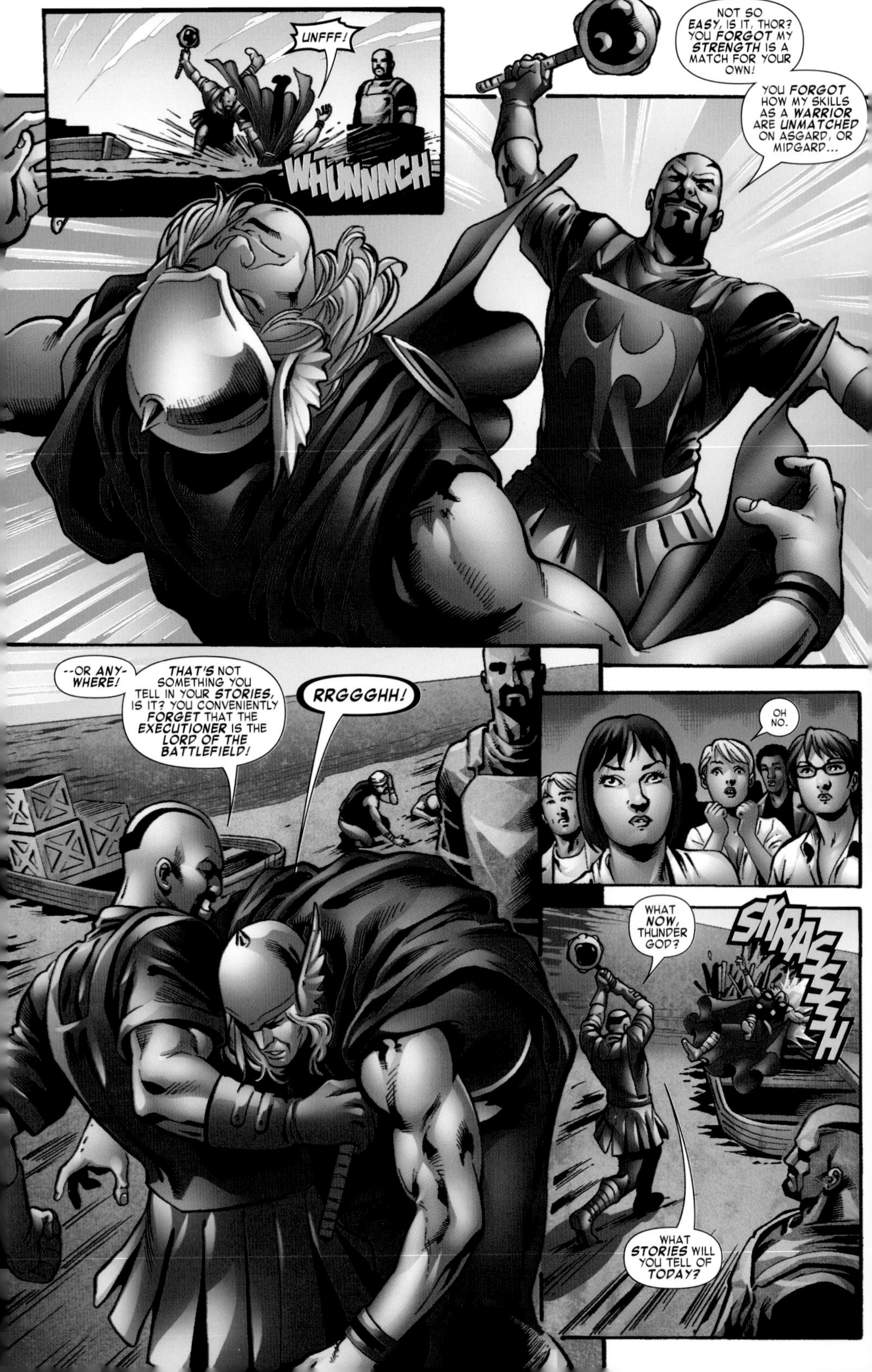
UNFFF!
WHUNNNCH
NOT SO EASY, IS IT, THOR? YOU FORGOT MY STRENGTH IS A MATCH FOR YOUR OWN!
YOU FORGOT HOW MY SKILLS AS A WARRIOR ARE UNMATCHED ON ASGARD, OR MIDGARD...
--OR ANYWHERE!
THAT'S NOT SOMETHING YOU TELL IN YOUR STORIES, IS IT? YOU CONVENIENTLY FORGET THAT THE EXECUTIONER IS THE LORD OF THE BATTLEFIELD!
RRGGGHH!
OH NO.
WHAT NOW, THUNDER GOD?
SKRASSSHH
WHAT STORIES WILL YOU TELL OF TODAY?

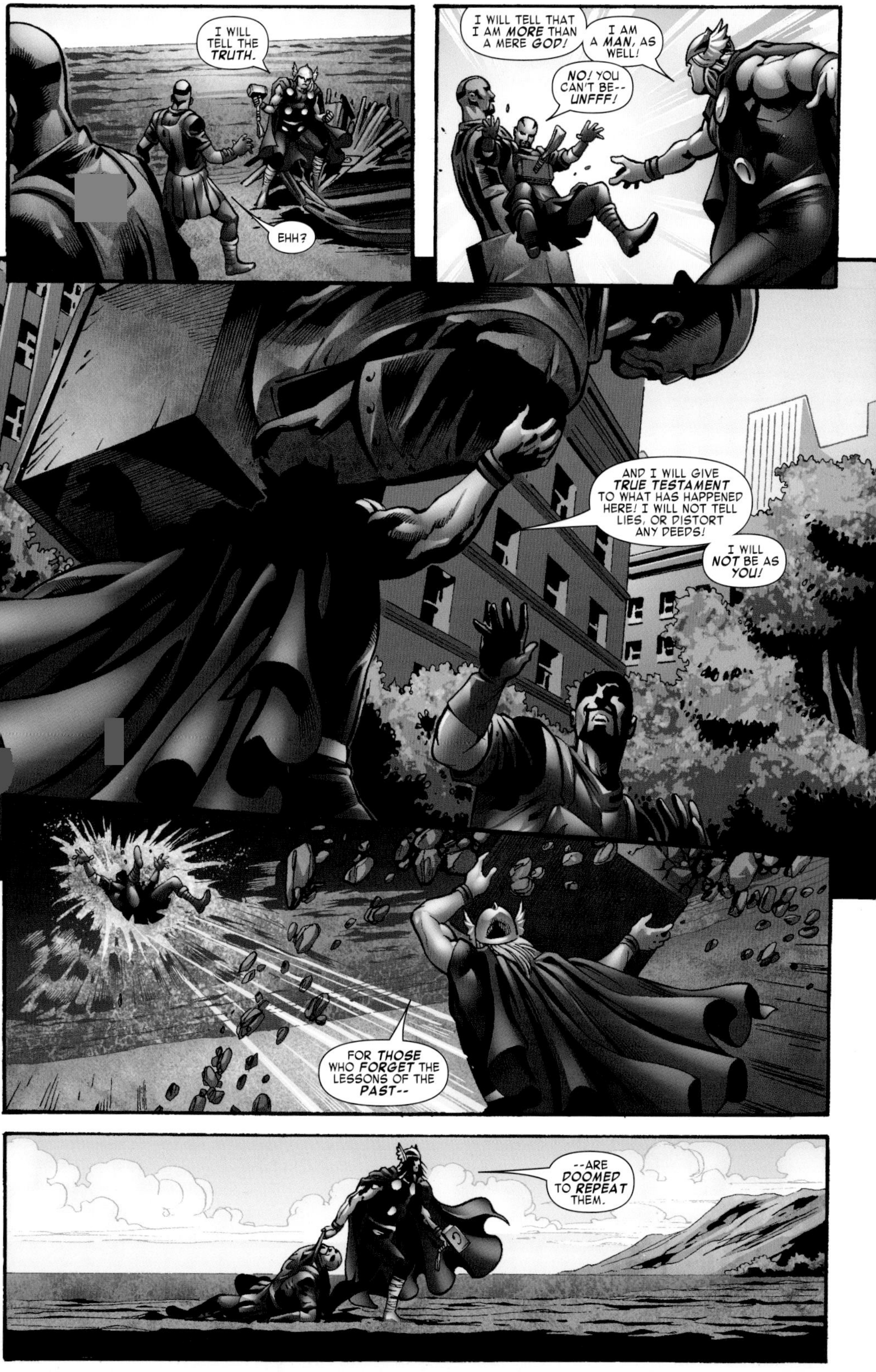
I WILL TELL THE TRUTH.
EHH?
I WILL TELL THAT I AM MORE THAN A MERE GOD!
I AM A MAN, AS WELL!
NO! YOU CAN'T BE-- UNFFF!
AND I WILL GIVE TRUE TESTAMENT TO WHAT HAS HAPPENED HERE! I WILL NOT TELL LIES, OR DISTORT ANY DEEDS!
I WILL NOT BE AS YOU!
FOR THOSE WHO FORGET THE LESSONS OF THE PAST--
--ARE DOOMED TO REPEAT THEM.

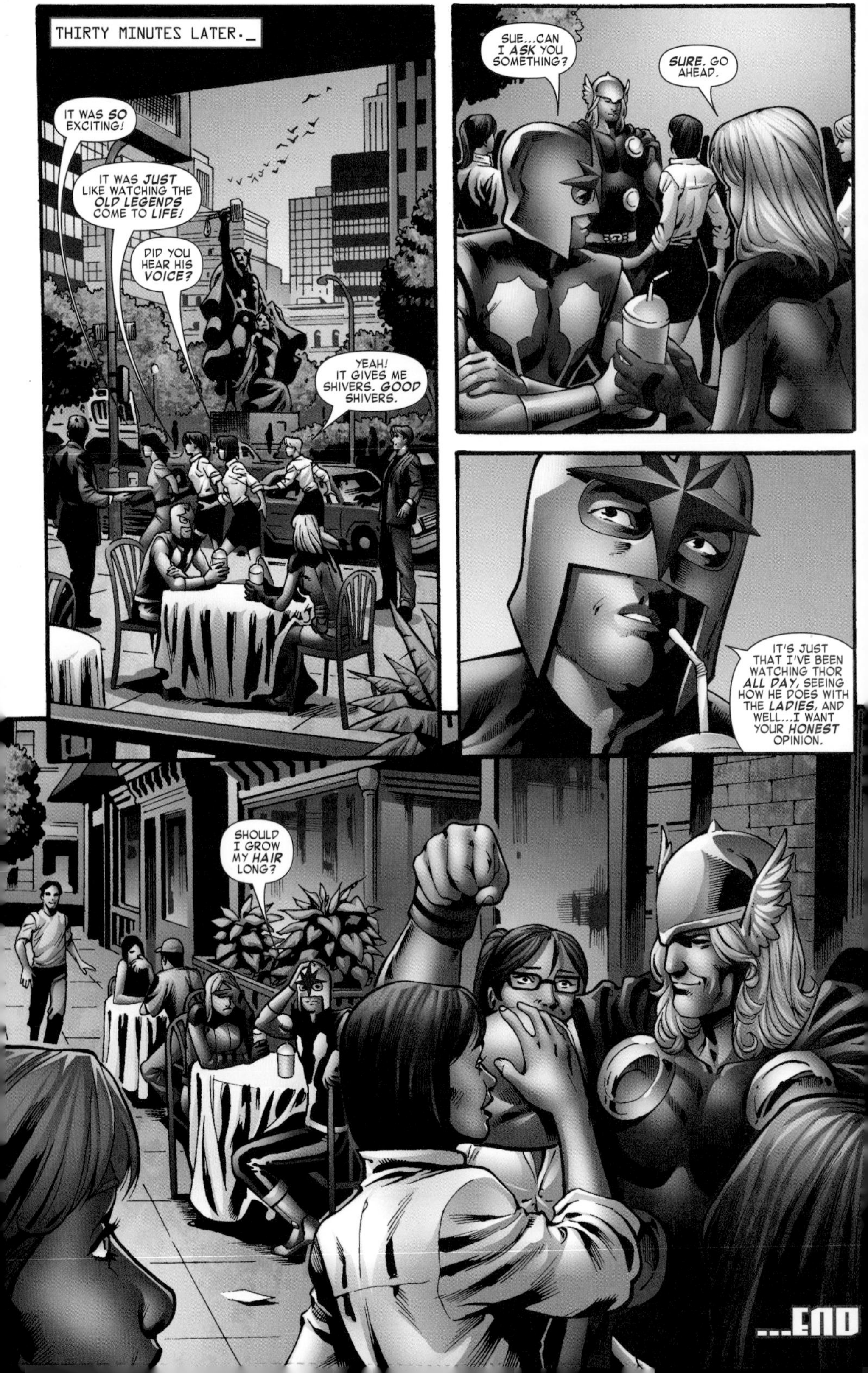
THIRTY MINUTES LATER._
IT WAS SO EXCITING!
IT WAS JUST LIKE WATCHING THE OLD LEGENDS COME TO LIFE!
DID YOU HEAR HIS VOICE?
YEAH! IT GIVES ME SHIVERS. GOOD SHIVERS.
SUE...CAN I ASK YOU SOMETHING?
SURE. GO AHEAD.
IT'S JUST THAT I'VE BEEN WATCHING THOR ALL DAY, SEEING HOW HE DOES WITH THE LADIES, AND WELL...I WANT YOUR HONEST OPINION.
SHOULD I GROW MY HAIR LONG?
...END

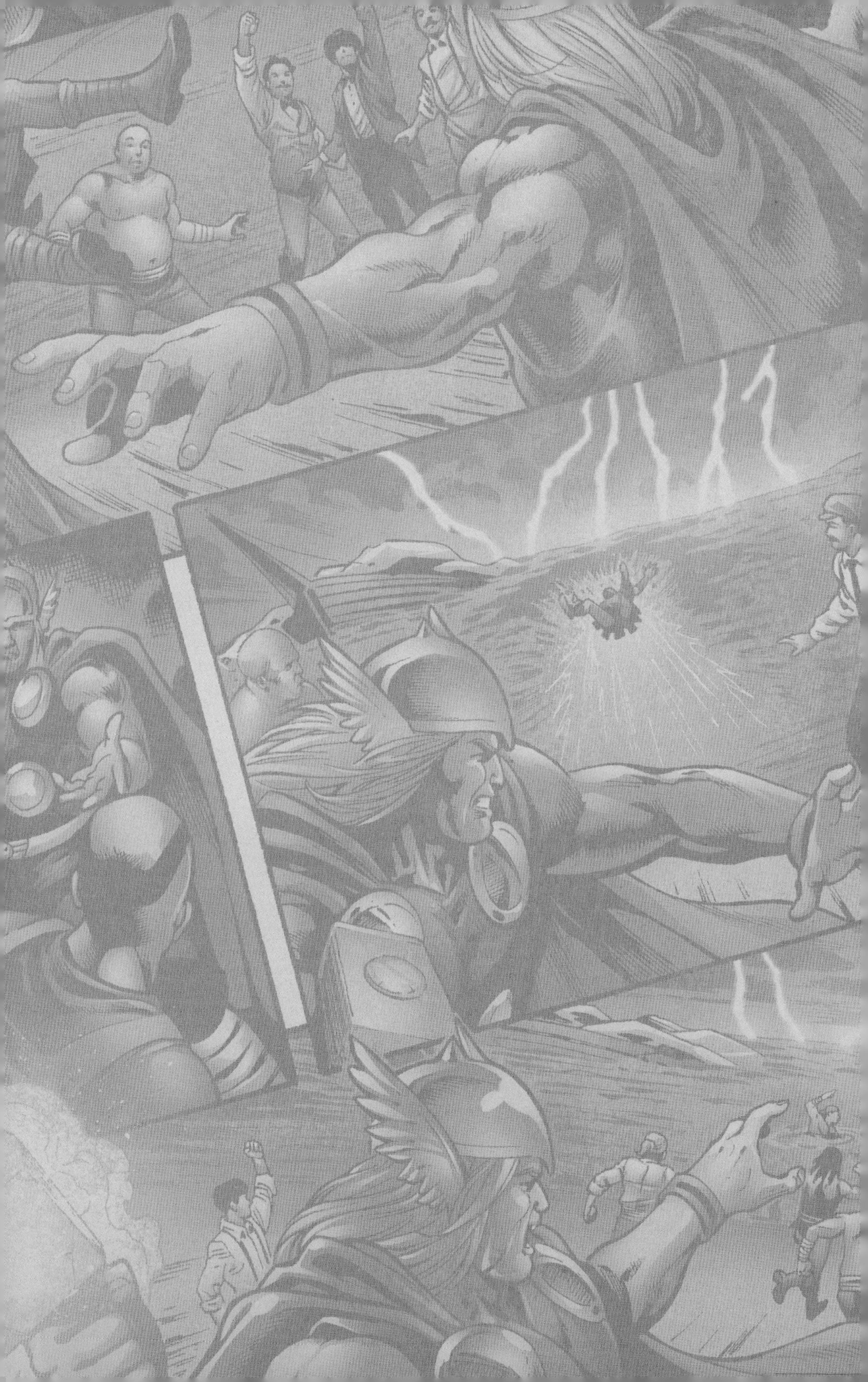

05

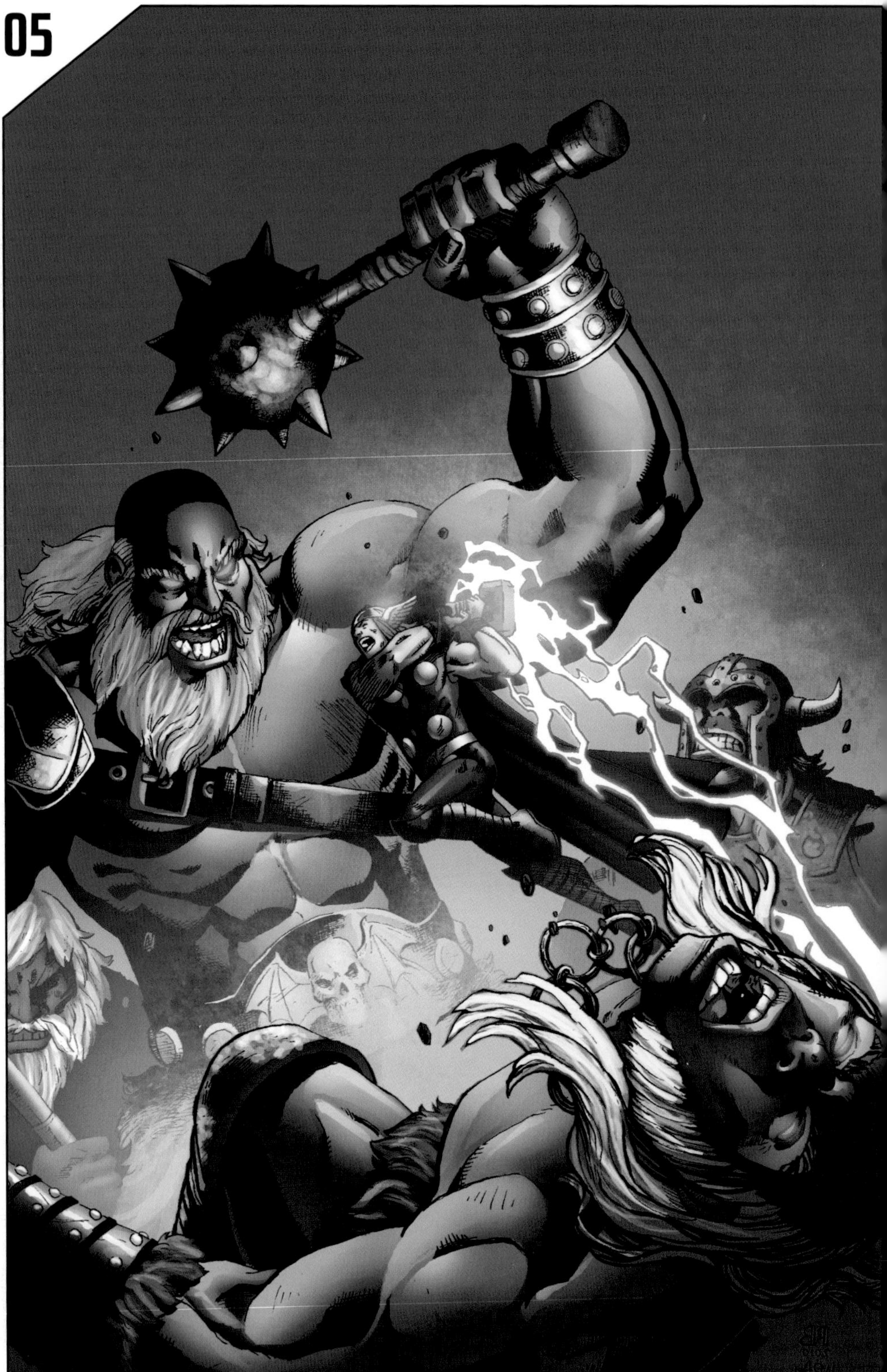

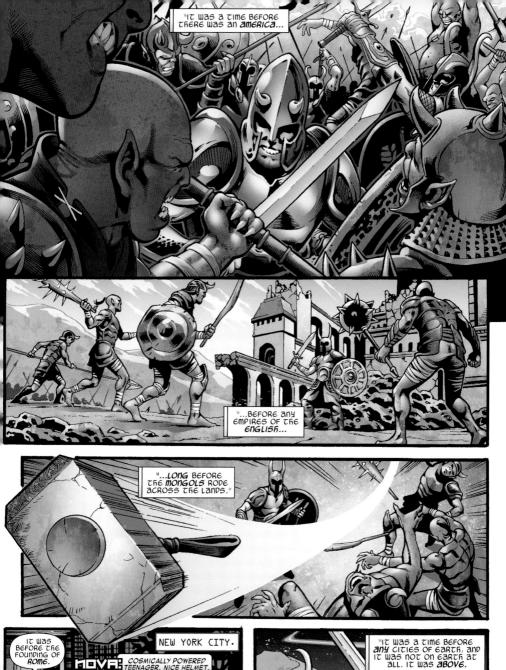

"IT WAS A TIME BEFORE THERE WAS AN *AMERICA*...

"...BEFORE ANY EMPIRES OF THE *ENGLISH*...

"...*LONG* BEFORE THE *MONGOLS* RODE ACROSS THE LANDS."

IT WAS BEFORE THE FOUNDING OF *ROME*.

AND BEFORE THE FIRST OF THE *GREAT PYRAMID'S* STONES WERE SET INTO PLACE.

"IT WAS A TIME BEFORE ANY CITIES OF EARTH, AND IT WAS NOT ON EARTH AT ALL. IT WAS *ABOVE*.

NEW YORK CITY.

NOVA: COSMICALLY POWERED TEENAGER. NICE HELMET.

THOR: GOD OF THUNDER. SON OF ODIN. REAL GOOD WITH A HAMMER.

VALKYRIE: ASGARDIAN DEMI-GODDESS. LEADER OF THE LEGENDARY VALKYRIOR...DOESN'T PUT UP WITH JERKS, WIMPS OR FOOLS.

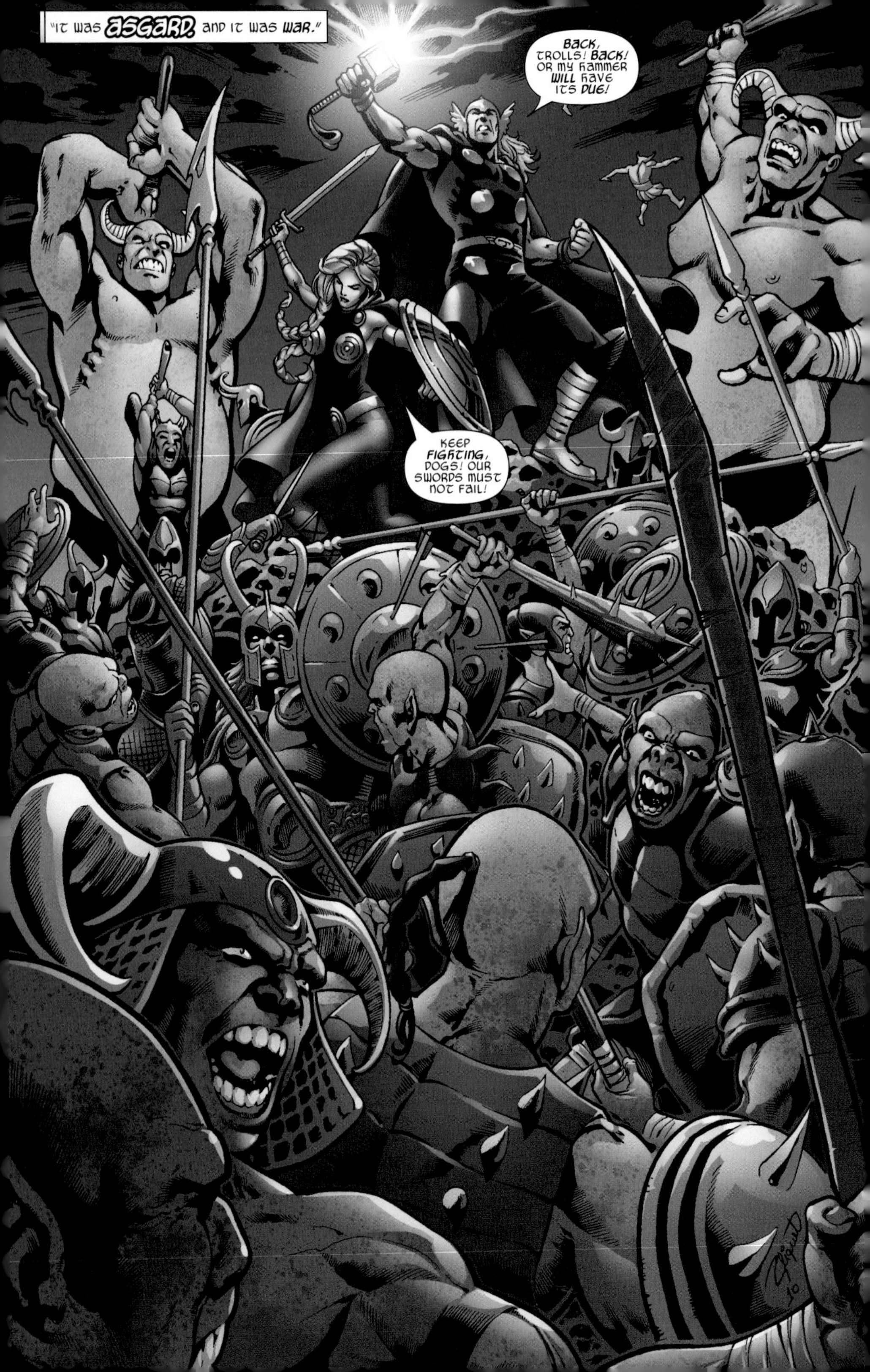
"It was ASGARD, and it was WAR."
BACK, TROLLS! BACK! OR MY HAMMER WILL HAVE ITS DUE!
KEEP FIGHTING, DOGS! OUR SWORDS MUST NOT FAIL!

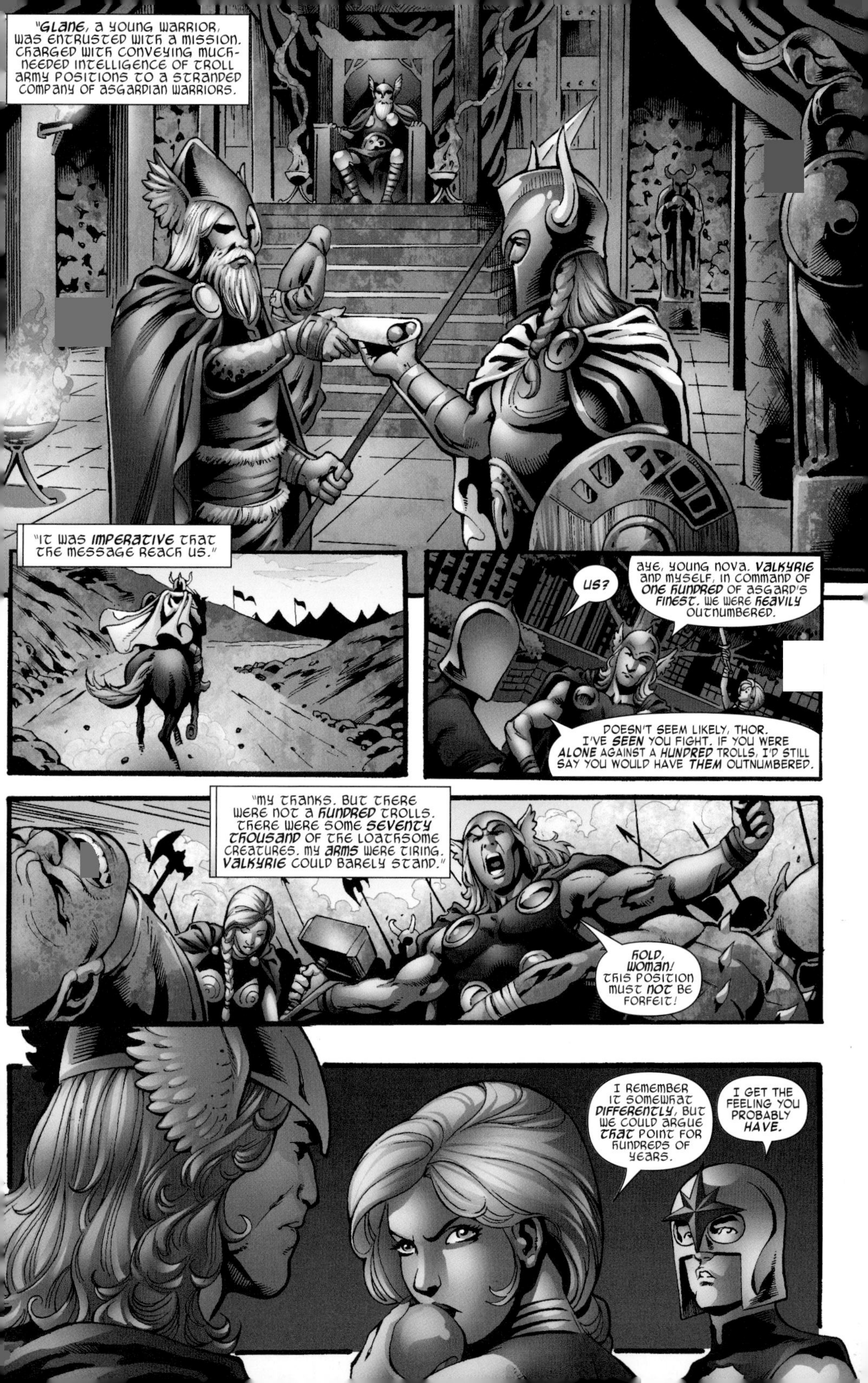
"GLANE, A YOUNG WARRIOR, WAS ENTRUSTED WITH A MISSION. CHARGED WITH CONVEYING MUCH-NEEDED INTELLIGENCE OF TROLL ARMY POSITIONS TO A STRANDED COMPANY OF ASGARDIAN WARRIORS.
"IT WAS IMPERATIVE THAT THE MESSAGE REACH US."
US?
AYE, YOUNG NOVA. VALKYRIE AND MYSELF, IN COMMAND OF ONE HUNDRED OF ASGARD'S FINEST. WE WERE HEAVILY OUTNUMBERED.
DOESN'T SEEM LIKELY, THOR. I'VE SEEN YOU FIGHT. IF YOU WERE ALONE AGAINST A HUNDRED TROLLS, I'D STILL SAY YOU WOULD HAVE THEM OUTNUMBERED.
"MY THANKS. BUT THERE WERE NOT A HUNDRED TROLLS. THERE WERE SOME SEVENTY THOUSAND OF THE LOATHSOME CREATURES. MY ARMS WERE TIRING. VALKYRIE COULD BARELY STAND."
HOLD, WOMAN! THIS POSITION MUST NOT BE FORFEIT!
I REMEMBER IT SOMEWHAT DIFFERENTLY, BUT WE COULD ARGUE THAT POINT FOR HUNDREDS OF YEARS.
I GET THE FEELING YOU PROBABLY HAVE.

"GLANE'S DASH THROUGH THE ENEMY FORTIFICATIONS WAS *SWIFT.*"

"BUT NOT *UNNOTICED.*"

"THERE WAS A BATTLE. SEVERAL OF THEM, IN FACT. *SCORES* OF TROLLS FELL IN THE WAKE OF HIS WAR HAMMER."

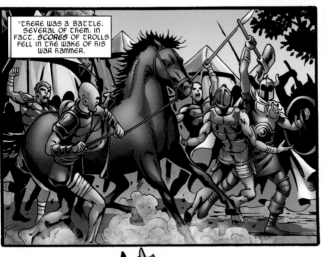

"BUT AT LAST, GLANE HIMSELF WAS *OVERWHELMED.* DRAGGED DOWN. THE MESSAGE WENT UNDELIVERED."

"VALKYRIE AND I, UNABLE TO RESPOND TO TROOP MOVEMENTS, *LOST OUR* POSITION. *AND OUR MEN.*"

BECAUSE OF HIS FAILURE, ODIN HAS *CONDEMNED* GLANE THESE PAST FEW THOUSAND YEARS TO TOIL IN THE *FIELDS* OF THE *FALLEN,* BARRED FROM ENTERING VALHALLA.

CONDEMNED HIM? HE...*SEEMED* TO HAVE DONE *FAIRLY WELL,* DIDN'T YOU SAY THAT LIKE A *HUNDRED TROLLS* FELL?

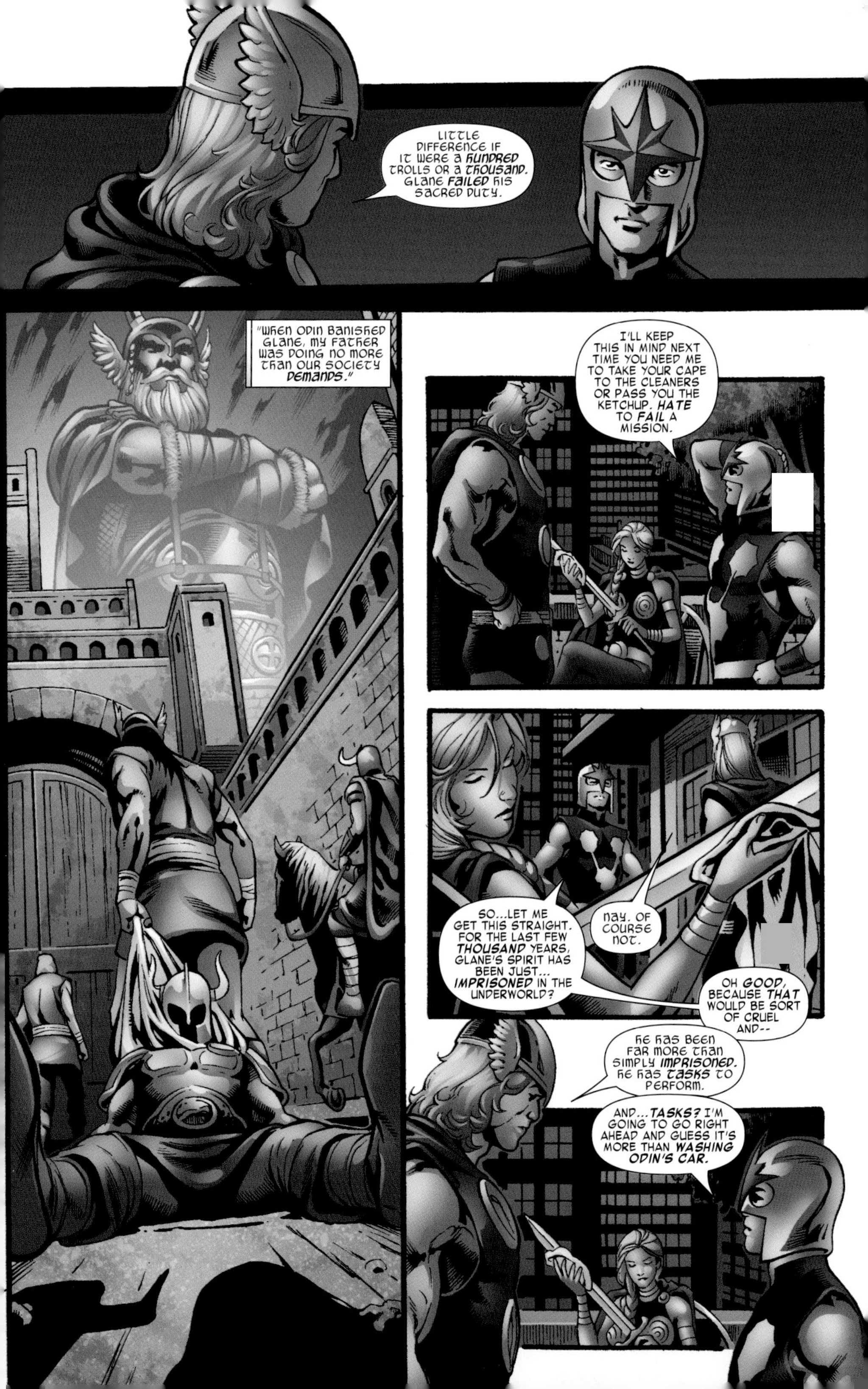
LITTLE DIFFERENCE IF IT WERE A HUNDRED TROLLS OR A THOUSAND. GLANE FAILED HIS SACRED DUTY.
"WHEN ODIN BANISHED GLANE, MY FATHER WAS DOING NO MORE THAN OUR SOCIETY DEMANDS."
I'LL KEEP THIS IN MIND NEXT TIME YOU NEED ME TO TAKE YOUR CAPE TO THE CLEANERS OR PASS YOU THE KETCHUP. HATE TO FAIL A MISSION.
SO...LET ME GET THIS STRAIGHT. FOR THE LAST FEW THOUSAND YEARS, GLANE'S SPIRIT HAS BEEN JUST... IMPRISONED IN THE UNDERWORLD?
NAY. OF COURSE NOT.
OH GOOD, BECAUSE THAT WOULD BE SORT OF CRUEL AND--
HE HAS BEEN FAR MORE THAN SIMPLY IMPRISONED. HE HAS TASKS TO PERFORM.
AND...TASKS? I'M GOING TO GO RIGHT AHEAD AND GUESS IT'S MORE THAN WASHING ODIN'S CAR.

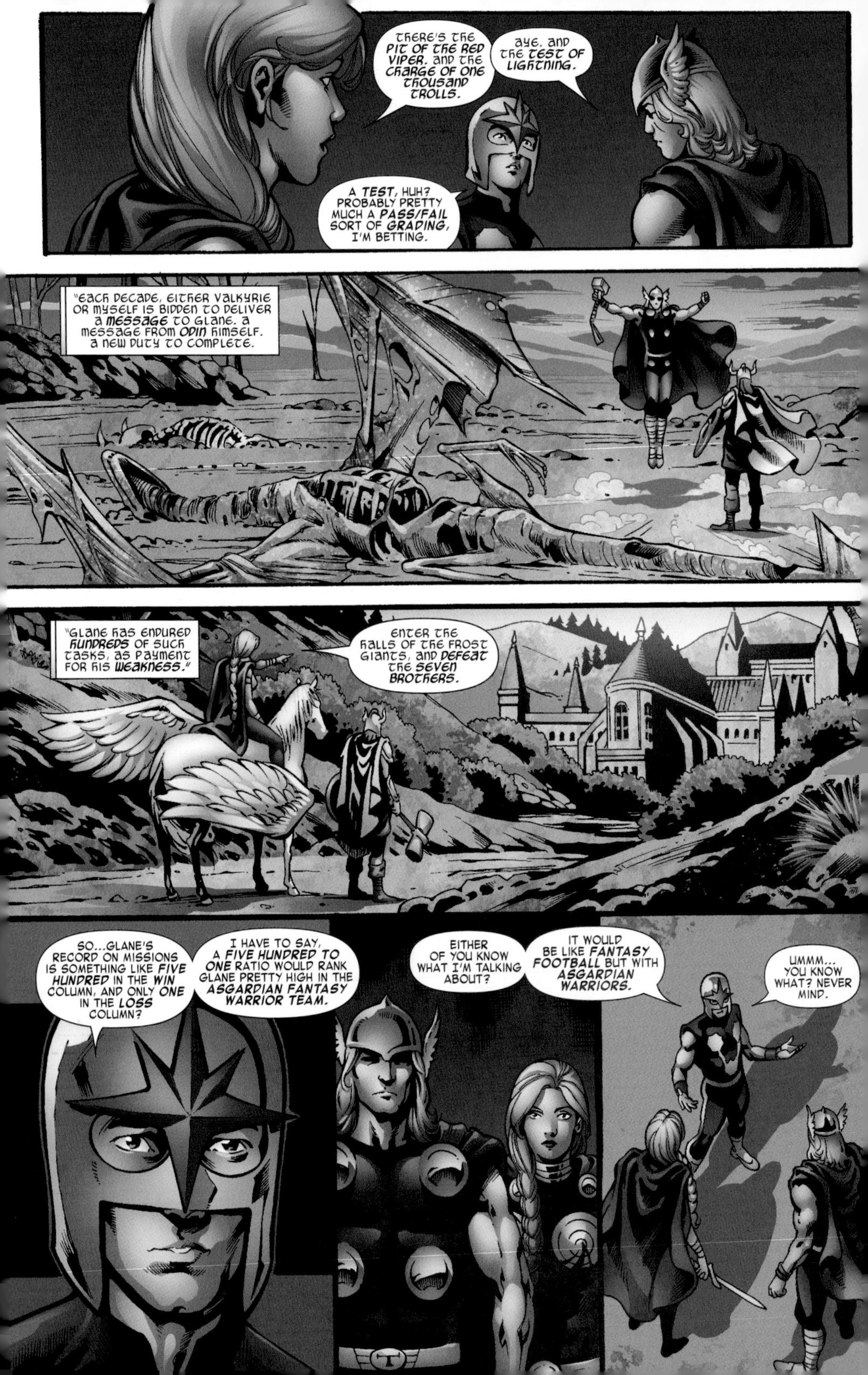
THERE'S THE PIT OF THE RED VIPER. AND THE CHARGE OF ONE THOUSAND TROLLS.
AYE. AND THE TEST OF LIGHTNING.
A TEST, HUH? PROBABLY PRETTY MUCH A PASS/FAIL SORT OF GRADING, I'M BETTING.
"EACH DECADE, EITHER VALKYRIE OR MYSELF IS BIDDEN TO DELIVER A MESSAGE TO GLANE. A MESSAGE FROM ODIN HIMSELF. A NEW DUTY TO COMPLETE.
"GLANE HAS ENDURED HUNDREDS OF SUCH TASKS, AS PAYMENT FOR HIS WEAKNESS."
ENTER THE HALLS OF THE FROST GIANTS, AND DEFEAT THE SEVEN BROTHERS.
SO...GLANE'S RECORD ON MISSIONS IS SOMETHING LIKE FIVE HUNDRED IN THE WIN COLUMN, AND ONLY ONE IN THE LOSS COLUMN?
I HAVE TO SAY, A FIVE HUNDRED TO ONE RATIO WOULD RANK GLANE PRETTY HIGH IN THE ASGARDIAN FANTASY WARRIOR TEAM.
EITHER OF YOU KNOW WHAT I'M TALKING ABOUT?
IT WOULD BE LIKE FANTASY FOOTBALL BUT WITH ASGARDIAN WARRIORS.
UMMM... YOU KNOW WHAT? NEVER MIND.

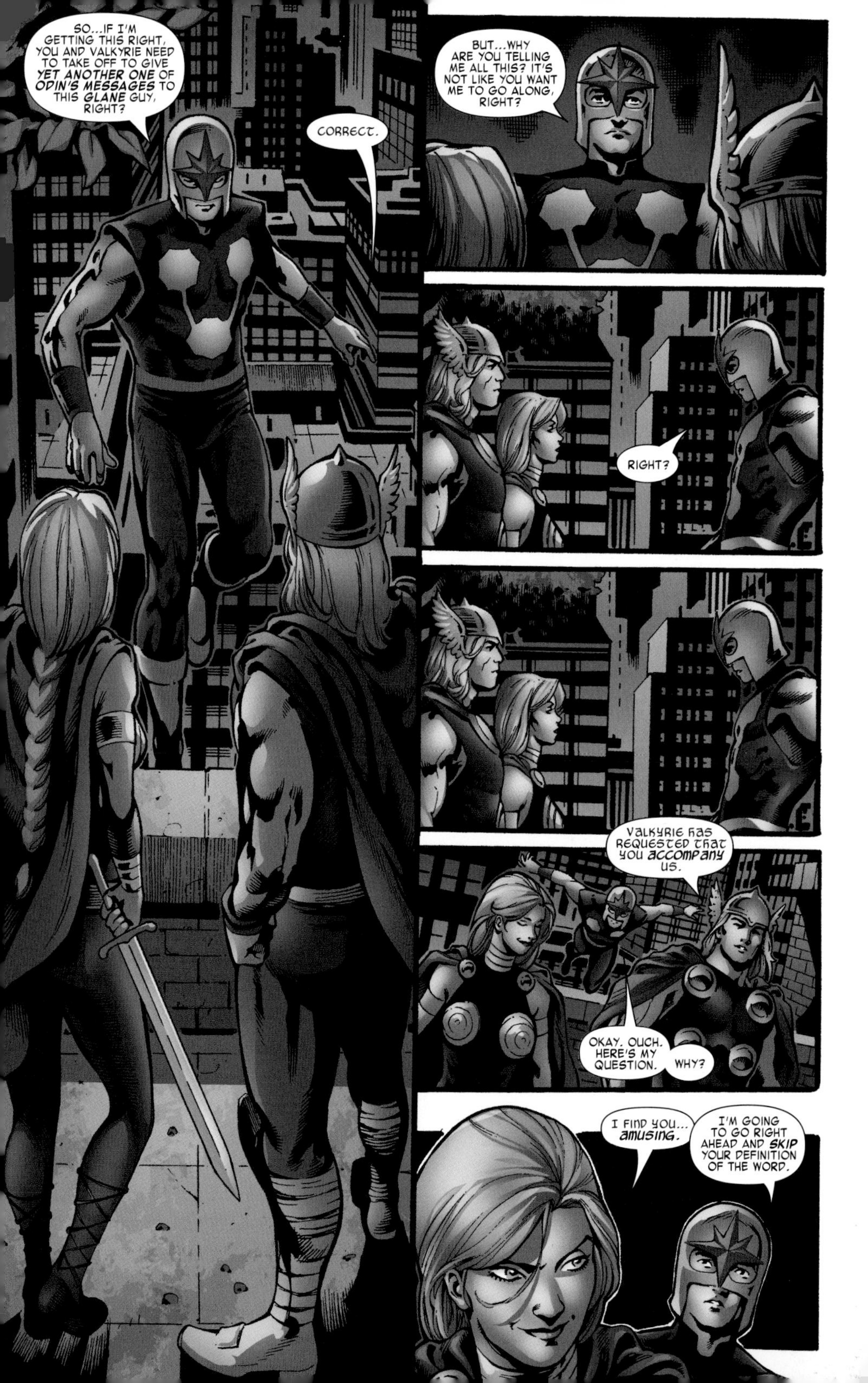
SO...IF I'M GETTING THIS RIGHT, YOU AND VALKYRIE NEED TO TAKE OFF TO GIVE YET ANOTHER ONE OF ODIN'S MESSAGES TO THIS GLANE GUY, RIGHT?
CORRECT.
BUT...WHY ARE YOU TELLING ME ALL THIS? IT'S NOT LIKE YOU WANT ME TO GO ALONG, RIGHT?
RIGHT?
VALKYRIE HAS REQUESTED THAT YOU ACCOMPANY US.
OKAY. OUCH. HERE'S MY QUESTION.
WHY?
I FIND YOU... AMUSING.
I'M GOING TO GO RIGHT AHEAD AND SKIP YOUR DEFINITION OF THE WORD.

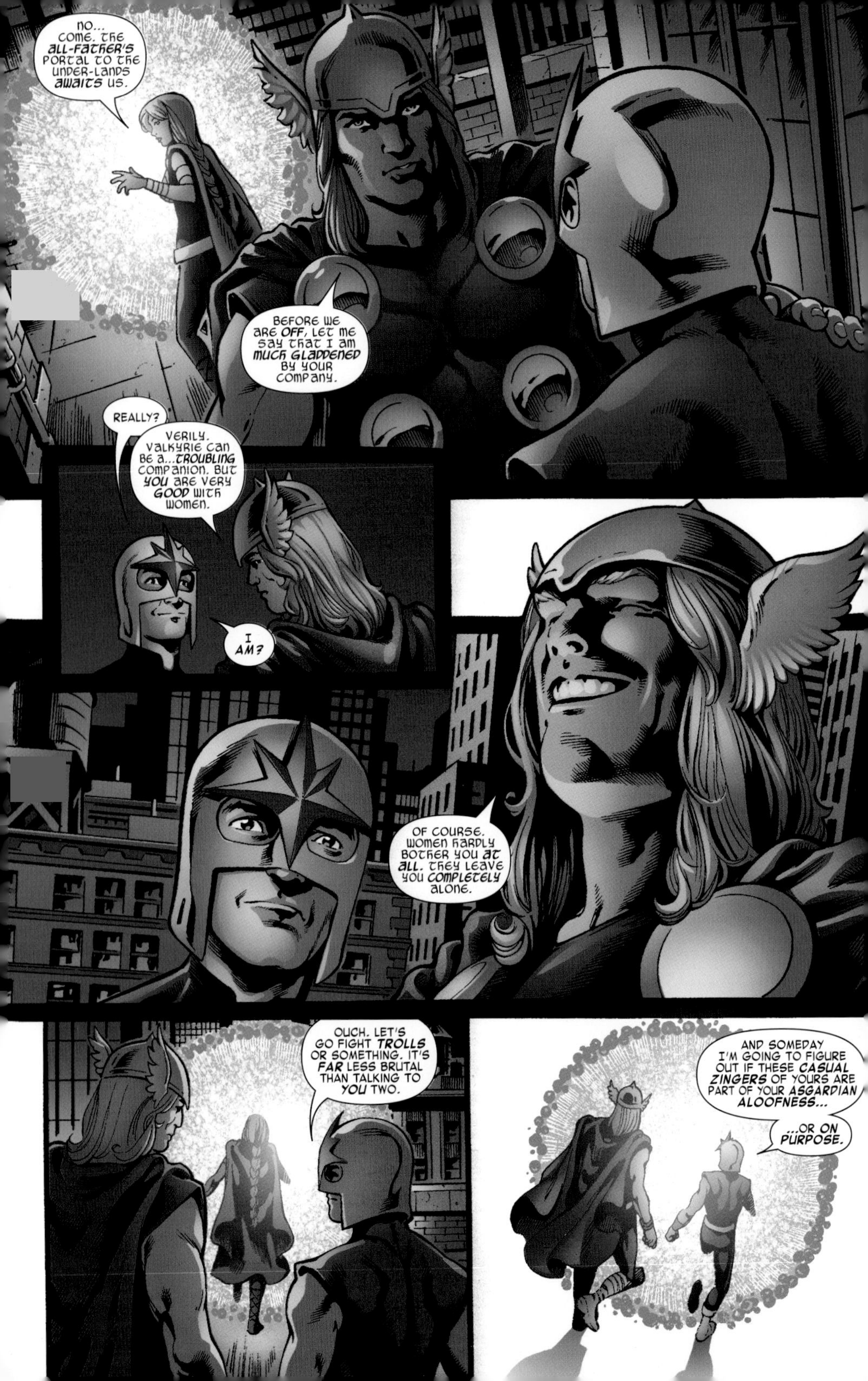
NO... COME. THE ALL-FATHER'S PORTAL TO THE UNDER-LANDS AWAITS US.
BEFORE WE ARE OFF, LET ME SAY THAT I AM MUCH GLADDENED BY YOUR COMPANY.
REALLY?
VERILY. VALKYRIE CAN BE A...TROUBLING COMPANION. BUT YOU ARE VERY GOOD WITH WOMEN.
I AM?
OF COURSE. WOMEN HARDLY BOTHER YOU AT ALL. THEY LEAVE YOU COMPLETELY ALONE.
OUCH. LET'S GO FIGHT TROLLS OR SOMETHING. IT'S FAR LESS BRUTAL THAN TALKING TO YOU TWO.
AND SOMEDAY I'M GOING TO FIGURE OUT IF THESE CASUAL ZINGERS OF YOURS ARE PART OF YOUR ASGARDIAN ALOOFNESS...
...OR ON PURPOSE.

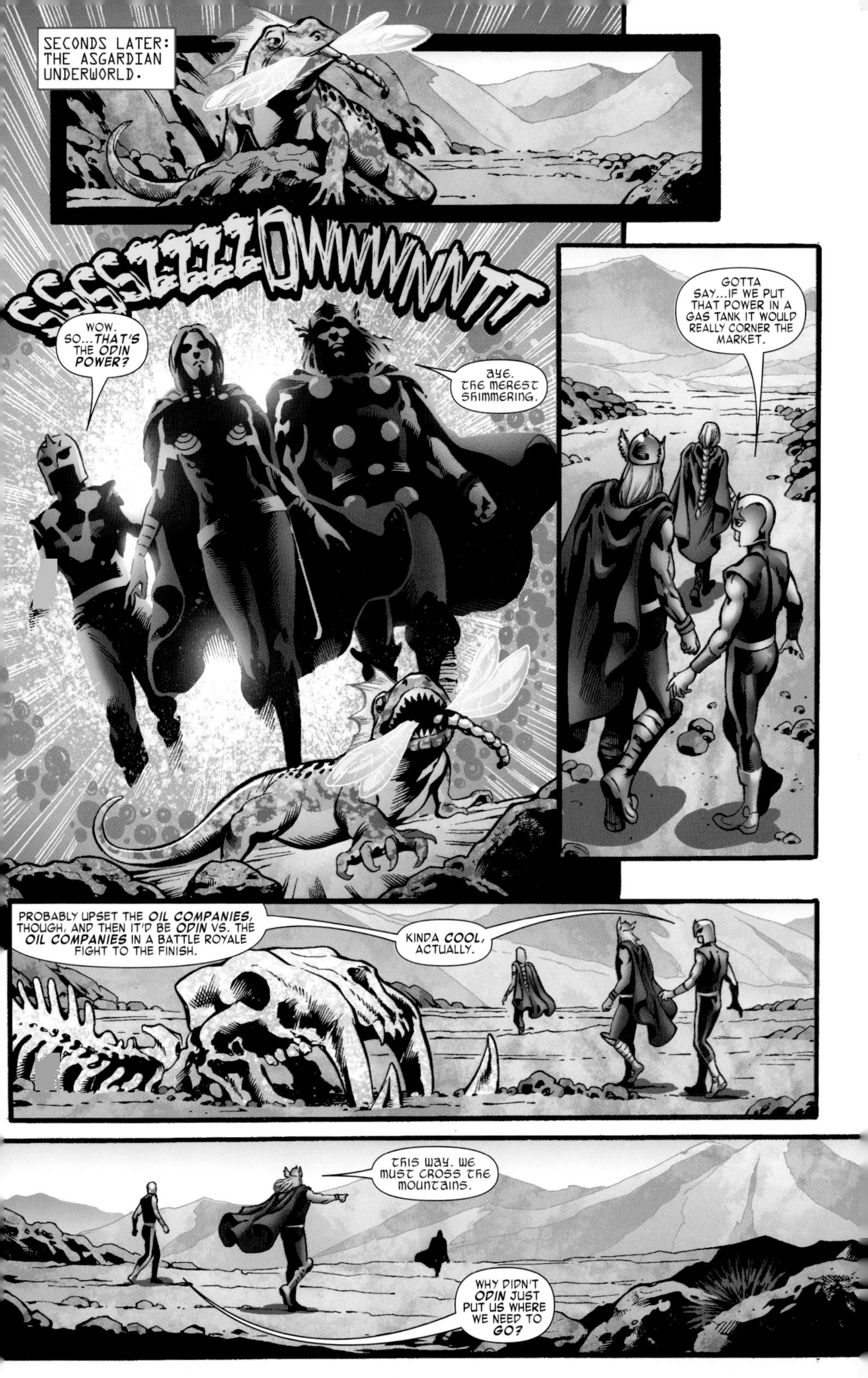
SECONDS LATER: THE ASGARDIAN UNDERWORLD.
SSSSZZZZZOWWWWNNTT
WOW. SO...THAT'S THE ODIN POWER?
AYE. THE MEREST SHIMMERING.
GOTTA SAY...IF WE PUT THAT POWER IN A GAS TANK IT WOULD REALLY CORNER THE MARKET.
PROBABLY UPSET THE OIL COMPANIES, THOUGH, AND THEN IT'D BE ODIN VS. THE OIL COMPANIES IN A BATTLE ROYALE FIGHT TO THE FINISH.
KINDA COOL, ACTUALLY.
THIS WAY. WE MUST CROSS THE MOUNTAINS.
WHY DIDN'T ODIN JUST PUT US WHERE WE NEED TO GO?

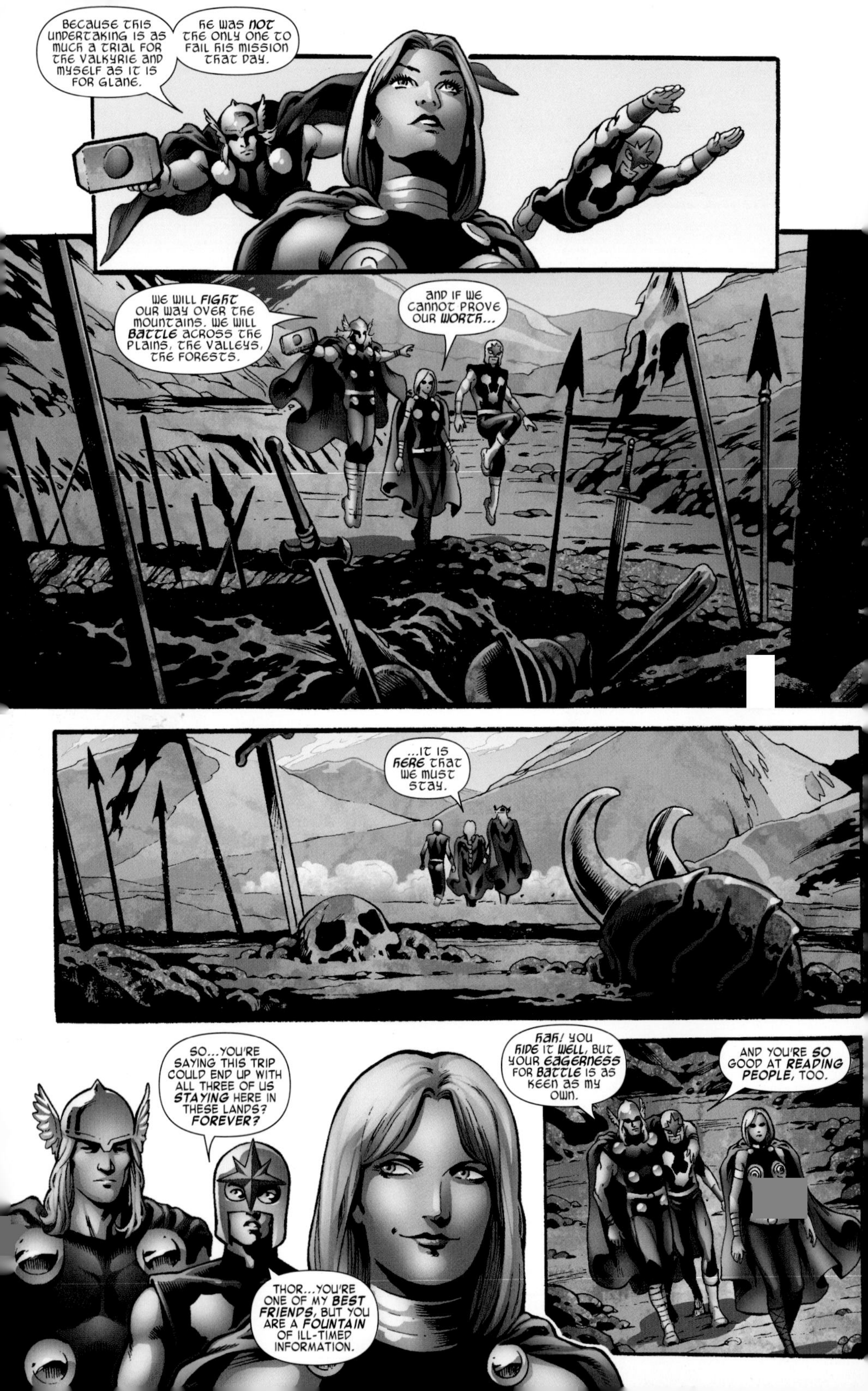
BECAUSE THIS UNDERTAKING IS AS MUCH A TRIAL FOR THE VALKYRIE AND MYSELF AS IT IS FOR GLANE.
HE WAS NOT THE ONLY ONE TO FAIL HIS MISSION THAT DAY.
WE WILL FIGHT OUR WAY OVER THE MOUNTAINS. WE WILL BATTLE ACROSS THE PLAINS, THE VALLEYS, THE FORESTS.
AND IF WE CANNOT PROVE OUR WORTH...
...IT IS HERE THAT WE MUST STAY.
SO...YOU'RE SAYING THIS TRIP COULD END UP WITH ALL THREE OF US STAYING HERE IN THESE LANDS? FOREVER?
THOR...YOU'RE ONE OF MY BEST FRIENDS, BUT YOU ARE A FOUNTAIN OF ILL-TIMED INFORMATION.
HAH! YOU HIDE IT WELL, BUT YOUR EAGERNESS FOR BATTLE IS AS KEEN AS MY OWN.
AND YOU'RE SO GOOD AT READING PEOPLE, TOO.

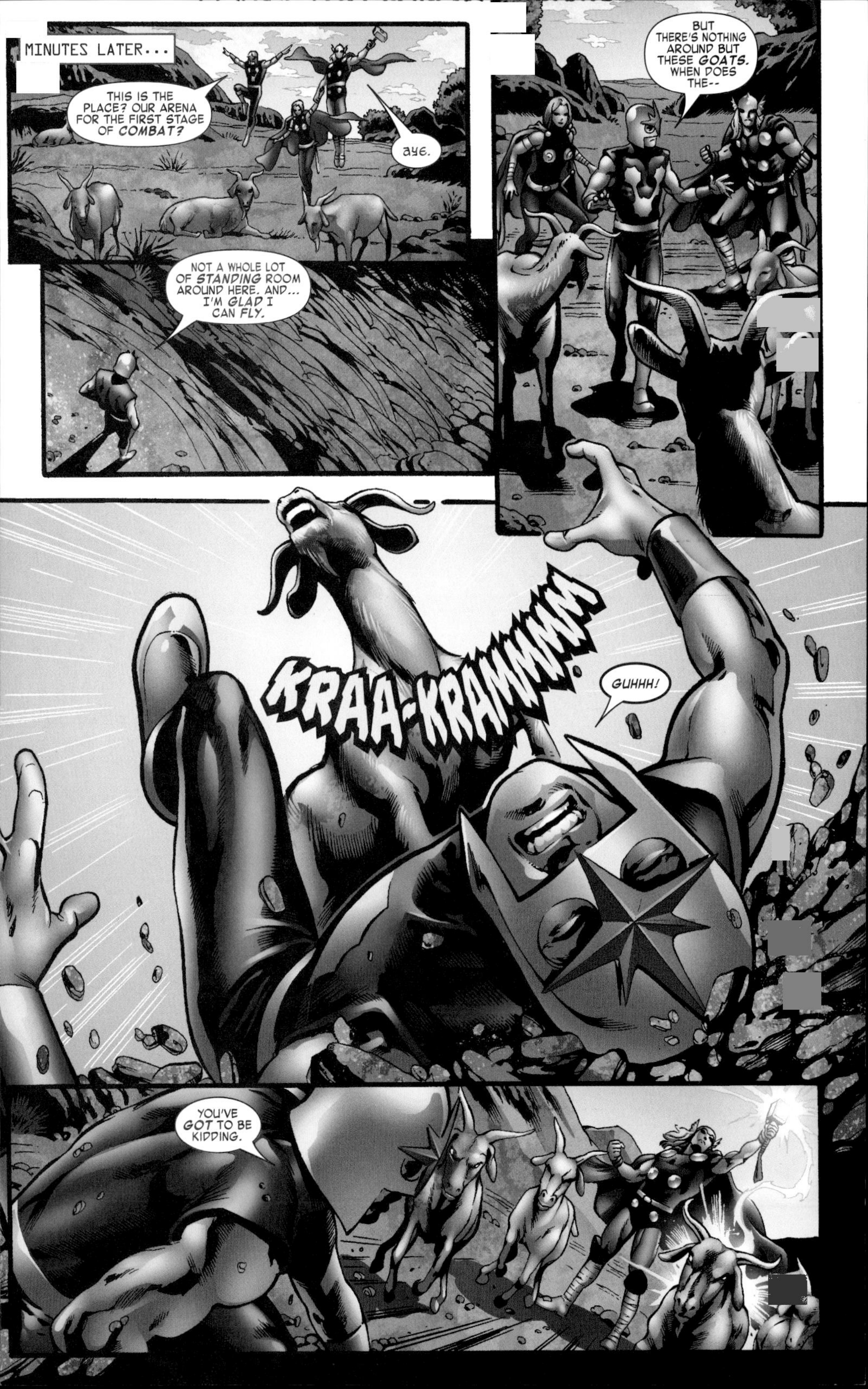

MINUTES LATER...
THIS IS THE PLACE? OUR ARENA FOR THE FIRST STAGE OF COMBAT?
AYE.
NOT A WHOLE LOT OF STANDING ROOM AROUND HERE. AND... I'M GLAD I CAN FLY.
BUT THERE'S NOTHING AROUND BUT THESE GOATS. WHEN DOES THE--
KRAA-KRAMMMM
GUHHH!
YOU'VE GOT TO BE KIDDING.

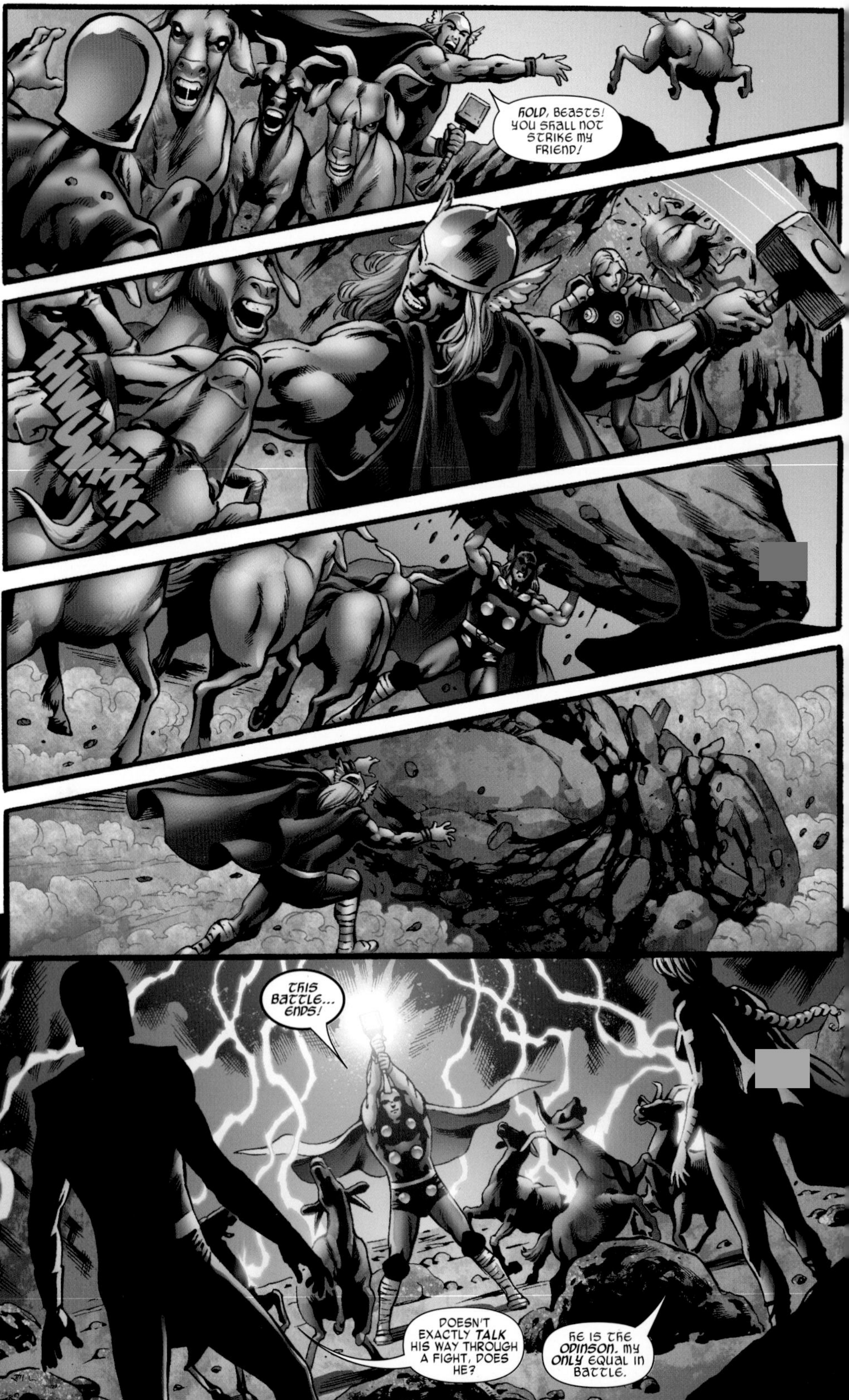
HOLD, BEASTS! YOU SHALL NOT STRIKE MY FRIEND!
THWUNKKT
THIS BATTLE... ENDS!
DOESN'T EXACTLY TALK HIS WAY THROUGH A FIGHT, DOES HE?
HE IS THE ODINSON, MY ONLY EQUAL IN BATTLE.

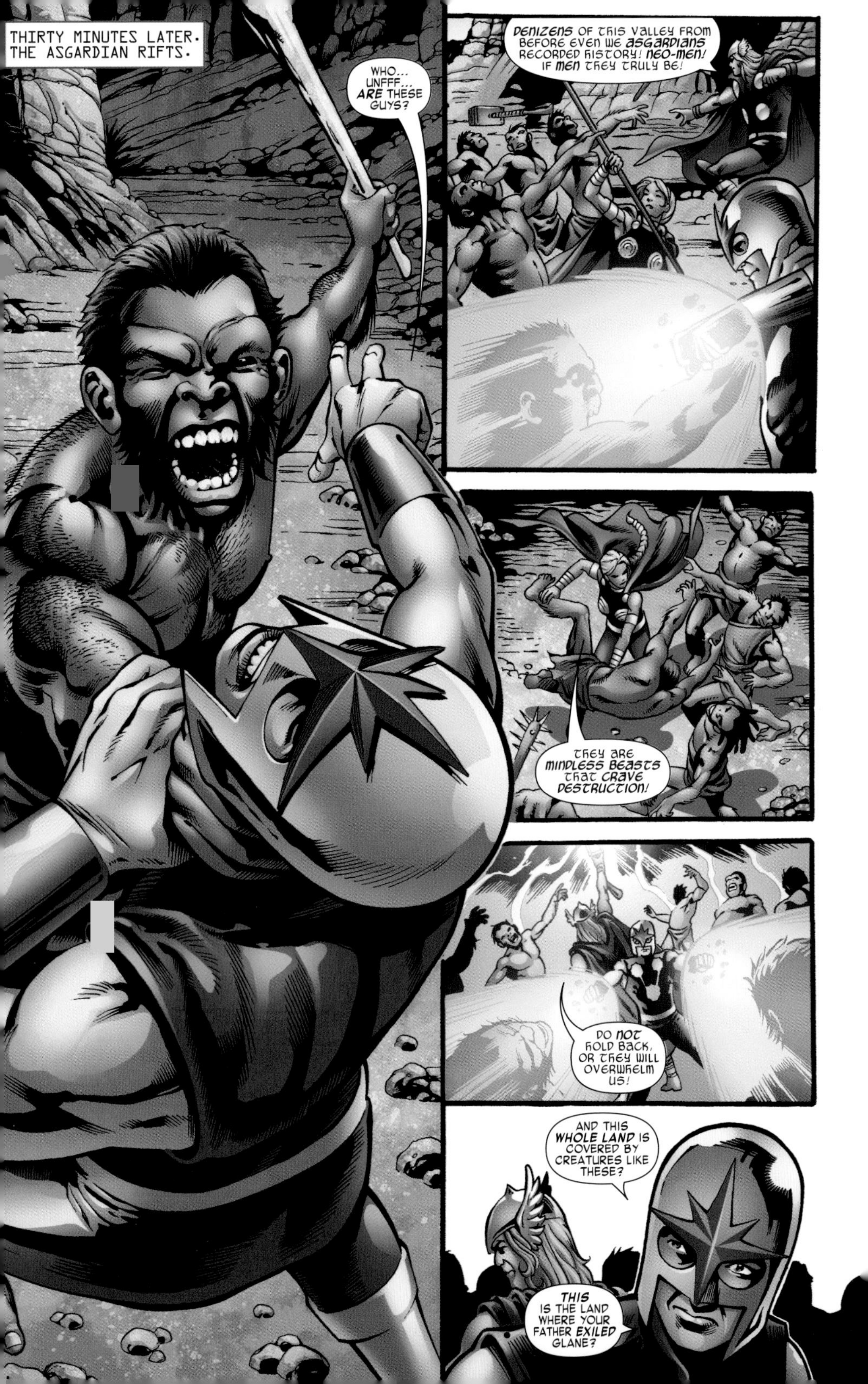
THIRTY MINUTES LATER. THE ASGARDIAN RIFTS.
WHO... UNFFF... ARE THESE GUYS?
DENIZENS OF THIS VALLEY FROM BEFORE EVEN WE ASGARDIANS RECORDED HISTORY! NEO-MEN! IF MEN THEY TRULY BE!
THEY ARE MINDLESS BEASTS THAT CRAVE DESTRUCTION!
DO NOT HOLD BACK, OR THEY WILL OVERWHELM US!
AND THIS WHOLE LAND IS COVERED BY CREATURES LIKE THESE?
THIS IS THE LAND WHERE YOUR FATHER EXILED GLANE?

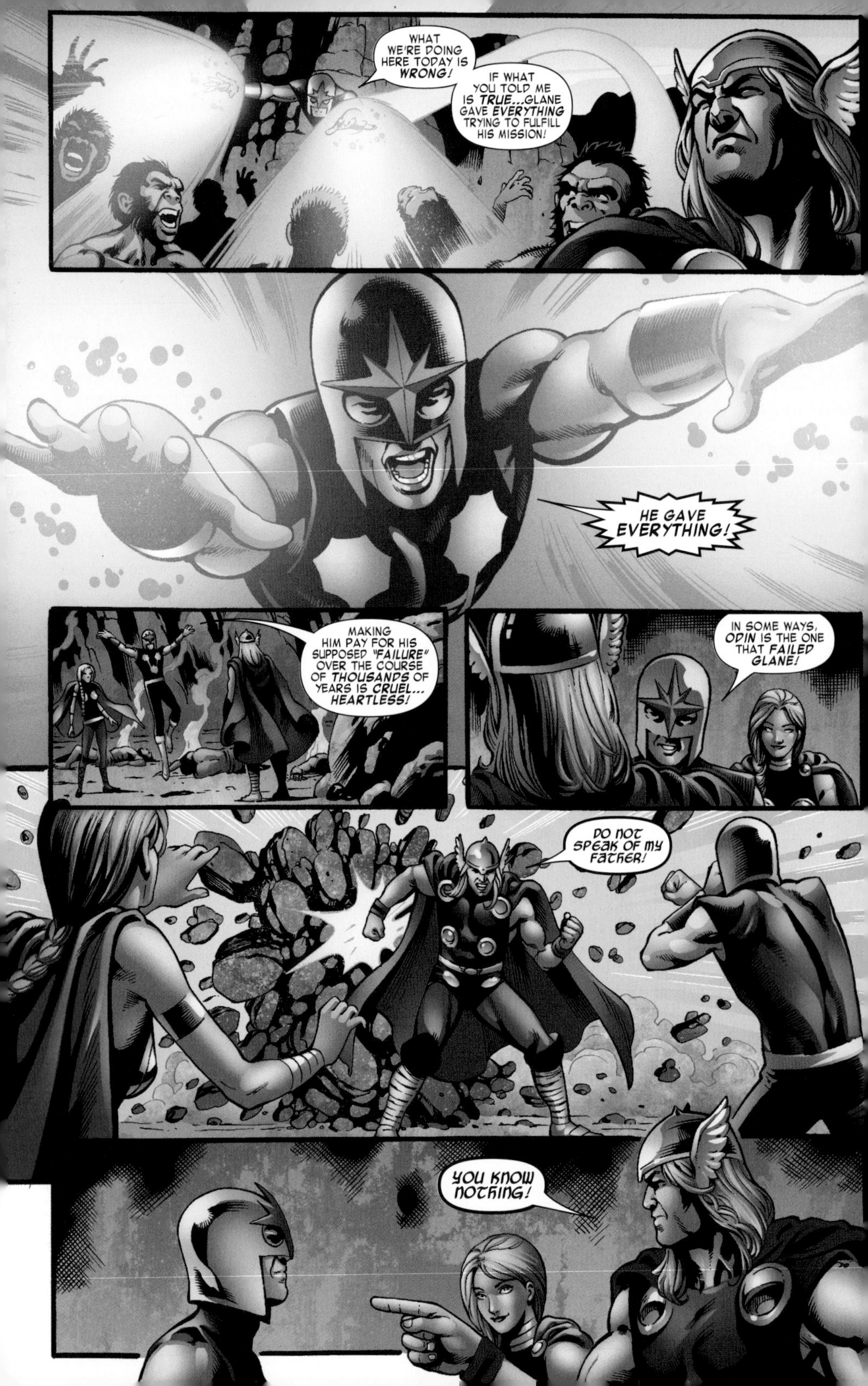
WHAT WE'RE DOING HERE TODAY IS WRONG!
IF WHAT YOU TOLD ME IS TRUE... GLANE GAVE EVERYTHING TRYING TO FULFILL HIS MISSION!
HE GAVE EVERYTHING!
MAKING HIM PAY FOR HIS SUPPOSED "FAILURE" OVER THE COURSE OF THOUSANDS OF YEARS IS CRUEL... HEARTLESS!
IN SOME WAYS, ODIN IS THE ONE THAT FAILED GLANE!
DO NOT SPEAK OF MY FATHER!
YOU KNOW NOTHING!

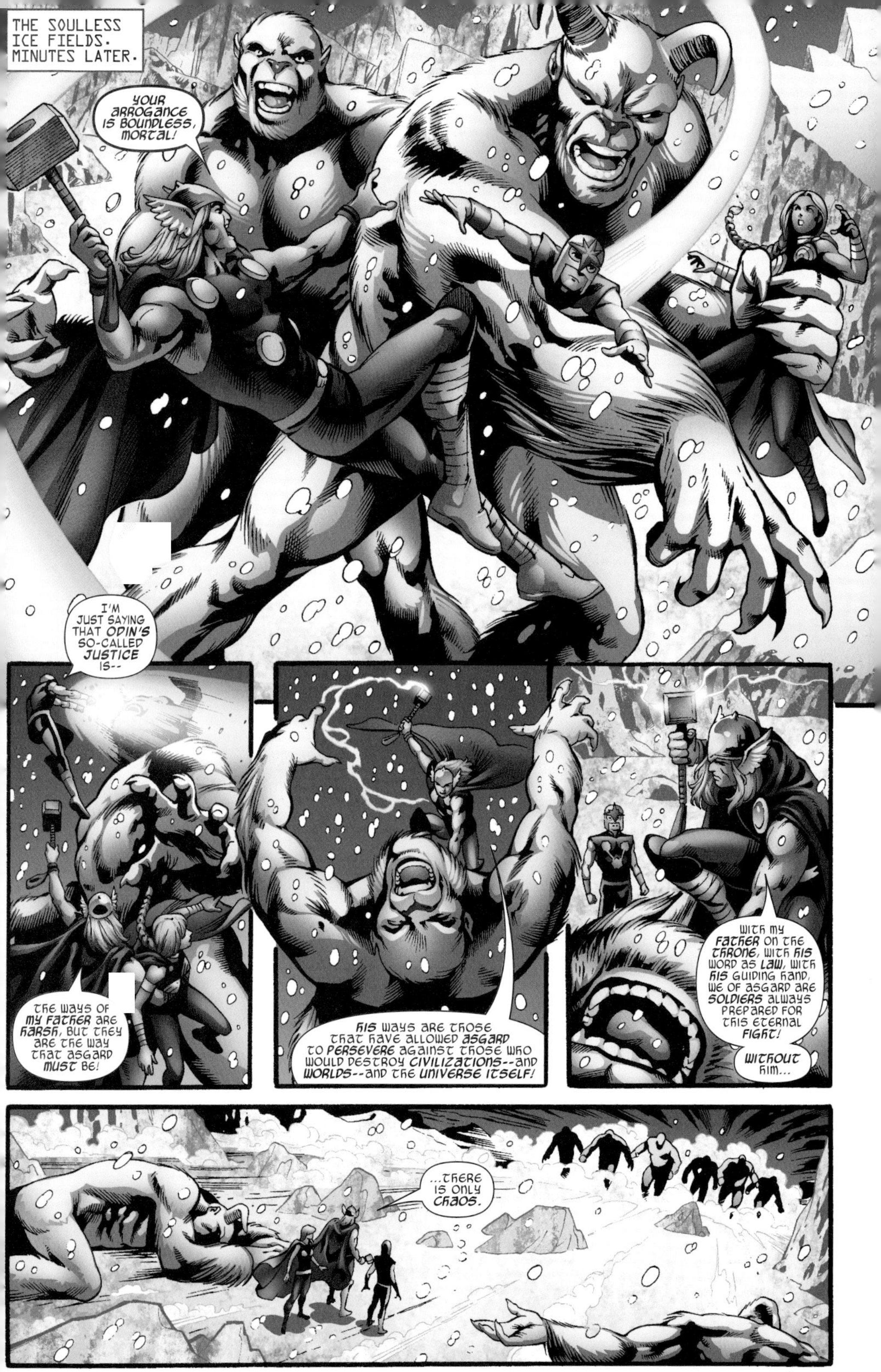
THE SOULLESS ICE FIELDS. MINUTES LATER.
YOUR ARROGANCE IS BOUNDLESS, MORTAL!
I'M JUST SAYING THAT ODIN'S SO-CALLED JUSTICE IS--
THE WAYS OF MY FATHER ARE HARSH, BUT THEY ARE THE WAY THAT ASGARD MUST BE!
HIS WAYS ARE THOSE THAT HAVE ALLOWED ASGARD TO PERSEVERE AGAINST THOSE WHO WOULD DESTROY CIVILIZATIONS--AND WORLDS--AND THE UNIVERSE ITSELF!
WITH MY FATHER ON THE THRONE, WITH HIS WORD AS LAW, WITH HIS GUIDING HAND, WE OF ASGARD ARE SOLDIERS ALWAYS PREPARED FOR THIS ETERNAL FIGHT!
WITHOUT HIM...
...THERE IS ONLY CHAOS.

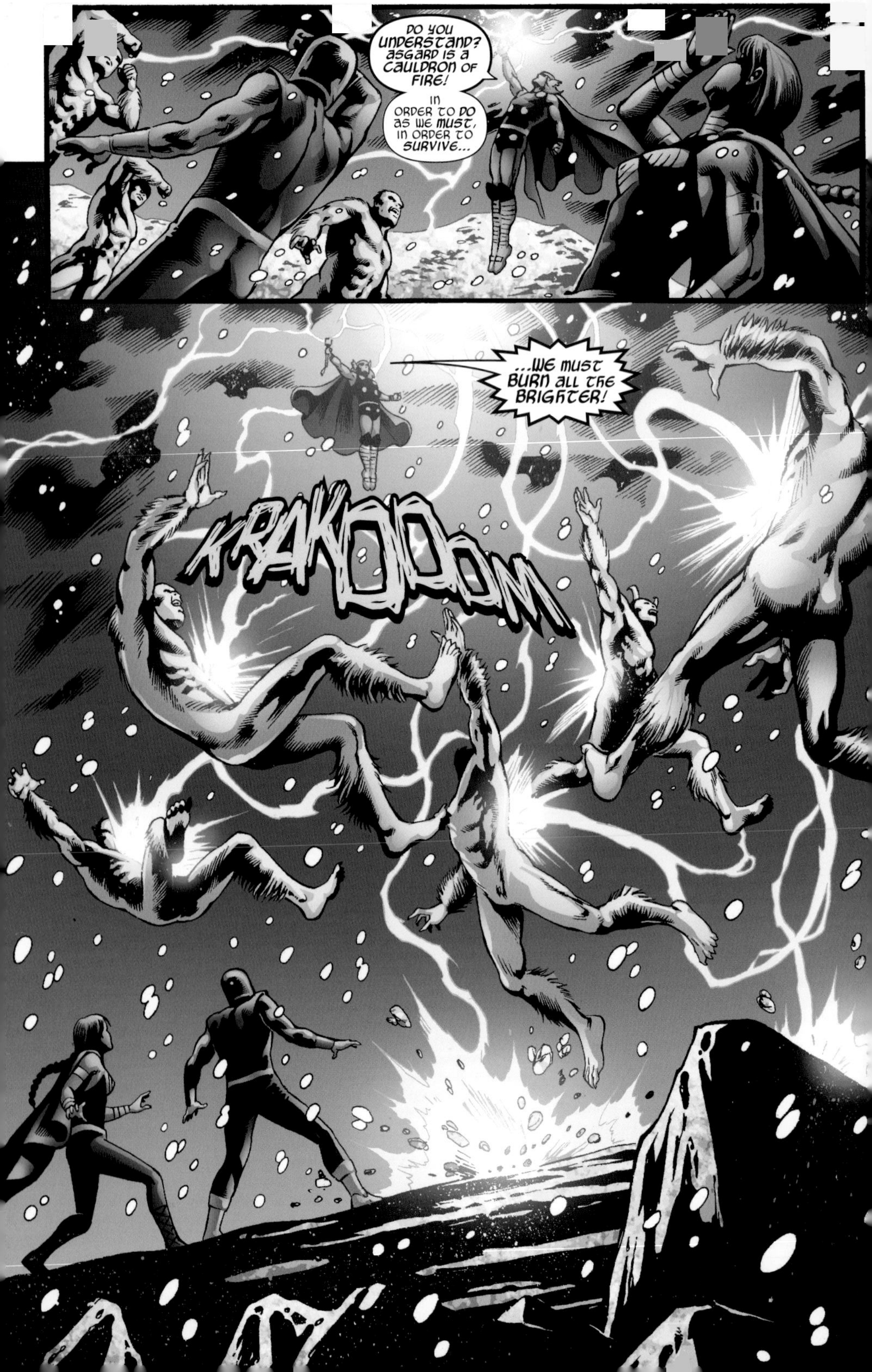
DO YOU UNDERSTAND? ASGARD IS A CAULDRON OF FIRE!
IN ORDER TO DO AS WE MUST, IN ORDER TO SURVIVE...
...WE MUST BURN ALL THE BRIGHTER!
KRAKOOOOM

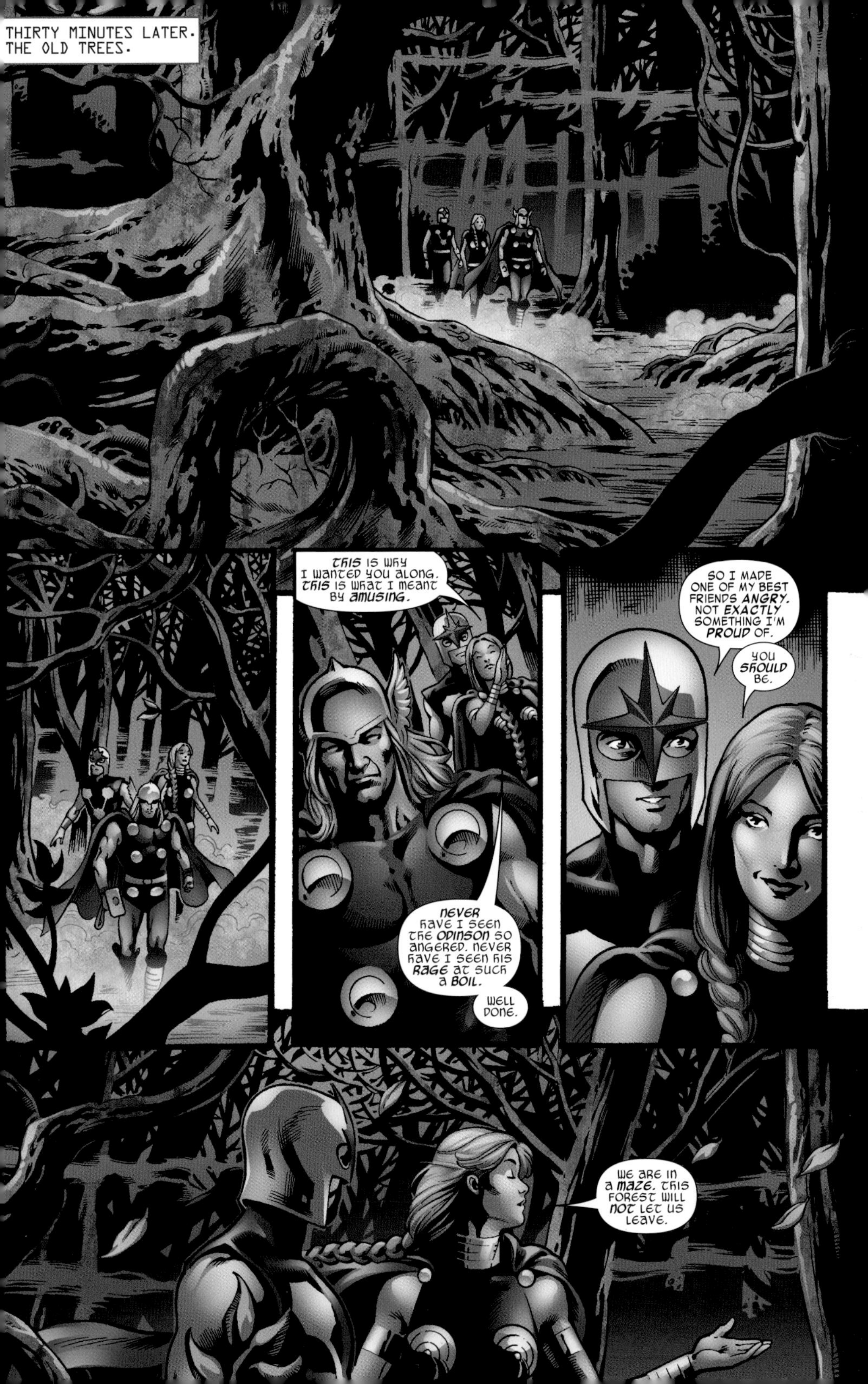
THIRTY MINUTES LATER. THE OLD TREES.
THIS IS WHY I WANTED YOU ALONG. THIS IS WHAT I MEANT BY AMUSING.
NEVER HAVE I SEEN THE ODINSON SO ANGERED. NEVER HAVE I SEEN HIS RAGE AT SUCH A BOIL.
WELL DONE.
SO I MADE ONE OF MY BEST FRIENDS ANGRY. NOT EXACTLY SOMETHING I'M PROUD OF.
YOU SHOULD BE.
WE ARE IN A MAZE. THIS FOREST WILL NOT LET US LEAVE.

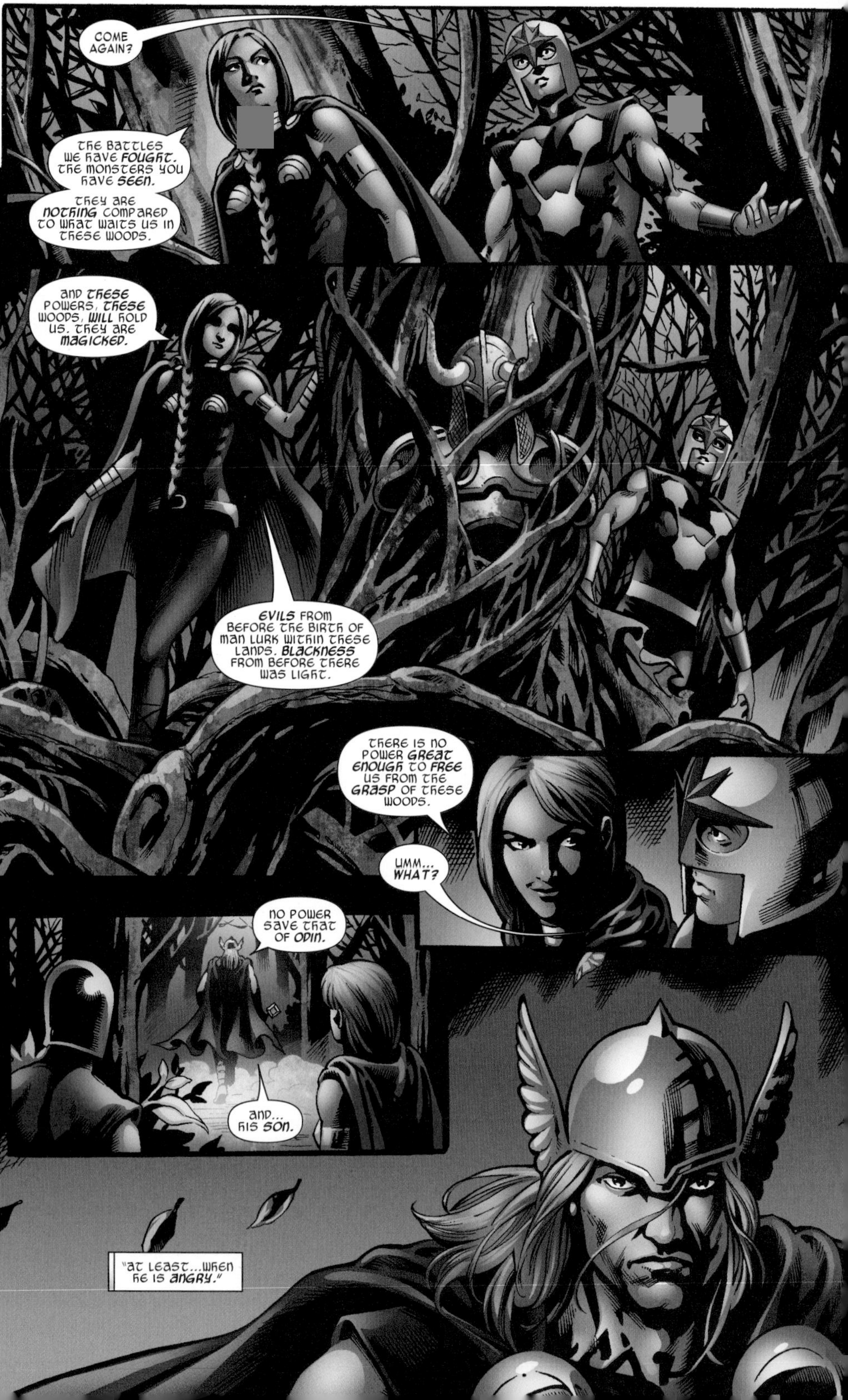
COME AGAIN?
THE BATTLES WE HAVE FOUGHT. THE MONSTERS YOU HAVE SEEN.
THEY ARE NOTHING COMPARED TO WHAT WAITS US IN THESE WOODS.
AND THESE POWERS, THESE WOODS, WILL HOLD US. THEY ARE MAGICKED.
EVILS FROM BEFORE THE BIRTH OF MAN LURK WITHIN THESE LANDS. BLACKNESS FROM BEFORE THERE WAS LIGHT.
THERE IS NO POWER GREAT ENOUGH TO FREE US FROM THE GRASP OF THESE WOODS.
UMM... WHAT?
NO POWER SAVE THAT OF ODIN.
AND... HIS SON.
"AT LEAST...WHEN HE IS ANGRY."

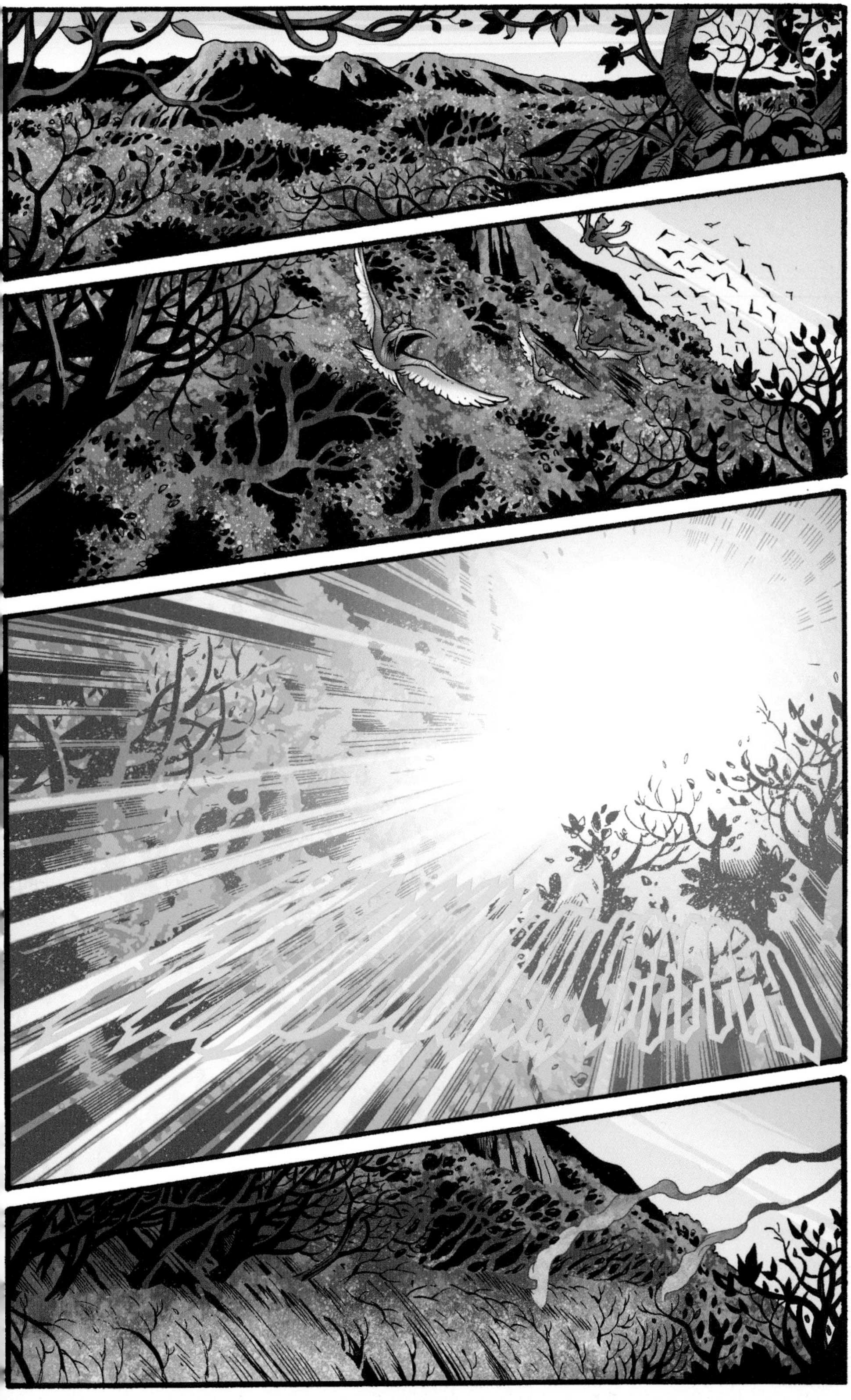

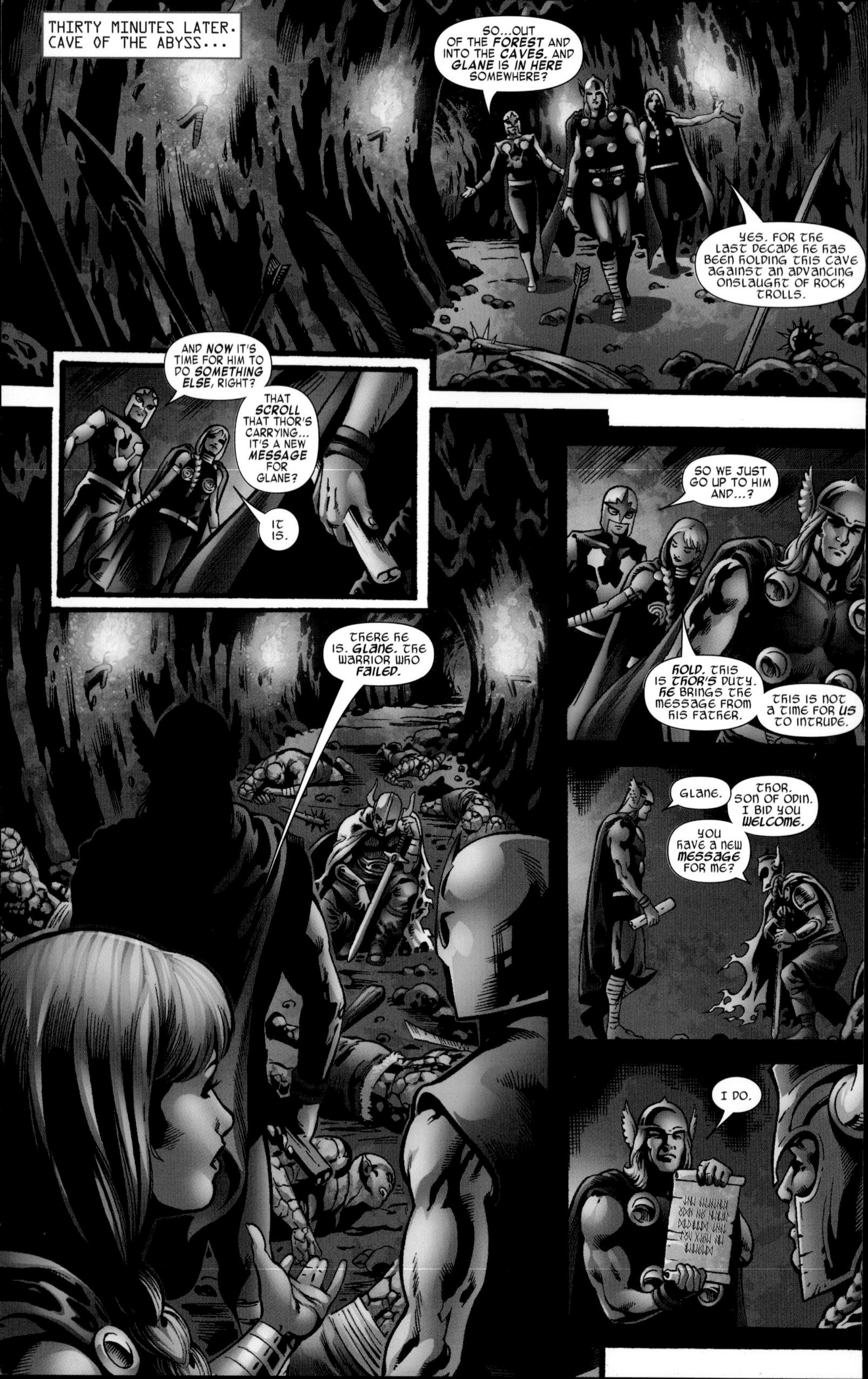
THIRTY MINUTES LATER. CAVE OF THE ABYSS...
SO...OUT OF THE FOREST AND INTO THE CAVES. AND GLANE IS IN HERE SOMEWHERE?
YES. FOR THE LAST DECADE HE HAS BEEN HOLDING THIS CAVE AGAINST AN ADVANCING ONSLAUGHT OF ROCK TROLLS.
AND NOW IT'S TIME FOR HIM TO DO SOMETHING ELSE, RIGHT?
THAT SCROLL THAT THOR'S CARRYING... IT'S A NEW MESSAGE FOR GLANE?
IT IS.
SO WE JUST GO UP TO HIM AND...?
HOLD. THIS IS THOR'S DUTY. HE BRINGS THE MESSAGE FROM HIS FATHER.
THIS IS NOT A TIME FOR US TO INTRUDE.
THERE HE IS. GLANE. THE WARRIOR WHO FAILED.
GLANE.
THOR. SON OF ODIN. I BID YOU WELCOME.
YOU HAVE A NEW MESSAGE FOR ME?
I DO.

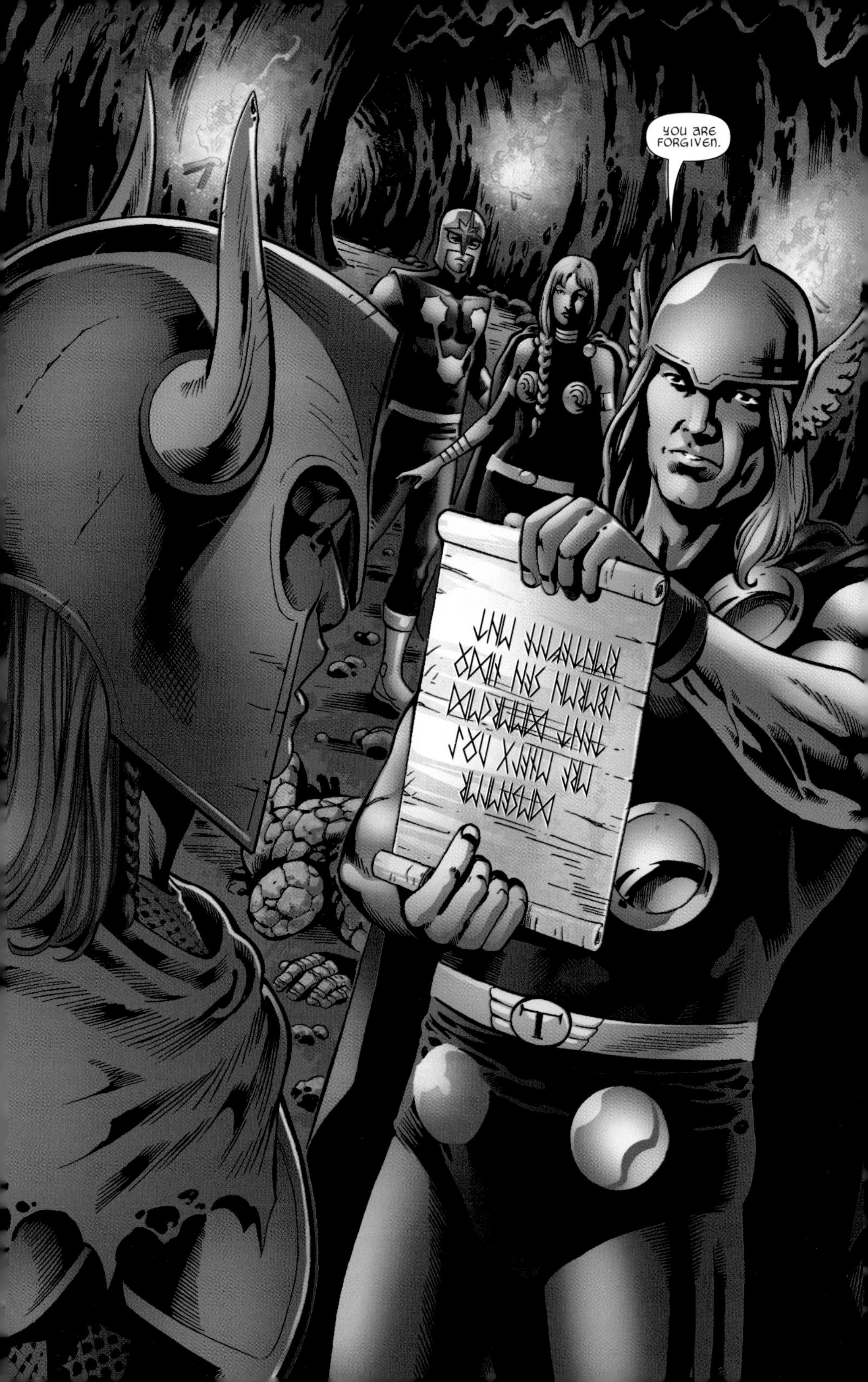
YOU ARE FORGIVEN.

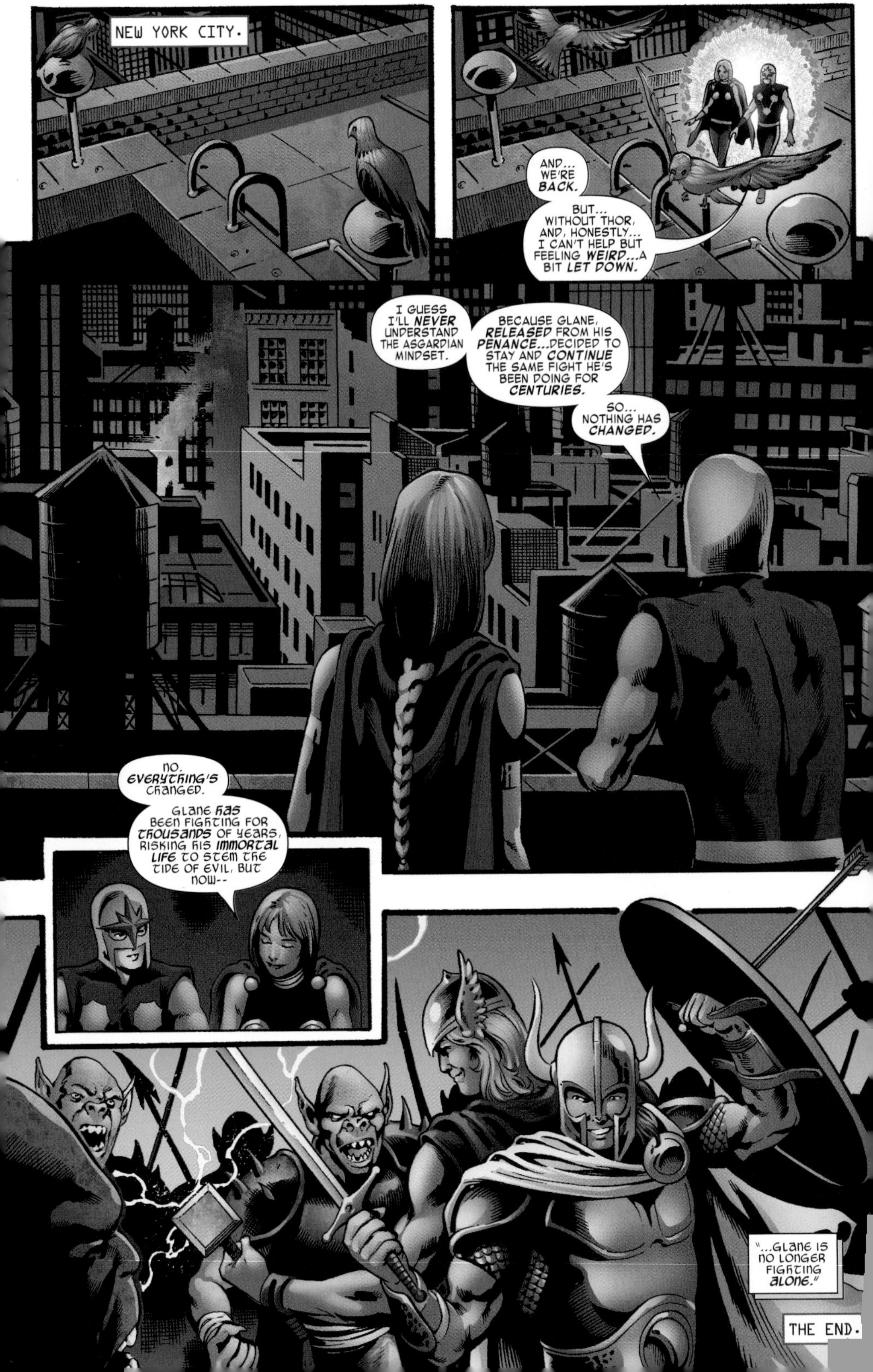
NEW YORK CITY.
AND... WE'RE BACK.
BUT... WITHOUT THOR, AND, HONESTLY... I CAN'T HELP BUT FEELING WEIRD...A BIT LET DOWN.
I GUESS I'LL NEVER UNDERSTAND THE ASGARDIAN MINDSET.
BECAUSE GLANE, RELEASED FROM HIS PENANCE...DECIDED TO STAY AND CONTINUE THE SAME FIGHT HE'S BEEN DOING FOR CENTURIES.
SO... NOTHING HAS CHANGED.
NO. EVERYTHING'S CHANGED.
GLANE HAS BEEN FIGHTING FOR THOUSANDS OF YEARS, RISKING HIS IMMORTAL LIFE TO STEM THE TIDE OF EVIL, BUT NOW--
"...GLANE IS NO LONGER FIGHTING ALONE."
THE END.

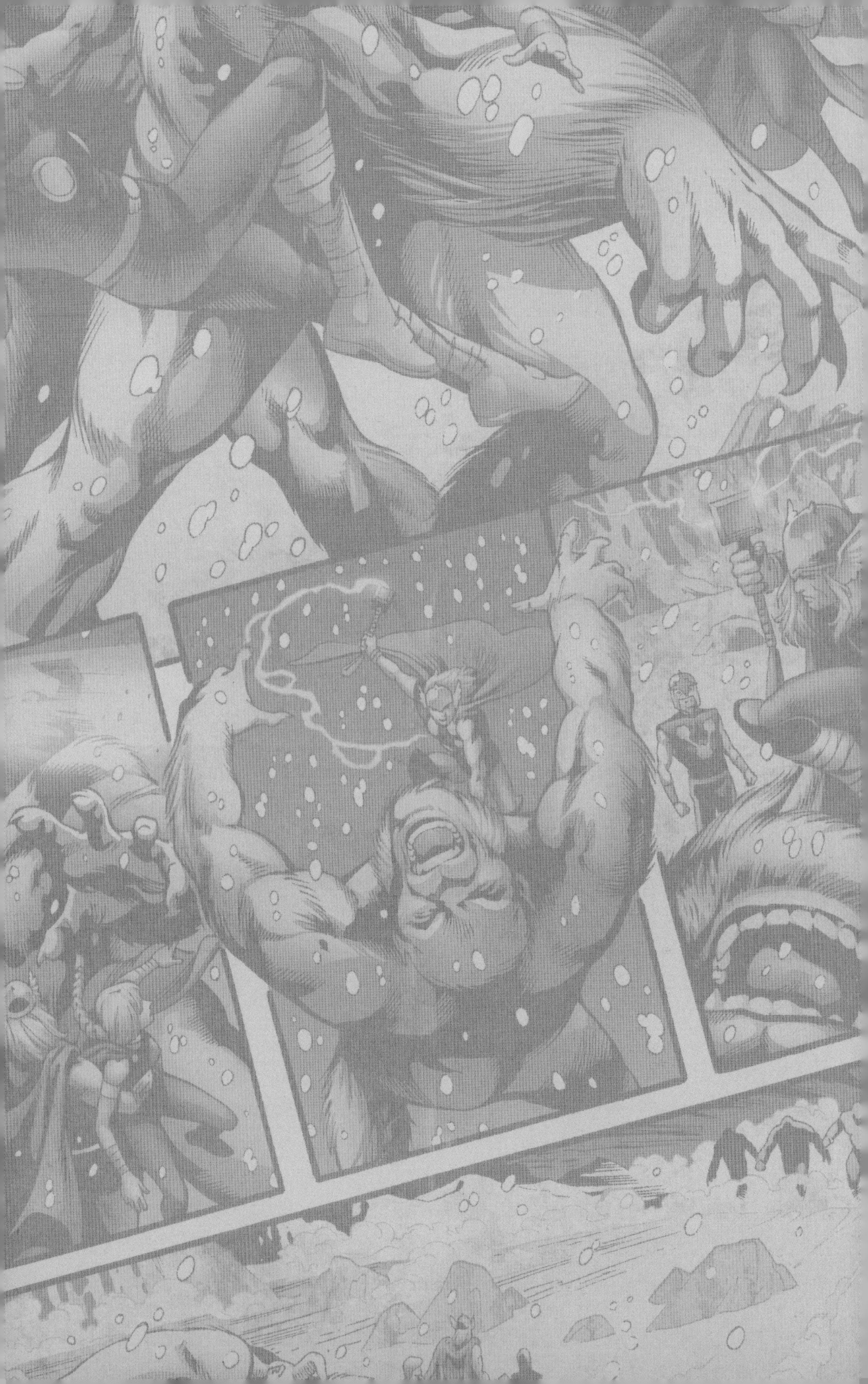

06

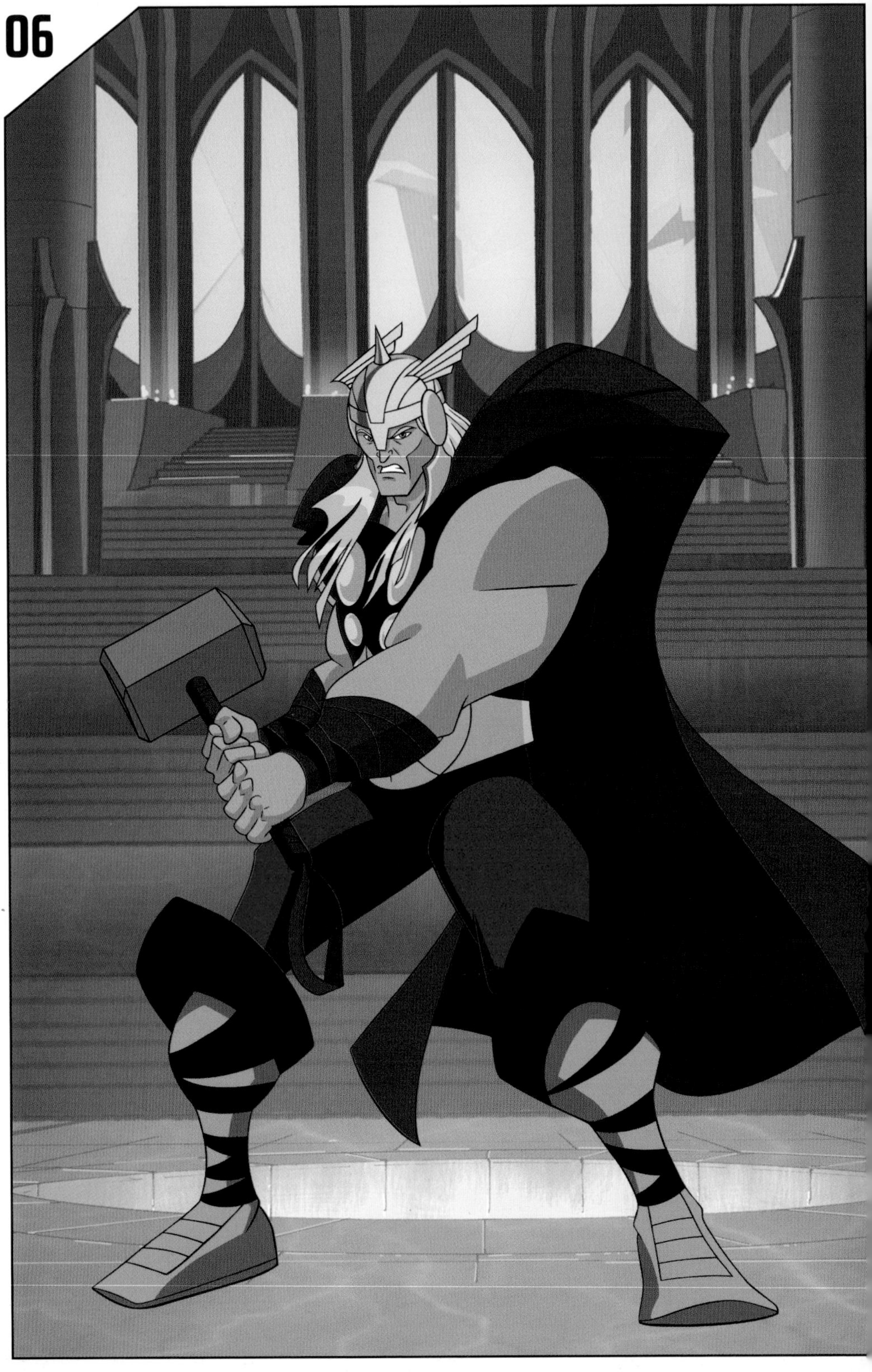

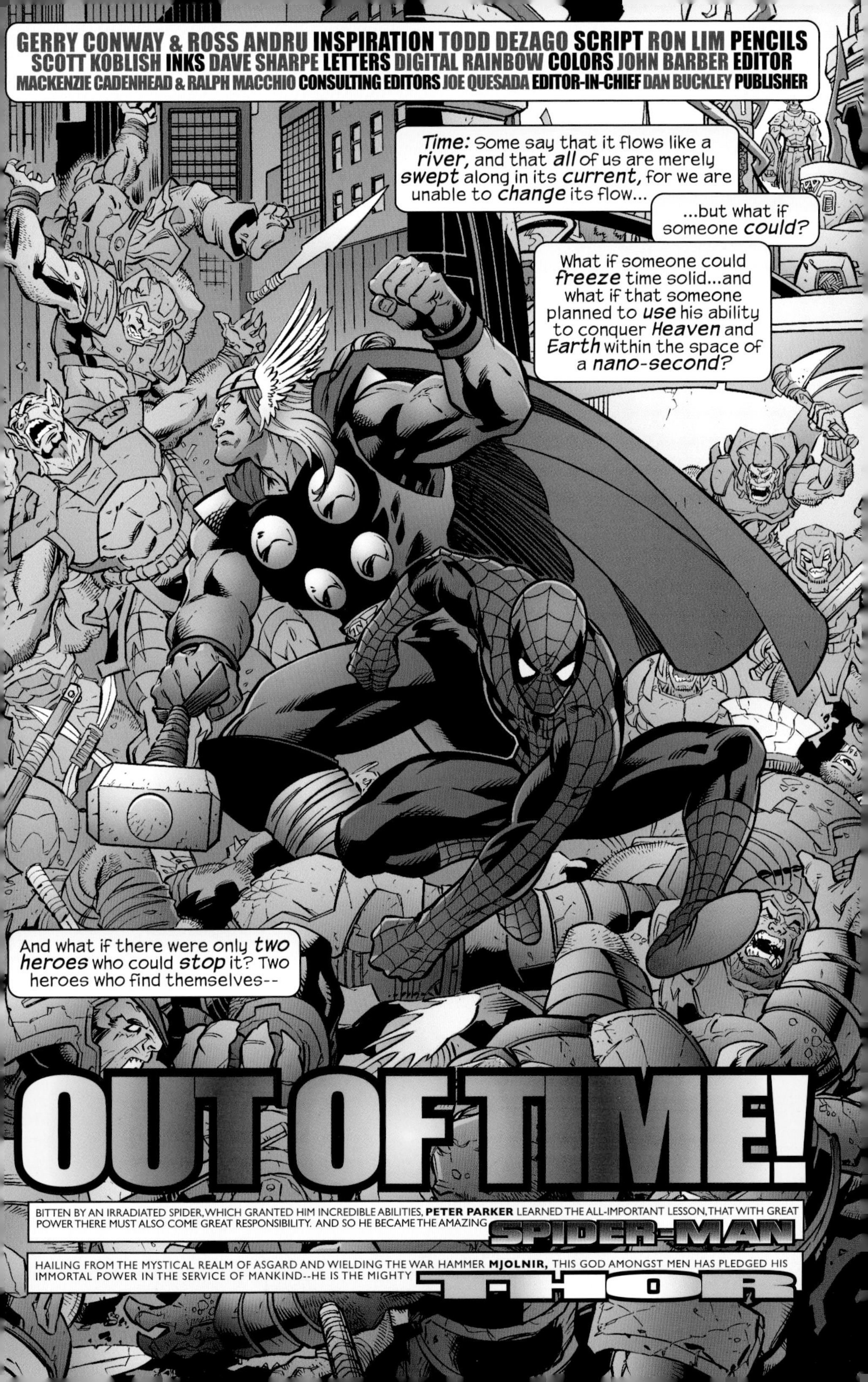
GERRY CONWAY & ROSS ANDRU INSPIRATION TODD DEZAGO SCRIPT RON LIM PENCILS SCOTT KOBLISH INKS DAVE SHARPE LETTERS DIGITAL RAINBOW COLORS JOHN BARBER EDITOR MACKENZIE CADENHEAD & RALPH MACCHIO CONSULTING EDITORS JOE QUESADA EDITOR-IN-CHIEF DAN BUCKLEY PUBLISHER
Time: Some say that it flows like a river, and that all of us are merely swept along in its current, for we are unable to change its flow...
...but what if someone could?
What if someone could freeze time solid...and what if that someone planned to use his ability to conquer Heaven and Earth within the space of a nano-second?
And what if there were only two heroes who could stop it? Two heroes who find themselves--
OUT OF TIME!
BITTEN BY AN IRRADIATED SPIDER, WHICH GRANTED HIM INCREDIBLE ABILITIES, PETER PARKER LEARNED THE ALL-IMPORTANT LESSON, THAT WITH GREAT POWER THERE MUST ALSO COME GREAT RESPONSIBILITY. AND SO HE BECAME THE AMAZING SPIDER-MAN
HAILING FROM THE MYSTICAL REALM OF ASGARD AND WIELDING THE WAR HAMMER MJOLNIR, THIS GOD AMONGST MEN HAS PLEDGED HIS IMMORTAL POWER IN THE SERVICE OF MANKIND--HE IS THE MIGHTY THOR

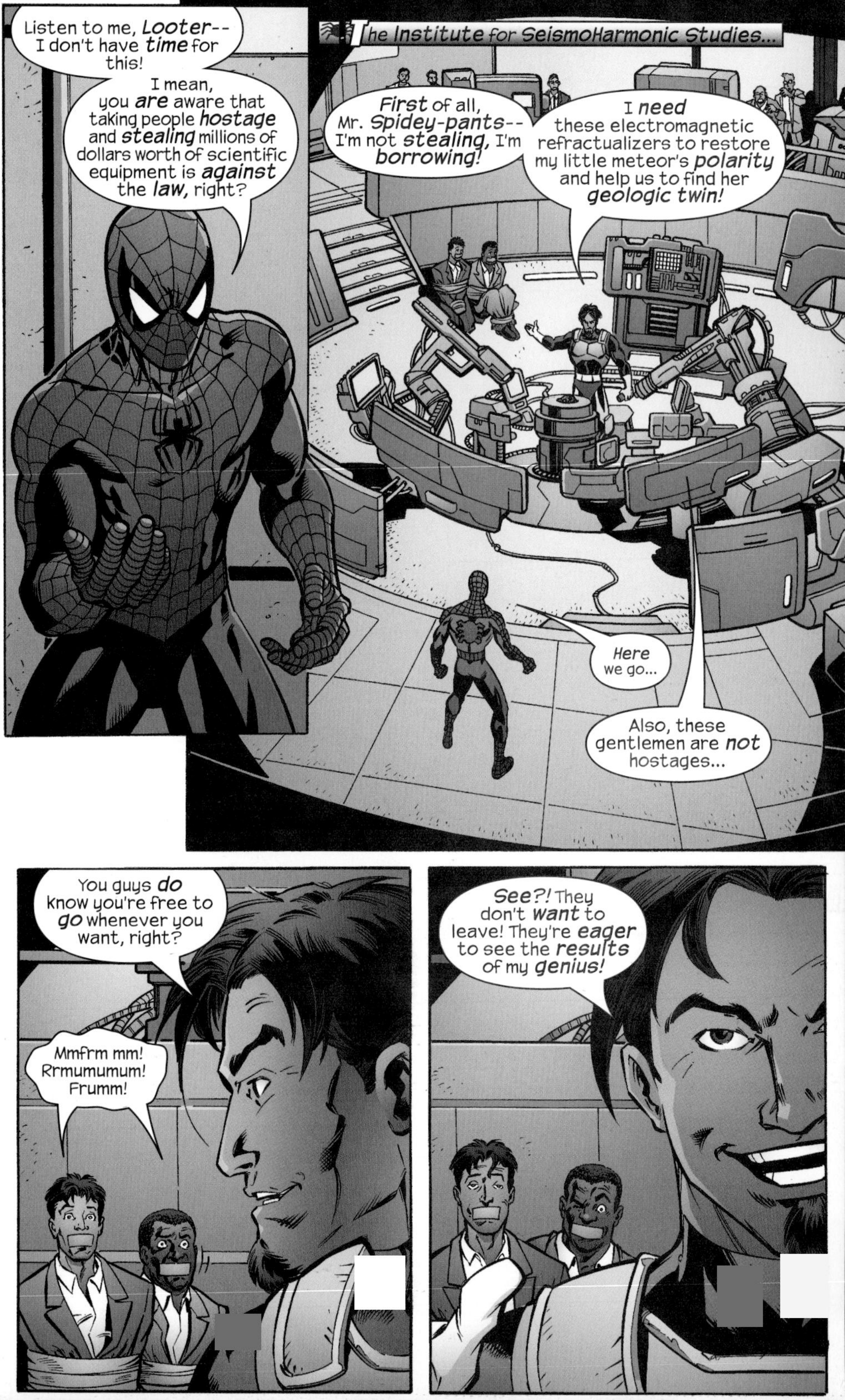
Listen to me, Looter-- I don't have time for this!
I mean, you are aware that taking people hostage and stealing millions of dollars worth of scientific equipment is against the law, right?
The Institute for SeismoHarmonic Studies...
First of all, Mr. Spidey-pants-- I'm not stealing, I'm borrowing!
I need these electromagnetic refractualizers to restore my little meteor's polarity and help us to find her geologic twin!
Here we go...
Also, these gentlemen are not hostages...
You guys do know you're free to go whenever you want, right?
Mmfrm mm! Rrmumumum! Frumm!
See?! They don't want to leave! They're eager to see the results of my genius!

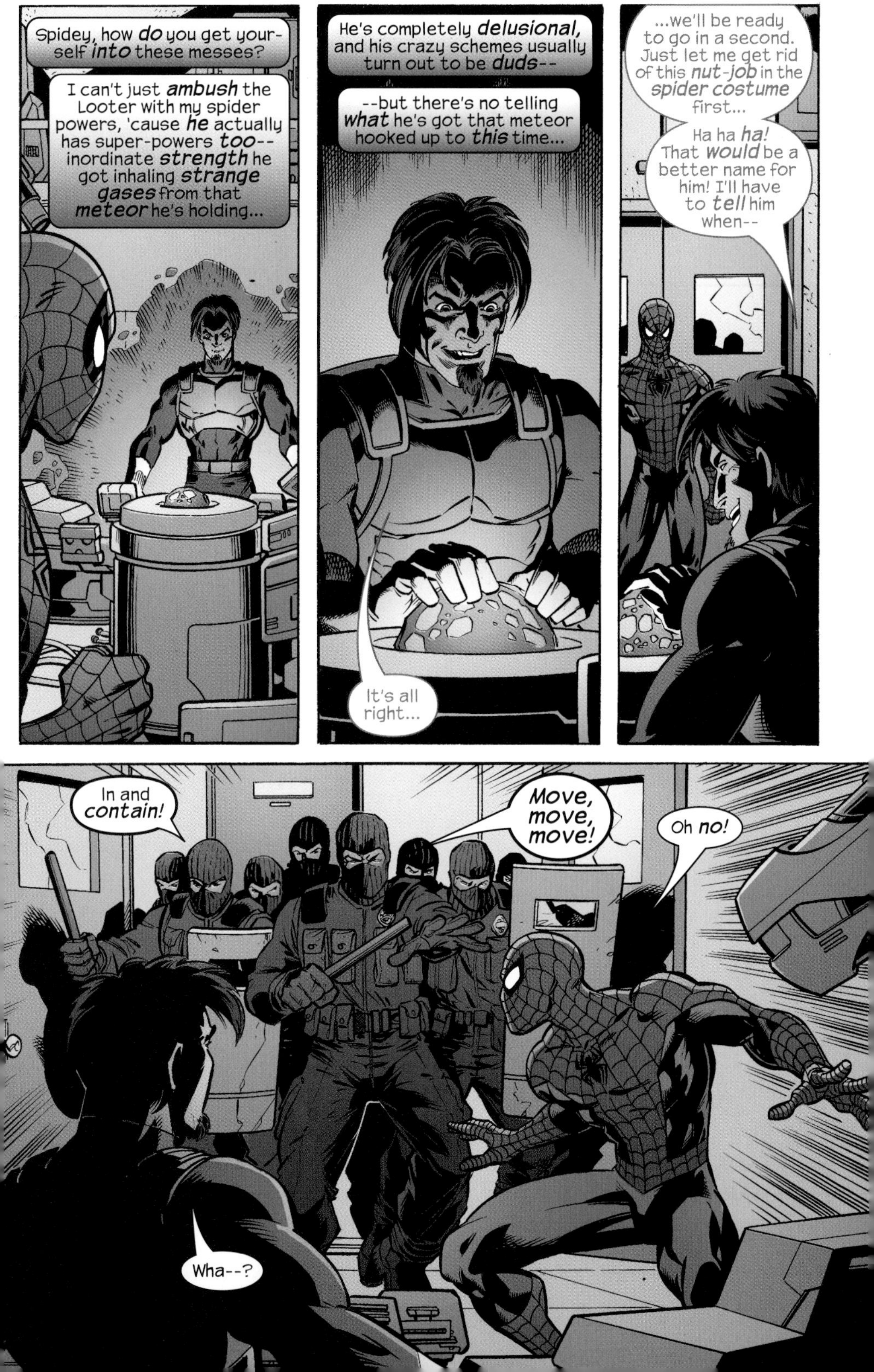
Spidey, how do you get yourself into these messes?
I can't just ambush the Looter with my spider powers, 'cause he actually has super-powers too--inordinate strength he got inhaling strange gases from that meteor he's holding...
He's completely delusional, and his crazy schemes usually turn out to be duds--
--but there's no telling what he's got that meteor hooked up to this time...
It's all right...
...we'll be ready to go in a second. Just let me get rid of this nut-job in the spider costume first...
Ha ha ha! That would be a better name for him! I'll have to tell him when--
In and contain!
Move, move, move!
Oh no!
Wha--?

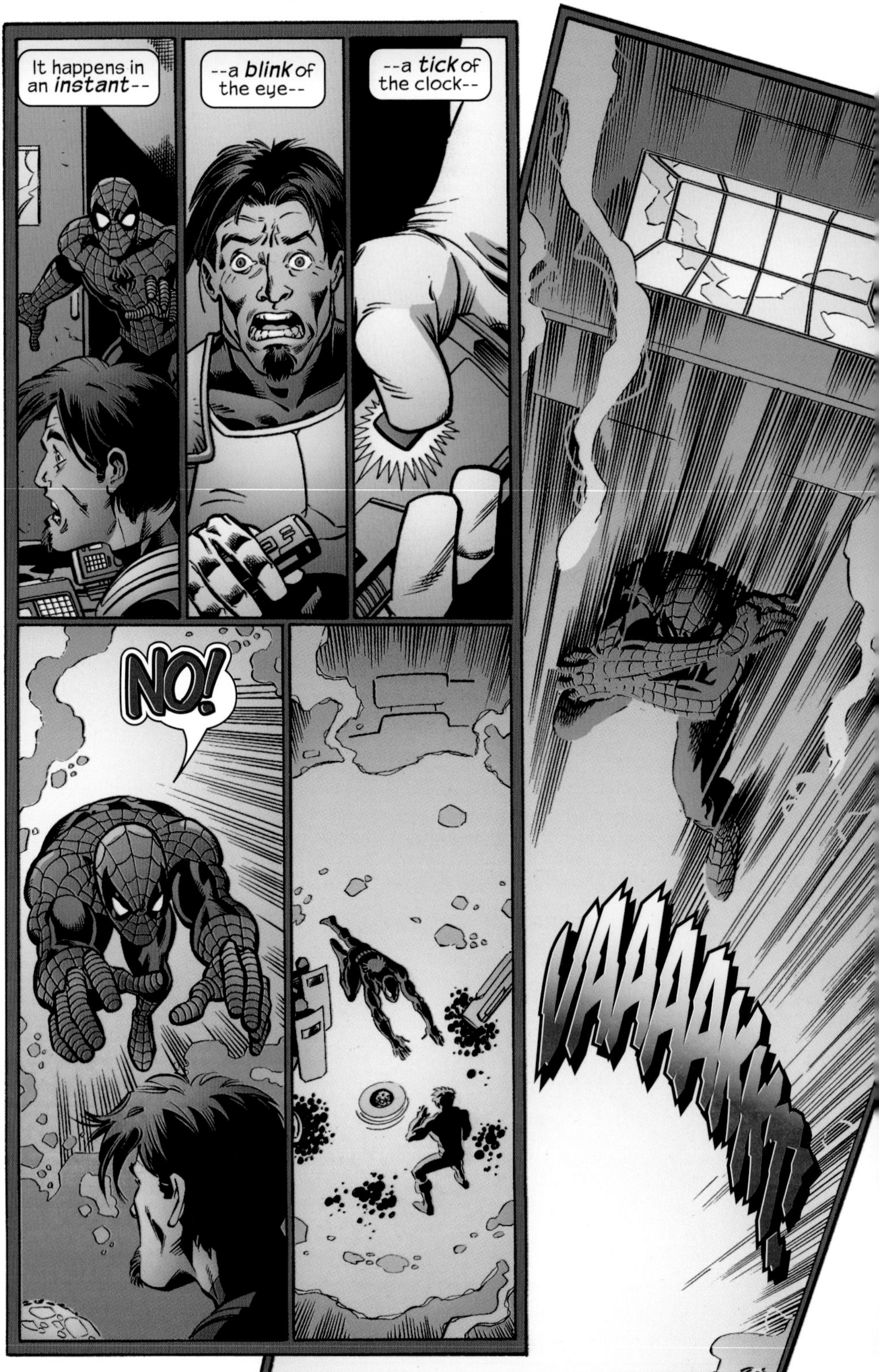
It happens in an instant--
--a blink of the eye--
--a tick of the clock--
NO!
VAAAKK!

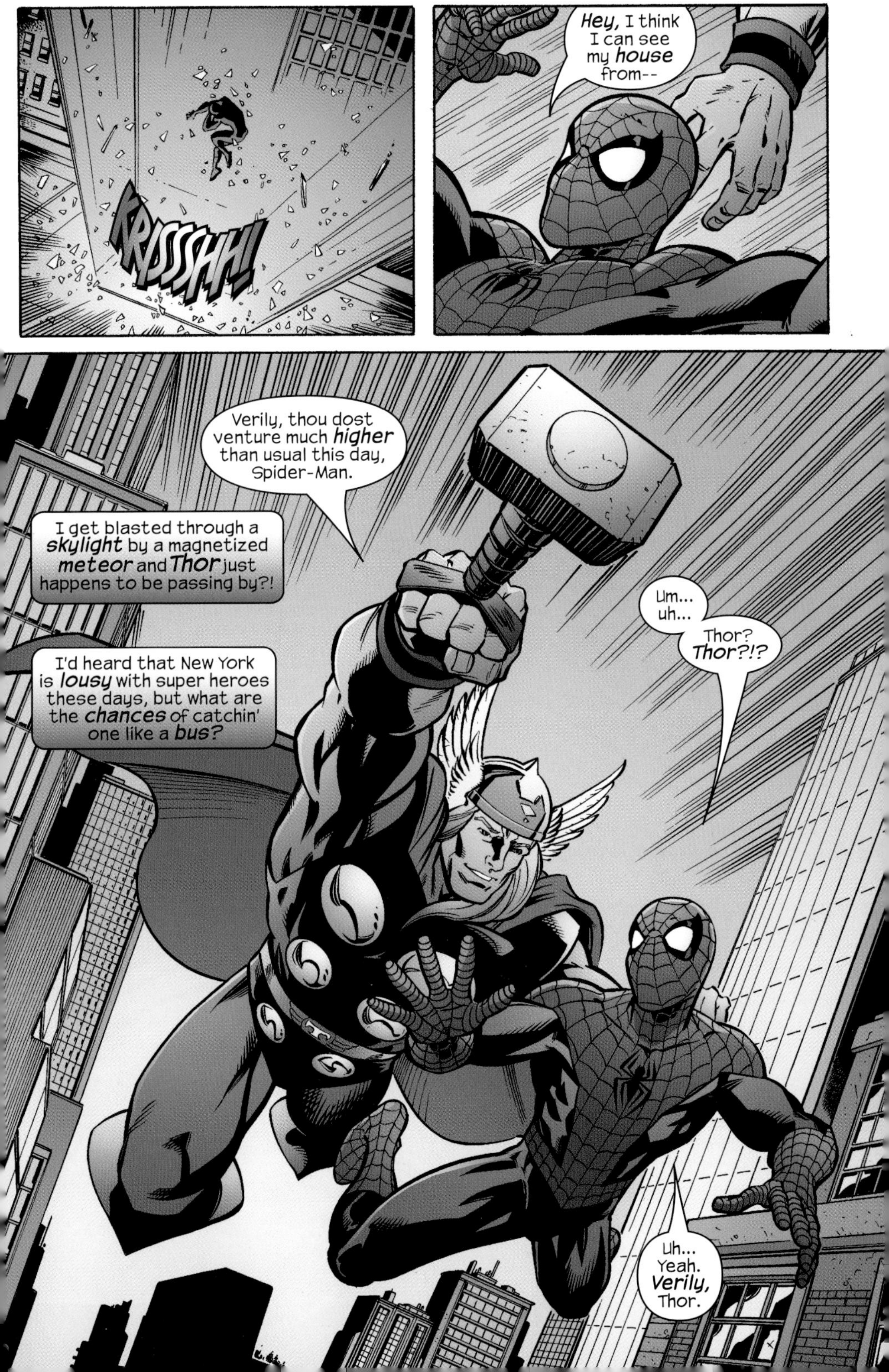
KRISSSHH!
Hey, I think I can see my house from--
Verily, thou dost venture much higher than usual this day, Spider-Man.
I get blasted through a skylight by a magnetized meteor and Thor just happens to be passing by?!
I'd heard that New York is lousy with super heroes these days, but what are the chances of catchin' one like a bus?
Um... uh...
Thor? Thor?!?
Uh... Yeah. Verily, Thor.

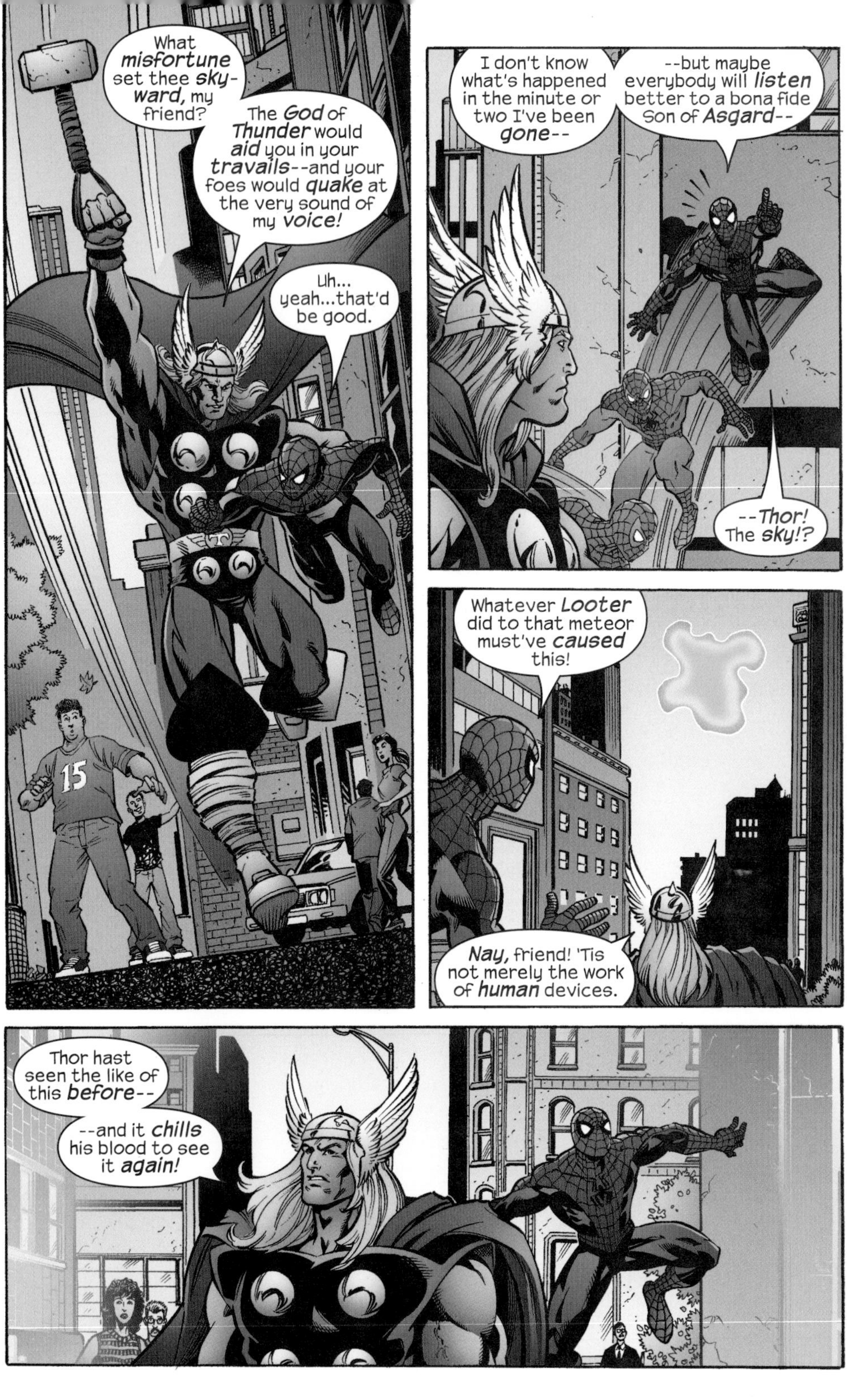

What misfortune set thee sky-ward, my friend?
The God of Thunder would aid you in your travails--and your foes would quake at the very sound of my voice!
Uh... yeah...that'd be good.
I don't know what's happened in the minute or two I've been gone--
--but maybe everybody will listen better to a bona fide Son of Asgard--
--Thor! The sky!?
Whatever Looter did to that meteor must've caused this!
Nay, friend! 'Tis not merely the work of human devices.
Thor hast seen the like of this before--
--and it chills his blood to see it again!
15

WUMWUMMMMMM!

Stand *by* me, Spider-Man—that I may wield mystic *Mjolnir* and safeguard us from the coming *cataclysm!*

What *is* it, Thor? What're you *doing?*

WUMWUMMMM!

WUMWUMMM!

I have transported us a half-step *beyond* the reality we know. For if yon anomaly is *truly* what I *take* it to be...

...t'would be better were we *not* within its chilling grasp.

Okay. Nothing's *moving!*

Time has *stopped?!*

Aye. 'Tis as I have viewed it *before...* ...aeons *past,* in the Realm of *Asgard.*

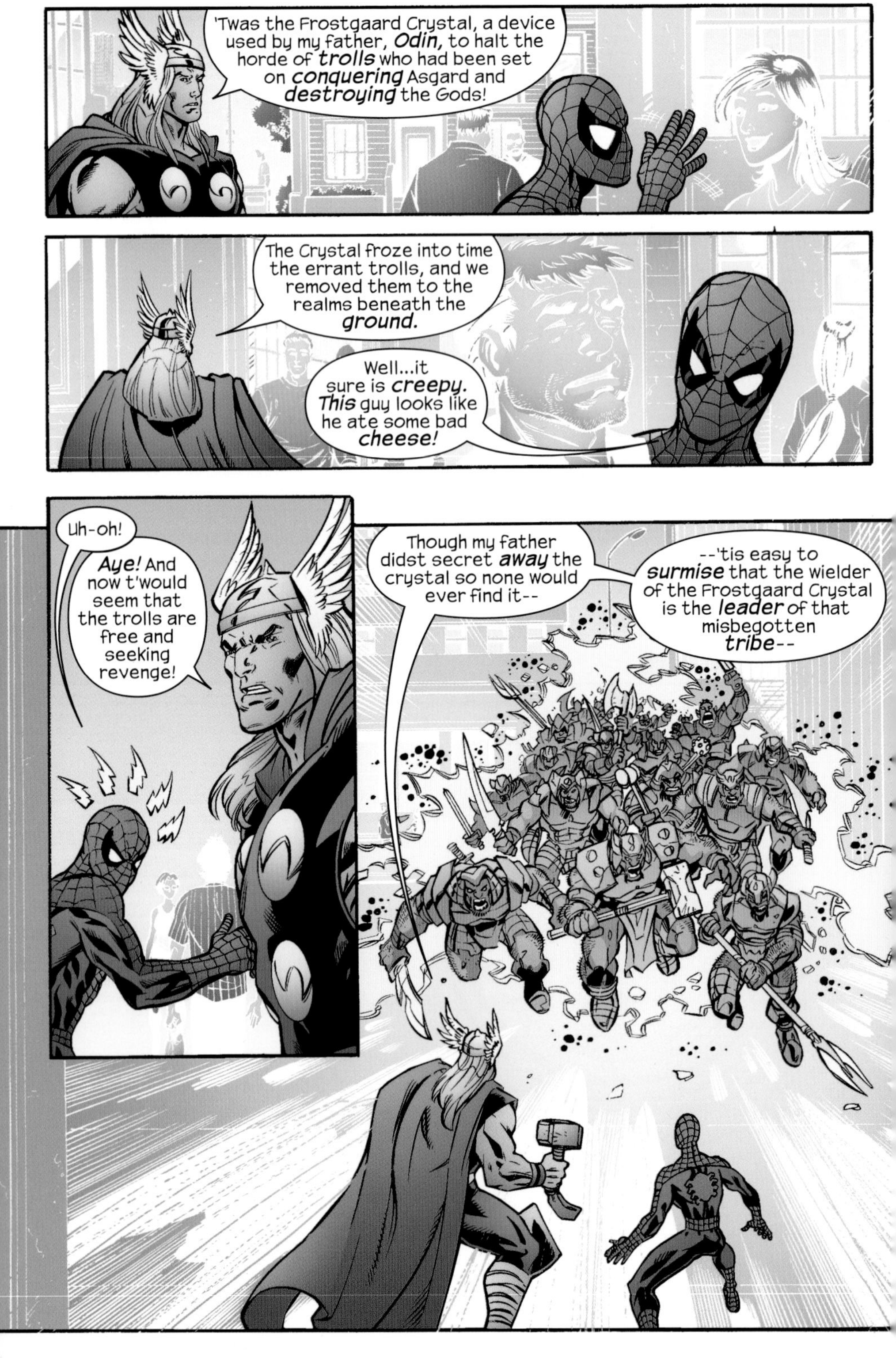
'Twas the Frostgaard Crystal, a device used by my father, Odin, to halt the horde of trolls who had been set on conquering Asgard and destroying the Gods!
The Crystal froze into time the errant trolls, and we removed them to the realms beneath the ground.
Well...it sure is creepy. This guy looks like he ate some bad cheese!
Uh-oh!
Aye! And now t'would seem that the trolls are free and seeking revenge!
Though my father didst secret away the crystal so none would ever find it--
--'tis easy to surmise that the wielder of the Frostgaard Crystal is the leader of that misbegotten tribe--

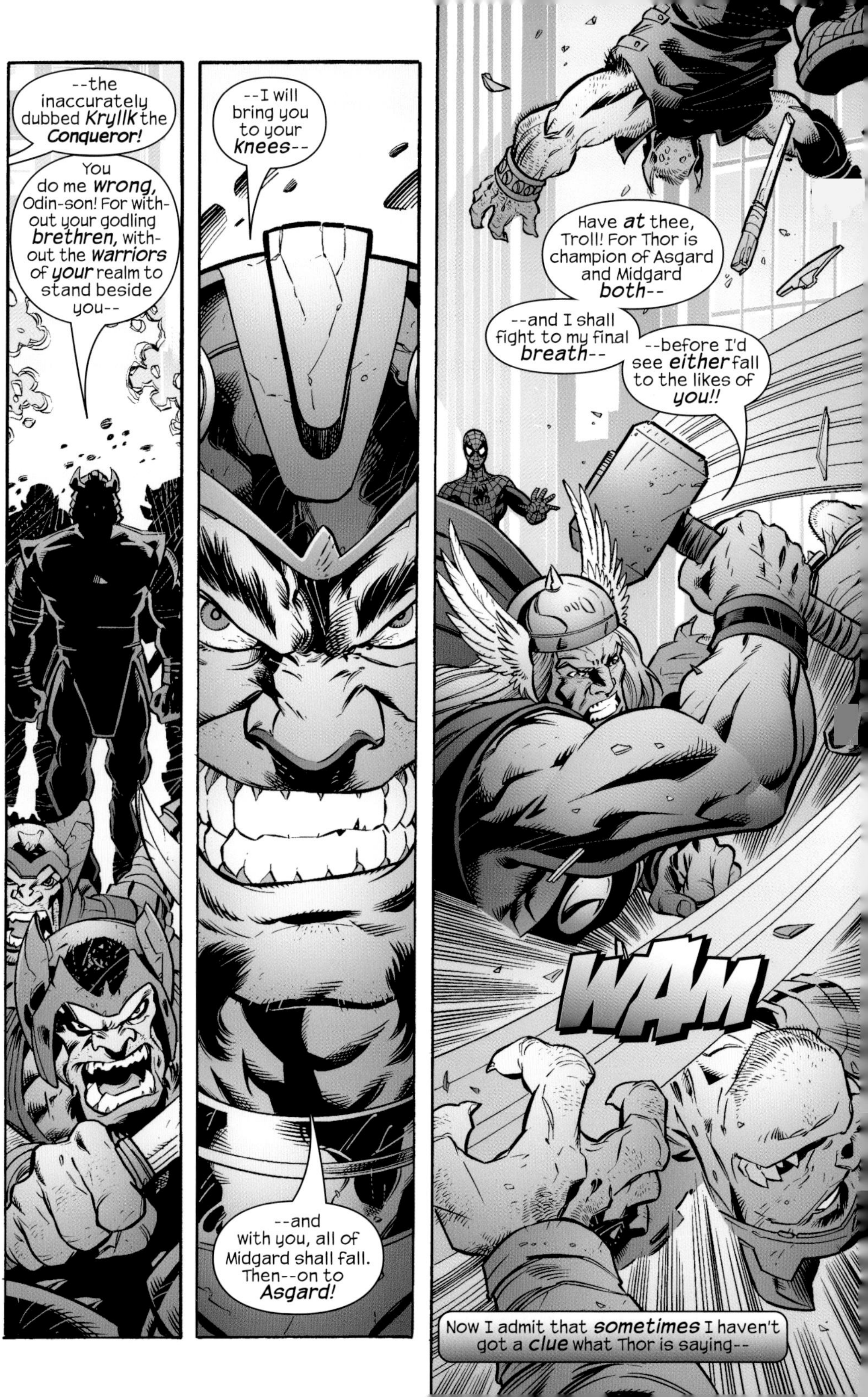
--the inaccurately dubbed Krylik the Conqueror!
You do me wrong, Odin-son! For with-out your godling brethren, with-out the warriors of your realm to stand beside you--
--I will bring you to your knees--
--and with you, all of Midgard shall fall. Then--on to Asgard!
Have at thee, Troll! For Thor is champion of Asgard and Midgard both--
--and I shall fight to my final breath--
--before I'd see either fall to the likes of you!!
WAM
Now I admit that sometimes I haven't got a clue what Thor is saying--

--and this *Kryllk* guy isn't too much *better*--

--but I'm pretty sure that *"Midgard"* means *"Earth."* And if that's what Thor is *fighting* for--

--then *that's* good enough for *me!*

Thou had best send in your *good* warriors, Kryllk--

WHUD!

CLUD!

--Thor is near *done* with these *practice* trolls!

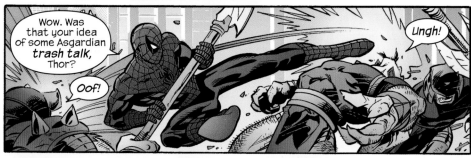

Wow. Was that your idea of some Asgardian *trash talk,* Thor?

Oof!

Ungh!

Oot!

'Cause that was *pathetic.* You need to get with the times!

Kuhhh!

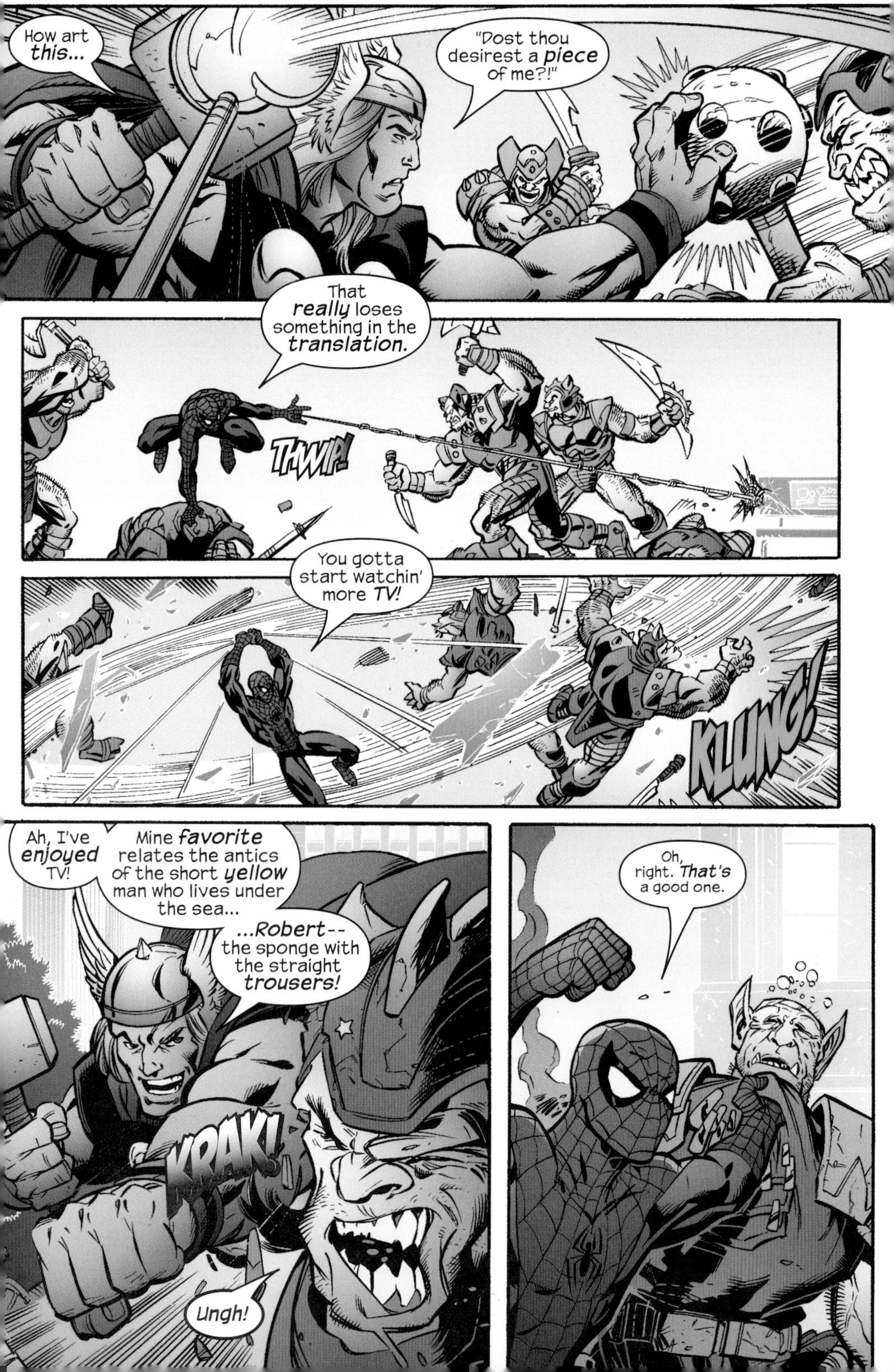
How art this...
"Dost thou desirest a piece of me?!"
That really loses something in the translation.
THWIP!
You gotta start watchin' more TV!
KLUNG!
Ah, I've enjoyed TV!
Mine favorite relates the antics of the short yellow man who lives under the sea...
...Robert-- the sponge with the straight trousers!
KRAK!
Ungh!
Oh, right. That's a good one.

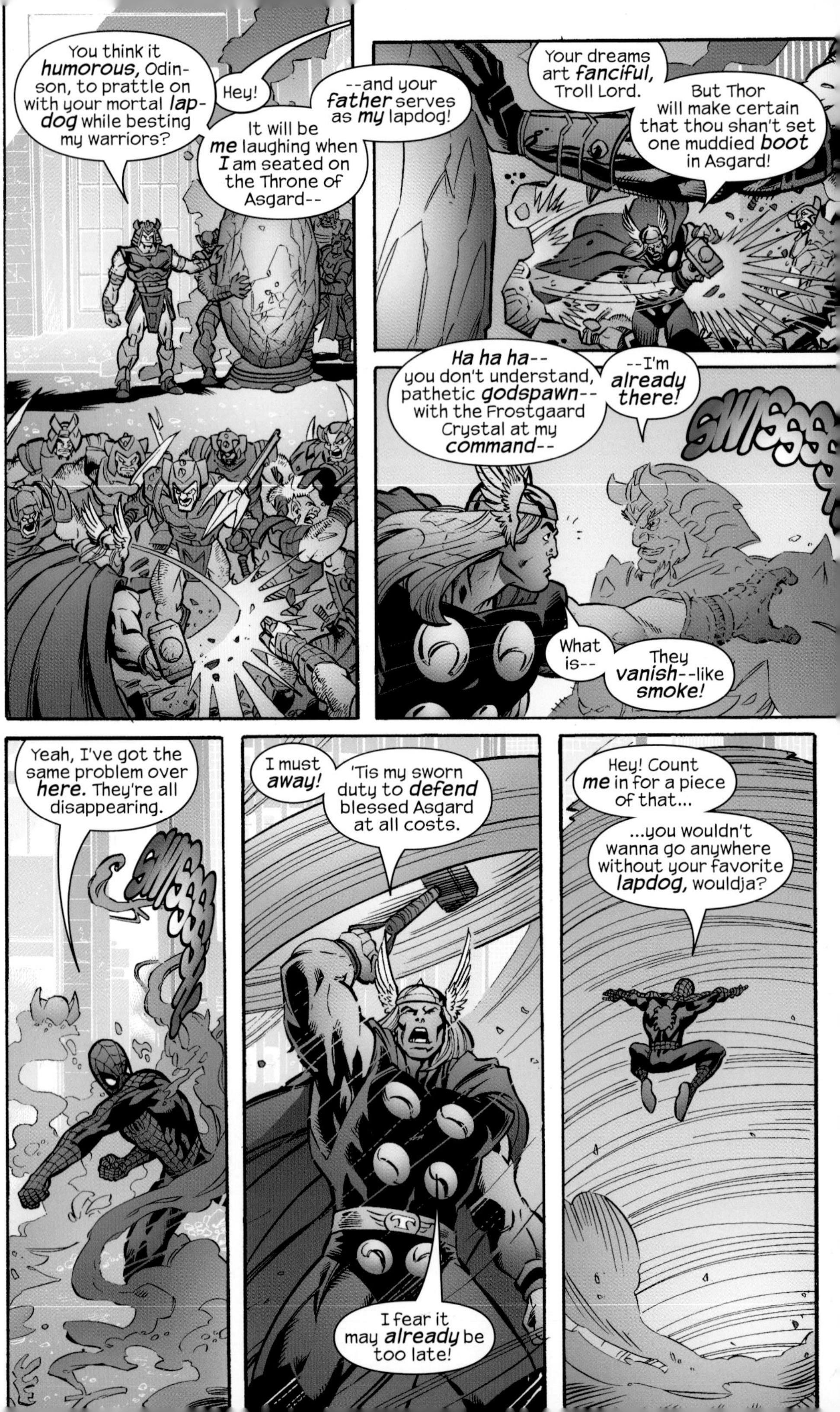
You think it humorous, Odinson, to prattle on with your mortal lapdog while besting my warriors?
Hey!
It will be me laughing when I am seated on the Throne of Asgard--
--and your father serves as my lapdog!
Your dreams art fanciful, Troll Lord.
But Thor will make certain that thou shan't set one muddied boot in Asgard!
Ha ha ha-- you don't understand, pathetic godspawn-- with the Frostgaard Crystal at my command--
--I'm already there!
SWISSS
What is--
They vanish--like smoke!
Yeah, I've got the same problem over here. They're all disappearing.
SWISSSS
I must away!
'Tis my sworn duty to defend blessed Asgard at all costs.
I fear it may already be too late!
Hey! Count me in for a piece of that...
...you wouldn't wanna go anywhere without your favorite lapdog, wouldja?

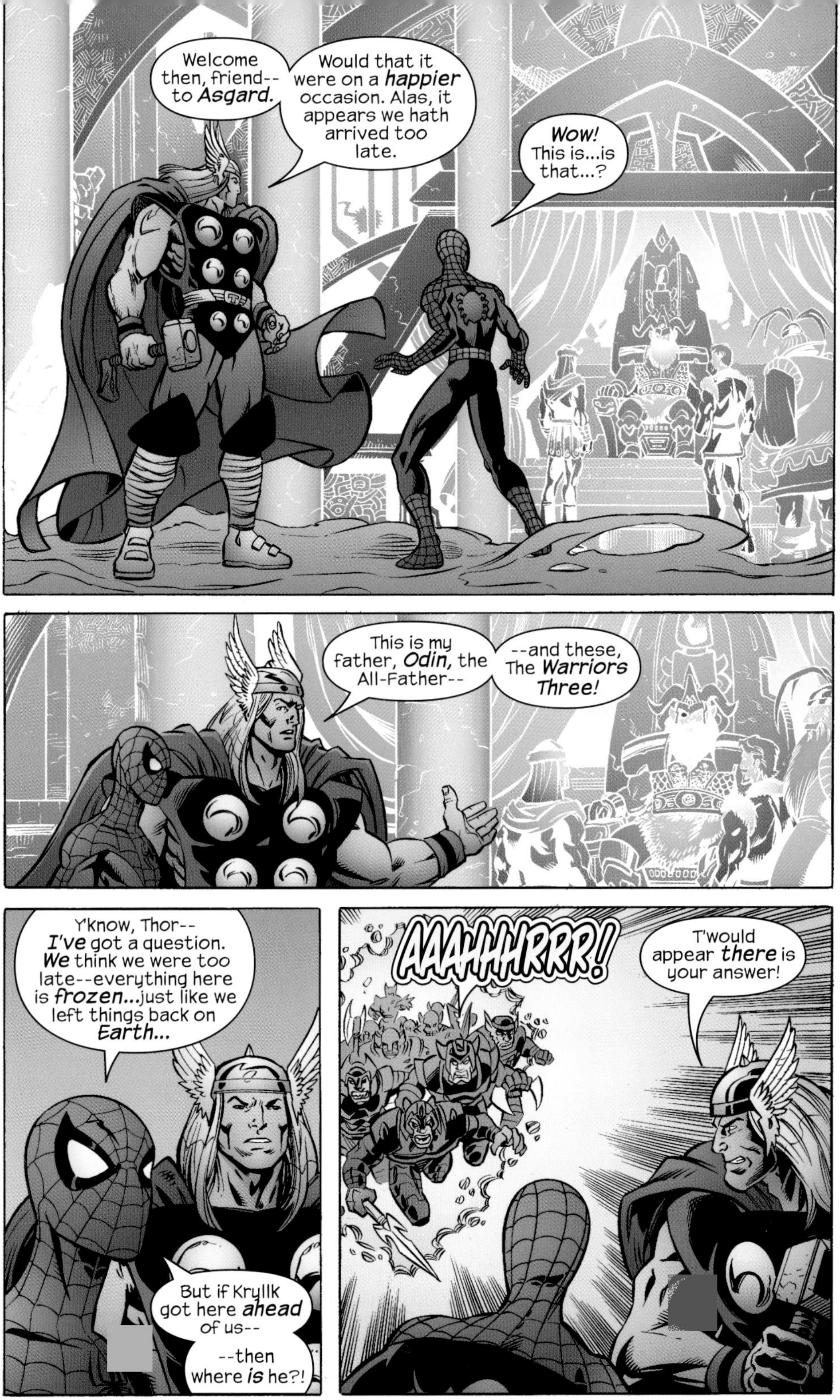
Welcome then, friend-- to Asgard.
Would that it were on a happier occasion. Alas, it appears we hath arrived too late.
Wow! This is...is that...?
This is my father, Odin, the All-Father--
--and these, The Warriors Three!
Y'know, Thor-- I've got a question. We think we were too late--everything here is frozen...just like we left things back on Earth...
But if Krylik got here ahead of us--
--then where is he?!
AAAHHHRRR!
T'would appear there is your answer!

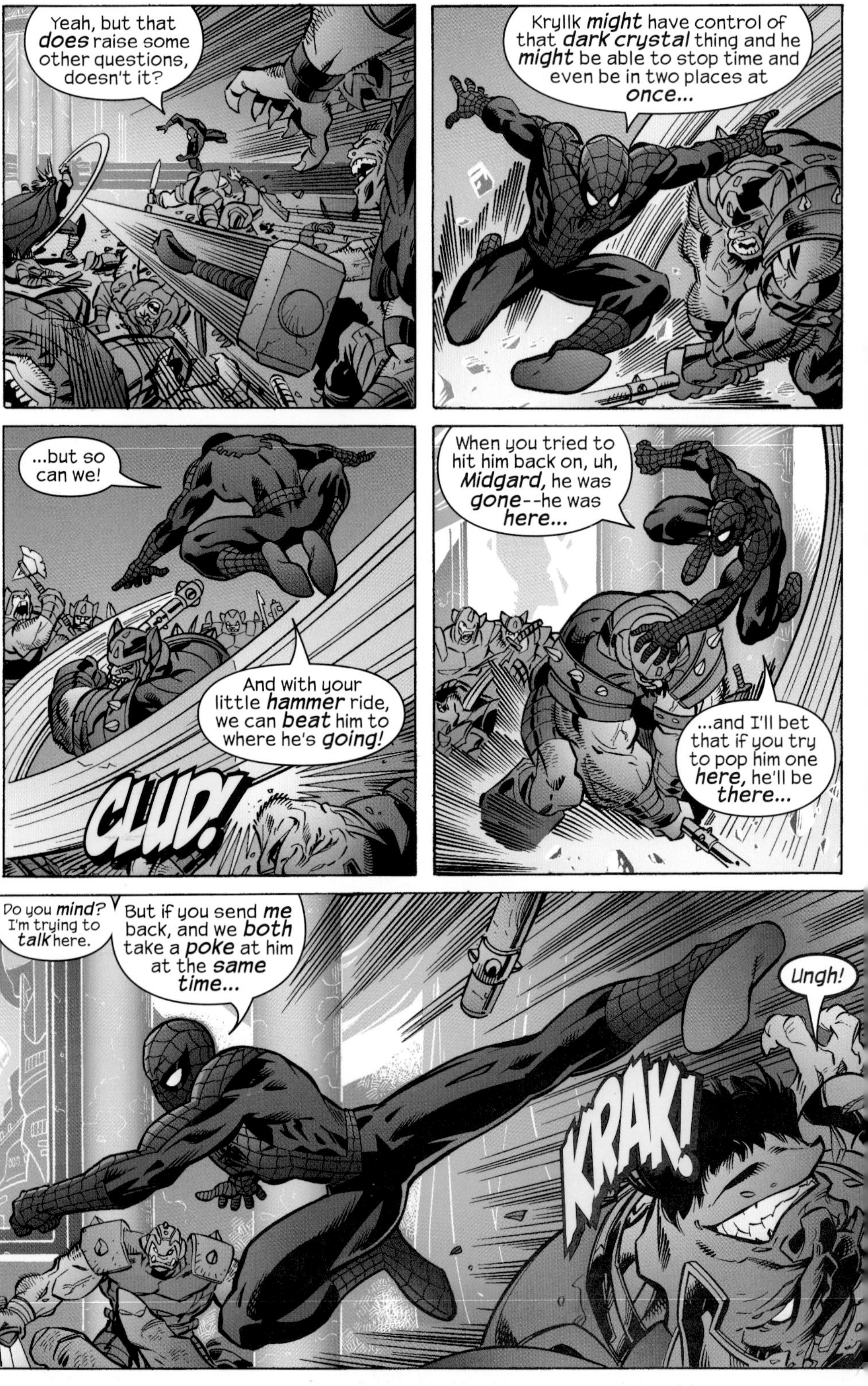
Yeah, but that does raise some other questions, doesn't it?
Kryllk might have control of that dark crystal thing and he might be able to stop time and even be in two places at once...
...but so can we!
And with your little hammer ride, we can beat him to where he's going!
CLUD!
When you tried to hit him back on, uh, Midgard, he was gone--he was here...
...and I'll bet that if you try to pop him one here, he'll be there...
Do you mind? I'm trying to talk here.
But if you send me back, and we both take a poke at him at the same time...
Ungh!
KRAK!

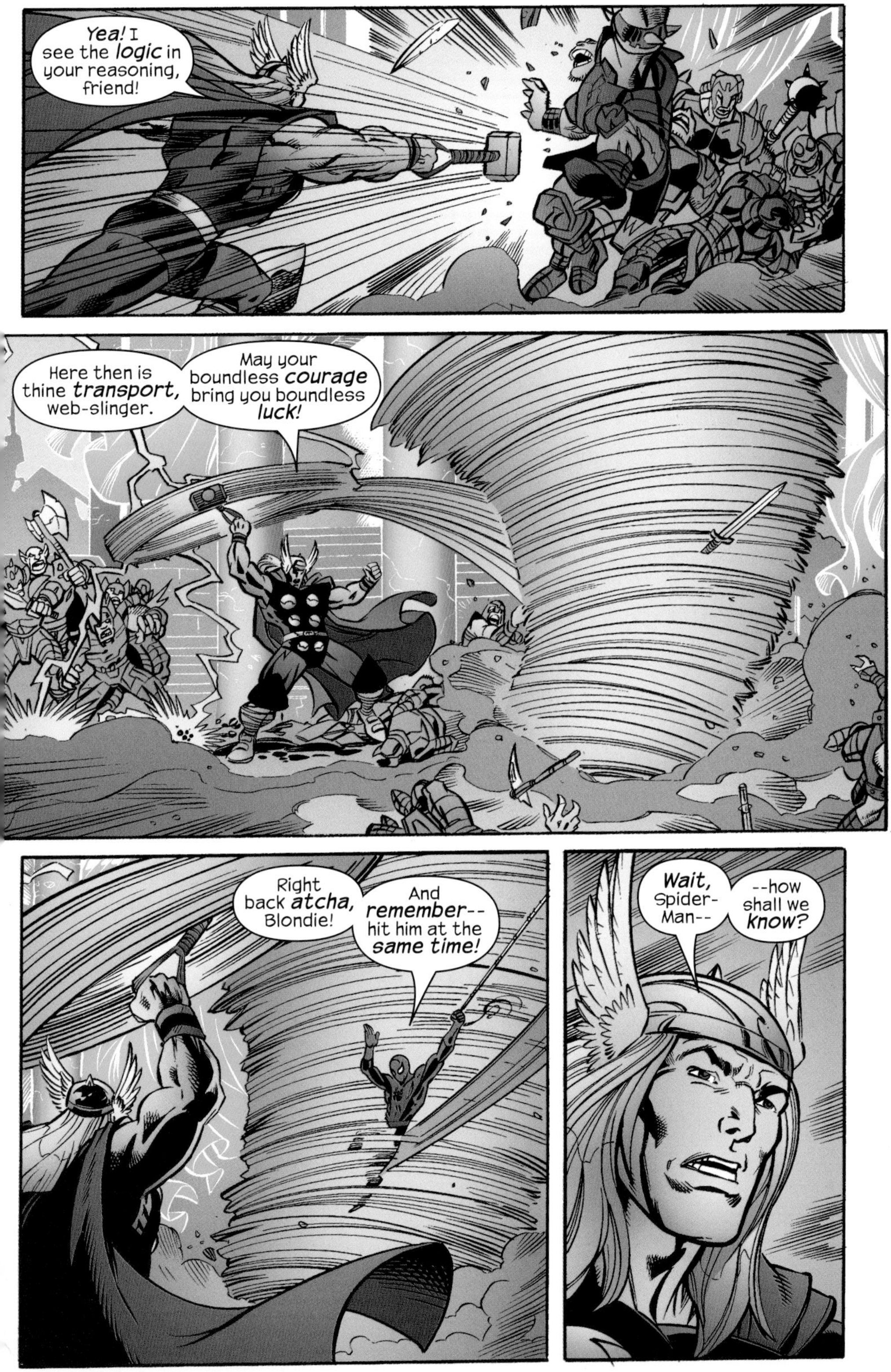
Yea! I see the logic in your reasoning, friend!
Here then is thine transport, web-slinger.
May your boundless courage bring you boundless luck!
Right back atcha, Blondie!
And remember--hit him at the same time!
Wait, Spider-Man--
--how shall we know?

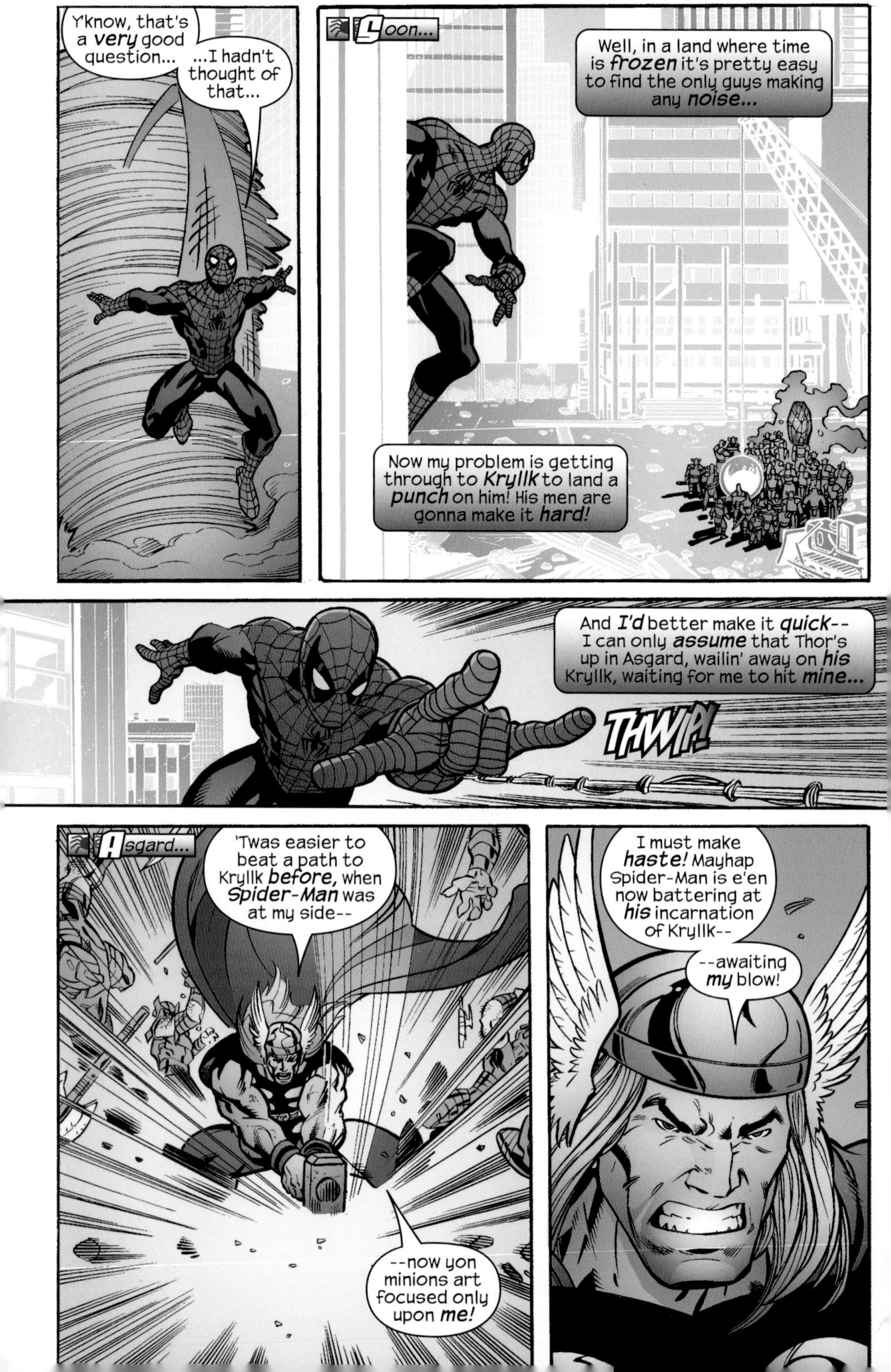
Y'know, that's a very good question...
...I hadn't thought of that...
Soon...
Well, in a land where time is frozen it's pretty easy to find the only guys making any noise...
Now my problem is getting through to Kryllk to land a punch on him! His men are gonna make it hard!
And I'd better make it quick-- I can only assume that Thor's up in Asgard, wailin' away on his Kryllk, waiting for me to hit mine...
THWIP!
Asgard...
'Twas easier to beat a path to Kryllk before, when Spider-Man was at my side--
--now yon minions art focused only upon me!
I must make haste! Mayhap Spider-Man is e'en now battering at his incarnation of Kryllk--
--awaiting my blow!

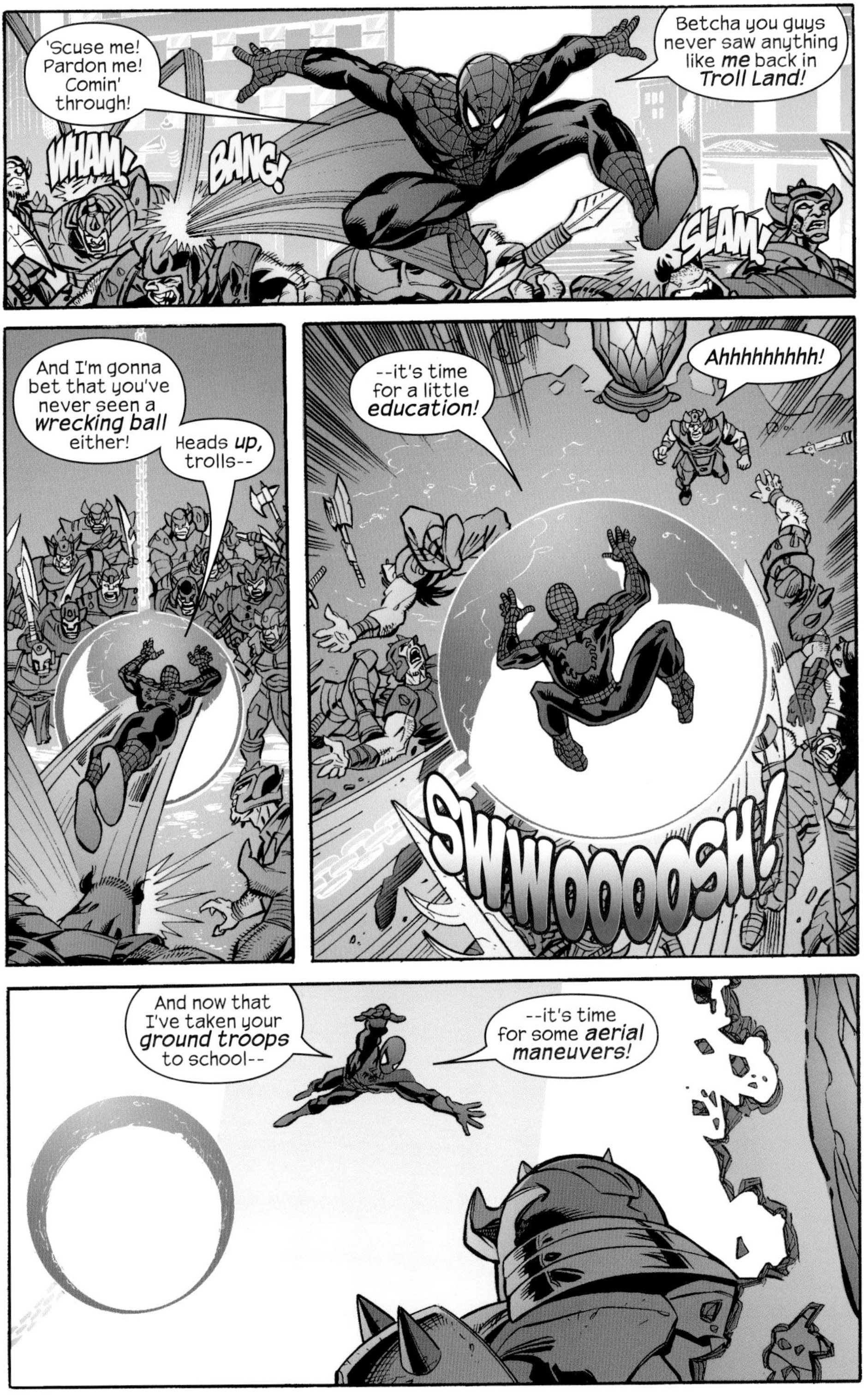
'Scuse me! Pardon me! Comin' through!
Betcha you guys never saw anything like *me* back in *Troll Land!*
WHAM!
BANG!
SLAM!
And I'm gonna bet that you've never seen a *wrecking ball* either!
Heads *up,* trolls--
--it's time for a little *education!*
Ahhhhhhhhh!
SWWOOOOSH!
And now that I've taken your *ground troops* to school--
--it's time for some *aerial maneuvers!*

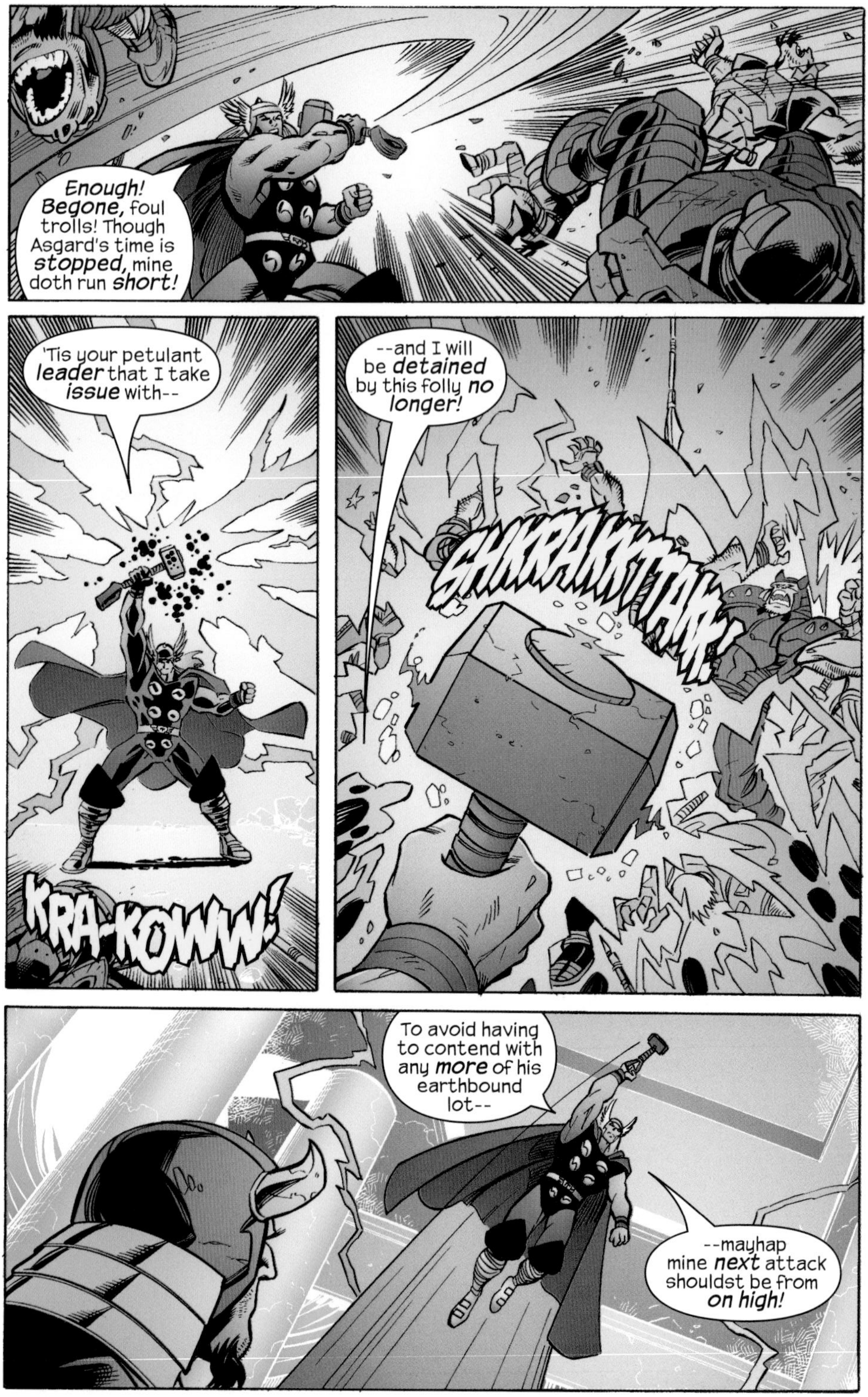
Enough! Begone, foul trolls! Though Asgard's time is stopped, mine doth run short!
'Tis your petulant leader that I take issue with--
KRA-KOWW!
--and I will be detained by this folly no longer!
SHKRAKKTAK!
To avoid having to contend with any more of his earthbound lot--
--mayhap mine next attack shouldst be from on high!

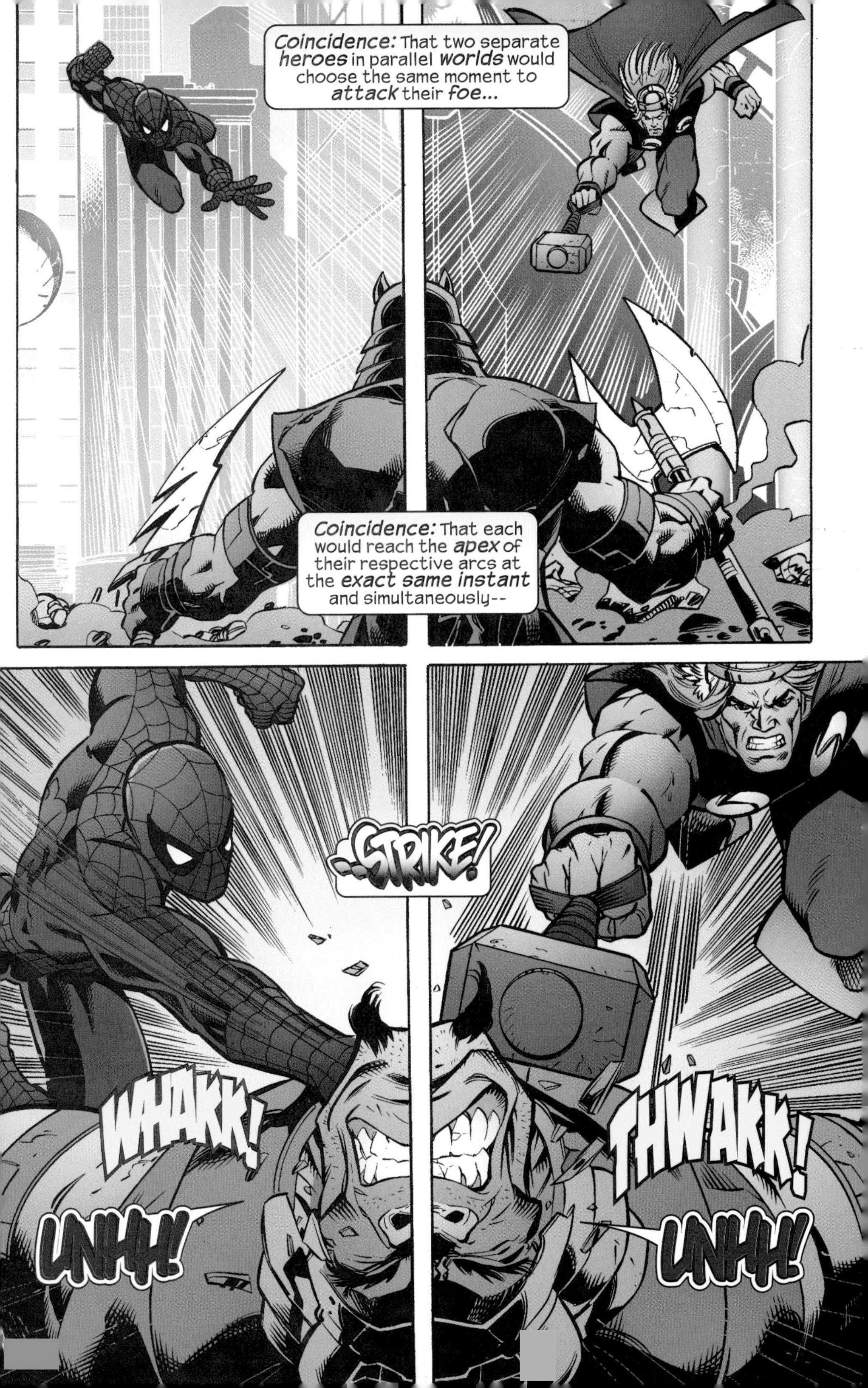
Coincidence: That two separate heroes in parallel worlds would choose the same moment to attack their foe...
Coincidence: That each would reach the apex of their respective arcs at the exact same instant and simultaneously--
--STRIKE!
WHAKK!
THWAKK!
UNHH!
UNHH!

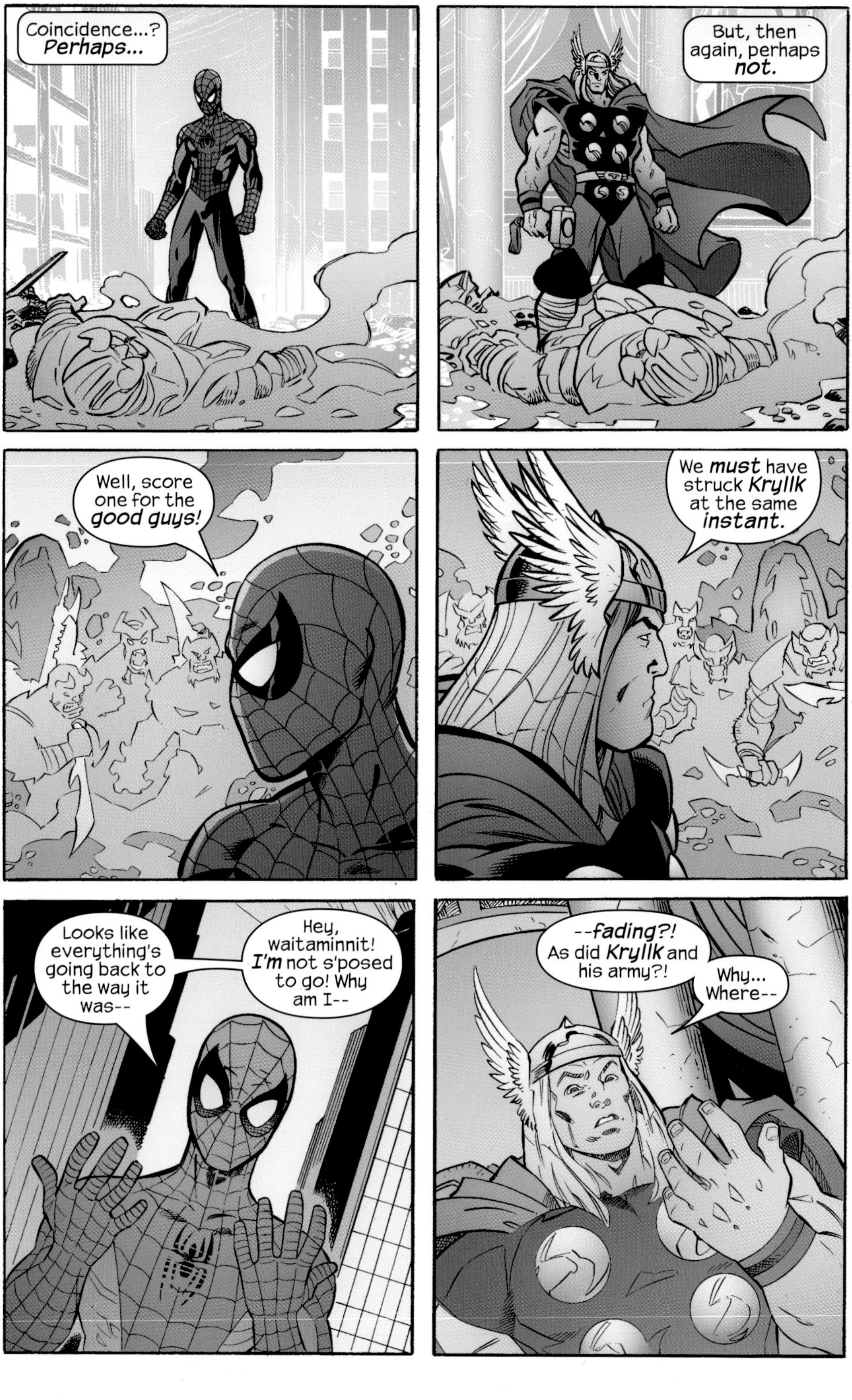

Coincidence...? Perhaps...
But, then again, perhaps not.
Well, score one for the good guys!
We must have struck Kryllk at the same instant.
Looks like everything's going back to the way it was--
Hey, waitaminnit! I'm not s'posed to go! Why am I--
--fading?! As did Kryllk and his army?!
Why... Where--

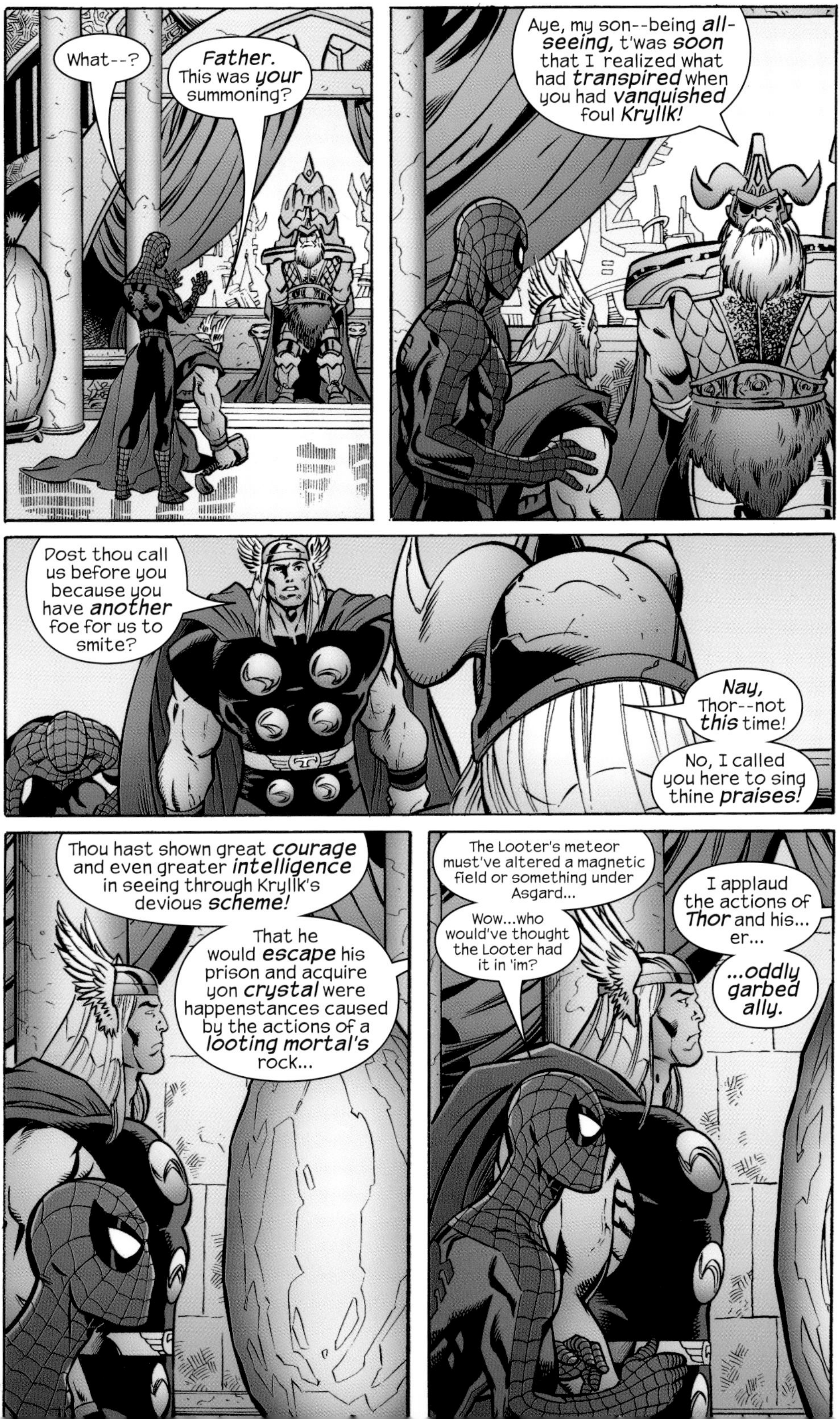
What--?
Father. This was your summoning?
Aye, my son--being all-seeing, t'was soon that I realized what had transpired when you had vanquished foul Kryllk!
Dost thou call us before you because you have another foe for us to smite?
Nay, Thor--not this time!
No, I called you here to sing thine praises!
Thou hast shown great courage and even greater intelligence in seeing through Kryllk's devious scheme!
That he would escape his prison and acquire yon crystal were happenstances caused by the actions of a looting mortal's rock...
The Looter's meteor must've altered a magnetic field or something under Asgard...
Wow...who would've thought the Looter had it in 'im?
I applaud the actions of Thor and his... er...
...oddly garbed ally.

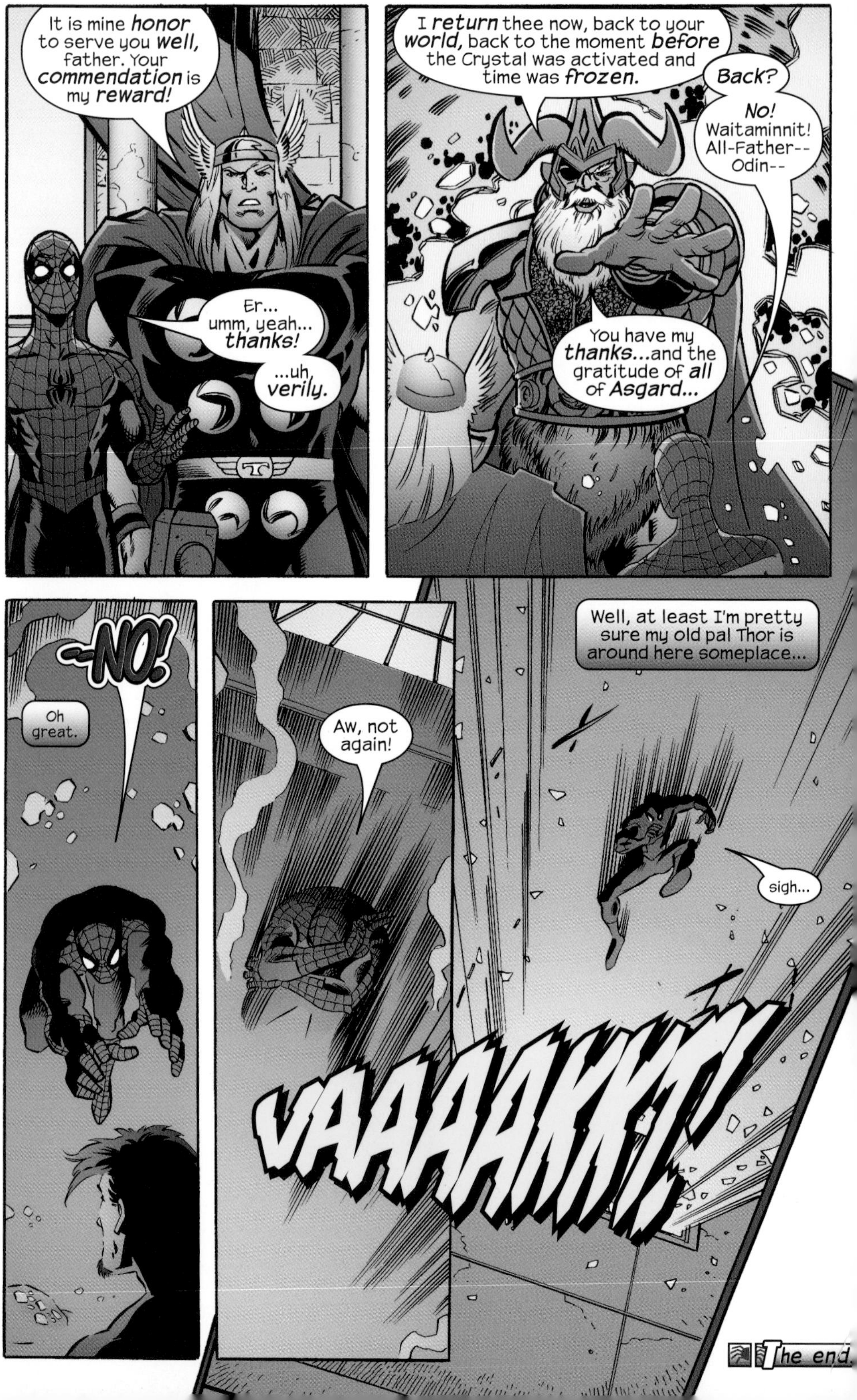
It is mine honor to serve you well, father. Your commendation is my reward!
Er... umm, yeah... thanks!
...uh verily.
I return thee now, back to your world, back to the moment before the Crystal was activated and time was frozen.
Back?
No! Waitaminnit! All-Father-- Odin--
You have my thanks...and the gratitude of all of Asgard...
--NO!
Oh great.
Aw, not again!
Well, at least I'm pretty sure my old pal Thor is around here someplace...
sigh...
VAAAAKKT!
The end.

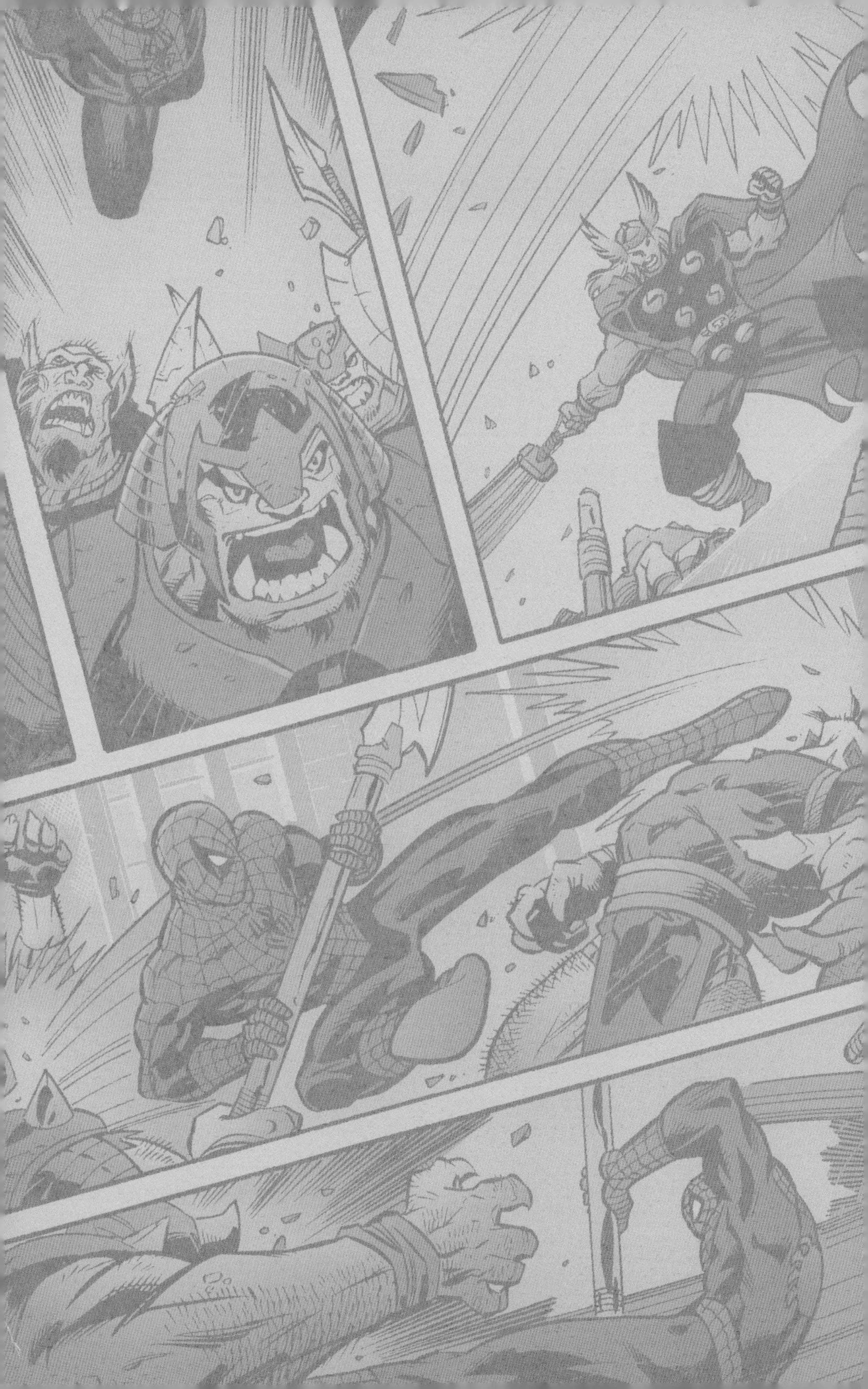

07

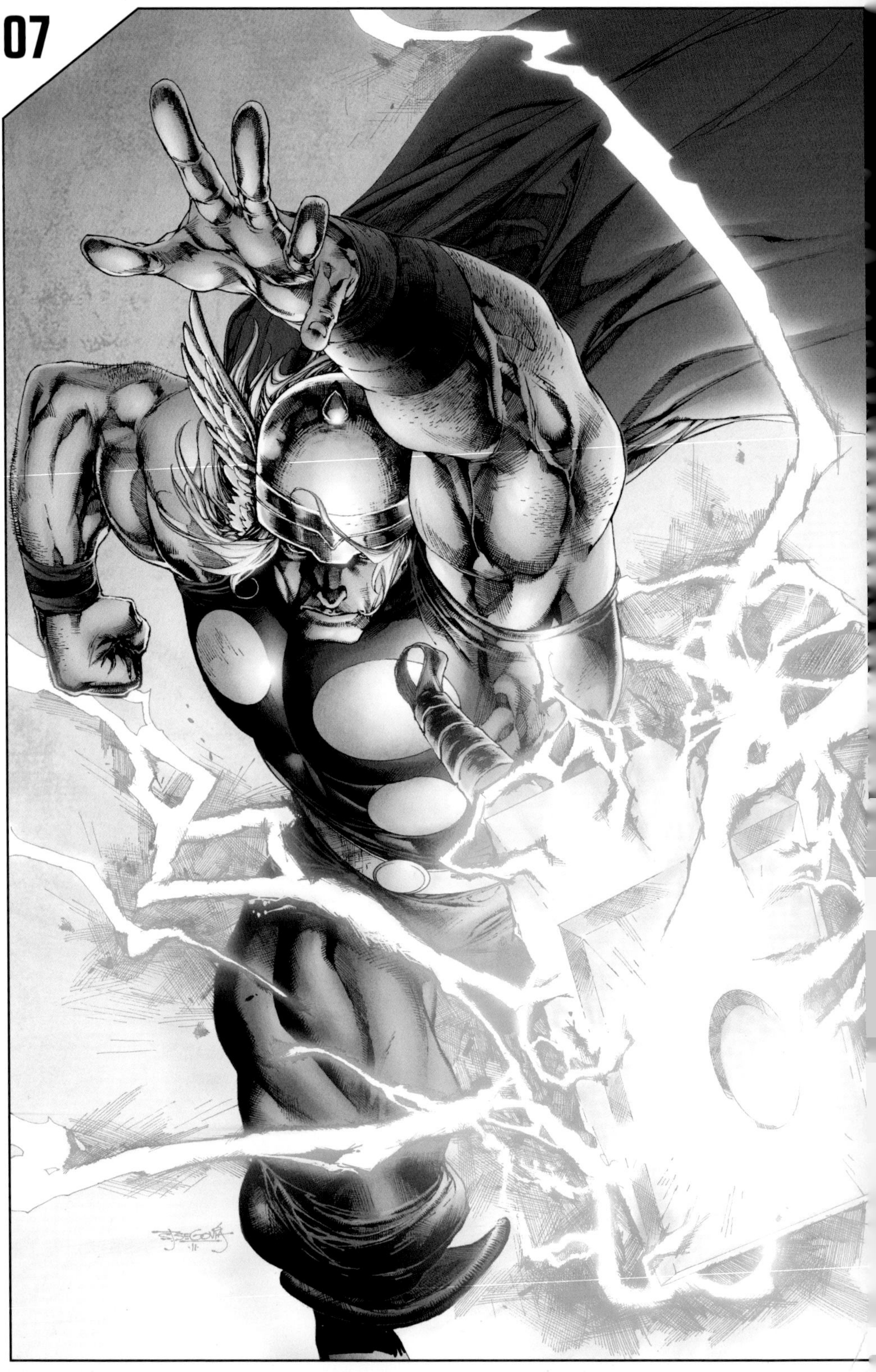

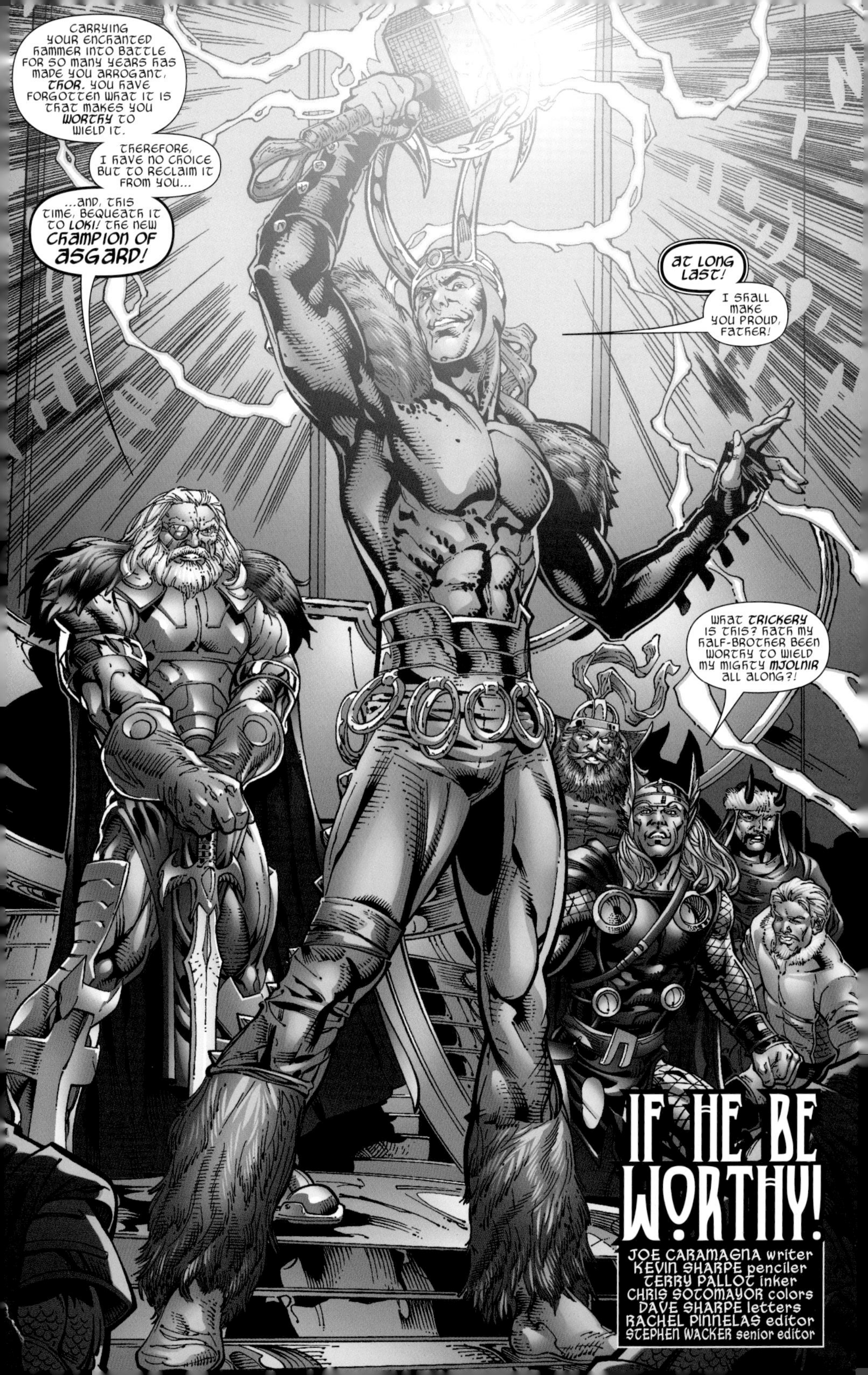
CARRYING YOUR ENCHANTED HAMMER INTO BATTLE FOR SO MANY YEARS HAS MADE YOU ARROGANT, THOR. YOU HAVE FORGOTTEN WHAT IT IS THAT MAKES YOU WORTHY TO WIELD IT.
THEREFORE, I HAVE NO CHOICE BUT TO RECLAIM IT FROM YOU...
...AND, THIS TIME, BEQUEATH IT TO LOKI! THE NEW CHAMPION OF ASGARD!
AT LONG LAST!
I SHALL MAKE YOU PROUD, FATHER!
WHAT TRICKERY IS THIS? HATH MY HALF-BROTHER BEEN WORTHY TO WIELD MY MIGHTY MJOLNIR ALL ALONG?!
IF HE BE WORTHY!
JOE CARAMAGNA writer
KEVIN SHARPE penciler
TERRY PALLOT inker
CHRIS SOTOMAYOR colors
DAVE SHARPE letters
RACHEL PINNELAS editor
STEPHEN WACKER senior editor

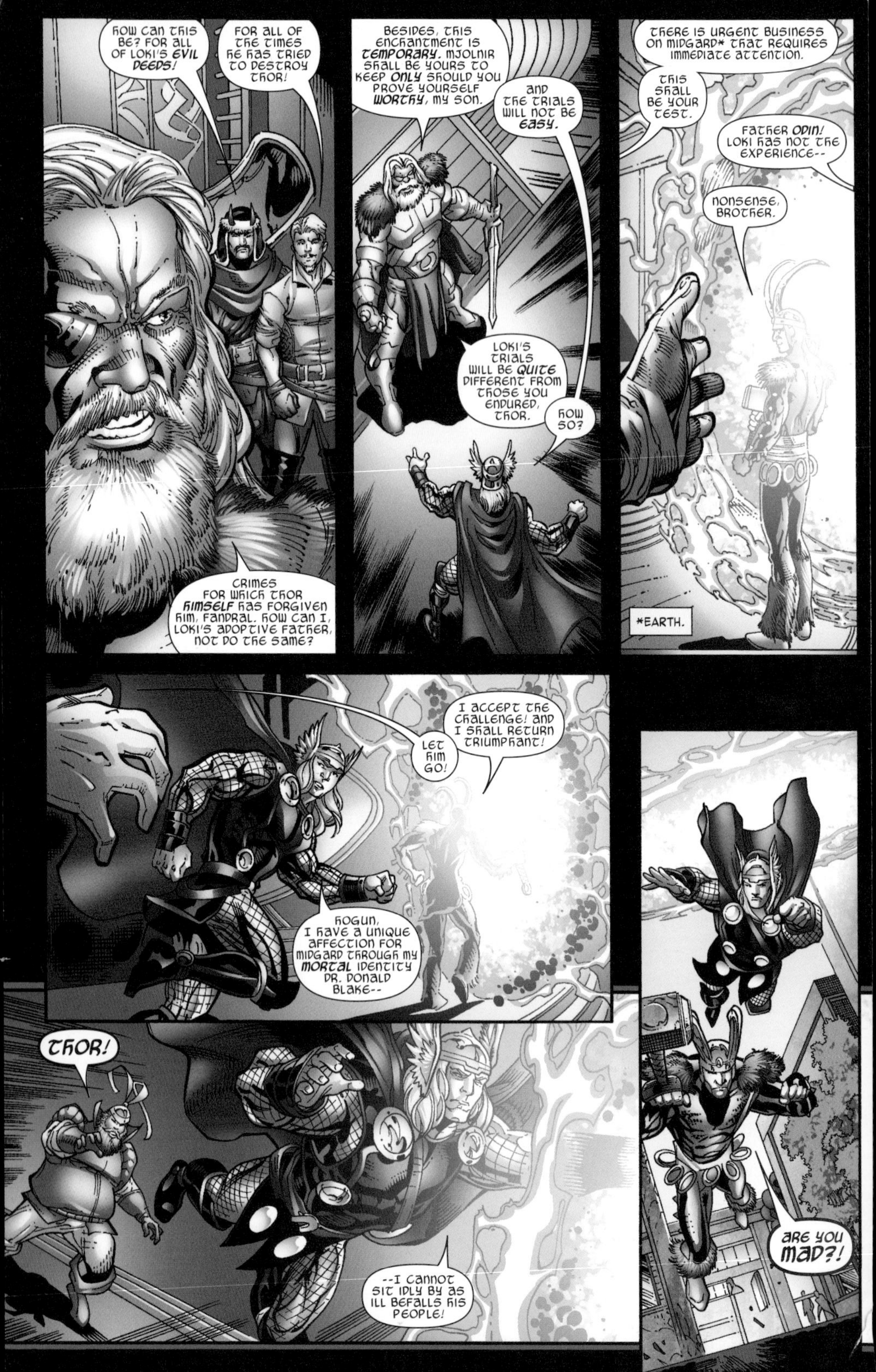
HOW CAN THIS BE? FOR ALL OF LOKI'S EVIL DEEDS!
FOR ALL OF THE TIMES HE HAS TRIED TO DESTROY THOR!
CRIMES FOR WHICH THOR HIMSELF HAS FORGIVEN HIM, FANDRAL. HOW CAN I, LOKI'S ADOPTIVE FATHER, NOT DO THE SAME?
BESIDES, THIS ENCHANTMENT IS TEMPORARY. MJOLNIR SHALL BE YOURS TO KEEP ONLY SHOULD YOU PROVE YOURSELF WORTHY, MY SON.
AND THE TRIALS WILL NOT BE EASY.
LOKI'S TRIALS WILL BE QUITE DIFFERENT FROM THOSE YOU ENDURED, THOR.
HOW SO?
THERE IS URGENT BUSINESS ON MIDGARD* THAT REQUIRES IMMEDIATE ATTENTION.
THIS SHALL BE YOUR TEST.
FATHER ODIN! LOKI HAS NOT THE EXPERIENCE--
NONSENSE, BROTHER.
*EARTH.
LET HIM GO!
I ACCEPT THE CHALLENGE! AND I SHALL RETURN TRIUMPHANT!
HOGUN, I HAVE A UNIQUE AFFECTION FOR MIDGARD THROUGH MY MORTAL IDENTITY DR. DONALD BLAKE--
THOR!
--I CANNOT SIT IDLY BY AS ILL BEFALLS HIS PEOPLE!
ARE YOU MAD?!

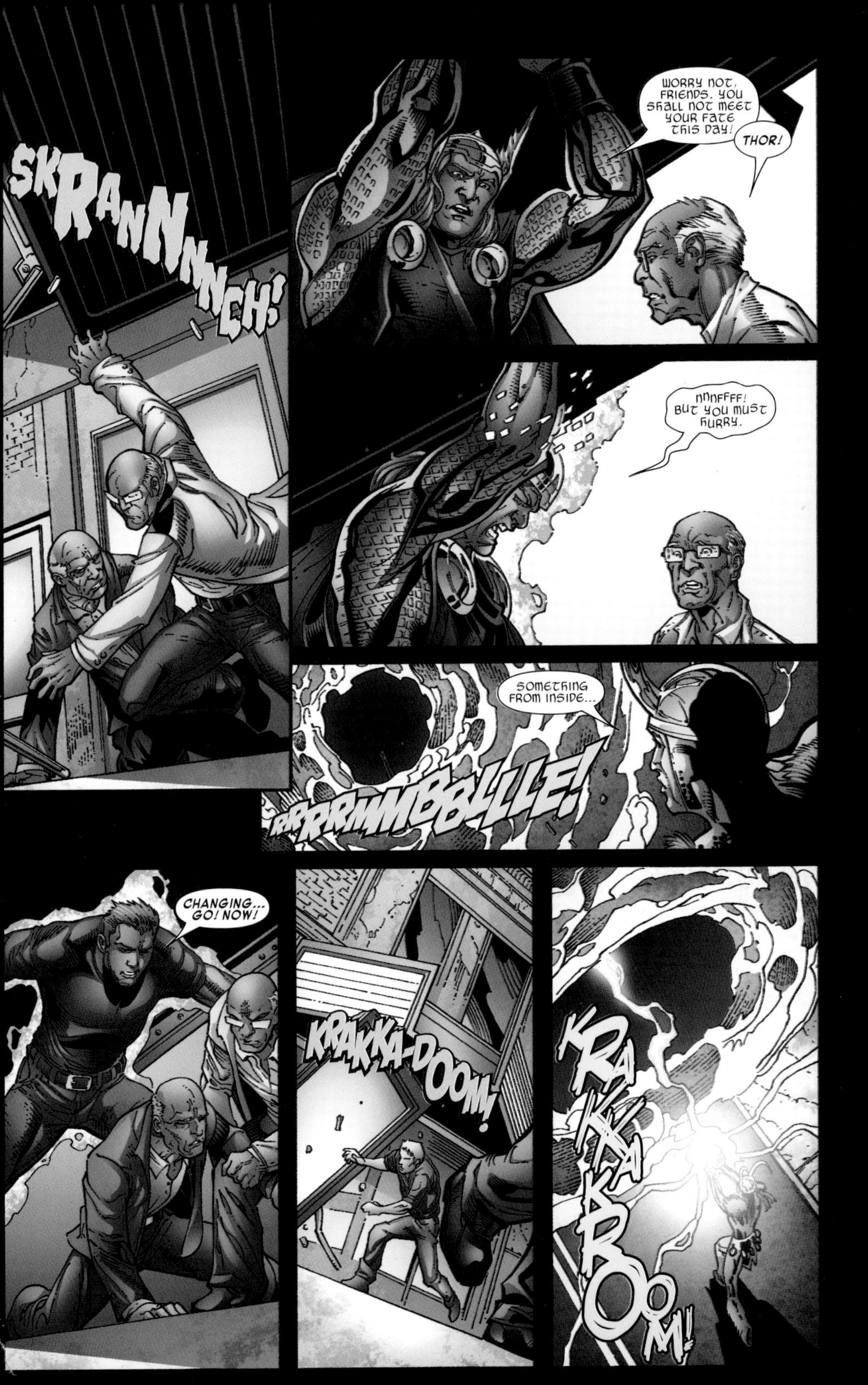
SKRANNNNNCH!
WORRY NOT, FRIENDS. YOU SHALL NOT MEET YOUR FATE THIS DAY!
THOR!
NNNFFFF! BUT YOU MUST HURRY.
SOMETHING FROM INSIDE...
RRRRMMBBLLLE!
CHANGING... GO! NOW!
KRAKKA-DOOM!
KRAKKAKROOM!

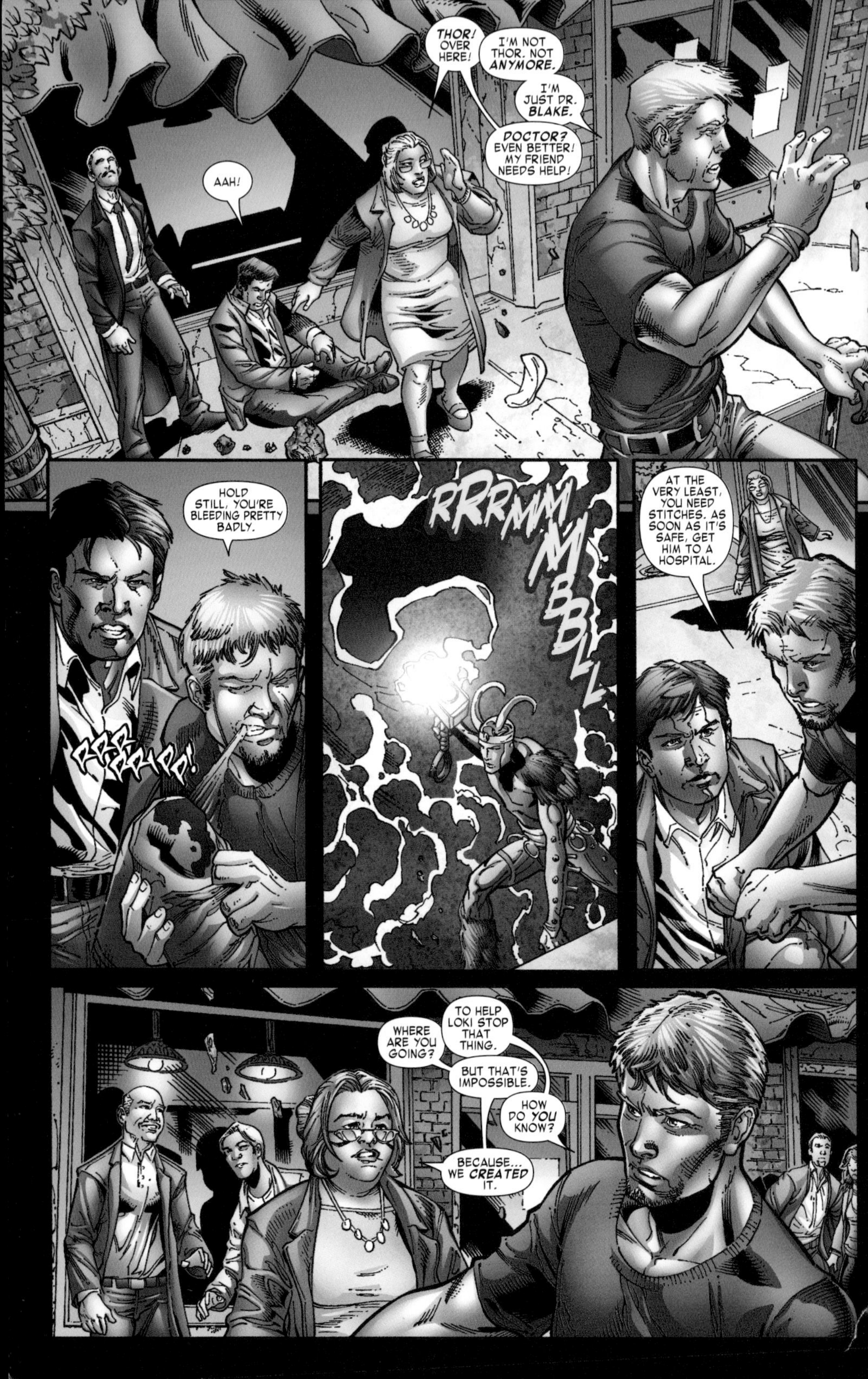
THOR! OVER HERE!
I'M NOT THOR. NOT ANYMORE.
I'M JUST DR. BLAKE.
DOCTOR? EVEN BETTER! MY FRIEND NEEDS HELP!
AAH!
HOLD STILL, YOU'RE BLEEDING PRETTY BADLY.
RRRRRIPP!
RRRRMMMMBBLL
AT THE VERY LEAST, YOU NEED STITCHES. AS SOON AS IT'S SAFE, GET HIM TO A HOSPITAL.
WHERE ARE YOU GOING?
TO HELP LOKI STOP THAT THING.
BUT THAT'S IMPOSSIBLE.
HOW DO YOU KNOW?
BECAUSE... WE CREATED IT.

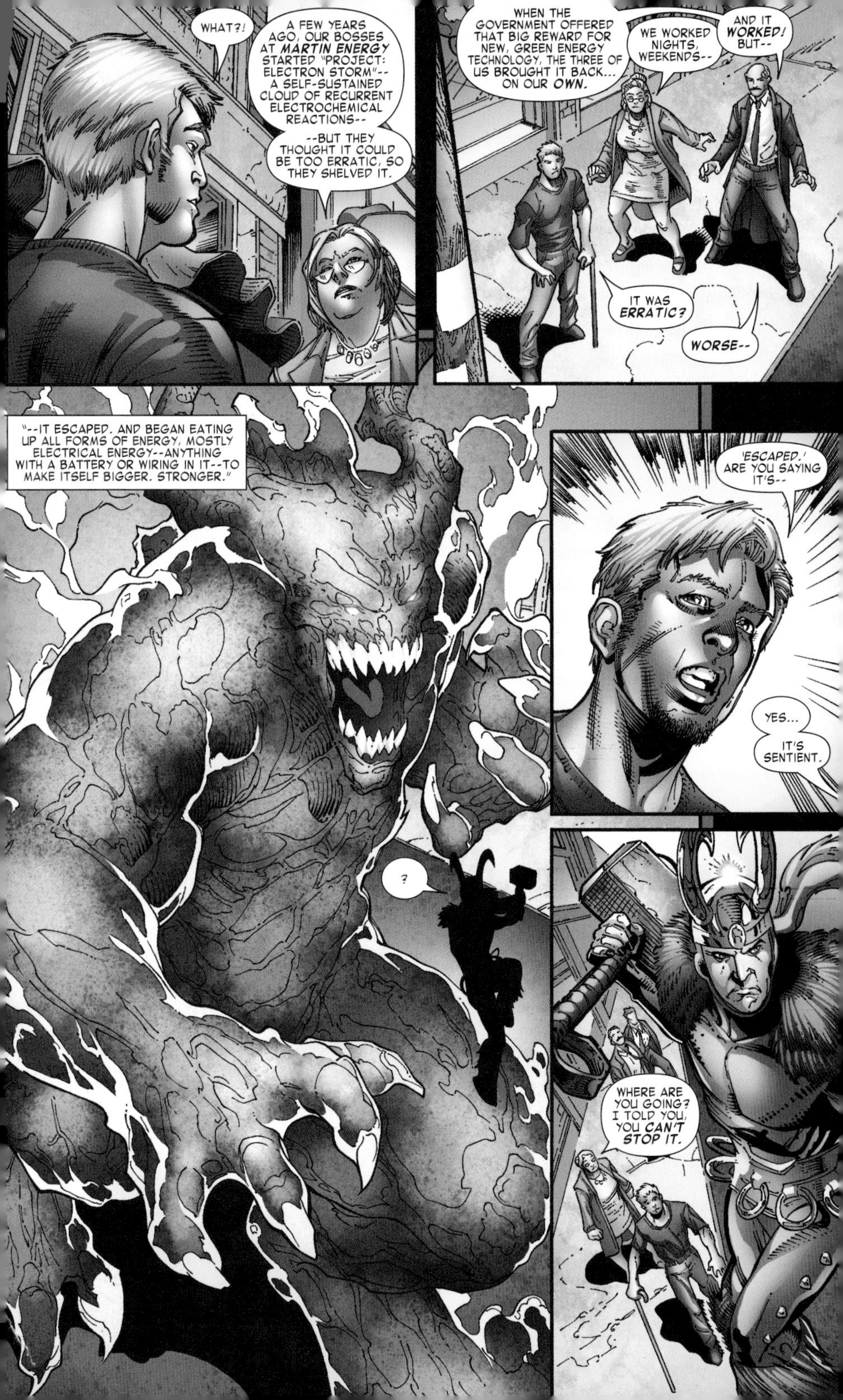

WHAT?!
A FEW YEARS AGO, OUR BOSSES AT MARTIN ENERGY STARTED "PROJECT: ELECTRON STORM"--A SELF-SUSTAINED CLOUD OF RECURRENT ELECTROCHEMICAL REACTIONS--
--BUT THEY THOUGHT IT COULD BE TOO ERRATIC, SO THEY SHELVED IT.
WHEN THE GOVERNMENT OFFERED THAT BIG REWARD FOR NEW, GREEN ENERGY TECHNOLOGY, THE THREE OF US BROUGHT IT BACK... ON OUR OWN.
WE WORKED NIGHTS, WEEKENDS--
AND IT WORKED! BUT--
IT WAS ERRATIC?
WORSE--
"--IT ESCAPED. AND BEGAN EATING UP ALL FORMS OF ENERGY, MOSTLY ELECTRICAL ENERGY--ANYTHING WITH A BATTERY OR WIRING IN IT--TO MAKE ITSELF BIGGER. STRONGER."
?
'ESCAPED.' ARE YOU SAYING IT'S--
YES...
IT'S SENTIENT.
WHERE ARE YOU GOING? I TOLD YOU, YOU CAN'T STOP IT.

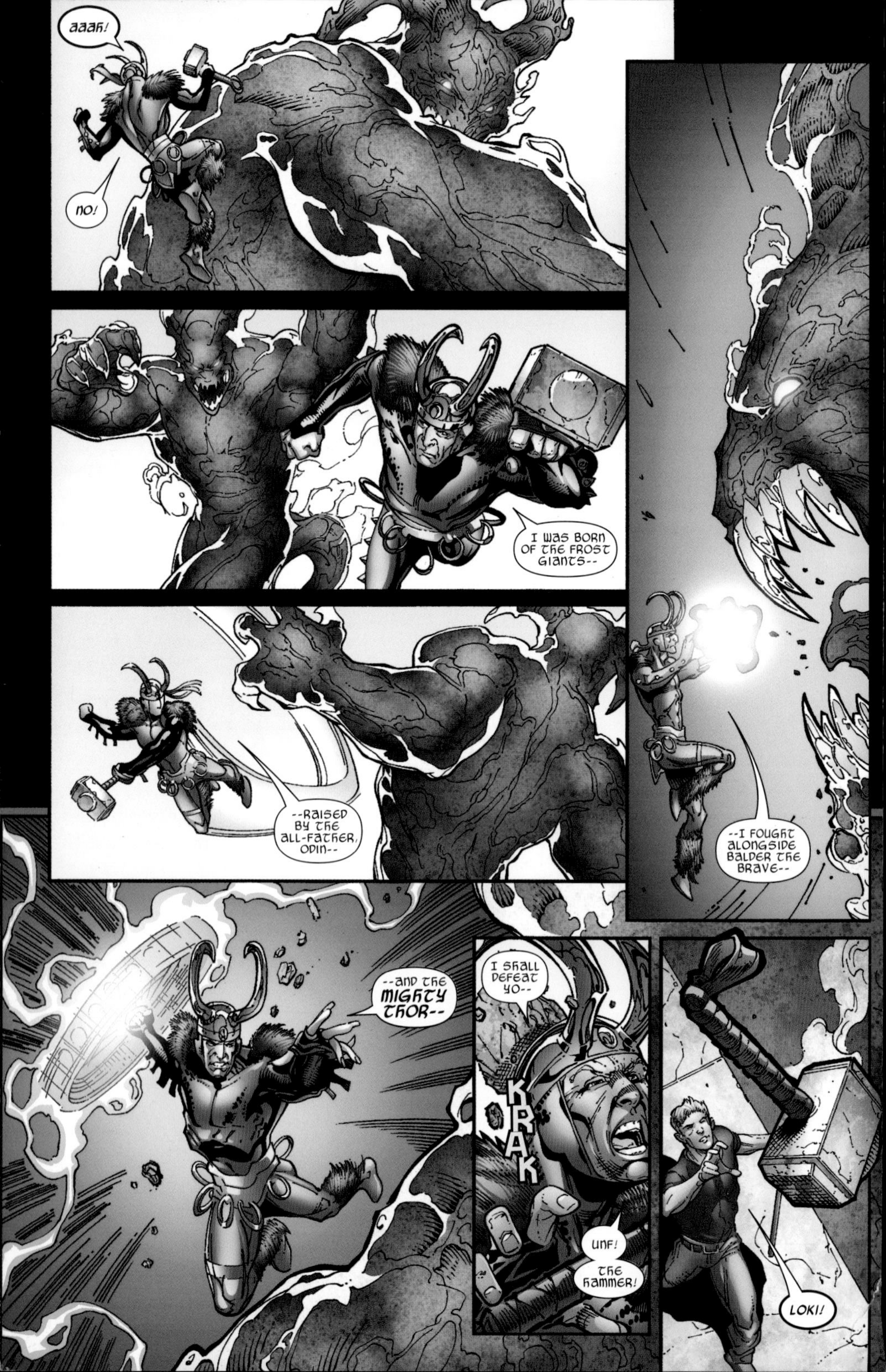
AAAH!
NO!
I WAS BORN OF THE FROST GIANTS--
--RAISED BY THE ALL-FATHER, ODIN--
--I FOUGHT ALONGSIDE BALDER THE BRAVE--
--AND THE MIGHTY THOR--
I SHALL DEFEAT YO--
KRAK
UNF!
THE HAMMER!
LOKI!

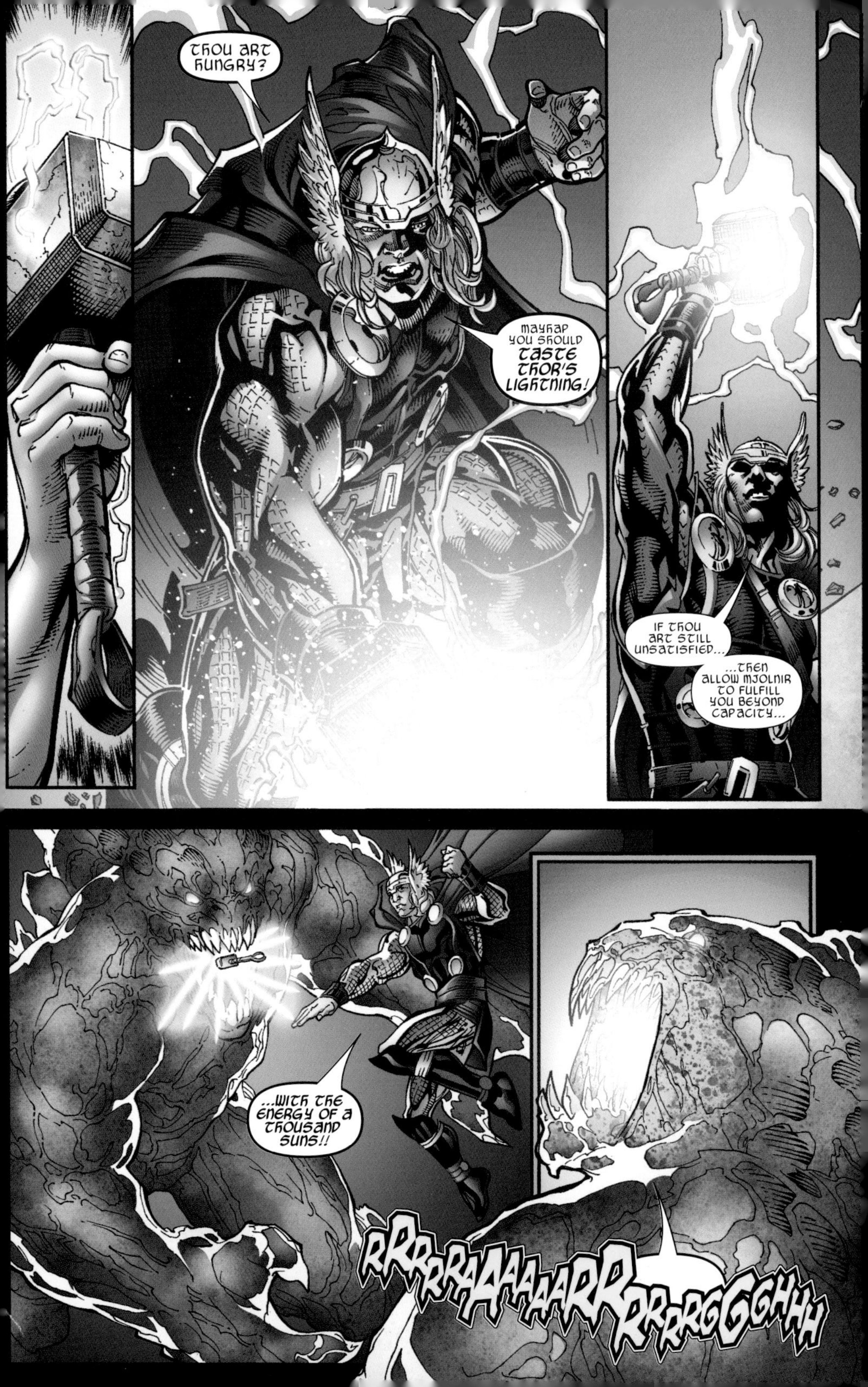
THOU ART HUNGRY?
MAYHAP YOU SHOULD TASTE THOR'S LIGHTNING!
IF THOU ART STILL UNSATISFIED...
...THEN ALLOW MJOLNIR TO FULFILL YOU BEYOND CAPACITY...
...WITH THE ENERGY OF A THOUSAND SUNS!!
RRRRRAAAAAARRRRRRGGGHHH

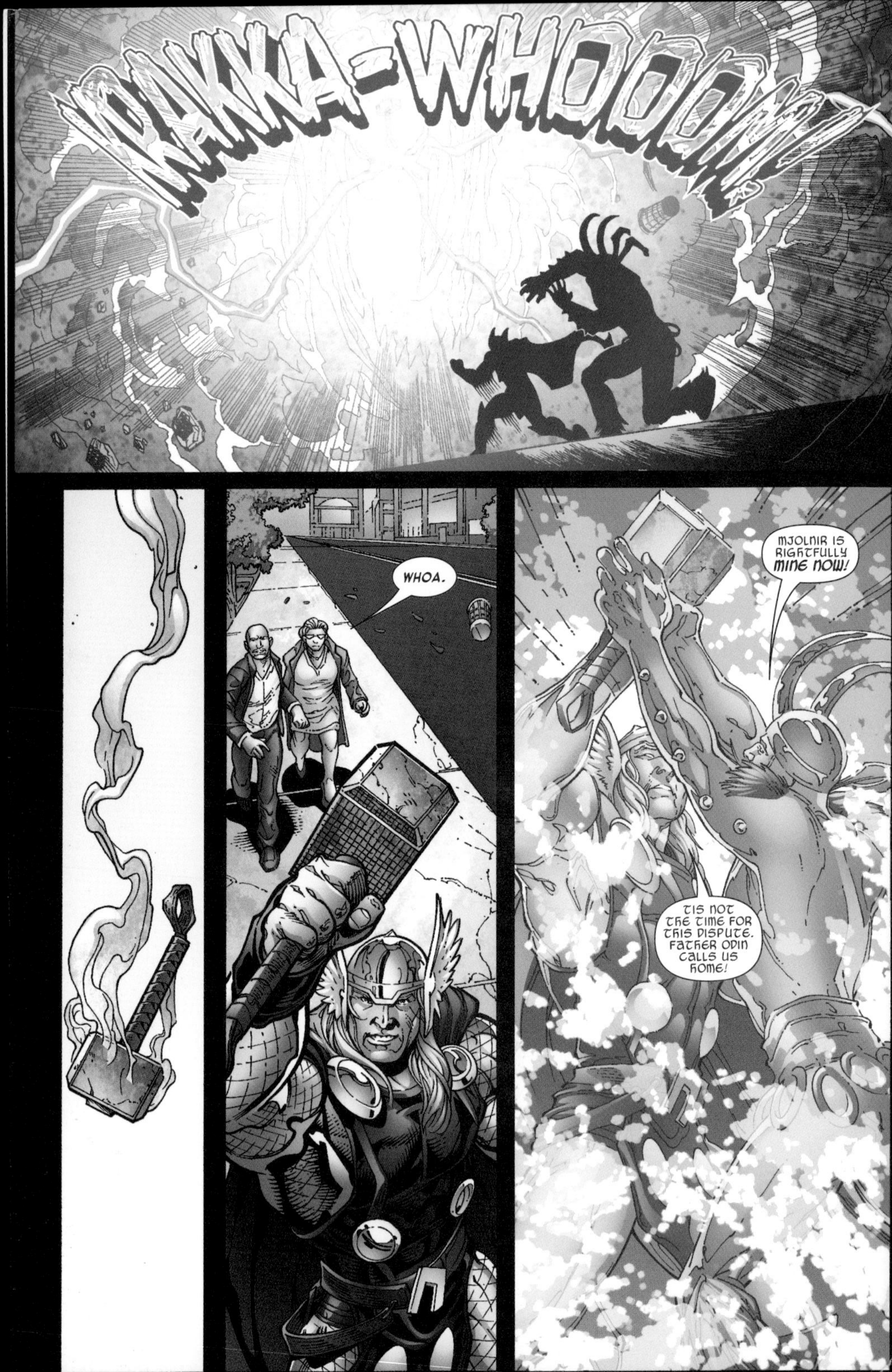

DAKKA-WHOOOM!
WHOA.
MJOLNIR IS RIGHTFULLY MINE NOW!
TIS NOT THE TIME FOR THIS DISPUTE. FATHER ODIN CALLS US HOME!

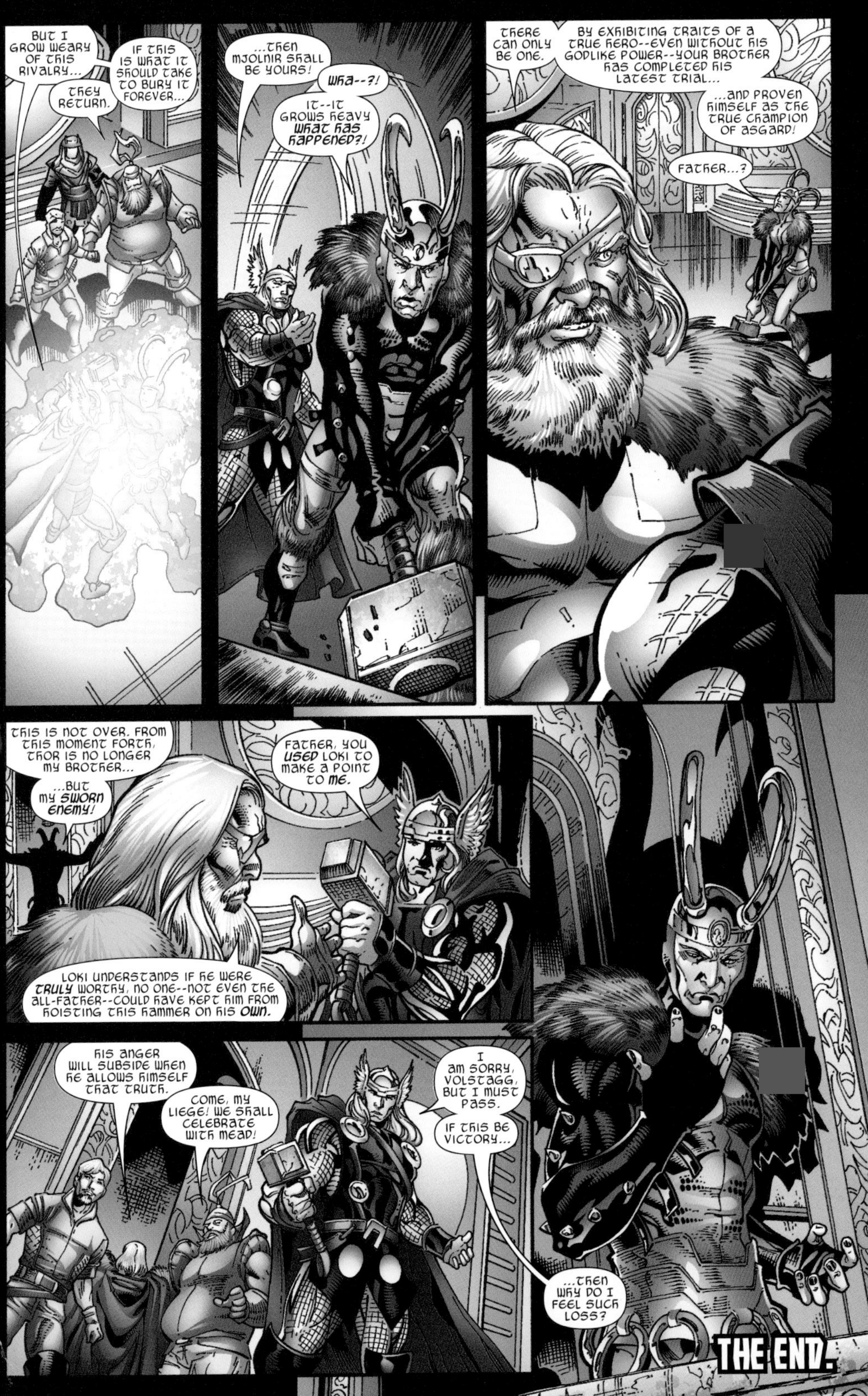
BUT I GROW WEARY OF THIS RIVALRY...
IF THIS IS WHAT IT SHOULD TAKE TO BURY IT FOREVER...
THEY RETURN.
...THEN MJOLNIR SHALL BE YOURS!
WHA--?!
IT--IT GROWS HEAVY WHAT HAS HAPPENED?!
THERE CAN ONLY BE ONE.
BY EXHIBITING TRAITS OF A TRUE HERO--EVEN WITHOUT HIS GODLIKE POWER--YOUR BROTHER HAS COMPLETED HIS LATEST TRIAL...
...AND PROVEN HIMSELF AS THE TRUE CHAMPION OF ASGARD!
FATHER...?
THIS IS NOT OVER. FROM THIS MOMENT FORTH, THOR IS NO LONGER MY BROTHER...
...BUT MY SWORN ENEMY!
FATHER, YOU USED LOKI TO MAKE A POINT TO ME.
LOKI UNDERSTANDS IF HE WERE TRULY WORTHY, NO ONE--NOT EVEN THE ALL-FATHER--COULD HAVE KEPT HIM FROM HOISTING THIS HAMMER ON HIS OWN.
HIS ANGER WILL SUBSIDE WHEN HE ALLOWS HIMSELF THAT TRUTH.
COME, MY LIEGE! WE SHALL CELEBRATE WITH MEAD!
I AM SORRY, VOLSTAGG, BUT I MUST PASS.
IF THIS BE VICTORY...
...THEN WHY DO I FEEL SUCH LOSS?
THE END.

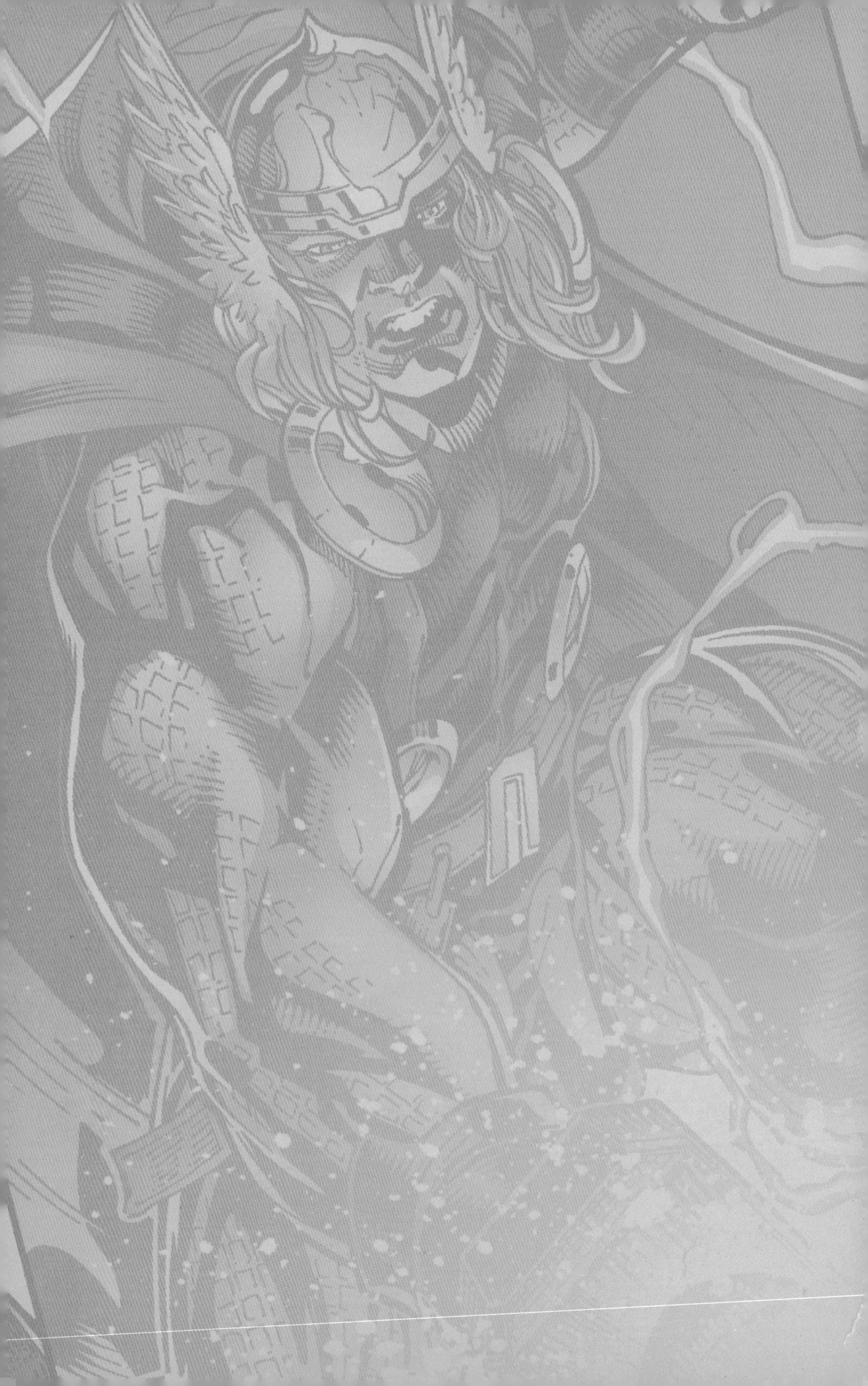